JODI TAYLOR

HEADLINE

The right of Jodi Taylor to be identified as the Author of
the Work has been asserted by her in accordance with the
Copyright, Designs and Patents Act 1988.

First published in Great Britain in 2015 by
Accent Press Ltd

This edition published in paperback in Great Britain in 2019 by
HEADLINE PUBLISHING GROUP

1

Cataloguing in Publication Data is available from the British Library

ISBN 978 1 4722 6433 6

Printed and bound in Great Britain by Clays Ltd, Elcograf S.p.A.

Headline's policy is to use papers that are natural, renewable and recyclable
products and made from wood grown in well-managed forests and other
controlled sources. The logging and manufacturing processes are expected
to conform to the environmental regulations of the country of origin.

HEADLINE PUBLISHING GROUP
An Hachette UK Company
Carmelite House
50 Victoria Embankment
London EC4Y 0DZ

www.headline.co.uk
www.hachette.co.uk

Warwickshire County Council

COL 1019			

This item is to be returned or renewed before the latest date above. It may be borrowed for a further period if not in demand. **To renew your books:**

- **Phone the 24/7 Renewal Line 01926 499273 or**
- **Visit www.warwickshire.gov.uk/libraries**

Discover ● Imagine● Learn ● *with libraries*

By Jodi Taylor and available from Headline

THE CHRONICLES OF ST MARY'S SERIES

JUST ONE DAMNED THING AFTER ANOTHER
A SYMPHONY OF ECHOES
A SECOND CHANCE
A TRAIL THROUGH TIME
NO TIME LIKE THE PAST
WHAT COULD POSSIBLY GO WRONG?
LIES, DAMNED LIES, AND HISTORY
AND THE REST IS HISTORY
AN ARGUMENTATION OF HISTORIANS
HOPE FOR THE BEST

THE LONG AND SHORT OF IT (short-story collection)

THE CHRONICLES OF ST MARY'S DIGITAL SHORTS

WHEN A CHILD IS BORN
ROMAN HOLIDAY
CHRISTMAS PRESENT
SHIPS AND STINGS AND WEDDING RINGS
THE VERY FIRST DAMNED THING
THE GREAT ST MARY'S DAY OUT
MY NAME IS MARKHAM
A PERFECT STORM
CHRISTMAS PAST
BATTERSEA BARRICADES
THE STEAM-PUMP JUMP
AND NOW FOR SOMETHING COMPLETELY DIFFERENT

ELIZABETH CAGE NOVELS

WHITE SILENCE   DARK LIGHT

FROGMORTON FARM SERIES

THE NOTHING GIRL   THE SOMETHING GIRL
LITTLE DONKEY (digital short)

A BACHELOR ESTABLISHMENT

To the best bunch of loyal and enthusiastic followers an author could ever wish for. St Mary's thanks you for your support and encouragement over the past four Chronicles. This, the fifth book, is dedicated to all of you.

DRAMATIS THINGUMMY

Dr Edward Bairstow	Director of the Institute of Historical Research at St Mary's Priory. Any resemblance to a bad-tempered bird of prey is not coincidental.
Mrs Partridge	PA to the Director and Kleio, daughter of Zeus, Muse of History. Critical and unforgiving. Probably easier to find the source of the Nile than any evidence of a sense of humour.
Maxwell	Chief Operations Officer. Responsible for re-establishing St Mary's after its exciting summer last year, and for organising the infamous Open Day this year.
Leon Farrell	Chief Technical Officer. A man of extraordinary patience and restraint – he says.
Major Ian Guthrie	Head of the Security. A man of extraordinary etc. – he says.
Mr Dieter	Second Chief Technical Officer. Because you can't have too much of a good thing – he says.
Dr Tim Peterson	Chief Training Officer in search of someone to train. The sensible one – he says.

Mr Markham	Guthrie's Number Two. In every sense of the phrase. Disaster magnet and mostly indestructible.
Dr Helen Foster	Chief Medical Officer. The only medical officer, actually. Not to be trusted with ten feet of rubber tubing and a jug of warm water.
Nurse Diane Hunter	Chief Nurse and recipient of Mr Markham's affections.
Prof Andrew Rapson	Head of Research & Development. Very unreliable with anything more flammable than a wet tissue.
Dr Octavius Dowson	Librarian and Archivist. Elderly and irascible. You wouldn't want to turn your back on either of these two.
Theresa Mack	Kitchen Supremo and former Urban guerrilla.
Mavis Enderby	Head of Wardrobe.
Elizabeth Shaw	PA to the Chief Training Officer. Highly valued for her cakes and biscuits. Not that historians are in any way shallow or easily bribed …
Rosie Lee	Supposedly PA to the Chief Operations Officer, but does pretty much as she pleases.
Mary Schiller	Senior Historian.
Greta Van Owen	Senior Historian.

The tea-sodden catastrophe cluster that is the
HISTORY DEPARTMENT

Mr Clerk	
Miss Prentiss	
Mr Roberts	
Mr Sands	
Tom Bashford & Elspeth Grey	Recently rescued historians. Currently at Thirsk University, acclimatising themselves after a ten-year absence.

CHANCELLOR AND MEMBERS OF THE SENIOR FACULTY

University of Thirsk	Nominal employers and purse-holders.
Dr Kalinda Black	St Mary's liaison officer with Thirsk University.
Professor Penrose	Retired physicist and appointed boat designer.
SPOHB	Society for the Protection of Historical Buildings. The provisional wing of English Heritage.

VILLAINS

Clive Ronan	Renegade historian and bad guy.
Isabella Barclay	Professional bitch and bad girl.

PROLOGUE

It always seemed strange to me that a building as old as St Mary's should have no ghost.

No Headless Monk.

No Grey Lady.

No sinister shade haunting the corridors, uttering blood-curdling warnings of vengeance and retribution – apart from Dr Bairstow distributing his 'Deductions from Wages to Pay for Damages' forms, of course – so when Markham claimed to have seen a ghost, no one believed him and the reason we didn't believe him was because he was the only person ever to see it.

Then it happened again.

And then again.

And still no one ever saw anything. No one except for Markham, bolting into my office, as agitated as I'd ever seen him, and gabbling about something that no one else could see.

We didn't realise that the reason he was the only person ever to see the ghost, was because he *was* the ghost.

Another all-staff briefing from Dr Bairstow. The first since our unpleasantness with the Time Police last summer. However, they'd gone – we were still here – most of the building had been restored, and St Mary's was open for business.

We work for the Institute of Historical Research at St Mary's Priory. We investigate major historical events in contemporary time. For God's sake – *do not* call it time travel. The last person to do that had her head thumped and then was inadvertently caused to fall down the stairs.

Anyway, the building had recovered from its wounds – we'd recovered from ours – and here we all were, slowly suffocating in the smell of new wood, damp plaster, and fresh paint. Not the best smells in the world, but still a big improvement on cordite, blood, and defeat.

Tim Peterson and I sat in the front row and assumed expressions of near-terminal enthusiasm and commitment. Once we would have sat at the back and played Battleships, but senior staff have to sit at the front and show willing. It makes the destruction of the enemy fleet that much more difficult, but we were willing to rise to the challenge.

Here came the Boss, limping to the half-landing and

standing in his usual position, leaning heavily on his stick. The cold winter sunshine streamed through the newly restored glass lantern above him as he surveyed his unit with the expression of an impatient vulture waiting for a dying wildebeest to get a move on.

'Good morning, everyone. Thank you for coming.'

As if we had any choice.

'As you can see, with effect from 10 a.m. this morning, St Mary's is up and running.'

There was a polite smattering of applause. Most of us had been working our socks off for the last three weeks, restoring the Library and Archive, and generally helping to put the building back together, so whether St Mary's was open or not actually made very little difference to us.

'There are a few staff changes to announce. If you care to consult the organisational charts distributed at the beginning of this meeting by Mrs Partridge ...' He paused for the traditional panic from those who had lost theirs already. Peterson and I were using ours to record the disposition of our respective armadas.

'Firstly, I would like to confirm Dr Maxwell in her position of Chief Operations Officer.'

He paused again. I fixed my attention on my imperilled destroyers and mentally crossed my fingers. There was a small round of applause and I breathed a sigh of relief. There had been that episode last Christmas, when Dr Bairstow had returned from a rare night of carousing in Rushford to find he had mysteriously acquired two additional historians. He'd taken it very well, all things considered. They were off now, reorienting and acclimatising themselves at Thirsk

4

University – a necessary procedure after such a long absence. They'd been missing for ten years. And Ian Guthrie, to whom one of the missing historians was very special indeed, had caught me in the corridor one day, held my hand very tightly, said, 'I owe you, Max,' and then walked away before either of us displayed any unseemly emotion.

Dr Bairstow was forging on. 'Dr Peterson assumes his original position of Chief Training Officer. Chief Farrell returns as joint head of the Technical Section, alongside Mr Dieter. Miss Perkins is appointed Head of IT, replacing Miss Barclay who has left us.'

Yes, she bloody had. She'd escaped in the confusion arising from the kitchen staff blowing up the building with flour-filled condoms. Long story. Still, a wrecked building was a small price to pay for ridding ourselves of Bitchface Barclay. Sadly, she hadn't gone for good. She was out there, somewhere. It was only a matter of time before we met again. She'd left me a note to that effect.

He continued. 'I would like to congratulate Mr Markham on his promotion to second in charge of the Security Section.'

No, I didn't think he'd be able to bring himself to utter the words, *Number Two* and *Mr Markham* in the same sentence. It would be asking for trouble. Markham sat up and beamed amiably at him. His hair, as usual, stuck up in irregular clumps. He looked like someone being treated for mange. And not for the first time, either.

'Mrs Partridge is confirmed as my PA and Miss Lee will return to her former position as admin assistant to the History Department.'

The History Department sighed. As did I. Yes, there she was, two rows along, her short dark hair waving around her head, just like Medusa's snakes, but slightly more intimidating. She turned her Gorgon stare upon the History Department who promptly shut up.

'I would also particularly like to welcome back our caretaker, Mr Strong.'

This time, the round of applause was enthusiastic and genuine. He was an old man and last year, he'd disobeyed instructions, pinned on his medals and stepped up to fight for St Mary's. He'd been injured – we all had. Some of us had died. The Boss had tried to send him away to convalesce and he'd respectfully refused to go and spent his time stumping around the ruins of the Great Hall, telling the builders where they were going wrong and infuriating the Society for the Protection of Historical Buildings, who were supposed to be overseeing the repairs. They'd complained and Dr Bairstow, in a few well-chosen words that echoed around St Mary's, had given them to understand that Mr Strong was one of his most valued employees and his long years at St Mary's made him a leading authority on the building and everything in it. They got the message. Mr Strong had, however, in the interests of good will, consented to a two-week visit to see his grandchildren.

'Mr Strong has asked me to remind you that this building is in better condition now than at any time during its long history – and certainly since we moved in – and he would be grateful if you could all use your best endeavours to keep it that way. As would I.'

He paused for this to sink in as Peterson whispered, 'B6.'

'Miss!'

'Normal service is to resume as soon as possible. The History Department will let me have their schedule of upcoming assignments and recommendations by tomorrow.'

'B7.'

'Bollocks!'

'Dr Foster, please confirm all personnel are medically fit to return to duty. Or at least as fit as they are ever likely to be.'

'B8.'

'You're cheating, aren't you?'

'The Technical Section is to confirm that all pods are serviceable.'

'B9.'

'Sunk.'

'Dr Peterson? Do we possess any trainees at this moment, or did they all run for the hills during our summer unpleasantness?'

'No and no, sir. We didn't have any trainees before the summer unpleasantness, let alone afterwards. Our last recruiting drive was … ineffective.'

He sighed, impatiently. 'I cannot understand why St Mary's finds it so difficult to recruit and retain staff.'

In my mind's eye, I saw the broken bodies, half-buried under the rubble, the blood, heard the thump of explosions …

'Please draw up ideas and suggestions for recruiting and, most importantly, retaining suitable personnel. Please do not construe this instruction as permission to roam the streets with nets and ropes, offering people the King's Shilling. Attempts to retain future trainees by nailing them to their own desks will be discouraged.'

'You are imposing unreasonable restrictions, sir, but I shall do my best.'

He started on about something else, but I'd discovered Peterson's cruisers, cunningly clustered together in the top left-hand corner of his A4 ocean. In the subsequent orgy of destruction, I completely missed what he said next, and was roused only by his traditional, 'Are there any questions?' which is Dr Bairstow-speak for 'I've told you what to do – now get on with it.' He had once been forced to attend a 'Caring Management' seminar, during which someone had courageously informed him that staff are more productive if they feel included and valued. Clearly, he hadn't believed a word of it. There were never any questions.

'Dr Maxwell, if you could spare me a moment, please? Thank you everyone. That will be all.'

Back in his office, he didn't waste any time.

'I'll leave you to set the date, Dr Maxwell. I think you'll agree that sometime during the coming summer seems most convenient – good weather and so on. There will be an enormous amount of work, of course, but farm it out as you think appropriate. I shall want weekly updates, but just a quick progress report will be sufficient. Draft in whomever you need. I'll be able to let you have details of the budget sometime over the next few days.'

I hadn't the faintest idea what he was talking about.

Behind him, Mrs Partridge smirked unhelpfully.

'I'm sorry, sir?'

'Mrs Partridge will handle the admin side – licenses, permits, insurance, etc. Pass all the details to her.'

'Um ...'

He handed me an already bulging file and dismissed me. 'Thank you, Dr Maxwell.'

My finely honed historian senses told me I'd missed something. And he knew it. There was no escape.

'I'm sorry, sir – perhaps you could elaborate a little?'

He sighed, and as one addressing an idiot, said, 'The Open Day.'

'What Open Day?'

'St Mary's Open Day.'

'What? When?'

'Whenever you select the date. St Mary's is to hold an Open Day and you are to organise it.'

'Am I? When was all this announced?'

'About twenty minutes ago. Just as you destroyed Dr Peterson's second submarine.'

I was back in my newly refurbished office. The windows had been heaved open, but even so, the stench of paint was making my eyes water. The smell reminded me of the polyurethane poisoning I'd had as a student, when I'd painted my room one weekend and had only a very rudimentary understanding of the words 'adequate ventilation'.

In reverse order of importance, I had something ergonomic in the way of a desk, a new, posh chair, and a new kettle. Sadly, I also had Miss Lee, who was peering at her screen and possibly frying a few circuits with her Gorgon glare.

I dropped the folder onto my desk with a thud and was about to request a cup of tea from Miss Lee – yet another example of blind optimism over experience – when Markham burst into the room.

'Max! Quick! Someone's fallen off the roof!'

I shot to my feet and followed him out. We ran down the corridor to the second window from the end. Unlike the others along the corridor, it was open. He thrust out his head and shoulders, leaning precariously over the low sill.

'It was here!'

I grabbed a handful of his green jumpsuit and yanked him back.

'Steady on or there'll be two of you stretched out on the gravel …'

There was nothing there.

I looked left and right but there was nothing there. The bare-stemmed Virginia creeper covered the walls, but other than that, there was no plant life for yards around. A wide gravel path ran along this, the eastern side of St Mary's. There was just the path and the frosty grass sloping down to the lake. The only sign of life was a few of our less traumatised swans, stumping up and down on the far side of the lake. Other than that – there was nothing.

I pulled my head in.

'Where?'

'Here. I saw it. They fell past this window. But when I looked, there was no one there.'

I didn't bother asking, 'Are you sure?' This was

Markham. To be sure, he was small, grubby, and accident prone, but he was also virtually indestructible and very, very tough. Yet here he was, standing in front of me now, so pale that I could see the blue veins in his temples. There was no doubt he thought he'd seen something.

He stuck his own head back out of the window, presumably in case the body had magically reappeared.

'Perhaps they weren't hurt – or not hurt very badly,' he said, 'and they got up and went for help.'

'Good thought.' I opened my com link and called Dr Foster. 'Helen – has anyone reported to you at any time in the last ten minutes?'

'No. Why?'

'There's a possibility someone may have fallen off the roof.'

'Check around. Especially those idiots in R & D. Sounds like the sort of thing they might do. I'll let you know if anyone turns up.'

She closed the link.

Markham was as near angry as I'd ever seen him. 'There's no "possibility" about it. I know what I saw.'

'What did you see? Tell me every detail.'

'I was standing just here.'

He pushed me aside and stood where I had been.

'I was walking towards your office.'

He mimed walking, just in case I was having some difficulty grasping the concept.

'The window was on my left. Just as I drew level, something black fell past. I was so surprised I couldn't move for a second.'

He mimed a level of surprise and horror that would

11

lead anyone else to believe he'd just witnessed the asteroid wipe out the dinosaurs.

'Then I heaved up the window, leaned out, and … and there was nothing there.'

'Is there a possibility they got up and ran away before you had a chance to see?'

'I don't know. It took me a while to get the window open, but you've seen for yourself – there's no cover. All right, they might not be dead since they only fell on gravel, but it's three floors up – they'd have broken a bone or two at least. And why would they hide? It doesn't make sense.'

He looked genuinely agitated, which was a first for him.

'I think,' I said slowly, 'that someone's pulling your plonker. Someone's up on the roof – they push off an old dummy and in between the time you see it and struggle to get the window up and look out, someone's leaned out of a downstairs window and pulled it in. I bet they're down there now, laughing their heads off and waiting for you to appear at any minute and start dashing about looking for bodies.'

His face cleared. 'Of course. Bastards! Good trick though. Talk about shitting bricks – I nearly evacuated a monolith. Thanks, Max.'

He strolled off, presumably to bring down retribution on persons unknown and I wandered back to my office.

The next day, he was back again and this time he wasn't alone.

They burst through my door, Peterson escorting Markham who looked – not to put too fine a point on it –

as if he'd seen a ghost.

'It did it again,' he said, not very coherently for someone brought up in the Major Guthrie tradition of concise reporting.

First things first. I opened my mouth to instruct Miss Lee to make him a cup of much-needed tea but she was already ahead of the game, gathering up two or three files at random and heading for the door, announcing she had to catch the post, which indeed, would be collected in about four hours' time.

Peterson made us all a cup of tea. I contemplated adding something comforting from my bottom drawer, but Markham was incoherent enough.

'I saw it again, Max,' he announced. 'A black figure falling past the window and when I looked out there was nothing there. Again. Dr Peterson was there. He saw it.'

'I saw you see something,' corrected Peterson. 'I didn't see anything fall, but I can confirm there was nothing there when we looked.'

'But you must have,' objected Markham. 'A black figure, silhouetted against the sky. I saw arms and legs. Just for a moment, true, but you can't mistake a falling body.'

I had a thought. 'What did you hear?'

He sat quietly, running through things in his mind. 'Nothing.'

'Nothing? No cry? No sound of impact?'

He looked suddenly thoughtful. 'No. There was no sound of impact. And if those buggers from R & D were playing silly devils and chucking things off the roof then you'd hear something, wouldn't you?'

13

Yes, you would. I looked at him again. I'd seen him wounded; I'd seen him running for his life; I'd even seen him in drag, but I'd never seen him like this before. I couldn't dismiss this lightly.

I stood up. 'Tim, can you check out R & D? Tactfully, please.'

He nodded. 'What are you going to do?'

'I'm going to talk to Dr Dowson.' I looked at Markham. 'You all right?'

'Yes. What shall I do?'

'Nothing for the minute. If someone is playing a trick on you then the best thing you can do is ignore it. We'll meet back here at half past three.'

Dr Dowson was our librarian and archivist. In most organisations, this means spending the day in an atmosphere of tranquil serenity. Books don't usually give you a lot of grief. Today, he was standing on his desk, pounding the ceiling with a broom handle and shouting curses. In Latin, Greek, and possibly Morse code, by the sound of it.

He broke off to greet me with a smile. 'Ah, Max. Can I help you?'

I knew better than to ask what was going on. He and Professor Rapson from R & D were old friends, which apparently was sufficient grounds for mutual abuse and recrimination at every opportunity. R & D occupied the rooms directly overhead and possibly inadvertently, but probably not, had done something to incur his wrath.

I helped him down off his desk and told him the story and feeling a little foolish said, 'Is it possible, is it just possible, that we have a ghost we didn't know about?'

14

He stood still for a moment, polishing his spectacles, lost in thought, and then disappeared briefly, returning with an old book, two modern pamphlets, and a file of loose photocopies.

He laid them on a table and we sat down.

'Right.' he said. 'A potted history of St Mary's.

'The first building, the original Priory of St Mary's, was raised by Augustinian monks towards the end of the 13th century. That building stood for more or less a hundred years. I think the location was too remote, however, and over the years, the monks just drifted away. St Mary's, the village, and all the land with it were eventually acquired – it doesn't say how – by Henry of Grosmont, 4th Earl of Lancaster. He did nothing with it, other than collect the rents, but his son-in-law, John of Gaunt, Duke of Lancaster, bestowed the manor upon Henry of Rushford, a comrade in arms, for services rendered during the 1386 campaign in Castile.

'This next bit is interesting. There was, apparently, a bit of a skirmish during the confusion of 1399. While Richard II and Henry Bolingbroke jostled for supremacy, it would appear another branch of the Rushford family took advantage of the confusion and attacked St Mary's. Despite a spirited defence, the attackers did gain entry, but were foiled when, in a last desperate effort, the defenders, led by Henry's granddaughter, attempted to burn the place down to cover their escape to Rushford. Exciting days, eh?

'Matters were obviously resolved satisfactorily, but St Mary's passed out of the Rushford family's hands a generation or so afterwards. No heir, as is frequently the case, I'm afraid. I really don't know why these things are always passed down through the male line – girl children are much more robust than their brothers, and let's face it, Max – while there may always be doubt about the identity of the father, most people are usually fairly clear about who the mother is.'

He brooded for a while on this unsatisfactory state of affairs, and who was I to disagree?

'Anyway, St Mary's had any number of owners, all of whom apparently lived perfectly peacefully, even during troubled times. The estate survived the Wars of the Roses, religious strife under the Tudors, and then, in the late 16th century, the Laceys of Gloucestershire moved in.'

He opened the book. 'The Civil War split them down the middle, with half of them supporting the King and the other half lining up for Cromwell. In 1643, a contingent of Parliamentary forces, led by Captain Edmund Lacey, left Gloucester for some reason, and rode here. Accounts are jumbled, and there are several versions of events, but they all agree that the Great Hall was torched and Margaret Lacey and her elder son, Charles, perished in the blaze. The younger son, James, who was only a very young boy at the time, escaped to the roof, was rescued by a servant, and taken safely to the village. Captain Lacey disappeared, was tried, and found guilty of murder in his absence and was never seen again. The Hall was rebuilt by James and is largely as we see it today. With the exception of the glass lantern, of course.

'St Mary's continued to change hands, shedding land as it went, until it fell empty in the late 19th century. It was too big for a family house and since there was no longer any land left to support it, it became a bit of a white elephant, I'm afraid. It was used as a convalescent home for soldiers during and after World War I, and then was a school, briefly and disastrously. Apparently, someone left a tap running and the ceiling came down in what is now Wardrobe. It was used as a hospital again during World War II. And that's it until we moved in, my goodness, some years ago now.' He tapped the documents. 'It's all here. And much more besides.'

I said slowly, 'Thank you, Doctor, but I think might I have what I need.'

He nodded. '1643?'

'Yes, I think so. The little boy ran up to the roof. He survived, but maybe someone did fall. Captain Lacey, maybe. Perhaps that's why he was never seen again. Because he died. Either in the fire or in the fall. Can you get me more details?'

He smiled. 'I expect so. Give me an hour.'

We reconvened. There being no sign of Miss Lee, I made the tea this time.

'You can't be doing it right,' said Peterson, smugly. 'My Mrs Shaw brings me chocolate biscuits as well.'

I ignored him.

'There seem to be two candidates for Mr Markham's falling body. In 1399, there was a minor skirmish over ownership. I suppose it's perfectly possible someone could have fallen from the roof.'

'Or possibly, someone had a mad wife and she jumped, like Mrs Rochester,' added Markham, never one to choose the obvious option. 'And she dashed her brains

17

out on the flags below.'

'When did you ever read *Jane Eyre*?' demanded Peterson, easily distracted.

'I broke my ankle.'

We waited, but that seemed to be it.

'Or,' I said, firmly dragging them back on track, 'in 1643, during the Civil War, the Roundheads arrived, threatened, and possibly murdered a woman and child. But, and this is the interesting bit, a second child sought refuge on the roof. Describe the body again.'

'There's nothing to describe. A black shape with arms and legs.'

'Could it have been a child?'

'It could, I suppose. It didn't look very big, but ...' He sounded doubtful. 'I don't know. And anyway, the kid survived, didn't he? It's a bit of a mystery.'

Silence. We slurped our tea.

'Well,' said Peterson. 'Now what? All very interesting, but what has this to do with us?'

There being no good answer to that one, we finished our tea and stood up. I walked with them to the door and out into the corridor.

'Sorry, mate,' said Peterson to Markham. 'There's just too little to go on. Apart from your daily hallucinations, we just don't have any – '

Markham stiffened, pointed, and cried, 'There! Oh, my God! Again!'

We stood paralysed, because we're highly trained professionals, and then rushed to the window. Peterson heaved it up and stuck out his head. I elbowed myself some room and did the same. Markham, realising he stood no chance, ran to another window and looked out.

The sun shone down on the frosty gravel. We looked to the north. We looked to the south. Markham thought to hang even further out of the window, twist himself around, and look up.

Nothing.

'Come on,' he said, and we headed for the roof, emerging through a tiny door in the north-east corner. Despite the frost, the roof was a bit of a suntrap and pleasantly warm. In the old days, it had been gabled and tiled, but at some point in its history, the roof had been replaced and flattened. Groups of tall chimneys stood around. The big glass lantern, which let some much-needed light into the Hall, was over there. Over to the right, we could look down on lower roof levels. There was even a fire escape, which Markham headed towards. We watched him go.

'What do you think?' said Peterson. 'It's astounding, isn't it?'

'I know. I'm still gobsmacked. Jane Eyre!'

'Are we going to check this out?'

'Are you kidding?'

'We'll never get permission.'

'Leave that to me. I've had a brilliant idea.'

He groaned.

Markham returned and crossed to the parapet, which was just above waist height and looked down. We joined him.

'Bloody hell,' said Peterson, stepping back.

'You all right?'

'Fine,' he said, averting his eyes and stepping four or

five paces back. 'Just tell me what you see.'

'Nothing. There's nothing.'

'And nothing's been up here today,' added Markham.

He was right. Our footprints were clearly visible on the frosty roof. And only ours. Unless someone had come up here barefoot …

We looked around, our breath frosty in the cold, sharp air.

I looked at Markham. 'Are you up for this?'

'How can you even ask?'

I spent the rest of the day putting things together and just as the lights were coming on and people beginning to drift towards the dining-room, I went to see Dr Bairstow. Who looked about as pleased to see me as he usually did.

'Dr Maxwell. Can I assume you bring me details of your progress organising our Open Day?'

'All in hand, sir,' I said with massive confidence and even more massive untruthfulness.

'Then you are here because …?'

'I'd like to claim my jump, sir. If you please.'

At the end of our unpleasantness last year, as an outright bribe, he'd offered me the assignment of my choice. At the time, I'd considered Thermopylae, but now …

'Really? Where and when did you have in mind?'

'St Mary's. 1643.'

He finished stacking his files and straightened, slowly.

'And interesting choice. May I ask why?'

'Ghost-hunting, sir.'

20

He looked at me sharply. 'There is no ghost at St Mary's.'

'We may have recently acquired one, sir.'

'How?'

I considered my options, remembered no good ever came of lying to the Boss, and said, 'On three occasions now, Mr Markham has seen someone fall off the roof. When we go to check it out, there's never anything there.'

'1643? That would be the dastardly Captain Lacey?'

'That's the one, sir.'

He moved the files around.

'Do we have a working pod?'

'I'm sure Chief Farrell will have one tucked away somewhere, sir.'

I waited. There was no need to remind him of his promise.

'Do not let the fact that I have pre-approved this assignment lead you to believe I will not wish to see the usual mission plan, Dr Maxwell.'

'Of course not, sir.'

'Or that the usual parameters will not apply.'

'No, sir.'

'And your team will consist of ...?'

'Me, Dr Peterson, and Mr Markham.'

'Ah. The usual suspects. Why Mr Markham?'

'It's his ghost, sir,' I said, more accurately than anyone realised at the time.

'Well, I suppose Mr Markham's absence from St Mary's is always a cause for celebration.'

'Well not really, sir. He'll still be here – just

four hundred years ago.'

He sighed. 'I don't really think that will be long enough.'

I held a briefing.

Since there were only the three of us, we held it in my office. I'd asked for tea to be served. Miss Lee had left out mugs, milk, lemon, sugar, tea bags, and even put water in the kettle. Sadly, she had made no attempt to assemble these component parts, all of which remained scattered around the room. It was like a treasure hunt.

'Your turn,' I said to Markham and to the accompaniment of the boiling kettle and clattering teaspoons, I laid out Dr Dowson's findings.

'OK, listen up. It's 1643 – right in the middle of the Civil War, just before the Siege of Gloucester gets under way. At some point, for reasons unknown, Captain Edmund Lacey slips away from the city and makes his way here, to St Mary's. His elder brother, Rupert,' I laid down a photograph of a very dim painting of a pouty man in a vast wig, 'is away fighting for the King.'

Markham gulped his tea. 'They were on opposite sides?'

'Yes. Something not uncommon in this particular conflict. Families divided. Some members fought for the King – others for Cromwell. Anyway, Captain Lacey fetches up here on ...' I consulted Dr Dowson's notes, '3rd

August. Sir Rupert, whereabouts unknown at this point, is away, leaving behind his wife, their two sons, and, presumably, one or two servants. Later that same day, there's a fire – probably set by the Roundheads. Perhaps Edmund wanted her to surrender St Mary's and she refused. Although it's hard to see how she could possibly have resisted. Anyway, there's a fire. A serious fire. It starts in one of the rooms off the gallery and spreads rapidly. Wooden floors, wooden furniture, hangings – it all goes up.

'Margaret Lacey and the elder son, Charles, don't survive. The younger boy, a lad of around six or seven, somehow gets away. He runs up to the roof. Maybe he's pursued by Edmund Lacey who died when the roof came down. We don't know. Edmund Lacey never rejoins his unit. In fact, he's never seen again, so yes, at this time, we'll assume he died in the fire, along with his sister-in-law and nephew.'

'What happened to James?'

'James was rescued by a servant and taken to the village for safety. Sir Rupert was killed later on in the war, so eventually James inherits St Mary's. The estate escaped the fines and imprisonment usually imposed on the losing side by virtue of his youth. When Charles II later restored the monarchy, he escaped the fines or imprisonment usually imposed for having a Parliamentarian in the family, by virtue of his father's service to the king. As far as everyone knows, he lived happily ever after.'

We drank our tea.

'So no one falls off the roof?' persisted Markham.

'Well, if anyone does, I'm betting it's Edmund Lacey.'

'Why did he desert his unit in the first place?'

'Dunno. Maybe he thought his brother was already dead and came to claim the property.'

'But there were sons to inherit.'

'Yes,' I said quietly, 'but there was also a fire in which one son died. The other escaped only thanks to their servant. Who knows for what purpose Captain Lacey chased him up onto the roof?'

Silence.

'A bit of a bastard, then,' observed Markham.

'Yep.'

'And that's who we're going to check out?'

'Yep.'

'Cool.'

We assembled outside my favourite pod, Number Eight, and checked each other over.

Peterson and Markham both wore unpadded jerkins, knee-length breeches, stockings, heavy leather shoes, and mirth-provoking hats. Fortunately for me, ladies' costumes were looser and more comfortable than the heavily embroidered portable torture chambers of Elizabethan times. However, I do have to say that for the short, mildly overweight ginger historian, the mid-17th century wasn't a good look. In addition to what Mrs Enderby from Wardrobe maintained was actually a very moderate bum roll, my ankle-length full skirt made me look wider than I was high.

I unwisely enquired whether my bum looked big in this.

There was a brief pause.

'Bloody massive,' said Peterson. 'I'm not sure we'll get you through the door.'

I glared at him. 'You could at least have tried for a tactful response.'

'That was the tactful response. Be grateful.'

'Yes,' said Markham, 'because I was going to say …'

'Just shut up and get in the pod.'

Once inside, we were joined by the centre of my universe. Or Chief Farrell, as everyone else called him. He wore the orange jumpsuit of the Technical Section and was, as usual, festooned with tools and implements. He had more silver in his hair than when we first met, but his blue eyes remained as bright as ever. He winked at me and began to check over the console.

Markham stowed our gear while Peterson and I ran our eyes over the read-outs.

'All laid in,' said Leon, stepping back. 'Return coordinates, too.'

Arising out of an assignment last year, I'd made two recommendations to Dr Bairstow. The first was that there were no more open-ended assignments. Peterson and I had jumped to 14th-century Southwark last year, and he'd carelessly picked up a touch of plague. 'Just a twinge,' as he was fond of saying, but I'd been unable to get him back to St Mary's.

Not normally a problem, they'd have sent out search parties soon enough, but in this case, being open-ended, we had no return date, so no one knew we were in trouble. By the time St Mary's realised something was wrong, it could have been too late. So now, every assignment had a specific return date and time, and if we didn't show up, they'd come looking for us.

The second recommendation concerned contamination. We always decontaminate on our return from every mission. It had occurred to me – actually, I'd been sniffing around Peterson's groin at the time, but never mind that – that our modern bugs could be as fatal to contemporaries as theirs were to us. Look at Cortéz and the South American natives. After some discussion, we now not only decontaminated on our return, but also when we left St Mary's as well. As a further precaution – Peterson getting the plague had been a nasty shock for everyone, especially for him – the inside of the pod was painted in that special paint that kills bacteria when lit with fluorescent lights and a strip across the floor ensured our shoes were treated as well.

Markham shut the locker doors and said, 'All done.'

'That's it,' said Leon. 'Good luck, everyone.' He held out his hand as he spoke. We shook hands, just as we always did when others were present. His hand was warm and rough and firm. 'Stay safe.'

'You too,' I said.

He smiled for me alone and then exited the pod. The door closed behind him.

I seated myself. 'Whenever you're ready, Tim,' and felt the familiar tingle of anticipation.

'Computer – initiate jump.'

And the world went white.

We stared at an unfamiliar St Mary's.

'It looks so small,' said Markham, eventually, and

27

he was right.

This was not the St Mary's we knew, with its flat roof and Virginia creeper, its sprawl of outbuildings, its car park, and neat grounds. This St Mary's was square and blocky, with a steeply gabled roof from which protruded randomly placed chimneys which wouldn't have been part of the original structure and must have been added on as required.

There were no formal gardens as we knew them, just trees, bushes, an orchard and extensive vegetable garden. Sheep cropped the ancestor of Mr Strong's beloved South Lawn. There was no drive leading to the house, just a wide grassy path, rutted with wagon tracks. The gates were high, wooden, and firmly shut. Most noticeably, there was no lake. A string of ponds had been built – by the monks, I guessed – to supplement their diet with the occasional carp. When Capability Brown or whoever got his hands on St Mary's, they and the surrounding boggy area would be excavated to make the familiar lake.

The silence was complete. I remembered what Dr Dowson had said about the monks drifting away. What was pleasant seclusion at our St Mary's was remote and lonely at this one. Everything looked small, rural, and at the moment, very peaceful.

That wouldn't last. In a day or so, much of this St Mary's would be gone.

There was no one around. The shadows were long. The sun was setting.

'Right,' I said, turning from the screen. 'Plan of action. We wait until it's dark and then nip across the grass. Do not fall over the sheep. We'll approach from the east, and see if we can get a window open. Then it's up the stairs to the attics and find a place from which to observe events. Tomorrow is the day the Roundheads turn up.'

'Are we likely to encounter any dogs?' said Peterson.

'Unlikely,' said Markham. 'Not if they have sheep outside, but in case my lady has a lapdog or similar ...' He flourished a small aerosol.

'Not pepper,' I warned. The last thing we wanted was a pack of hysterical, sneezing, panic-stricken spaniels yelping all over the house.

'No, it's something the professor knocked up. It's quite harmless. It just ... confuses them.'

'Well in that case, for God's sake don't spray it on Peterson.'

'Don't spray it at all,' warned Peterson. 'Remember the professor's hair lacquer?'

He had a point.

Responding to the many complaints from female historians about the difficulties of managing the enormous lengths of hair with which they were cursed, the professor had given the problem some thought and then announced the invention of a hairspray guaranteed to hold in place even the most unruly locks. Delighted historians had given it a go until the whole lot was confiscated by Dr Bairstow when it was discovered to be so inflammable you couldn't even walk under a streetlight without featuring in the next scientific paper on spontaneous human combustion.

I interrupted the discussion between Peterson and Markham who had gone on to dispute exactly who had been responsible for the small fire in the copse behind our big barn, and why Peterson couldn't land a pod without bumping it, which was threatening to become wide-ranging and noisy.

'The sun's going down. I'm going to decontaminate now,' and operated the lamp. The cold blue light glowed and I felt the hairs on my arms shiver.

'I swear that bloody thing makes you sterile,' muttered Markham.

Nobody fell over a sheep. A minor miracle in itself.

The moon came up, sending long blue shadows over silver grass. We flitted from tree to tree in a magical landscape. The woods came down much closer to the house than in our time and we hugged the treeline as far as we could.

I'm not sure we needed to. There were no signs of life anywhere. No lights showed from the blank windows. No dogs barked. Even the stables seemed deserted. Had Sir Rupert taken all his horses off to war? Not even leaving his wife the working horses for the land?

We paused for a final check before approaching the house.

'This is suspiciously easy,' murmured Peterson. 'Are we even sure anyone's at home?'

'We're not sure of anything,' I whispered, which was true. Our assignments usually had a stated purpose. To observe the fall of Troy. To carry out an in-depth study of the Cretaceous period. To catch a glimpse of Isaac Newton. Today we'd just turned up. To see what, if anything, happened next. To solve a mystery we weren't sure even existed. And, of course, to discover why something or someone only Markham could see kept falling from the roof.

It seemed likely that out here in the country, the household went to bed at sunset and rose at dawn. The house certainly looked bedded down for the night.

'Come on,' I said. 'Before we lose the moonlight.'

We made a final dash to the side of the house, standing in its shadow as clouds scudded across the sky. The wind felt cool on my face.

Peterson and Markham felt around the windows while I kept watch. They didn't seem to be having any luck until suddenly, in the dark, I heard a quiet tinkle of broken glass.

'What?' I said, managing an outraged whisper with no trouble at all.

'Relax,' said Markham. 'I was doing this when I was in my cradle.'

'What?' said Peterson. Ditto with the whisper.

'That's why I had to join the army.'

'You're a felon?' It takes talent to hiss when there isn't a single 's' in the sentence.

'Well, yes. Aren't you?'

'You had to join the army?' persisted Peterson.

'Yeah. It was that or – something else.' He was working the catch. 'Served under Major Guthrie. Didn't you know? There we go.'

He eased open a small window.

We paused for irate householders, watchdogs, patrolling servants, crying children, whatever, but apart from the odd owl, we could hear nothing.

Markham was fastidiously picking up the glass.

'What are you doing?'

He tossed the shards under a bush. 'We don't want some servant noticing a broken pane and raising the alarm.'

'Oh. Good thinking.'

'I offer a complete service,' he said smugly.

We pushed the curtain aside and clambered in, dropping silently to the floor. Risking a little light, Peterson flashed a tiny torch.

We appeared to be in a small, wood-panelled room. I wondered if this was Sir Rupert's study. Just faintly, I thought I could make out the smells of wood, leather, and tobacco. Like most rooms of the period, it wasn't over-cluttered with furniture and what there was of it was dark and heavy. Markham crossed to the door, opened it a crack, and peered out. Peterson and I remained motionless.

He watched and listened for what seemed a very long time then signalled us forwards. From now on, there would be no talking.

We glided across the Great Hall, keeping to the shadows. There was no glass lantern in the roof. Massive hammer beams supported the high ceiling, but the smell was just the same – dust and damp stone. I listened to St Mary's talking to itself in the darkness. Boards creaked. Timbers settled. Somewhere, a mouse skittered along the floor.

The staircase was unfamiliar, being long and straight and running up the wall. The famous half-landing, the centre of St Mary's life, had yet to be born. We eased our way around the gallery, silent apart from the swish of my skirts. From somewhere in the dark, I could hear the murmur of a woman's voice. A high, childish voice answered. We veered silently away, past closed doors, heading for the narrow staircase in the corner. Our plan was to spend the night in the attics and that was all the plan we had. We had no idea what to do next. We've had missions fall apart around us – that happens all the time – but this was the first time we'd set out with no clear course of action. It was quite exciting, actually.

The attics were tiny. We could barely stand up in our little room. Peterson flashed his torch and I stared in wonder at the treasure trove of broken household goods, unfashionable portraits, bric a brac … and it would all be gone in a day or two when the place went up in flames. We found a corner. Markham indicated he would take the first watch and I settled down to sleep.

I had the last watch. I sat against the wall, watched the patterns of light travel across the floor as the sun rose, and then woke them for breakfast. We sat on the floor and munched a couple of those shitty high-energy biscuits they keep shoving in our ration packs and listened to the house stir. A door opened and a woman's voice called outside. Someone must be in the hen house because I could hear chicken noises. Faintly, a child shouted and there were running footsteps on a wooden floor. They were up and about. Time to get cracking.

We were just packing everything away when we heard the hoof beats. Someone was approaching – and at great speed. It had begun.

'Bloody hell, he's early,' muttered Peterson. 'Leave all

this. We'll come back for it later.'

We crept down the stairs and oozed out onto the gallery, grateful, for once, for the bad lighting. Correctly guessing that everyone's attention would be on the front door, we wriggled forwards. Lying on our stomachs and peering through the bannisters, we had an excellent view of the front doors below and most of the Hall. There was no vestibule. The front doors opened directly into the Great Hall. Whoever was there – whatever was about to happen – we would be able to see everything.

Peterson and I are historians. We get caught up in what's happening. That's why we usually bring a member of the Security team with us. They watch our backs because we forget to. My attention was fixed on downstairs. I never thought to look behind us.

Markham nudged me and nodded over my shoulder. Two little boys, dressed well but soberly, stood in the doorway to what I guessed might be Lady Lacey's own sitting room. They held hands and both of them looked terrified. Galloping horsemen arriving just after dawn during a civil war – that's never reassuring.

The eldest boy was very pale, and slender and delicate looking in his blue jacket and breeches. His blond curls hung around his face. His brother was stockier, darker, and dressed in similar material. Idly, I wondered if it was his brother's outgrown suit. These must be Charles and James, the two boys.

They both stared at us in silence. Given that the sight of three complete strangers lying on their stomachs, peering through the bannisters couldn't possibly be something they'd ever seen before, we probably had only seconds before one or both of them raised the alarm.

Down below, someone pounded on the front door, demanding admittance. The boys stopped staring at us and turned their attention to the Great Hall instead. Then back to us again.

Markham rolled over onto his back, winked at them, put his finger to his lips, and gestured them back into the room again. Amazingly, they did as they were told. In fact, they seemed glad to go.

Downstairs, the pounding redoubled. No servant came to answer the door. Had they already fled? In all our time there, we never saw a single one.

Lady Lacey – at least I assumed that was who she was – slowly crossed the Hall. I could only see her rear view. She wore something light on her head – I couldn't make it out. Her dress was of some dark, stiff material, caught up over a lighter underdress. Her skirt was even fuller than mine was and the wide sleeves gave her that fashionable narrow back. In the sudden silence, I could hear the sound of silk swishing over the stone flags.

The pounding began again. Visibly squaring her shoulders, she pulled back the bolts. The door crashed back against the wall. Echoes boomed around the building. I risked a look over my shoulder. The boys had gone.

A dusty figure tumbled into the Hall, bent forwards, and panted for breath.

Margaret Lacey stepped back, her hands to her face. '*Edmund*?'

I suddenly had a very bad feeling about all of this.

Straightening, he seized both her hands. 'Margaret – I

have come to warn you. He is coming. He is on his way. I came across the fields, but he will be here at any moment.'

She half turned and I could make out her white face.

'Rupert? Coming here? But why?'

I couldn't see his face clearly – he was outlined against the light behind him, but I heard him take a deep, shuddering breath.

'Because he knows, Margaret. God help us both – he knows!'

You see, this is the problem with legends. They're legends. A bunch of colourful facts bundled together to make a good story. This is why the world has historians. We jump back to a given event, sort out the real facts, escape whatever peril(s) is (are) menacing us at the time, and return in triumph. That's what historians do. It's not all sitting around drinking tea and blowing things up, you know.

Anyway, it seemed that even St Mary's gets their facts wrong occasionally. From the way they were clinging to each other, it was obvious that Edmund Lacey and his sister-in-law had a greater affection for each other than had previously been known.

And who was 'he'? And what did 'he' know? These were not difficult questions to answer, and 'he' was on his way here. We were in uncharted territory now.

I glanced at Peterson, immersed in the human drama below, and at Markham who was still keeping watch behind us. He cocked his head, listening. Then I heard them too. More hoof beats. And more than one horseman this time. Markham melted away into the shadows, reappearing moments later to whisper, 'Four of them. Riding hard. Don't like the look of this.'

Neither did I. I twisted round to make sure both boys were safely out of the way.

Back down in the Hall, both Margaret and Edmund Lacey had also heard the sound of approaching riders. She uttered a small shriek and clung to him.

He pushed her towards the stairs. 'I will speak with him. Calm him down. Go upstairs and stay with the boys.'

Her face was a mask of fear. 'He will kill you. He will kill us both.'

'No. He will be angry, but he is my brother. He will not harm me.'

He should have listened to her.

I wondered why he left the front door open, but that was just common sense. When an enraged Rupert Lacey eventually arrived, his mood would not be improved by having to hammer on his own front door for admittance. On reflection, however, they might have been better off barricading themselves inside and taking their chances. Angry was not the word to describe the burly figure striding through the open door, sword drawn.

We all have our illusions about Roundheads and Cavaliers. Roundheads – right but repulsive. Cavaliers – wrong but wromantic.[1] Roundheads were bullying killjoys headed by the charmless Oliver Cromwell. Cavaliers served their king and were tall, handsome, well dressed, and charming.

Not in this case. These two brothers were definitely doing things the wrong way round.

In the brief glimpse I'd had of him, Captain Lacey was

---

[1] *1066 And All That*, W C Sellar & R J Yeatman. Methuen & Co., 1930

tall and slender, with fine, light-coloured hair and Rupert Lacey looked like your typical Roundhead. Short, square, blunt features, large hands. There couldn't have been a greater contrast between the two brothers. Almost as great as that between the next generation of brothers, young Charles and –

Oh, shit!

I knew what this was about. Everyone must know what this was about. The physical evidence was there for everyone to see. Including Sir Rupert. He must have had his suspicions for years, but now something had happened – some stupid joke at his expense, maybe, we'd never know – and he'd left the King's army, left everything, to come here today and – what?

All right, it was a promiscuous age, especially amongst the aristocracy. Things would quieten down a little during Cromwell's Commonwealth, but since football hadn't really got off the ground yet, adultery was still the national sport. Lady Lacey, however, had made an unforgiveable mistake and if her husband killed her for it – and he would, by the looks of him – there wasn't a soul in the land who would condemn him. Because she'd committed the cardinal sin. She'd played around before presenting her husband with an heir and you just don't do that. The rules are very clear for wives – husbands, of course, can do as they please – but if you're a wife then you do your duty. You present your husband with an heir – and possibly a spare, just to be on the safe side. Then, if you want to, you can have a little discreet fun afterwards, but there must never, ever, be any shadow of doubt over who fathered the first son. With titles, land, and money at stake, no one can afford any questions over the heir's paternity.

She'd broken the rules and she was about to pay the price. And possibly her children would, too.

How strong must their passion have been for Captain and Lady Lacey to take such a risk? Was it love? Captain Lacey was a handsome man. Her husband wasn't. Even from here, he looked boorish and bad tempered. Vicious, even. She'd married the wrong brother. Yes, this was probably love. She didn't look like a strumpet and neither did Edmund; there was a war on and he'd abandoned his post and risked his life to warn her.

I felt Peterson's hand on my shoulder, and we inched backwards into the shadows with which St Mary's was so liberally provided.

Lady Lacey hurried up the stairs and around the gallery. She passed so close to me that her skirt brushed my face as I crouched in the shadows, and I could smell some sort of spicy orange smell from the stuff she rubbed into the folds to keep it fresh. I doubt she would have seen me even if I were standing directly in front of her. She was blind with fear: her dark eyes distended and desperate. She couldn't have been much more than twenty-four or twenty-five and the little knots of curls on either side of her face made her look even younger. She swept into her room and closed the door behind her. I waited in vain for the sound of the key turning but it never came. She couldn't lock herself in.

We wriggled forwards again.

Sir Rupert halted just inside his own front doors, his chest heaving. Captain Lacey walked slowly to the middle of the Hall and stood, waiting for him.

'You!' It came out as a roar. 'You dare show your face here? In my house?'

Captain Lacey held out his hands. 'Rupert, be calm.'

He was wasting his time. Rupert Lacey advanced down the Hall like a one-man cavalry charge. Captain Lacey stepped back warily, keeping out of sword range and that would have been a very sensible move indeed, had not his brother whipped out a pistol and shot him.

The sound of the shot echoed around the Hall, followed by screaming from Lady Lacey's room. I could hear her shouting, 'Edmund! Oh God, Edmund! May God and his saints preserve us' and I couldn't help feeling that given her current situation a little more wifely concern for her husband, however insincere, might have been more prudent.

Edmund fell with a crash and lay still.

'Shit,' whispered Peterson, which was a bit of an understatement, all things considered. None of this was right. There should be a contingent of Roundheads pillaging the place as fast as they could go. Sir Rupert definitely shouldn't be here at all, and as for Lady Lacey and her children ... I remembered she was to die today.

No time to think. Without even a glance at his fallen brother, the wronged husband was heading for the stairs, gun in one hand, and sword in the other. He shouted, 'Margaret! I come for you now,' and she broke off in mid-shriek. The silence was terrifying.

Under cover of his footsteps on the wooden stairs, I said, 'Markham, stay with Captain Lacey. Peterson, watch out for the youngest kid. He'll bolt for the roof. I'll stick with Margaret.'

Peterson made a slight sound that I had no difficulty in interpreting as 'I'd really rather not go up there, if you don't mind.'

I smoothly changed gear. 'On second thoughts, Markham to the roof and Peterson, you see to the captain. Remember there are three other men somewhere around.'

They vanished and I pulled myself to my feet and silently followed Sir Rupert along the gallery.

His family had made a sad little attempt to barricade themselves inside. It didn't slow him down at all. Finding that the door wouldn't open, he put his shoulder to it. He was a powerful man and the door jerked open. I could hear furniture scraping across the boards as he heaved. It didn't take him long to force a gap wide enough not only for him to squeeze through, but for me to see what was happening.

He burst into what was obviously her private sitting room. The spicy orange smell was stronger in here. Two wooden seats with comfortable cushions stood one on each side of the empty fireplace. There was no library as such, not yet, but a row of some half dozen books stood on one table, held up by two very amateurishly carved wooden horse's heads. Perhaps a gift from one of her sons.

A good carpet lay in the middle of the room and a small Flemish tapestry hung along the inside wall, well away from damaging sunlight.

Her needlework lay where it had been hurriedly discarded. A set of toy soldiers sprawled across the floor in front of the fire. It was a light, sunny, pleasant family room. I could easily imagine Lady Lacey and her sons spending their time here, quietly happy.

She stood, seemingly trapped, on the far side of the room, between the fireplace and the window. Both boys clung to her skirts. James had buried his face in them. Not taking her eyes from her silently advancing husband, she groped frantically at the panelling behind her, found what she was looking for, and twisted a wooden boss.

A whole section of panelling slid aside.

They had a priest hole. Of course they did. A tiny, supposedly secret room where Catholics could hide during Protestant oppression. And vice versa, of course. And where erring wives could take the children to keep them safe. A 17th-century panic room.

Except that, at this point, everything went wrong for her. The younger boy lost his head. Perhaps he didn't like the look of this tiny, dark cave. Even as Lady Lacey drew her elder son backwards into the priest hole, young James gave a terrified cry and tore himself free from her grasp.

She screamed, 'James!' and lunged for him. Sir Rupert seized his arm and for a few dreadful seconds, they tugged the little lad back and forth. He was screaming. She was screaming. Lacey was roaring like a bull. I wouldn't have been surprised to see him start frothing at the mouth.

If he'd concentrated on James, he would have had him, but although he'd dropped his pistol, he still had his sword in his other hand and he couldn't resist the chance to have a stab at his wife. She screamed again and jerked back, releasing her son. James fell forwards and Sir

43

Rupert lost his balance and tripped over a footstool. Before he could pick himself up, Margaret flung herself backwards into the priest hole, and James dodged past his cursing father, squeezed easily through the partially open door, and disappeared.

I heard footsteps his footsteps, clattering along the gallery. He was heading for the roof.

Sir Rupert heaved himself to his feet, swore viciously, kicked the footstool aside, strode to the area of panelling between the fireplace and the window, and began to beat on it with his sword hilt.

'Margaret! Come out! Come out, I say!'

I'm paraphrasing. That wasn't actually how he expressed himself at all. I learned several new words that day. Including the meaning of the verb to swive.

Wisely, she did no such thing. She'd secured the priest hole from the inside and if she had any sense, she'd never come out.

Again, if he'd kept his head, he'd have gone after his younger son – although strictly speaking James was his only son – and used him as a hostage. My guess was that Lady Lacey would not have remained concealed for long. Unless, of course, her affection for her lover's child was greater than that for her husband's. We'll never know, because tiring of battering uselessly at the panels, he strode to the window, flung it open, and shouted.

I just had time to conceal myself at the end of the gallery – actually, just where Dr Bairstow's office would be, one day – as his two henchmen came piling up the stairs. From the lack of commotion in the Hall, I guessed that Peterson had somehow managed to get Captain Lacey away and Markham was elsewhere, keeping an eye on James.

They clattered up the stairs and presented themselves for orders. Where was the third man? What was he up to?

These were no Cavaliers. They weren't in any army. Even the worst type of army wouldn't accept these men. I could smell them from here. Both of them were in a state of high excitement and I suddenly realised why Lady Lacey had been so terrified and why she had seemingly abandoned one of her children. What had her husband planned for her? And possibly the elder boy, Charles, as well.

He barked a series of orders, spit flying from his mouth with the violence of his words. The men disappeared in a hurry and he began to tear down the curtains and hangings and pile them against the entrance to the priest hole. The books were tossed contemptuously onto the pile. Even her needlework was ripped to shreds and flung to the floor.

My God, was he intending to burn them alive?

The two men reappeared – one with kindling and the other with two oil lamps. At his instructions, they piled it all against the panelling. Sir Rupert relieved some of his feelings by smashing such furniture as he could and that was added too. They emptied the oil lamps on the heap and one of them produced a tinderbox.

Finally, with a contemptuous laugh, he tossed a lighted rag onto the bonfire. With a whoosh and a flash of blue and yellow flame, the whole lot went up.

He *was* going to burn them to death. They couldn't escape now even if they wanted to. He must be mad.

Insane with rage. He stood in the light from the window, his face working with emotion. Such was the depth of his fury that I honestly think if he could have laid hands on her, he would physically have torn her apart.

The three men strode from the room. I could hear their voices fading down the stairs.

I was a little surprised he hadn't waited around to gloat, but it dawned on me – of course, there would be an exit. There had to be, otherwise soldiers looking for religious dissidents just had to wait outside the priest hole until the fugitives either surrendered or went mad with thirst. The things religious people do to each other never fail to amaze me.

That accounted for the third man. He was outside, covering the exit. I wondered briefly where it came out – and now they'd all gone to ambush Margaret Lacey and her son as they were driven from the priest-hole either by the smoke or by the heat.

Downstairs in the Hall, I heard Captain Lacey raise his voice in challenge. He wasn't dead, then. And if he was there, where was Peterson? And what of Markham? Was he on the roof?

Back in the sitting room, I could hear the crackle of burning wood and the roar of flames. Smoke began to fill the room.

I pulled the door shut in a vain attempt to prevent the fire spreading and ran around the gallery. I hoped to God that Margaret and Charles had escaped, even if only to run straight into a sword as they emerged. It would certainly be a far more merciful death than slowly cooking to death in what would be little better than an oven.

Looking over the gallery, I could see Sir Rupert, flanked by the other two men, facing Captain Lacey, who, sword drawn, was somewhat lopsidedly barring their way. His uniform jacket was gone and underneath, he wore a plain linen shirt. His left sleeve was red, and blood ran down his fingers onto the floor, but his right arm was undamaged and rock steady.

They laughed at him.

Until Peterson stepped out of the shadows, chairleg in hand, and stood alongside him.

Oh, Tim!

Sir Rupert hadn't had time to reload, so they had only swords. It was still three to two, but one of those two was Peterson.

Actually, whom are we kidding? It was three to three. I pulled out my two hairpins and prepared – as they say – to take them from behind.

The two brothers were engaged down at the other end of the Hall, swords flashing, and had no eyes for anything other than each other, which suited me just fine. Peterson was engaged with the other two. Time to render assistance.

I heard Markham's voice in my ear and stepped back, hissing, 'Report. Quick.'

'The kid's on the roof. There's smoke coming out from between the tiles. What's going on?'

'We're on fire. Do *not* let anything happen to that kid.'

'You and Peterson OK?'

I watched the vicious street fight going on in the Hall.

'Yeah. Peachy.'

I ran down the stairs and crouched behind one of

Peterson's assailants. Peterson pushed hard and the guy fell backwards over me. I scrambled onto his chest and jabbed a hairpin into the fleshy part of his upper arm. He screamed and went to slap me away and it really was just his bad luck that his swinging hand encountered the other hairpin, which went straight through his palm. He screamed again and I scrambled to my feet, kicked him in the head, and stamped hard on his wedding tackle. I swear there was a rather nasty squelchy sound. He stopped screaming. He stopped everything. In fact, he just curled up and disappeared into his own world.

At the other end of the Hall, the two brothers were still going at it. Even to my inexperienced eyes, Captain Lacey was by far the better swordsman. Sir Rupert had obviously come to the same conclusion. He stepped back. At once, Captain Lacey lowered his sword, which was a big mistake because in one smooth movement, Sir Rupert reversed his sword and fetched his brother a vicious blow across the face. The captain fell to the ground. Sir Rupert hesitated a moment over his body, caught sight of me and Peterson heading towards him, recalculated the odds, and headed for the stairs.

I let him go and called Markham. 'Report.'

'Can't stop. Kid's running along the eaves. Can't get to him.'

'Sir Rupert's on his way. Heads up!'

'Copy that.'

Peterson was wiping the sweat from his face, standing over his fallen foe. He had a swollen eye and a split lip but the other guy looked worse. You don't want to mess with a pair of historians. We're not nice people.

I was already racing towards the stairs. 'There's another one outside, Tim. Probably guarding the priest hole's exit. Waiting for Margaret and Charles. Go.'

Thank God he understood all that and headed for the door. I raced around the smoky gallery and found the narrow stone stair in the north-east corner. As I rounded the first bend into almost complete darkness, I realised I'd forgotten to bring a light.

It's little things like this that always bring home to me that I'm out of my own time. A contemporary would automatically have picked up a candle on the way. I groped my way up. The stairs were uneven and irregular and designed expressly to trip those stupid enough to attempt to climb them in the dark. In the end, I tucked up my skirt and went on all fours. There's no dignity in my job.

The last part was easier, because they'd left the door open at the top, giving me enough light to see by. I emerged cautiously, blinking in the bright summer sunshine.

Subconsciously, I suppose, I'd been expecting the vast, flat expanse that was the roof at our St Mary's and it wasn't like that at all. The roof was steep, tiled, and irregular. Bits stuck out all over the place. A small walkway around the very outside was the only way to get around without actually having to climb up the tiles. A very inadequate parapet, only just over knee-high, gave no illusion of safety whatsoever. On the contrary, it was a trip hazard. I thought again of Markham's ghost. Someone was going off the roof today. Bloody hell – it might be me!

I couldn't see anyone from where I was standing. Bugger! I was going to have to go out there.

I made my way slowly along the narrow walkway, definitely not looking down. Peterson was down there, somewhere. He could cope. I should concentrate on what was happening up here. Because, not to put too fine a point on it, this kid had to survive. Captain Lacey, Lady Lacey, and Charles Lacey – they all died today, but this kid had to live.

I leaned inwards, trailing one hand along the tiles, keeping as far from that parapet as I could. Where could they be? I scrambled over a gable and there they were. The kid had climbed up the roof and was crouched, terrified, up near the ridge. Markham stood at the bottom, back to him, stun gun drawn, facing down Sir Rupert. And he was right; smoke was curling up through the tiles.

I thought of the fire in her sitting room. All that oil they'd thrown around. The attics above, stuffed with pictures, broken furniture, old hangings … all tinder dry. I thought of the wooden floors, wooden staircase, those hefty wooden hammer beams in the Great Hall … This was no place for gentle, inoffensive historians. Actually, it was no place for anyone. It would be a really good idea to get everyone off the roof and continue the discussion about who'd slept with whom and whose kid belonged to whom at a safe distance away from this burning building. Before someone fell off this bloody roof. And we had to save the kid. James Lacey definitely inherited. The records said so. Therefore, if no one else did, he must survive today.

I wished I could say the same about us.

Markham was calling to Sir Rupert, warning him to stay back. He flourished his stun gun, but of course, a man from the 17th century would have no idea of its purpose and his sword gave him the longer reach. He kept coming. I had no idea what would happen. The two were equally matched. It could go either way.

I shouted. They both looked at me, but I was too far away. I threw caution to the winds and tried to run along the walkway. My skirt caught on the roof tiles to one side and the parapet on the other and then tried to wrap itself around my legs. I was forced to slow down. I wasn't going to get there in time.

And then, it was all taken out of our hands.

The smoke, curling lazily out from around the edge of the roof, had given no indication of the inferno raging below. Fire burns upwards. Flames began to lick eagerly through the tiles. All around, I could hear the pinging noises as they cracked and below me, I could hear the roaring flames.

I heard Markham shout a warning to the kid and hold out his hands. Sir Rupert did a quick risk assessment, decided he could always sire another heir another day, and turned back the way he'd come. He'd have to pass me on this narrow walkway and he wouldn't mess about. I didn't either, getting out of his way by going up the roof like a rabbit. Do I mean rabbit? Some animal that climbs roofs easily. A goat, maybe?

Anyway, I went up that roof like a rocket. And it was hot. I could feel the heat coming up through the tiles. Were the roof timbers ablaze already?

Below me, Sir Rupert was heading for the little

doorway in the north-east corner. I watched anxiously, in case he thought to lock it behind him and block our escape, but he was more interested in getting away. And killing his wife, of course.

I opened my com. 'Tim. He's on his way. He's coming back.'

No reply. Bloody hell, Tim!

I slid down the roof on my bum. Please see my previous comment about dignity.

The kid, James, alas, didn't possess my calm, good sense. He was frozen with fear. Fear of his father. Fear for his mother. Fear of heights. Fear of fire. Nothing even remotely like this could ever have happened to him before and he couldn't deal with it, poor little lad. He couldn't be much more than six or seven.

Markham was amazing. Holstering his stun gun, he began to climb the roof. I've said before, he's not big, but he was considerably heavier than James was and I worried the weakened roof wouldn't hold him. He halted just below the kid and held out his hand.

I could hear the roaring flames quite clearly now. I stayed quiet because Markham was doing very well without any interference from me, so I stood still and held my breath.

After an endless moment, the boy reached out his arms. Markham grabbed him, slithered back down the roof, paused for a moment to settle him more securely on his hip, and set off towards me.

I heaved a sigh of relief.

That was when it happened.

He so nearly made it. I was only about ten or fifteen

feet away. An entire section of the roof between us just dropped. Like a stone. Great orange and yellow flames whooshed up towards the sky, greedily reaching out for everything around them.

I shouted. The heat was enormous. I held up my arm to shield my face and tried to think what to do. I had no idea whether there was another way off the roof. I doubted it.

Markham shouted something that I never caught. He took two long paces forwards and threw the kid at me. He must have been desperate, but what else could he do? His orders were to keep James safe. The kid caught me squarely in the chest and for one heart-stopping moment, I flailed helplessly and then fell back onto the hot tiles.

The boy clamped himself to me. Arms round my neck in a stranglehold and legs wrapped around my waist. Which was good – he obviously wasn't going to let go and it left my arms free.

For what? What could I possibly do? Markham was trapped. He knew it. I knew it. His famous luck had run out. I scrambled to my feet and stared at him through the leaping flames. This could not be happening. This was Markham. He was indestructible. He was famed for it. He couldn't die today.

Yes, he could. He was going to die. With sick certainty, I suddenly realised who it was who fell from the roof. And why he fell from the roof. And why only Markham could see it. Yes, it was a ghost. Or an echo of some kind. An echo from the past. And only Markham could see it because Markham was the ghost. Markham was the very last person I should have brought with us today.

All this was my fault. I clutched at young James, experiencing the paralysing, brain-numbing despair you can only feel when you've led a dearly loved friend into a stupid situation and lost him his life. After everything that had happened to us over the years, I was getting into the habit of thinking we were immortal and now, too late, I realised we bloody weren't.

I called his name. I don't know why. The tears running down my cheeks dried instantly in the heat. I heard him shout something, but the roar of the flames was too great to hear anything else.

He had a choice. He could jump or he could burn.

He jumped.

There was a time when I never thought I'd have any close friends. That I would even want close friends. Those days were gone. Over the years, I'd rescued colleagues and they'd rescued me. I'd built relationships and grown fond of people. I even had a few individuals, other than Leon, who were special to me. Peterson – always. Guthrie. Helen – whether she liked it or not. Even, sometimes, Mrs Partridge …

And Markham. Grubby, disastrous, loveable, brave as a lion. No one ever talked much about their time before St Mary's, but I could make an educated guess. Something had happened to him – I could guess what – and he'd had to make a choice. How to deal with it. You can get angry – I did – but that wouldn't have worked for him. He was small. He'd have been beaten to a pulp. So he'd become a clown. Self-preservation. People don't hurt you if they're too busy laughing at you. Obviously, it had served him well and even though he didn't need it at St Mary's, he'd kept up the charade. He was, in fact, intelligent, tough, and as Major Guthrie had once said, very, very good at his job. I suspected our Mr Markham, even when extricating himself from whatever disaster he had just instigated, had often enjoyed a quiet laugh at our expense.

In my mind, I saw him − defying Clive Ronan at Alexandria. Performing conjuring tricks in front of Mary Stuart, as cool as a cucumber. Stealing a Trojan chicken and shoving it down the front of his tunic. That final charge against the Time Police ... And then − suddenly − he was gone. My friend, Markham.

I buried my head in James's shoulder and we both cried.

The crash of falling timber brought me back. We weren't out of the woods yet. Or off the burning roof, if you want to be more accurate.

I heard a shout behind me. Peterson was here somewhere. What fears had he overcome to force himself up here? And how would I tell him about Markham?

I inched my way along the walkway. Scrambled over the gables. Felt the heat. Heard parts of the roof give way around me. It seemed a very long way to the north-east corner.

Peterson came to meet us. He was white-faced and tense and I'll swear he had his eyes shut most of the time. He couldn't do anything except be with me but I appreciated it, all the same.

'I'll take the kid. You go first.'

I set off down the narrow stairs, rounded the first bend, plunged into darkness, missed my footing, and, because the day wasn't bad enough, fell down the stairs. I fell quite slowly, rolling from step to step. If there had been a rail, or bannisters, I could have stopped myself quite easily, but there was nothing to get a grip on and so I fetched up, half way around the final bend, bruised, shaken and with every bone in my body broken.

Or so it felt.

'You all right?' called Peterson, winning today's award for Most Idiotic Question.

'Yes,' I shouted, winning today's award for Most Inaccurate Answer.

'Turn right at the bottom. There's a small outside door.'

There was too, and it was open. I stumbled out into bright morning sunshine. Unbelievably, it wasn't even lunchtime yet.

I could hear Peterson behind me. I looked left and right, trying to get my bearings. Where would he have fallen?

As I looked frantically around, Peterson caught me up. 'Where's Markham?'

I couldn't tell him. I put my hand on his and rested my forehead against his arm.

He got an arm free from young James and put it around me. 'Oh God, Max', and we stood, the three of us, in the sunshine, just for a moment, until we were roused by the sound of falling tiles and breaking glass.

What to do next?

Someone had to get the kid to the village. That should be Peterson. He could easily pose as 'the servant' who was supposed to have saved James, and I should go and find Markham's body. Somehow, we'd have to get it back to the pod.

And what had happened to Margaret? And where was Rupert? And actually, did I care?

Peterson was looking down at me. 'Do you want to take James to the village?'

57

I shook my head. I was mission controller. It was my duty to stay with Markham.

'If you can, Max, pull him away from the building. I know the walls stand, but the roof's going to come down any minute now.'

I nodded.

'I'll be back as soon as I can.'

We separated and I set off around the building.

Unbelievably, it was still a lovely summer's day. Flames were erupting from the roof and from a few upstairs windows, but in the distance, birds still sang, the sun still shone, the wind still stirred the leaves in the trees. You think the world should stop and join you in your grief, but it never bloody does.

Unlike our St Mary's, this building was surrounded by a thick shrubbery. Laurels were the only bushes I recognised. I couldn't see Markham anywhere. I'd become completely disoriented, tumbling down that twisty stair, and I have the sense of direction of a sponge, anyway. I had to run all the way around the building before I found him. And I didn't find Margaret or Charles at all. Had they preferred to bake to death rather than face what the loving father and husband had in mind for them? Nor did I see any henchmen. Whatever had happened was all over now and I'd been so busy getting Markham killed that I'd missed it.

There he was. A limp, sad little shape, lying in a heap on the ground.

I ran towards him, my breath catching in my throat and gently rolled him over. His face was dirty, but that was nothing new. In addition to smoke and sweat stains, he'd obviously fallen into one of the bushes because his face was covered in scratches, blood, and sap. Leaves and twigs had caught in his hair.

Professional detachment flew straight out of the window. I don't know why, but I tried to wipe his face clean.

He opened his eyes.

I was so shocked, I screamed and dropped him.

His voice was hoarse and weak, but even a near-death experience can't shut Markham up for long. 'Bloody hell, Max!'

Relief flooded through me like a tsunami. I cried. I couldn't help it. He wasn't dead.

He said feebly, 'You're dripping snot on me.'

'Sorry. Sorry. I thought you were dead.'

'No. Fell in that swiving bush.'

I looked to my right. A battered laurel had broken his fall. Looking at it, Markham had emerged from their encounter with slightly less damage. He wasn't unscathed, however. His right leg shouldn't look like that.

He clutched my arm. 'The kid?'

'On his way to the village. Safe.'

He looked past me. 'Yeah. He is. We're not.'

I looked behind me. Oh, shit! Would this day never end? All I wanted to do was get Markham back to the pod and leave the bloody Laceys to sort out their own bloody marital problems, and now there was no chance, because here came Sir Rupert and his one remaining henchman.

Bloody bollocking hell!

I groped for my pepper spray and Markham handed me his stun gun. Sir Rupert had his sword, still dramatically wet with his brother's blood and the henchman had the standard henchman cudgel.

I appreciated that Markham didn't tell me to run. He knew I wouldn't leave him.

They saw me and stopped.

If I'd had a functioning Markham, it would have been a piece of cake, but I didn't. I could hear him making efforts to sit up and the pain it was causing him.

'Watch the one with the cudgel, Max. He'll try to get behind you.'

I stood over Markham, stun gun in my right hand, pepper in my left, and wondered how long it would take Peterson to get back from the village. It seemed safe to assume longer than the ten or so seconds it would take them to reach me.

My plan was to stun cudgel man, who'd already been in a fight, and disable Rupert with the pepper spray. After that, I'd just wing it. And because fire doesn't stop for anything, while all this was going on, windows were exploding along the top floor. Sparks flew through the air to land on our clothing. Scraps of glowing ash drifted silently past us. We'd really bitten off more than we could chew with this assignment.

I tightened my grip and bared my teeth. They wouldn't be accustomed to aggressive women. I hoped.

Ten feet away, they paused. Sir Rupert nodded and just as Markham had predicted, cudgel man began to circle behind me. I half turned to face him. Sir Rupert matched my movement. Cudgel man moved to my left, brushing against the bushes. I tried to keep both of them in my vision. I couldn't afford to turn my back on either of them.

There was a sound that was exactly the same as a piece of wood bouncing off someone's skull and that must have been exactly what it was, because cudgel man fell to the ground.

Sir Rupert grunted in surprise and turned. I seized the opportunity and fired off the pepper spray. He shrieked another mighty oath, bent double, dropped his sword, and clawed at his eyes. I took two steps forwards and gave him another blast. He fell to the ground, eyes streaming, and snot bubbling from his nose. Already, his face was red and swollen. I felt a certain sense of job satisfaction.

Captain Lacey pushed his way through the remains of Markham's laurel still clutching Peterson's chairleg. Bloody hell – this man was indestructible. Behind him stood Lady Lacey and young Charles. Smoke-streaked, hair plastered to their heads with sweat, but very much alive.

The way today was going, I wasn't the slightest bit surprised. Only a group of highly trained, professional historians with years of experience under their belts could get things this wrong.

Peterson arrived back from the village, breathless and astonished, and we assembled the wounded together in one place. His brother's pistol shot had only grazed Edmund's left arm and was soon dealt with. He also had a shallow sword wound to his right shoulder, a really deep gash across his cheekbone, which was going to spoil his pretty-boy looks, and extensive cuts and bruises. All of which he would survive.

Markham had well and truly broken his right leg. In several places, by the looks of it. Peterson went off to find something we could carry him on, returning with a broken gate and the small med kit. While Peterson shielded me from view, I shot Markham the pain-killing injection he was certainly going to need.

Lady Lacey was suffering from smoke inhalation and shock. Charles clung to her. He was frightened, but unhurt. I took advantage to say to her, quietly, 'James is safe and well. He is in the village. I think it best he remains there.'

She looked at me for a while, opened her mouth, and then nodded. She was a sensible woman. He would be safe and well, but only if she never saw him again.

'You should leave. Now. Don't stop to take anything. Everyone will think you and Charles died in the fire. You can be safe. Go far away and never come back.'

She looked across at Edmund who was having his wounds treated by Peterson. 'He will not come with us.'

'He must. You will need his protection. He cannot return to his unit. He can never return here. Wherever he goes, sooner or later his brother will find him.'

I couldn't tell her that Rupert would soon be dead, killed by a stray cannonball at the Battle of Cheriton, next year, because that was something she must never know. The records say she was never seen again. Killed in the fire along with her son and possibly Captain Lacey as well. The three of them must disappear. Start a new life in a strange, new, foreign world. America, maybe. Or Manchester.

We both turned to look at Sir Rupert, stretched out on

the grass, still incapacitated after a discreet but thorough tasering. She nodded.

They found the horses, tied up in the stable yard. Peterson heaved Edmund onto his horse and helped Lady Lacey mount her husband's. I was pleased to see she sat astride. I would definitely be having a word with Dr Bairstow about the amount of unnecessary sidesaddle hours we had to log each month.

Charles took another horse. It was too big for him and he could easily have ridden behind Captain Lacey, but I guessed they would head to the nearest port and sell them to buy their passage. To wherever they would go.

We let the other horses go. Wherever they came from, Sir Rupert and any surviving henchmen would be walking back. Together with cuts, bruises, swollen bollocks, and a disjointed nervous system. Served them right.

We watched the Laceys leave. They set off through the woods and were soon lost to sight. They had said hardly anything to us. I think we frightened them. They didn't know who we were or where we came from. I suspected, in some way, they were convinced some of this was our fault.

Markham was woozy but happy and so we sat on the grass and recorded as much of the burning of St Mary's as we could. It had burned before and it would again, especially if Professor Rapson had anything to do with it. Even so, it's sad to see your home go up in flames. We waited until Rupert Lacey heaved himself to his feet, looked around, and then staggered off unsteadily in the direction of the village. I have no idea what happened to the henchmen.

'We can go now,' I said.

'Not a very tidy ending,' observed Peterson. 'Still, at least we now know which idiot fell off the roof.'

Markham grinned lopsidedly, eyes wandering in all directions. From past experience, any moment now he would start singing.

'And we lost all our gear,' I said, staring at the burning roof.

'And you broke me, too,' slurred Markham.

'Save your breath,' advised Peterson. 'We still have to get you back to the pod.'

The trip back was no fun for any of us. Markham bore it all bravely by closing his eyes and singing a song about the Mayor of Bayswater's daughter. What a gifted girl she turned out to be!

There wasn't much of him, but he was heavy and so was the gate. Something metal was cutting into my hands, but I wouldn't let go, and Peterson, whose facial injuries were more severe than they looked, began to complain of a headache.

We gave the burning St Mary's a wide berth and staggered up into the woods. Peterson and I had to swap ends because he couldn't see very well.

'Nearly there,' I said, ignoring my aching body and throbbing hands. Then we were.

I called for the door and we lifted Markham in as gently as we could. Peterson initiated the jump, sat back, and closed his eyes.

I poked him.

'Don't close your eyes.'

'With you around, chance would be a fine thing.'

I activated the decon lamp and requested a medical team.

Duty done, I slumped to the floor alongside Markham and we got our breath back.

Nurse Hunter went ballistic. Why? What had we done?

It was all right for Markham – he was only semi-conscious and missed most of it, and Peterson clearly couldn't sustain any more damage to his head, so that just left me.

I cowered in the treatment room, holding my bandaged hands high, half in surrender and half so she might actually remember I was a patient. I'm sure nurses aren't supposed to carry on like this.

I said hopefully, 'Any chance of a cup of tea?' A remark carefully calculated either to recall her to her nursing duties, or, more probably, topple her over the edge completely so I could make my getaway.

To my horror, she began to cry, instead.

I scrambled off the treatment table. 'Oh God, Di. Don't cry.'

I didn't even want to speculate on my fate should Helen come in and find I'd somehow reduced her toughest nurse to tears. Hunter was the Schwarzenegger of the nursing profession and here she was now, gulping into a wad of blue medical wipe.

She blew her nose with the thoroughness for which she was famed. 'No, it's OK. I'm fine. Sorry.'

I regarded her with misgiving. I didn't even know she could cry. 'What's the problem?'

She stamped on the pedal bin opener and hurled the medical wipe inside. 'Nothing. Well, not nothing, obviously, but not anything I can do anything about.'

I gestured over my shoulder to the next cubicle where the young master was lying, drugged to the eyeballs and alternately singing a song about an engineer and his mechanical contrivance, and inviting her to stroke his fevered brow. At least I hoped it was his brow.

'Di, this is Markham. He is indestructible, you know.'

She batted my hand away angrily. 'One day he won't be.'

I saw again the billowing smoke, felt the heat, heard the flames, watched him jump …

I took a deep breath. 'Did he ever mention that he kept seeing …?'

'Something falling off the roof. Yes he did.'

'Well, then Di, you'll know why he went. Why he had to. Why he kept seeing something fall from the roof. Something only he could see, because he was the important one today. If he hadn't been there today, a young child would certainly have died. And if I'd found the courage to cross that roof, then I'd have died too. And Peterson, big idiot that he is …'

'Hey!' said an indignant voice from further down the corridor.

'… would probably have tried to save us and he might have died as well. And if we hadn't dealt with Sir Rupert and his henchmen then they would almost certainly have overpowered Captain and Lady Lacey and young Charles, too. I don't know what he had in mind for them, but it wouldn't have been good. I know you're a bit miffed with him at the moment,' (a slight understatement there), 'but it's very possible he saved six people today. He's a bit of a hero, you know. And it's his job. He loves it. You know that.'

'Yes, I do know.' She slammed a cabinet door. 'I know. I know that you tumble back to St Mary's burned, bloody, broken, and full of good reasons why you had to act as you did and I don't think any of you ever – ever – give a thought for those left behind. Or who have to pick up the pieces afterwards. It's no fun, you know. And no, I'm certainly not going to make him choose, any more than Leon Farrell would ever ask you to choose, but please, Max, any of you, just stop occasionally, and think what it must be like for the rest of us. Now, I'm not going to say any more.'

She squared her shoulders and when she turned to face me, her face was back to normal.

'Twelve hours' observation for you and Peterson. Markham's off to what Peterson unwisely referred to as "a proper hospital", a remark which is about to cause him untold suffering – silly ass.'

'Hey! You do know I can still hear you, don't you?'

I refused to be deflected. 'Have you mentioned any of this to Markham?'

'On the contrary – I've told him it's only the glamour of working here that renders him even remotely attractive.'

'He doesn't deserve you.'

'Finally – the History department gets something right.'

After that little lot, I thought we'd better try for something a touch more sedate. I had a look through our outstanding assignments, discarding (for the time being) battlefields, revolutions, major geological and meteorological events, and anything even remotely connected with riots and civil disturbances or assassinations.

Pretty well the only thing left was a basic bread and butter jump to the Crystal Pa lace Exhibition in 1851. I stared at it without enthusiasm. My speciality is Ancient Civilisations with a bit of medieval and Tudor stuff chucked in for luck. As far as I was concerned, 1851 was practically yesterday, but it was our first major assignment since the unpleasantness with the Time Police and really, it was ideal. Although the Exhibition itself is more than well documented, Thirsk had requested visuals and since they were our employers ... A boring but necessary assignment that I could use to get the entire History Department back out there – it would almost be a works outing – and best of all, there should be no violence.

I thought very long and hard about stepping back from this one. Either of my senior historians, Schiller or Van Owen, could easily head up this assignment. It would be safe, sedate, and probably utterly boring. On the other hand, both Roberts and Sands had only just been declared medically fit. Sands had lost a foot. I mean, he'd lost part of his leg, not that he'd suddenly become shorter. This would be his first assignment with his prosthetic and I had the unenviable task of assessing his physical fitness and recommending whether to keep him on. He swore to me that his bionic foot could easily mimic the function of a normal foot. That he could walk, run, dance, chase girls, whatever. I knew he was desperate to stay at St Mary's and I certainly didn't want to lose him, but, to be blunt, if he was unable to cope with rough ground, if he couldn't run, if he was any sort of liability then I would have no choice but to make the appropriate recommendation to Dr Bairstow. Not only for his sake – if he fell or was left behind, the entire team would go back for him, so he wasn't just a danger to himself, but to us as well.

He wasn't stupid. He knew all this and still he bounced – literally – around the building, showing off his foot and inflicting his ghastly knock-knock jokes on anyone who had the misfortune to cross his path. I really, really didn't want to be the one to carry out the assessment, but there was no way I could farm it out to anyone else. Being the boss is a bitch, sometimes. And then there was Roberts. I needed someone just to keep a quiet eye on him, as well. No, I wasn't looking forward to this assignment at all.

Sighing, I divided us into groups. Maxwell and Sands. Schiller and Roberts. I put those two together because they were both desperate to see the elephant that was supposedly part of one of the exhibits. Historians and an elephant, all together in a giant glass greenhouse! I made a note to put the god of historians on full alert. The third team comprised Clerk and Van Owen. No one from the Security Section would accompany us. We didn't need them this time. What sort of trouble could we possibly get into during what might be the most boring assignment in History?

We assembled in Wardrobe. I wanted everyone checked over very carefully. Victorian dress is intricate and complicated.

I wore an outfit similar to the one in which I'd encountered Jack the Ripper, but with stiffened petticoats instead of a bustle. A huge number of stiffened petticoats. In fact, more stiffened petticoats than one woman could reasonably be expected to endure. No matter in which time period I found myself, female apparel is never conducive to comfort and easy movement.

'I can't lift my arms above my shoulders,' I said.

'Why would you want to?' asked Mrs Enderby. 'Are you going to be turning cartwheels?'

My corset gave me the requisite tiny waist, but only at the expense of breathing. I wore a tight-fitting V-shaped bodice in a dark blue material. The skirt was flounced to within an inch of its life. I was offered an embroidered Paisley shawl, which I declined on the grounds I was encumbered enough, and a grinning Van Owen snapped it up. I discovered why when Mrs Enderby attempted to drape a dead fox over my shoulders.

'No!' I said, aghast.

'It's the height of fashion.'

'It's dead.'

'Well of course it is. Do you know how difficult it would be to persuade a live animal to stay in place for hours on end?'

'Can't we give this one the day off? What was it anyway?'

'A silver fox. And it's not alive.'

'So I should hope.'

'I mean it never was. It's artificial. Look.'

I lifted the end with the face. Beady glass eyes peered at me and, I suspected, found me wanting. The other end was probably even more unpleasant. Realism is overrated.

Without hope, I said to Van Owen, 'Want to swap?' and she pretended she'd gone suddenly deaf.

Sands appeared and recoiled. 'Why are you wearing roadkill?'

'Dear God, what's happened to your face?'

He preened. 'Victorian whiskers.'

'Are they your own?'

'Of course not. No one outside the Victorian era could possibly grow this amount of facial hair. I think they're made from the same material as your polecat.'

I pulled out an imaginary clipboard and made an imaginary giant cross.

'Failed. Go and pack your bags.'

'Sorry,' he said, hastily. 'You look lovely. Not everyone can pull off the dead animal look, but you …'

'Shut up.'

He, of course, looked pretty good, wearing a soft linen shirt, a floppy bow tie, an elaborate waistcoat, a thick dark coat, and lighter trousers in a different material. Suits hadn't been invented yet. A glossy top hat completed his look.

I had a blue bonnet with a deep poke and a bunch of depressed flowers pinned to one side. One consolation, however, muffs were fashionable. Mine was made of soft, cream-coloured velvet, into which I had stuffed my recorder, two copper pennies for emergencies, a handkerchief, a small can of pepper spray, and my stun gun.

'Yes, I know we're only visiting a trade fair,' I said, not meeting Mrs Enderby's reproachful gaze. 'But you never know when things will go pear-shaped. Suppose the elephant gets frisky?'

'It's stuffed,' she said.

Muttering, I compromised by leaving the stun gun at home.

Down in Hawking, we assembled in front of our pods. Schiller and Roberts were in Number Four, Clerk and Van Owen in Number Five, and Sands and I were in Number Eight.

Schiller turned to Van Owen, winked, and said, 'Love your muff.'

Every techie head jerked around.

Van Owen smiled demurely and I tried to pretend I couldn't hear any of this.

'I love how soft they are.'

'I know. I've been stroking mine all morning.'

'And, its capacity is amazing. You wouldn't believe what's nestling in mine.'

Someone, somewhere, dropped a tool.

'Is it loaded?'

'Locked, loaded, and ready to go.'

Young Lindstrom looked as if he was ready to faint.

It was a shame to tease him. He hadn't been with us that long and was still finding his feet, although Leon spoke highly of him. He stood now, Adam's apple bobbing uncertainly. Sands and Roberts were grinning.

Leon stepped forward. 'Much as I hate to break up this discussion on female apparel ...' He held up Van Owen's muff. 'A muff, Mr Lindstrom, is a cylinder of warm material or fur, into which the wearer can insert her hands to keep warm, or, if you are an historian, carry her own personal arsenal of pepper spray, stun gun, flick knife, flame thrower, and surface-to-air missiles.'

I twinkled at him and said quietly, 'Muff man?'

'If you don't know the answer to that one then I may have to initiate a rigorous refresher session tonight.'

I caught my breath and turned away before my own muff burst into flames.

Just time for one last word to the troops.

'Right, you lot. I know we've been through this already, but a final reminder. This is a very rigid and very formal society. Everyone knows their place. Ladies, do not speak unless spoken to. Do not offer to shake hands. Do not make eye contact with members of the opposite sex. Curtsey when spoken to.

'Gentlemen, raise your hats when speaking to ladies. You can get away with just a careless flick of the brim if speaking to a member of your own sex. Offer your arm to your partner. Steer her around obstacles and muddy ground, because, of course, she won't be able to do that for herself. Victorian society genuinely feels that never having to open a door in your life more than compensates for not having your own job, your own money, or any sort of control over your own life, so remember that. Above all, be discreet with your recording. Any questions?'

Nope. They were itching to be off.

I turned to find Dr Bairstow at my elbow. Nothing strange in that – he often comes down to see us off. I suspect he just wants to reassure himself we're actually off the premises.

I waited, but he said nothing.

Finally, I said, 'Was there something, sir?'

He seemed to debate with himself for a moment and then said, 'No, I've just come to wish the History department well on its first full assignment after the Time Police.'

'Thank you, sir.'

He nodded. 'Good luck, everyone,' and stumped away.

Inside the pod, I seated myself comfortably and said, 'In your own time, Mr Sands.'

The world went white.

We landed in a very remote corner of the park; surrounded by sheds, outbuildings, compost heaps, and a great steaming pile of horse manure. Says it all, really.

Sands looked at me. I nodded for him to continue. He verified we were in the right place, carried out the coms check and decontamination, and we were all set to go.

We set off in our pairs – respectable middle-class Victorians come to celebrate the British Empire and, just for one afternoon, to identify with its glories. I could catch tantalising glimpses through the trees, and then, suddenly, there it was.

Ahead of us, I could see a giant glittering structure, taller than the trees around it. In fact, in the centre of the ground floor, adjacent to the Crystal Fountain, real trees had actually been incorporated into the design. This was the snappily named Great Exhibition of the Works of Industry of All Nations. Dreamed up by Victoria's husband, Prince Albert, to celebrate Britain's success as a manufacturing nation, and all of it incorporated into a palace made of glass – The Crystal Palace.

We paid the full price for admission – three guineas for gentlemen and two guineas for the ladies. There were days set aside for the hoi-polloi at vastly reduced entrance fees, but not today. I stood back and let Mr Sands pay for me. Commercial transactions were far beyond the capability of women.

We entered through the West Entrance and stopped dead in astonishment.

My first thought was that we really should have brought Kal on this one. With industrial history as her speciality, she would have loved this; but she was at Thirsk now, safeguarding our interests and terrorising harmless academics.

I hadn't expected to be impressed, but it was amazing. Absolutely bloody amazing.

Ten miles of displays, according to the statistics. Over a hundred thousand exhibits from fifteen thousand exhibitors around the world. Britain, of course, head of the empire and host nation, occupied the biggest space, but almost every nation was there. Flags hung above individual exhibitors in a riot of many colours.

'Elephant!' said Roberts, and he and Schiller

disappeared towards the Indian exhibit.

'The Koh-I-Noor,' said Clerk, and seizing Van Owen's arm in not quite the approved Victorian manner, they too disappeared into the crowd.

The noise was tremendous. Hundreds, possibly thousands of people milled around us, but there was no impression of overcrowding. People moved smoothly from one exhibit to the next, or paused to greet friends and show off the latest fashions. Most were family groups, headed by father and mother and accompanied by what seemed vast numbers of tiny replicas, which I subsequently discovered to be children. These pale copies of their parents seemed very well behaved although that might possibly be due to the enormous amount of clothing weighing them down.

We walked a little further down the central aisle, pausing by the steam hammer exhibit. Yes, Sands was limping a little and leaning on his ornate walking stick, but he seemed very cheerful, bright-eyed, and interested.

Well, here we go.

I indicated that our route was up to Mr Sands.

'In that case,' he said, 'I think we'll check out the South Side first, then up the stairs, up one side of the gallery, down the other, back downstairs again, pause for a quick cup of tea and then finish up with the North Side. What do you say?'

'The cup of tea appears a little late in the schedule and we'll delete the word "quick", but otherwise, fine.'

We set off and I forgot all about the tea. It was fabulous. All of it. Wonderful. An Aladdin's cave full of treasures and wonders and delights and magic and light and colour. I was entranced.

The plan went straight out of the window in our excitement.

We saw the Machinery in Motion exhibits. Huge machines from all over the world. Steam hammers, printing presses, pumps, looms, massive machinery, all pounding away. Valves hissed. Pistons ... pistoned. I assumed that was their function. Sands gestured with his stick, explaining all the workings to the tiny female brain, exactly as every other man-sized little boy was doing to his female companions.

From there we zigzagged haphazardly to the South Side of the exhibition area and saw fabulous shimmering fabrics from every corner of the Empire and beyond. There was furniture, made from exotic woods. Jewellery, china – even musical instruments.

Upstairs was a special area devoted to French velvets and lace and opposite that, on the North Gallery, fabulous examples of stained glass coloured the floor with their rich, dark colours.

Brilliant glass chandeliers hung above our heads, winking and gleaming in the bright sunshine.

Further along were even more musical instruments. At the invitation of a smiling exhibitor, I sat at a beautiful harpsichord, inlaid with mother of pearl. I dredged through my childhood memories and played 'In an English Country Garden', very badly. He tried so hard to induce Mr Sands to buy one for his talented and lovely – I saw him falter on the word 'wife', mentally substitute 'sister', lose his nerve, baulk at 'mother,' and settle for 'charming companion'. Mr Sands declined, but politely.

'I've been well brought up,' he said, as we moved away.

'But not by me,' I said, feeling that the mother issue should be made absolutely clear.

I couldn't help staring back wistfully at the little harpsichord. I wondered what had happened to it. Had it survived the two hundred years between then and now? Was it perhaps in a museum, somewhere? Was it someone's cherished possession? Who played it now? I'd never know.

We strolled back downstairs again, intending to spend some time under the trees admiring the Crystal Fountain and favouring the refreshment area there with our patronage. The crowds, however, were particularly thick. This was obviously a popular watering hole and so we settled for the Western Refreshment Court instead.

I have nightmares in which we didn't. Nightmares in which we did push through the crowds to the North Transept and sit down there for a cup of tea. How long would we have had? How long before time unravelled? Would we ever have known anything about it? I would have lifted a perfect cup of tea to my lips – and then what? Would everything have gone white? Where would I be when I opened my eyes? Would I even have eyes to open?

But we didn't. I remembered Mr Sands, and although he would drop down dead rather than admit it, he must be tired by now. I know I was, so we entered the Western Refreshment Court instead, which wasn't that busy. I went off to visit the Ladies and to experience using the very first public convenience ever – and the origin of the phrase, *spending a penny*, leaving Mr Sands to select a table and instruct the waiter to bring us afternoon tea.

Everyone should spend ten minutes in a Victorian lavatory. The word 'bog' does not apply. The fixtures and fittings were of brass, mahogany, and marble. There were mirrors. And red plush seats. To sit on, I mean, not the lavatory kind. And discreet attendants – presumably in case the more frail ladies were overwhelmed by their own clothing.

I joined him a few minutes later, picking my way carefully through the tables because these skirts could get away from you if you weren't careful.

The restaurant was lovely. Round tables were covered with crisp, white damask tablecloths. The china was exquisite. We're St Mary's – the concept of unchipped, matching china is completely alien to us. Ladies poured tea from silver pots. Cake stands were piled with sumptuous looking cakes and pastries. Gruesomely ugly potted palms and aspidistras were scattered around the place, but this was Victorian England after all – a bit of a taste-free zone. Besides, we weren't here for the landscaping. We were here for Afternoon Tea.

Mr Sands rose as I joined him and held my chair for me. Exactly as a contemporary would do.

I sat back in my chair, sighed with contentment, laid aside my muff, looked around, and found myself staring straight at Dr Bairstow.

It took a second or two to register, but once it did, there could be no doubt. I was looking at a very young Dr Bairstow. Good grief, he was younger than me. I stared. I couldn't help it. There could be no doubt. This was

Edward Bairstow. He even had hair – dark hair – brushed back from his forehead. Actually, he was rather handsome in a young eagle sort of way. He was accompanied by a young woman who, like me, looked slightly out of place in her Victorian costume. She wore a sea-green dress with wide sleeves and a fabulously embroidered Paisley shawl. Such hair as I could see under her matching bonnet was honey-blonde, gathered around her head in smooth bands and secured in a knot at the base of her neck. I knew who this must be. This was Annie Bessant.

I'll tell the story as Leon told it to me.

Once upon a time, there were three young historians. Three young, gifted historians. Edward Bairstow, Annie Bessant, and Clive Ronan. They were a team. The dream team. Only they weren't. They were a triangle, which is never a good situation and all the more serious because no one ever realised they were a triangle until it was far, far too late.

Matters came to a head during an assignment to the 16th century. James VI of Scotland. It was the time of the witch-hunts and for some reason, Annie was arrested. Edward Bairstow and Ronan got her back, but she'd picked up some sort of sickness while in gaol and developed a fever.

Protocol states you shoot the patient with every antibiotic known to man and wait and see. When you consider some of the diseases flying around at that time, you definitely don't want to bring any of them back to modern times. To be fair, most of these things aren't a huge threat to modern historians who are vaccinated against everything under the sun and beyond, and it's just

81

a case of waiting for the antibiotics to kick in, seeing what you're dealing with, and then returning to strict quarantine. Contrary to protocol, Ronan wanted to return immediately to St Mary's. Edward Bairstow refused and Ronan shot him. Just like that. He took out a gun and shot him in the leg, pitched him out of the pod to die, alone and abandoned, and returned to St Mary's telling everyone he'd been killed during Annie's rescue. Annie, at this point unconscious, was unable to refute his story.

I don't know how he thought he'd get away with it, because when Annie woke up, which she did because a course of antibiotics sorted things out, she told the truth and Ronan was arrested. They charged him with contravening St Mary's protocols and attempted murder. In that order.

He escaped custody, killing someone in the attempt, grabbed Annie from Sick Bay, tried to get to Hawking with her and escape in a pod, and Annie was shot in the crossfire. She died. Ronan got away. A rescue team went back for Edward Bairstow who was found in a bad way, hiding under someone's cart. They saved his life but he's limped ever since.

And here were two of that dream team, sitting a few tables away and on assignment, presumably, just like us. Like us, they were enjoying Victorian afternoon tea. They'd tucked into cakes and pastries. The table was littered with crumbs and empty plates. Any minute now, they'd be calling for the bill. This was obviously before their disastrous James VI assignment, when they were still a team, so where was the third one? Where was Clive Ronan?

I looked around and found him immediately, because he was sitting directly behind them at a separate table and they had no idea he was there.

It was very obvious that he wasn't with them. He was older. He was so badly dressed that I was surprised the waiter had served him. An untouched pot of tea stood on the table in front of him. He never took his eyes off them, and most worryingly of all, I couldn't see his hands. Both were below the table.

I had an awful, awful feeling about this. I had met our Mr Ronan on several occasions, and on none of them had he impressed me with his concern for others. Or even his sanity. On the other hand, his ruthless determination to get his own way at whatever the cost was more than impressive. There was going to be trouble.

I asked myself why he was here and I really don't know why I bothered, because the answer was painfully obvious, even to me. He was here to kill Edward Bairstow. I could follow his reasoning perfectly.

If Edward Bairstow died, right here, right now, then he wouldn't be around to prevent a sick Annie Bessant being returned to St Mary's. Maybe that assignment wouldn't even happen. So Ronan wouldn't have to shoot him. So he wouldn't be arrested. So he wouldn't have to flee. So Annie wouldn't die in the crossfire as he tried to force her into a pod. Edward Bairstow dies – here and now – and Annie lives. For him it was simple.

Except it wasn't and what was I going to do about it? Should I tell Mr Sands? Would that help? How much time did I have? People kept walking between Ronan and his targets, who were oblivious to his presence. Even if they turned around, he was partially obscured by potted palm trees.

He'd tried this sort of thing before. The man's a bloody nuisance and we can't kill him because his future is our past. If we change his future then we'd be changing our past. So killing him was out of the question. Somehow, he had to be neutralised before he could do any damage here today.

I put down my tea because my hands weren't quite steady, drew a deep breath, and smiled at Sands.

'Mr Sands. Please show no reaction of any kind. We are in very serious trouble. Sitting at a table over there is a very young historian named Edward Bairstow, together with his colleague, Miss Bessant. More importantly, behind them, near the exit, is a man named Mr Ronan, of whom you will have heard.'

He knew better than to turn and look. 'Is this a test?'

'No. Listen carefully. I strongly suspect he is here to kill Edward Bairstow. We cannot allow that to happen. You may be about to see and hear things that you will never, ever, under any circumstances, divulge to a living soul. Is that perfectly clear?'

He smiled pleasantly, nodded as if we were discussing the weather, and stirred his tea. He was a good lad.

I settled my dead animal firmly around my shoulders. 'If anything goes wrong, approach Dr Bairstow, identify yourself, and escort them both immediately from the building. Your priority – both our priorities – is to ensure the safety of Edward Bairstow and his colleague. Is that clearly understood?'

He smiled again, as if he didn't have a care in the

world, but his voice was tense. 'What about the others?'

'Leave them for the time being. We can't go at this mob-handed. If everything goes horribly wrong, try and get everyone back to St Mary's.'

Fat lot of good that would do them.

Sands had worked it out. 'If anything happens to Edward Bairstow here ... If he doesn't live long enough to found St Mary's ... Then none of us will be here for it to happen in the first place ... Bloody hell, Max. Paradox.'

I nodded. Trying to sound confident, I said, 'It won't come to that. Ready?'

'You're doing this alone?'

'If possible. You're first reserve. If I touch my bonnet, take whatever action seems appropriate.'

I rose from the table. He stood politely and passed me my muff.

I carried out a quick weapons check. I had two hatpins in my bonnet. A small can of pepper spray, which was almost useless here. I could spray him – but it would attract attention and make a scene. I suspected a stun gun would be my best bet but, of course, I hadn't brought mine with me today because this was supposed to be the most boring assignment ever. I really should be slapped round the side of the head on a regular basis.

I remembered to thread my way slowly between the tables. Firstly, because that's what women did in this time; secondly, because I still wasn't completely in control of my wide skirts, but mostly because the last thing I wanted to do was push Ronan into precipitate action. He had his back to the wall and a potted palm tree sheltered his right side, so I could only approach from an angle. He paid me no attention at all, never taking his eyes from the two people sitting at the nearby table, who were still talking quietly with their heads together. As I passed them, Edward Bairstow gently placed his hand over hers. They were completely unaware of his presence. In a world of their own.

I was very conscious of the murmur of conversation around me, the genteel clink of china, the tinkle of teaspoons, the sounds of the string quartet playing quietly in the corner.

Making no attempt at concealment, I pulled out a chair opposite him, thereby blocking his view to some extent and making it difficult for him to get past me.

I sat carefully and laid my muff on the table in front of me, keeping both hands inside it so he wouldn't be nervous and I could get to my pepper spray easily.

'Good afternoon, Mr Ronan. Or is it Dr Ronan? I've never been quite sure.'

The last time I'd seen him, he'd been an old man; desperate and diseased; a jumping, jerking, nervous wreck. If he showed the slightest sign of instability, I'd have no choice but to spray him immediately and just deal with the consequences. At the moment, however, he seemed relatively calm. Well, as calm as a man contemplating murdering his former colleague and good friend can be, but then, he was never one for the dramatic reaction.

He went very still and then said, 'You!'

I nodded.

'From Edinburgh.'

I nodded again. We'd encountered each other in the mean streets of 16th-century Edinburgh. There had been a certain amount of rolling around in the rain. Being unarmed, I'd had to resort to biting him and it wouldn't have ended well for me but Leon turned up and slugged him with a Maglite. And even then, the bastard had still managed to get away.

We regarded each other over the silver tea service.

'Are you armed?'

I nodded for a third time. Unless he had X-ray vision, he wouldn't know it was only pepper spray.

'What now? Have you come to take me in?'

'No.'

He seemed surprised.

I smiled slightly. 'I'm so sorry to damage your ego, Mr Ronan, but I'm not part of a major task force come to arrest you. I'm here on another assignment and just happened to recognise you. This is a friendly warning to move on. I don't want to have to take any action today and you don't want to be arrested. Or shot. Or killed. So, I'm giving you a chance. Stand up slowly, leave this place, return to your pod, and jump away. This is a once-in-a-lifetime offer.'

'And if I don't?'

'Then make no mistake, I'll neutralise you.'

'No,' he said, urgently. 'Wait. Please wait.'

I waited.

'Let me explain.'

'Explain what? Your plan to murder your colleague?'

He seemed thunderstruck. 'Murder? I'm not going to murder anyone. Why would you think I want to murder someone? Who would I want to murder?'

'Well, Edward Bairstow, for one.'

'Why would I want to murder Edward Bairstow? I don't want to kill anyone – I just want to ...'

'Yes?'

He swallowed. 'I just want to take Annie.'

Ah. Not murder. Another attempt at kidnapping.

He forged on. 'If you let me take her I swear I'll go away quietly. I'll never trouble anyone again. That's all I want. Just Annie.'

I shook my head.

'Please, please, just let me explain ...'

I said gently, 'I know your story.'

'Then how – how can you find it in yourself to stop me today? I don't want to kill anyone. No one has to die. Just let me take her and go. You'll never see me again, I promise. Just give me Annie.'

'Annie is not mine to give. You've tried that once. She wouldn't go then and she won't go now. I'm offering you a chance to leave quietly. Go now, before it's too late.'

He shook his head in frustration. 'How can I make you understand? You don't know what it's like to lose someone you love. The despair of waking every morning to face another day alone. There's no joy, no light, no life in the world. And it never goes away. Not for one moment does her memory ever leave me. But I can have her back. We'll go away quietly. I swear you'll never see us again. Please – to be so close. To see her again. To touch her. I can't bear it any longer.'

His voice cracked. Despite everything he had done and

would do, I felt so sorry for him. I knew a little of his suffering. I'd once lost Leon, and how well I remembered that blessed moment of non-remembrance every morning just before I opened my eyes. When, just for one second, Leon was still with me, before the full realisation of his loss would crash down upon me again, together with the knowledge I had to face another day alone.

How could I abandon anyone, even Clive Ronan to that pain? I'd had friends and a place in the world to help me through it. He had nothing and no one. I had it in my power to save him.

For a moment, I wavered. Looking back, I can't believe I did that, but I wavered. I stared at the table, formulating plans, trying to think of ways through this. Long seconds ticked by as I struggled to find a way in which, somehow, in some way, everyone would get what they wanted.

I came that close to disaster.

In the end, however, I didn't have to do anything. I didn't have any decision to make. He blew it. All by himself. If only he'd waited another five seconds ... That's how close I came to disaster.

He mistook my silence for refusal and just as I lifted my head to speak, his eyes narrowed and he said bitterly, 'I should have killed you when I had the chance.'

'There's a coincidence,' I said cheerfully, hoping he couldn't hear my heart pounding away. 'I was just thinking the same thing.'

Almost as if he was talking to himself, he said, 'So why didn't you?' and I realised I'd just made a big mistake.

I rummaged desperately for something to say but it didn't matter because he already had the answer. He wasn't a stupid man.

Slowly, working it out as he went along, he said, 'That's it. We meet again, don't we? In my future and your past. So you can't kill me, can you? Because if you kill me now then your past starts to unravel – which would be interesting, I'll admit, and I'd like to be around to appreciate that, but the important thing is that you can't kill me now, which means I can do as I please and there's not a thing you can do about it. Is there?'

I remained calm. 'I didn't say you would be killed. I said I'd neutralise you, which isn't quite the same thing at all, although I hear it's considerably more painful. Shall we give it a go?'

He paused. For all he knew I had some super-duper weapon tucked away somewhere. I kept my expression pleasant and interested, hoping he couldn't hear my thumping heart.

He leaned back in his chair. I heard the wood creak. 'Well, what shall we do now? You might have some sort of weapon in that muff of yours – how very improper that sounds – but I have a weapon now, under this table and it's pointed directly at you. Suppose I shoot you. In the ensuing panic, I seize Annie and we're out of the door while everyone is concentrating on you.'

If he snatched Annie now, she would never go on the James VI assignment. She wouldn't fall sick. So no need for him to shoot Edward Bairstow. Who could still go on to found St Mary's. No paradox. I'd underestimated him. In just a few seconds, he'd worked out a near-perfect solution. Edward Bairstow would survive. I wouldn't.

He saw my hesitation and switched back to Mr Reasonable again.

'Look. I don't want to kill you. I don't want to kill anyone. I just want Annie. Let me take her and go. You don't have to do anything. Pretend you never saw me. Just get up and leave. Visit the Ladies. By the time you come back, we'll be gone.'

'And Edward Bairstow? He'll defend her, you know. Will you shoot him again? And Annie – do you think she'll go willingly? Have you thought this through?'

'Of course I have. Annie will go willingly enough to save Bairstow. Once I get her away to somewhere quiet and explain how the events of today have saved both her life and his, she'll understand.'

I doubted it. Ronan was sitting behind them. He hadn't seen their faces as they looked at each other ...

For a moment, I felt sympathy again. The James VI assignment had gone wrong – which could happen to any of us. Fear and panic had led to him shooting Edward Bairstow and the whole situation had just escalated from there, hurtling headlong to a desperate confrontation in Hawking and Annie's death.

He wouldn't give up. 'Think about it. I won't have to shoot Bairstow. He'll have two good legs for the rest of his life. There is no downside to this. I don't want to shoot you. I don't want to shoot anyone. Please. I just want to save Annie.'

There was no mistaking the passion in his voice. He was no longer leaning back in his chair, careless and in control. He leaned forward, his eyes bright with emotion.

For a moment, I thought I saw tears. He spoke very quietly.

'I'm alone. I'm so alone. Do you know what it's like to be on the outside? Wherever I go, to whatever time I go, I'm always alone. Do you know how lonely Time can be? Do you know how many times I've visited towns, villages, settlements? I watch them. The people. Greeting one another, laughing, making plans, arguing, and living their lives. Everyone has a place. They may not like it or be happy with it, but everyone fits perfectly into the space and time allocated them. Except me. I don't fit in anywhere.'

He pulled his hand out from under the table and rubbed the back of it angrily across his eyes.

'And even if I did find somewhere, it would be of no use to me, because every waking minute of every day, I hear the rattle of gunfire that ended her life. I feel her go limp in my arms. See the reproach in her eyes. I couldn't be with her at the end. I had to run. She was dying in her own blood on the floor in Hawking and I had to leave her. And that's just when I'm awake. You don't want to know about my dreams.'

I leaned forward and said quietly, 'Clive ...' because he was beginning to raise his voice. A definite social no-no. And suppose Edward Bairstow or Annie Bessant just happened to glance around ...

I wanted to calm things down a little. Choose a neutral subject. 'Just as a matter of interest, why aren't you with them on this assignment? Where are you at the moment?'

'Off the active list. Broken elbow.'

'Painful.'

'Very.'

He leaned back in his seat, took a couple of deep breaths, and was, once again, in control of himself. Maybe I'd missed an opportunity to spray him but what could I do? Because his words had touched a nerve. I'd once had to jump wildly around the timeline, trying to escape the Time Police, desperately looking for somewhere to come to rest, just for a minute, to have time to stop and think ... It hadn't been a pleasant experience and I hadn't even been alone, so God knows what it was like for him. All he wanted was someone to be with. And Dr Bairstow could still go on to found St Mary's. Annie would live. And who, given the opportunity, wouldn't seize the chance to change the events leading to a loved one's death. Surely, Dr Bairstow would understand. Would it be a consolation for him to know that somewhere out there, Annie was still alive?

I shook myself. Who was I to play life and death with Annie's future?

'You'd be saving her life,' argued that treacherous little voice that gives me such a hard time on a regular basis. 'She might not be happy, but she'd still be alive.'

No. You can't change History. The price is too high. I'm not bright, but that's one thing I have learned.

It's not changing History, argued the voice inside my head. It hasn't happened yet. Annie dies in the future.

What could I do? Never mind that. What *should* I do? The answer to that was easy. I'm an historian and the rules are very clear. In a crisis, deal with the now. Sort out the future later. Save Annie now and let events take their course. I couldn't let him get away with it. I couldn't let him take Annie and even if I did, Edward Bairstow would pursue him to the end of time. There might not be violence now, but, ultimately, there would be and God knows how many others would die.

He was watching me very carefully. 'I'm begging you. Let me save her life. Let me take her today. History ripples, and suddenly, Annie doesn't die.'

Slowly, so as not to alarm him, I reached up, tucked a wisp of hair back under my bonnet, and said, as calmly as I could, 'No. Annie still dies. Whatever you do, Annie will always die. The only difference is how many people die with her. I'm sorry for you, Clive, but you have to face this. Annie dies and there's no way to change that. You know very well that there's no way Edward Bairstow will let you take Annie today. You'll have to kill him. You say you won't, but you know you will. He won't let you take Annie. I won't let you take Annie. None of my team will let you ...'

He tried to interrupt, but I swept on. 'If Edward Bairstow doesn't go on to found St Mary's then St Mary's never exists. So you can't jump back to change History. Paradox. And we both know what that means.'

He leaned suddenly across the table. The desperate, heartbroken man had disappeared and in his place was the Clive Ronan I knew. It took everything I had not to let him see me rear back in fright.

'Stupid bitch! You really haven't thought this through at all, have you? It doesn't have to be Edward Bairstow who jumps back to found St Mary's. It could be anyone.' He smiled coldly. 'It could even be me.'

I didn't know what to say. I could really do with a few

minutes just to stop and think this through. Could that happen? It seemed horribly probable. And if St Mary's was founded under the auspices of Clive Ronan rather than Edward Bairstow ...? The implications were enormous. I could imagine what a St Mary's under Ronan would be like. What the hell should I do?

Save Edward Bairstow was the answer to that one. Whatever happened this afternoon, either to Annie or to me, whatever the result of this deadly little duel in these incongruous surroundings, Edward Bairstow must – *must* – survive.

But how? All I had was a small pepper spray concealed in my muff. By the time I pulled it out and sprayed, I'd be dead. I so desperately wanted to believe he didn't have a gun under the table, that it was still in his pocket, but he never bluffed. He wasn't the type. He didn't gloat, either. If he wanted you dead then five seconds later, that's what you were.

My death wasn't actually important. What was important was what would happen after he fired. Like everyone else, Dr Bairstow would look around for the source of the shot. He would leap to his feet and turn round. The last thing he would see would be Clive Ronan putting a bullet between his eyes. There would be chaos, confusion, screaming women, panic. He'd be out of the door – with or without Annie. He'd get away and everything would change. Everything I'd ever known would be gone and there was nothing I could do about it.

We stared at each other in silence. I made one last effort. 'Clive. Please. Listen to me. You don't have to shoot anyone ...'

He smiled without humour or affection. 'I'm going to pull the trigger now. It will be a belly shot, I'm afraid. Messy and painful. Agonizing, even. You'll be glad to die, believe me. But you'll live long enough to see Edward Bairstow die too.'

I saw his arm shift fractionally. I tensed myself, unable to believe I was about to die ... He had no gun ...

A quiet voice said politely, 'Knock-knock ...'

I heard a familiar sound and Ronan went limp.

Mr Sands caught him and eased him gently back in his chair. Something clattered to the floor. Bloody hell, he had had a gun after all. I bent and picked it up, glanced around to make sure we were still unobserved, and tucked it in my muff. Now that it was over. I found myself beginning to shake.

'Sorry to leave it so long,' said Mr Sands, pulling up another chair and sitting down. 'I was a little worried that stunning him would cause him to fire the gun involuntarily. I know Dr Bairstow would probably have got away, but it wouldn't have done you any good and it would certainly have buggered my chances of passing this test with flying colours. Would you like some tea?'

I nodded. Words were beyond me at that moment.

He poured me a cup from Ronan's pot and I added most of the contents of the sugar bowl.

'You stunned him?'

'Yes. Oh God, shouldn't I have?'

I strove for nonchalance. 'No, no. Stunning is fine. But where is it?'

He looked shifty. 'Where's what?'

'Your stun gun.'

He looked guiltily around and then held up his cane. 'Professor Rapson said that since I couldn't run quite as fast as everyone else – yet – I'd better have a little something to even the odds.' He pulled the stick into two pieces and poking out of the end was the familiar stun gun electrical contact point.

I shrugged, determined not to be impressed.

He grinned. 'OK, then how about this?'

The handle was shaped like a duck's head. He did something to the beak and a shot of amber fluid tipped into my teacup. 'For emergencies only, of course.'

Actually, in my life, pretty well every day is an emergency.

I chugged back a suddenly very enjoyable cup of tea.

'What's going on behind me?'

'Dr Bairstow's paying the bill. What shall I do?'

'Let them go.'

'What about Ronan?'

Good question. We both looked at Ronan who was sagging untidily in his seat. A stream of drool ran down his chin. We could lug him out through the crowds, explaining he was an uncle who'd had a funny turn, whatever, get him back to the pod and take him back for Dr Bairstow to deal with. Or, more likely, the Time Police. But what good would that do? He had to be at liberty to commit the crimes in his future. Our past. It makes my head ache, it really does.

'The thing is, Max, he knows you now. He's seen you in daylight. You can't afford to let him go free. You're the one who ruined his chance today. He'll hate you for ever more.'

I already knew that was true. Today was the day I had made a powerful enemy. One day he would pay someone I considered a friend of mine to throw me off a cliff. He would try to shoot me in the Alexandrian desert. And who knew what else that hadn't happened yet. How much easier just to shoot the bastard.

With regret, I shook my head. 'Come on, let's get out of here.'

'We're going to leave him? He's going to get away with it?'

'Well, we are sticking him with the bill.'

'Fair enough.'

Safely out in the main boulevard, I called in the troops. I could see them making their way unobtrusively through the crowds.

'Please don't discuss this with anyone, Mr Sands. And your report is for my eyes only.'

'Understood. Did I pass?'

'Maybe,' I said, striving to maintain at least the appearance of authority as his head of department.

Water off a duck's back. 'Great. Hey, knock-knock …'

'Shut up.'

I took our reports to the Boss, personally.

He took them from me and grinned. He actually grinned. I didn't know he could do that.

'Well?' he said. 'Did you see us?'

'We did, indeed, sir.'

'You should have come over.' His smile faded. 'I would have liked to introduce you.'

'We were busy, sir.'

I sat quietly and looked out of the window at the rain while he read first Mr Sand's report, and then mine. Finally, he laid them both on his desk and looked at me.

'I really am not sure what to say.'

I said, 'No, sir,' because that seemed a safe bet and left it at that.

'I remember being in the Western Court. Miss Bessant and I.'

He paused for a moment and I made sure to shuffle some papers.

'And Ronan just happened to be there as well?'

'I don't think that was coincidence, sir. I think he'd been following you. He would be familiar with your assignments, after all. I think he chose the Crystal Palace because he could escape easily in the crowds.'

'And all this was going on behind us? We had no idea.'

No, they wouldn't. They had been in their own little world.

'No, sir,' seemed a tactful response.

'Well, that will be a lesson to me always to sit with my back to the wall in future,' He smiled and suddenly, that young historian wasn't so far away after all. 'How did I look?'

I remembered his hand on hers. The eagerness of a man snatching at a few unexpected minutes with the only woman he would ever love.

'Unfamiliar, sir.'

He smiled.

'Sir, what are we going to do about him? About Ronan, I mean. He's rampaging up and down the timeline, always causing trouble. He leaves a trail of dead bodies wherever he goes and we can't touch him. We can't do anything except foil whatever dastardly scheme he's concocted this time and wait for our paths cross again.'

'I shall pass on the coordinates to the Time Police, of course. There might be something they can do. Although I don't know what ...'

He sat silently for a while. I wondered if he was thinking through the implications of Ronan's appearance. Or were his thoughts more personal? Eventually, he roused himself.

'Am I to understand that Mr Sands performed adequately?'

'He did, sir. He carried out my instructions to the letter but was able to act promptly on his own initiative when required. I think he's aware of his own limitations. With your permission, I shall inform him he's back on the active list, but that the responsibility for declining any assignment in which he might have trouble will rest solely with him. He's a sensible lad, sir. He'll tell me if he thinks he can't hack it.'

'He saved St Mary's, Max. As far as I'm concerned, he has a job for life.'

'Just wait until he starts telling you interminable knock-knock jokes, sir.'

I stood up.

'Just one moment.'

'Sir?'

He picked up his own cane and stared at it, twisting it in his hand.

'I wonder if you could ask Professor Rapson to call in

and see me. When he has a moment to spare, of course. No rush.'

I grinned. 'Yes, sir.'

At the door, I looked back. He was sitting at his desk, staring back down the years. Back to the time when he was young and handsome. To when he was a brilliant historian with his whole future ahead of him. Back to the time when he had two good legs. Back to when Annie was still alive.

I let myself out quietly.

Now that we had an important assignment under our belts, we really felt we were up and running and I no longer had any excuse not to get to grips with Dr Bairstow's blasted Open Day. I assembled my carefully selected victims and once they were all present, got Miss Lee to lock the door. By exercising my fabled management skills, I alternately teased, bribed, threatened, called in favours, drowned them in tea, and refused to release them until I got what I wanted. I really can't understand why some managers find it so difficult to motivate their teams.

Four long hours later and after a prolonged and much needed unit-wide comfort break, I was able to present the Boss with a rough outline.

There would be, as they say, something for everyone. The Boss himself would kick things off with a short speech of welcome before declaring the proceedings officially open.

Peterson and Schiller had volunteered to give an archery demonstration, and with luck, no one would be punctured – or at least, not until after they'd parted with their money.

Professor Rapson was dusting off his trebuchet and would be firing missiles into the lake. What could go wrong with that?

Miss Lee would hire a marquee in which Polly Perkins from IT would show our legendary dinosaur holo. (When, eventually, the programmes were printed, a misprint informed us a marquis would be erected on the South Lawn. We all looked forward to seeing that.)

Messrs Clerk and Roberts from the History Department and Messrs Evans and Guthrie from the Security Section would dress as medieval knights and give us a demonstration of sword fighting. It seemed fair to assume that the opportunity to settle old scores and invent new ones would be enthusiastically seized. The medical team would be on high alert.

Miss Van Owen was to give a sidesaddle demonstration, along with Dr Maxwell, who had better get some practice in if she didn't want to make a complete arse of herself in public.

There would be static displays, too. Mrs Enderby was to mount a display of Costumes through the Ages along three sides of the Gallery, featuring the award-winning costumes she and her department had supplied for the BBC's latest Sunday-night historical bodice-ripper.

Dr Dowson, in addition to manning the public address system – for which he had enthusiastically volunteered and them become distressingly deaf to our attempts to dissuade him – would give guided tours of the suitable bits of St Mary's, pointing out areas of architectural interest. His team nodded wisely. I suspected they would go their own way and by the time they'd finished, the walls of St Mary's would run with blood and echo to the screams of tortured souls. There was talk of setting up a dungeon complete with skeletons and rats. Traumatised kids wouldn't be able to sleep for a week. Good stuff!

Mrs Mack was in charge of refreshments. There would be a pig roasting on a spit. There would be burgers, ice cream, jacket potatoes, exotic sausages, and an enormous tea tent. A picnic area would be set up by the lake, and in the evening, there would be a medieval banquet in the Great Hall for 'selected guests', the definition of which was either people from whom we wanted to extort large sums of money, or those with whom we needed to mend a few fences. The Parish Council, for instance. And the Chief Constable, who, for some reason, persisted in regarding us as a bunch of irresponsible nutters, despite all the evidence to the contrary. And, of course, SPOHB. The Society for the Protection of Historical Buildings with whom we did not enjoy a close relationship. Apparently, they have a kind of blacklist, and of the twelve organisations that figure prominently, St Mary's is five of them. Which is, I think, not only a little unjust, but mathematically incorrect as well.

Schoolchildren would be invited to draw a picture of their favourite moment in History and prizes would be presented by Dr Bairstow. It was really very remiss of me not to mention that to him. Apart from the joy of watching him deal with a sticky six year old, it meant all the schools would show up with proud relatives to view their talented offspring's work, which would be exhibited in the library.

There would be bouncy castles. The donkey sanctuary people would bring half a dozen of their most adorable guests. The nutters from the Castle Hendred re-enactment

105

society would mount a display. Various local traders had been persuaded to rent space. A display of vintage cars would line the drive. There would be a crafts tent and a small local farmers' market for anyone who wanted to buy a small local farmer. It was looking good.

Mrs Partridge was handling the publicity. Posters would be designed, along with adverts to be inserted in the paper. A reluctant Dr Bairstow was to be wheeled out to give a TV interview. It didn't have to be him – I could have done it – but the temptation to make him a star was too great.

Mr Strong was to organise car parking. The plan was to let people in for free and then take them for every penny they possessed once we actually had them. Someone suggested charging to let them out.

All members of the History Department were to wear historical costume. I had charged Mrs Enderby with the task of making sure they were all clean, authentic, and decent. I didn't want Mr Roberts turning up in his Lady Godiva gear.

Markham, who reckoned he had a gift for this sort of thing, would set up a small tent and tell people's fortunes. He had two already prepared. Women would meet a tall dark stranger and travel across water towards the sun. Men would have a lucky encounter at the time of the full moon, which would lead to money. It all sounded very dodgy to me, but apparently he'd already procured a crystal ball and in his new incarnation as Madame Zara, All-Seeing Daughter of the Gods, was prepared to dispense enlightenment and confusion in equal quantities.

The whole thing was to be rounded off with a

spectacular outdoor fireworks display – which caused Dr Bairstow some concern until I was able to reassure him that the fireworks were being procured from a reputable source and not in any way manufactured by R & D, and that the manufacturers themselves would be in charge of the display. I didn't actually say so, but I definitely gave him the impression that Professor Rapson would be locked in the basement for this part of the entertainment.

'I've chosen the first Saturday in August, sir. The start of the summer holidays, so we're not competing with other Bank Holiday events at the end of the month. It will be St Mary's who kicks off the holiday season and sets the standard for everyone else to beat.'

'I want spectacle, Dr Maxwell, excitement, thrills, crowds of people, and most of all, I want their money.'

'We could dress Markham as Dick Turpin and he could hold them up at pistol point. "Your money or your life."'

He frowned. 'I don't think we need go that far ... yet ...' He tailed away.

I paused from putting my papers away. 'Problem, sir?'

He sighed. 'The cost of rebuilding St Mary's is frightening. Small countries have been invaded for less expense than it took to put us back together. The expenditure has been remarked upon, and after we rescued part of the Great Library at Alexandria with all the fame and fortune that brought to Thirsk, they're clamouring for a repeat performance. To justify the cost. So I shall be looking to you to address that issue later this year, Max.'

I just couldn't keep my mouth shut, could I? When I

think of the grief that could have been avoided if I'd just gone quietly away at that point …

'Actually, sir …'

'Yes?'

'Actually, I've had a brilliant idea.'.'

He regarded me warily. God knows why. 'Continue.'

'Well, I've been thinking about another salvage assignment and I thought – what about Old St Paul's. The one destroyed in the Great Fire of London.'

'Go on.'

This was encouraging. I ploughed on.

'Well, I was thinking, we nip back and rescue what we can in terms of artefacts, regalia, documents, bury it all safely, inform Thirsk and let them make another spectacular discovery. That and the stunning success of our Open Day should ensure funding for at least the next couple of years.'

'An excellent idea on the face of it, but I'm not sure we could guarantee that anything buried in London would will be undisturbed long enough for us to retrieve it.'

I allowed myself to smirk. 'Ah, but that's the beauty of it, sir. We don't bury it in London. We bury it here. At St Mary's. We know it'll be safe and we'll get a share of the publicity too, when it's discovered.'

'Here?'

'Indeed, sir. It was our little adventure with the Laceys that gave me the idea. By 1666, Charles II is king; young James has grown up and is busy restoring and rebuilding St Mary's. And the gardens, too. How easy it would be to bury something in the grounds then, to be dug up by us some four hundred years later. We could even arrange for the Chancellor and some of the Senior Faculty "coincidentally" to be present for the discovery. For authenticity and respectability. Funding problems solved, sir.'

'Why on earth would treasures from Old St Paul's end up here?'

'Why not, sir? We've already dug up a lost Shakespeare play. Why not religious artefacts as well?'

He sat back for a while, drumming his fingers on his desk. Always a sign of deep thought.

'Why is it, Dr Maxwell, that the more outrageous your scheme, the more natural and logical you manage to make it sound?'

I grinned. 'No idea, sir.'

'Very well. If you can find the time, draw me up a mission plan.'

'Yes, sir.'

I handed over the St Paul's assignment to Van Owen and Schiller for two reasons. The first was that I had my hands full with this bloody Open Day and it was taking over my life. The second was that I wouldn't be able to go. St Paul's burns on 3rd September 1666, and on that date, I was in Mauritius chasing dodos, and you can't be in the same time twice. Yes, I know I hadn't been in this world then, but I'd checked the records, and a Maxwell had been in Mauritius on that date and no one was prepared to take the chance. So sadly, this one would be happening without me.

I handed over all my notes and data stacks. Van Owen took the London part of the assignment. Schiller liaised with Dr Dowson on the treasures we were likely to be able to retrieve and the best methods of preserving them for the four hundred years it would take for us to find them again.

And I was relegated to organising this bloody Open Day.

The next bit was nothing to do with me.

It was all Dr Bairstow's fault.

Just for once, I was completely blameless.

Actually, that should be made perfectly clear. I was completely blameless. It was – all of it – Dr Bairstow's fault.

Thirsk University had come to visit. They wanted to inspect the repairs. As they were perfectly entitled to do since, since they'd paid for most of it and, in their minds at least, they were our employers. They had a quick tour. I reported on the progress with our Open Day. They were graciously pleased – it was all going well and the Boss, sensibly wanting to get them off the premises as quickly as possible, took them into Rushford for lunch. It probably seemed a good idea at the time. They all waltzed off and we breathed a sigh of relief and carried on with the working day.

They were pretty late back, and noisy with it. We could hear them shouting and laughing and the car doors slamming as they drove away and then peace descended. But not for long.

I was settled nicely in the library, building my data-stack and doing no harm to anyone when Mrs Partridge tracked me down.

'Dr Bairstow would like to see you at your earliest convenience.'

By which she meant at his earliest convenience, which meant now. I searched my conscience. There were a few things, but he couldn't possibly know about any of them, so I entered his office with the confident tread of the very nearly innocent.

'Good afternoon, sir.'

He sat bolt upright in his chair. The curtains were half-pulled across the window. He looked like a silhouetted vulture.

'Ah. Dr Maxwell. Sit down please.'

I sat, yanked out my scratchpad to show willing, and waited expectantly.

And waited.

And waited.

Somewhere, a new galaxy formed.

The door opened behind me and Mrs Partridge, exuding disapproval from every pore, placed a tray containing a coffee pot, cup, and saucer on his desk in a very meaningful manner. I wouldn't have thought it possible to pour coffee with a snap, but she managed it, no problem at all, and the manner in which it was placed in front of him spoke volumes.

There was nothing for me. Was I in the outer darkness of her disapproval again? It was very possible, although as far as I was aware, I hadn't done anything very terrible recently. Maybe I was about to and this was pre-emptive action. After all, as Kleio, the Muse of History, she'd know better than anyone would. But no, it wasn't me. Not this time.

The silence went on. And on.

Mrs Partridge cleared her throat menacingly, and he appeared to make an effort.

'I've just returned from lunch with the Chancellor.'

'That's nice, sir. How did it go?'

'The Red Lion.'

I ran that answer past the question asked and picked my way carefully.

'I hope it went well, sir.'

'Oh, yes. Yes. Very well indeed. They are most interested in the Old St Paul's assignment. They are even looking forward to attending our Open Day.'

'Excellent news, sir.'

'Dr Black appears to have the entire Senior Faculty either bemused, bewitched, or just plain terrified.'

Kal never has any difficulty getting her own way. She simply states her desires and waits for the universe to arrange things accordingly.

Silence fell again. The clock ticked. The coffee cooled.

'Was there anything else, sir?'

He pulled open a drawer and took out a bottle and a glass, tipping a good measure into the glass for me and an even better one into his coffee.

Mrs Partridge looked at me. I felt like Odysseus caught between Scylla and Charybdis.

'Your very good health, Dr Maxwell.'

'And yours, sir,' I said, sipping something fiery.

And from that moment on, it probably became my fault as well, because I really shouldn't drink in the afternoon. Actually, I probably shouldn't drink at all. No good ever comes of it.

The silence from Mrs Partridge was deafening.

'Now then,' he said, briskly, tapping the desk. 'To business.'

I grinned at Mrs Partridge who compressed her lips in such a way that made me glad she wasn't compressing them at me.

'So – the Chancellor and her gang have gone back happy, sir?

'It would appear so, yes. However, I fear I may have allowed myself to be – ambushed.'

'You, sir?'

He pulled himself together. 'I won't bore you with the details, but it would appear that I – we – have accepted a challenge.'

I had a blurred vision of the really rather pleasant Chancellor leaping from her seat and slapping his face with her glove. Pull yourself together, Maxwell.

'To what have you been challenged, sir?'

'We, Dr Maxwell. To what have *we* been challenged?'

'I don't know, sir. I wasn't there.'

'What?'

I raised my voice a little in case he was becoming hard of hearing. 'I wasn't there, sir.'

'Where?'

'What?'

Mrs Partridge coughed. She probably had an afternoon she wanted to get on with.

He continued. 'There was some discussion over lunch – a variety of opinions were expressed and a challenge offered.'

He breathed heavily. I was enjoying myself so much

that I gave no thought as to where all this might be leading me.

'It would appear that last year, during a week of fund-raising activities, the University of Thirsk enjoyed considerable success in an event concerning the propulsion of aquatic vessels along a body of water. The first one to arrive at a designated finishing point is deemed the winner. Although apparently, in terms of crowd entertainment, it appears the journey is more important than the arrival. A great deal of horseplay must occur before what one can only describe as "the surviving team" reaches the finishing post. The Thirsk entry was joined in this adventure by boats designed and manned by the local police force, a branch of the Royal Engineers, and the Rugby Club. They still managed to emerge triumphant, so we can, I think, draw the conclusion that they are a force to be reckoned with.'

His enunciation was perfect. His movements perfectly coordinated but I realised at that moment, that Dr Bairstow was as drunk as a skunk. As a newt, even.

'A raft race? Sir, that is so cool!'

I could see I had joined Dr Bairstow under the cloud of Mrs Partridge's displeasure.

'According to an inappropriately self-satisfied Chancellor, they swept all before them. Of course, up there in the Danelaw, they're all descended from Caledonian cattle robbers, invading Vikings, and whippet-racing black-pudding eaters, so that probably doesn't amount to much.'

I heard an unwise voice say, 'The University of Thirsk attracts staff and students of the highest calibre, sir, and its reputation is internationally recognised,' and realised, with some concern, that it had been me.

Fortunately, he wasn't listening. 'And when I say swept all before them, I mean just that. Apparently they affixed some sort of contrivance to the front of their – craft – that simply swept aside all opposition and they cruised to victory – literally – waving to the crowds and broadcasting a ditty, entitled "We are the Champions" to the detriment of ear drums, glass edifices, and music lovers everywhere.'

My God, he was really worked up.

'Deplorable,' I said.

'Over lunch, the entire Senior Faculty insisted on demonstrating their victory utilising a variety of cruets, glasses, and cutlery dredged not only from our table but also from the unfortunates sitting nearby. I believe an entire family went without black pepper and Parmesan cheese on their penne, simply so the Chancellor could demonstrate the superiority of their tactics.'

His eyes closed as he relived the outrage.

'Disgraceful, sir.'

'So there you have it, Dr Maxwell.'

I peered into my glass. I'd missed something. 'Do I?'

'The University of Thirsk has challenged St Mary's to a race. Their boat against ours. The event to be held here, on the lake, during the afternoon of the Open Day.'

'Really, sir? Awesome!'

He assumed his Churchillian pose. 'We must win, Dr Maxwell. And not just win. We must crush them! We must epitomise the spirit of the Armada! The little boats at Dunkirk! The valiant actions of the *Revenge*!'

115

'I believe the *Revenge* was outnumbered fifty-three to one, suffered catastrophic damage and the loss of most of her crew, sir.'

He wasn't listening. 'We must relive Trafalgar! St Mary's expects every man to do his duty! Think of Drake at Cadiz! The Battle of the Nile! The Fighting Temeraire!' He thumped his desk. 'Failure is not an option!'

I allowed myself to be caught up in the moment. 'How can we fail, sir? We're St Mary's! We will channel our maritime heritage! We will blow them out of the water! Rule Britannia!'

I have got to stop drinking.

He regarded me silently for a moment and then slumped. 'I admire your optimism, Dr Maxwell, but they have resources far beyond anything we can muster here. An engineering department ...'

'We have Chief Farrell and Mr Dieter, sir. They can make a flotation device out of a concrete box lined with lead.'

'... Some of the finest minds in the country ...'

'We have Professor Rapson. A man whose thought processes defy close examination.'

'... And an apparently limitless supply of cannon fodder. Or the student body, as I suppose we should refer to them.'

'We have the History Department,' I said with boundless but groundless confidence. 'Or, if the worst comes to the worst we can launch Mr Markham as an underwater missile.' I recklessly knocked back the last of the fire juice. 'Leave this with me, sir,' and realised, too late, I'd walked straight into his trap.

I stared, reproachfully, and there was ten seconds of my life I was never going to get back again, because this time there was no response at all. I waited a while, but I think he might have dropped off. I wobbled to my feet and looked for the door. As I left, I could hear Mrs Partridge asking coldly whether she should cancel his afternoon appointments.

Deciding to strike while the iron was hot, I staggered off to Hawking to see Leon, who took one look and shouted for someone to put the kettle on. I sat in his office with him and Dieter and eloquently and succinctly recounted as much as I could remember, adding gestures and doing the voices where appropriate. At the end, they simply stared and Leon said, 'Dr Bairstow was drunk?' and it occurred to me that my report might not have been as crystal clear as I had thought. It took yet another cup of tea before they were able to grasp the full impact of my communication.

To my disappointment, they did not immediately leap into action. Dieter stared thoughtfully at the wall, and Leon subjected the floor to close scrutiny. I waited a while, but as far as I could see, the pair of them were very nearly comatose. The Technical Section at work is not a spectator sport. I stood up and headed for the door. As I was leaving, Leon asked if he could borrow Professor Rapson for a while. I indicated my immense enthusiasm for such an action and promised to despatch him forthwith. Then I thought I might have a bit of a lie-down.

I didn't take the briefing for the Old St Paul's assignment, although I did attend. Schiller made an excellent job of it.

We assembled in the Hall. She stood on the half-landing with the sun lighting up her fair hair. She spoke without notes.

'Good afternoon, everyone. Thank you for coming. As we're all aware, our next assignment is a salvage operation – 3rd September 1666. The Great Fire of London and the destruction of Old St Paul's Cathedral. I shall begin with some background on the cathedral, describe the Great Fire, give details of the pods and teams, and then outline our plan of action. Questions at the end.'

She paused, but everyone was busying themselves scratchpads or notebooks. Eventually, silence fell.

'Right, old St Paul's occupies the same site as the new building. It's fallen into disrepair and disrepute. The interior is used for commercial and social purposes. You could even pick up a prostitute there. The Nave is known as Paul's Walk and that's where you'll find the cream of society strutting their stuff and gossiping and the captains of industry wheeling and dealing. You probably can't hear yourself pray for the sound of money being made and reputations demolished. Cromwell's troops used it as stables during the Civil War, which probably didn't do it any good, either.

'It couldn't be more inflammable. Former religious buildings in the churchyard have been sold off to printers and booksellers. If you look at your plans, you will see the nearby churches of St Faiths and St Gregory's. They will be used to store vast quantities of books. St Faith's is so stuffed that it burns for a week. It's never rebuilt.

'To make things even worse, when it looks as if the fire is heading their way, citizens bring their important papers and household treasures to store inside St Paul's where they thought they would be safe and so they might have been, but Christopher Wren's proposed refurbishment means that the entire building is encased in wooden scaffolding. The summer has been long and dry and there's a stiff wind. It couldn't have been worse.

'I'm sorry the interior plans of the cathedral are a little short on detail. We have no clear idea of what to expect once we're inside. There will probably be very little in the way of religious artefacts or regalia. However, there should be wooden tablets to the memories of Sir Philip Sidney and Walsingham, and there are almost certain to be hangings, vestments, candlesticks, and the like. We'll just have to do our best.'

She paused for everyone to catch up and I took a moment to think of the tomb of John of Gaunt, destroyed in the fire. I would really have liked to see that. I've always been a big Lancastrian fan. Peterson had promised me an image.

She pointed to a street map shown on the big screen above her head. 'Paternoster Row, Warwick Lane, Old Change, all the cramped lanes and courts surrounding the cathedral go up, too. All of this area will be completely devastated. So be aware of your surroundings at all times.

'Moving on to the fire itself. The fire breaks out in Pudding Lane on the night of the 1st to the 2nd September. As I said, there's been a drought. Everything is tinder dry. There's a strong easterly breeze blowing and St Paul's is only half a mile from Pudding Lane.

'King Charles himself, together with his brother, the Duke of York, takes control of the fire-fighting. People are evacuated to Hampstead Heath. The Thames is full of tiny boats, ferrying people to safety. The King orders buildings to be blown up to create firebreaks. They are desperate to contain the fire and stop it spreading across the river. Thirteen thousand houses and ninety-three churches will be destroyed. By some miracle only five people die.

'By 3rd September, Ludgate Hill is a firestorm and St Paul's goes up like a torch. According to Evelyn, stones fly like grenades. Melted lead streams down the street. The pavements are red with it. We must be long gone by then.'

She paused again for people to catch up again.

Evans said, 'For how long does it burn?'

'Until the 7th September.'

'Wow!'

'We'll be in four teams, taking pods Three, Four, Five, and Eight. Chief Farrell, Mr Peterson, and Mr Roberts will be in Number Three. Major Guthrie, Mr Clerk, and Miss Prentiss in Number Four. Miss Van Owen and Mr Evans and I will be in Number Five and Mr Dieter, Dr Foster, and Mr Sands are in Number Eight which has been designated the medical centre.

'If you consult your layouts – we will land near Augustine's Gate, east of the building, work our way around and enter through the Crypt on the north side. Once we enter the building itself, control of the mission passes from me to Major Guthrie. You will obey his commands as if your life depends upon it – which it will. We've done this before and we've always come back safely so let's not screw it up now. When Major Guthrie says, "Jump!" your feet should already have left the ground.

'Once inside, we'll have to wing it. We have no idea of the contents, or where and how they are stored. We'll go for small, portable stuff that's easily shifted. If we get it right, it's perfectly possible that Londoners will be bringing their treasures through one door and we're shunting them straight out of the other.'

'Treasures?' enquire Evans.

'Don't get excited. The treasures of one century are not necessarily those of another. For instance, Samuel Pepys buried his wine and Parmesan cheeses.'

'Were they ever found?'

'No idea. The usual rules apply. We stay in our teams. If anyone is hurt, report to Dr Foster *in your teams*. No one wanders off alone. Do not race about like frantic ferrets. Organise yourselves into chains and always stay in sight of each other. And for God's sake, be aware a cathedral is about to fall on you. Be aware of yourself, your team, and the nearest exit. Study your handouts, plans, and schedules. We go the day after tomorrow. Any questions so far?'

Nope!

'Right – the second stage. Having loaded everything away, we jump sideways from Old St Paul's to St Mary's, where our big pod, TB2 will be waiting in the woods. Most of the Site One team will unload everything into TB2 and return home immediately. The fewer people milling around, the better. Dr Dowson will select his own team for this part of the assignment and from that moment, everyone takes their instructions from him.

We've chosen St Mary's because, in 1666, it's still undergoing rebuilding after a major fire in 1643. As far as we know, the family are not in residence and the workers are billeted in the village. This work will be done at night when we should have a free hand. We will take our time with this. There's no point in us risking life and limb at St Paul's and then finding nothing has survived the centuries because we cut corners when we buried it. We bury whatever we've managed to retrieve, record the location very carefully, and return to St Mary's.

'Those working at Site One, Old St Paul's, report to Wardrobe. We're kicking historical accuracy into touch for this one. We'll be wearing fireproof suits with some kind of cloak thrown over the top. Those at Site Two, St Mary's, will draw the usual paper suits. Cotton gloves and headgear, people. I don't want anyone shedding modern epithelials over 17th-century artefacts. Any questions, anyone?'

'Do we have any idea of what we'll be able to salvage?'

She shook her head. 'Not really, no, but stick with reasonably small stuff. Don't go trying to dismantle rood screens or uproot the font.'

'How long will we have?'

'Not long. Probably less than an hour. The time that everyone else has decided it's too dangerous to remain any longer is when we move in.'

'When do we move out?'

'When I say so,' said Major Guthrie, standing up and turning to face the room. 'Be very clear. Any historian not clearing the building when I give the word will be shot.

We will have a timekeeper. Mr Sands will remain in Number Eight to monitor the situation from outside. Either after one hour, or when he judges evacuation is necessary, whichever comes first, I will give the order to move. And you *will* move.'

'Any more questions?' said Schiller.

There weren't.

'Good luck, everyone.'

7

Twelve people set out for Old St Paul's and twelve people didn't come back.

It was a disaster. It was unprecedented. Twelve people lost in one mission.

We stood on the gantry with our stupid welcome home banners and waited.

No one came back.

We waited an hour. The techies frantically ran diagnostics, checked their equipment, and shouted at the IT Section. The IT Section stared at their screens and shouted back. Two hours later and four plinths still stood empty. No sign of TB2, either. Something had gone horribly wrong.

Finally, Mr Lindstrom reported to Dr Bairstow, who was still waiting with us on the gantry. I'd brought him a chair, which he'd gently refused, standing quietly with his hands crossed on his walking stick.

There was no malfunction, said Mr Lindstrom. Everything was working perfectly. There was no reason under the sun why four pods shouldn't be sitting quietly on their plinths. No reason at all. The fault lay at the other end. In London, 1666.

It was unthinkable that all four pods should have

developed a simultaneous fault, and certainly not with Leon and Dieter there. And even if they'd been in serious trouble, Mr Sands, at least, could have jumped back for assistance, but there was nothing. No pods. No people.

I stood on the gantry, gripping the safety rail and trying to get my thoughts in some sort of order. Something had gone hideously, horribly wrong and no one was coming back from this assignment.

Dr Bairstow said quietly, 'Dr Maxwell, Mr Markham, my office please. Ten minutes,' and limped from the gantry.

I looked down into the hangar. The technical team was still at it. Polly Perkins and the IT team were running more diagnostics. Up on the gantry, people looked at me.

'We may be worrying unnecessarily,' I said, quietly. 'No matter how big a catastrophe, someone is always able to get back to St Mary's and report. The fact that no one is here at all might simply mean they're too busy and have forgotten. You know how things are when historians are caught up in the moment.'

I'm not sure if anyone believed me. Leon, Guthrie, Dieter – there were cool heads there who would have driven oblivious, obsessed historians back to their pods with chairs and whips if they'd had to. And I'd put David Sands in Number Eight just to prevent this very occurrence. He was their timekeeper and observer. Any command from him was to be instantly obeyed. I'd given him the authority to override everyone and everything, deferring only to Major Guthrie.

So where were they?

More importantly, what were we going to do about it?

I looked at us. Markham and me. There are dream teams – and then there is Markham and me. He was still limping slightly from his unassisted leap from the roof in 1643. I was fit but ineligible. I couldn't go back. Not safely, anyway.

'Let's go and see what Dr Bairstow wants to do,' said Markham, and off we went.

Mrs Partridge was waiting for us and followed us in, closing the door behind her.

The Boss was sitting behind his empty desk. Brisk and business like. I did my best to swallow my own fears and pulled my scratchpad from my knee pocket.

'Yes, sir?'

'Tell me again, on which day were you in Mauritius?'

'Sept 3rd, 1666, sir.'

'All day?'

'No, we arrived mid-afternoon, Mauritius time.'

'Can you be more specific?'

'Not really, sir. Around three o'clock, I would say.'

'London is three hours behind … so about noon, our time.' He trailed off and stared at his desk. 'For how long were you there?'

'A little under three hours, sir. I could jump to London any time after, say, three o'clock.'

'By three in the afternoon, St Paul's will be ablaze. I dare not wait that long.' He did the desk-gazing thing again. 'You and Mr Markham will take a pod and jump back to investigate.'

I opened my mouth. He held up his hand. 'I am aware of the risk, Dr Maxwell. I am aware of the risk to you personally and I am especially aware of the risk to the timeline if two living versions of the same person try to inhabit the same period of time.'

He sighed. 'I cannot do nothing. I must make at least some attempt to mount a rescue. Therefore, I give you one hour. One hour only. You will be on the clock. You will use the time to locate and, if possible, extricate our colleagues. Their safety is your secondary concern. If necessary, you will instruct them to abandon their assignment and return to St Mary's. Whatever treasures they are endeavouring to rescue are valueless compared with the lives of the people in this unit. Is that clearly understood?'

'Yes, sir. So what's my primary function, then?'

'The timing of your Mauritius assignment is vague and it's impossible to be as accurate as I would like, so your primary function is to return to St Mary's by 11.30 regardless of whether you have located your colleagues or not. Is *that* clearly understood? I am concerned with the possibility you may have arrived in Mauritius earlier than you think.'

'Yes, sir.'

'I mean it, Max. There are some differences of opinion as to exactly what would happen should two incarnations of the same person appear at the same time, but everyone agrees it will not be good. You must, therefore, adhere to the thirty-minute safety margin. There will be no misunderstanding over this.'

'No, sir.'

'Mr Markham, you will accompany Dr Maxwell in your usual capacity.'

'Yes, sir.'

'Dr Maxwell, that will be all. Mr Markham, if you could remain behind for one minute, please.'

One minute he said, and one minute it was. Markham emerged looking rather pale. I guessed Dr Bairstow had been frightening him with the current thinking on what would happen if two versions of me tried to occupy the same time.

'What did he say?'

'A short and brutal lecture on what he personally will do to me if I don't get you out by the specified time. I know you don't care about yourself, Max, but for God's sake, spare a thought for what will happen to me.'

I laughed.

We sat on the stairs in the deserted Great Hall. All around us were whiteboards, data tables, and files. Piles of paper were strewn around the floor and stuck on the walls. The only thing missing was the historians themselves. All of them, except me. I pushed that thought to the back of my mind.

'Right,' said Markham, uncharacteristically business like. 'I think we can agree that whatever has happened to them has happened to all of them. Even Mr Sands.'

I nodded. Jagged pictures flashed through my head. A massive stone edifice, ablaze from top to bottom, running red with molten lead, slowly imploding and helpless historians trapped inside, their screams lost amongst the sounds of crashing masonry and roaring flames …

I pushed all that away. Not helpful. Markham was outlining a course of action.

'We'll land as close to the cathedral as we can get.

We'll check in with Sands, find out what's gone wrong. It might be something simple. Depending on what he tells us, we'll go after the others.'

I agreed. 'We should arrive around 10.30 in the morning.'

'We could go in earlier.'

'We're not sure where they'll be. By 10.30, they'll definitely be inside St Paul's so we'll know where to look for them. If, for some reason, they're not there, we'll initiate a widening search around the cathedral. We'll take tag readers – if they don't melt. It's going to be hot, I'm afraid.'

'The only reason they wouldn't be inside St Paul's is if they've been trapped elsewhere. Or maybe …' he trailed off, but I knew what he meant.

In a desperate attempt to save all London, Charles II would order vast numbers of houses to be demolished to prevent the fire spreading even further. A building could have come down on them. A whole street could have come down on them. Even if they'd sought safety inside their pods, they could have been buried under a vast pile of burning rubble, slowly suffocating … stifling in the immense heat …

'OK,' I said. 'We'll take water, tag readers, fire axes to clear a pathway. And rope. Anything else?'

'Blasters. To defend ourselves.'

'Against what?'

'We don't know. That's just the point. We'll wear fire suits, helmets, gloves, and boots – the usual stuff. Like we did at Alexandria.'

That had been our first salvage assignment. The Great

Library at Alexandria. That had been burning to the ground as well. Maybe one day we could embark upon a salvage assignment that involved vast amounts of cool, clear water.

'Meet you in Hawking in an hour,' he said.

We met in Hawking. We wore fire suits, heavy boots, and helmets. My gloves were stuffed into my belt, along with a fire axe. The suits were stiff and heavy. I was already sweating heavily and we hadn't even started yet.

Like Markham, I carried a cloak. They're so useful – you can tear them up for bandages, carry things or people in them, use them as a disguise – even actually wear them as cloaks to keep warm and dry. I don't know why we ever abandoned them. You try ripping up a waxed jacket to make a tourniquet.

We walked to Number Six. We were silent. The whole hangar was silent. There was no Leon around to give everything a reassuring last-minute check.

Mr Lindstrom was nervous. I think exactly the same thought had occurred to him.

'I've checked everything thoroughly, Max. Remember, you must be out by 11.30.'

I nodded. Markham was stowing our gear.

Lindstrom gulped nervously. 'I've laid in the coordinates and Miss Perkins has verified them.' He swallowed again. 'Just in case of error.'

'Thank you, Mr Lindstrom. I'm sure there was no need, but we both appreciate your attention to detail.'

'Yeah,' said Markham. 'And you can buy us a drink when we get back. Mine's a pint and they don't call this lady the Margarita Monster for nothing.'

'Do they?' I said, surprised.

'Well, not to your face, obviously.'

Poor Lindstrom was looking a little taken aback. In the absence of Leon and Dieter, he'd suddenly been propelled into the front line. I was more confident in his abilities than he was. None of Leon's or Guthrie's teams were idiots, no matter how many times we told them they were.

'Look on the bright side,' said Markham, making himself comfortable at the console. 'If neither of us comes back then you'll have a cheap evening. Albeit a lonely one.'

He didn't look particularly comforted.

'I tell you what,' I said. 'If we do make it back, Markham will buy you a drink instead, and if we don't, then I'll buy you one.'

We shunted him outside while he was still thinking about it.

We landed on the north side of St Paul's, in Paternoster Row, just outside Paul's Gate. Excellent work, Mr Lindstrom.

'Max. Listen. We have one hour. Not a second longer. We must be gone by 11.30, which will be about half past two in the afternoon in Mauritius. We dare not cut it any closer. No arguments. No excuses. After sixty minutes, we're out of here.'

I nodded. He didn't have to tell me. If, for any reason, I was still here   when I was due to arrive in Mauritius … what would happen?

It struck me that he was looking unusually serious. I

know that we were in the middle of the biggest fire London had ever seen, and that we would be poking around a cathedral whose roof was about to fall in on us, and that I was pushing our safety protocols to their limit, but all this sort of thing was meat and drink to Markham. As far as he was concerned, all assignments were like this. Maybe Hunter had consigned him to the outer darkness of her affections again and he was feeling gloomy. He slapped a gun on his sticky patch. 'Let's go.'

We had one hour.

We slipped out of the pod and my heart sank. We'd hugely underestimated the severity of the blaze. The heat was overwhelming. The entire north side of Paternoster Row was ablaze. The roar of the flames was deafening. Inside my helmet, I could feel the sweat running down my face. I could even feel the heat of the ground up through my heavy boots.

Our priority was to find the pods.

As we stood getting our bearings, a pleasant female voice said, 'Sixty minutes remaining to terminal event.'

I turned to Markham and could see jumping flames reflected in his visor. 'What the hell was that?'

'Countdown. Down here,' he said, tersely, and we set off at a run.

The pods were exactly where they should be, clumped together in their usual configuration, a neat three-sided square, just inside the East Gate, Augustine's Gate, and, as far as we could see, completely unscathed.

I called up David Sands.

No reply.

'Behind me,' said Markham, and we inched forwards to check them out.

Numbers Three and Five were empty. I checked the consoles and everything was just as it should be. Markham even checked the toilets, presumably in case they were all hiding in a three feet by three feet space.

Number Eight, however, contained an unconscious David Sands. He sprawled face down on the floor, breathing heavily. Blood had seeped from a wound on the back of his head.

I looked around. 'What happened here? Was he overcome by smoke? Did he fall backwards and hit his head on the console? Where are Helen and Dieter?'

Markham was bending over him. 'Check the console.'

I scanned the read-outs. Everything was normal. 'The next set of coordinates has been accessed, but he would have been prepping for a quick getaway.'

'Maybe. We'll check it out later. Come on.'

We heaved him into the recovery position and left, closing the door behind us.

'Fifty-five minutes remaining to terminal event.'

We set off, working our way back to the north side of the cathedral. Faintly in the distance, we could hear the sound of explosions. The ground shook and even above the roar of the flames, I could hear buildings coming down.

I activated my com.

'This is Maxwell. Can anyone hear me? Report.'

Static crackled in my ears.

I shouted to Markham. 'They're around here somewhere, I think. I just can't get a clear signal.'

He looked up at the huge edifice, towering above us, wreathed in burning wooden scaffolding and at the solid wall of fire in the streets around us.

'Really? You astonish me. '

All the time, we were working our way around St Paul's. More explosions in the distance caused pieces of burning wood to cartwheel through the air, scattering sparks on landing and starting their own individual little fires, which would eventually join up and become the huge conflagration that would kill us all. Bloody hell, this really was no place to be. Sod the artefacts. We'd get our people out. We'd laugh at them for having to get themselves rescued and get them straight back to St Mary's for something long, cold, and extremely alcoholic.

Another explosion, bigger and much closer. Were they blowing up the nearby streets in an effort to save St Paul's?

'Bloody hellfire,' said Markham, appropriately. 'We're going to be burned *and* blown up. It only takes one of us to fall into the Thames and drown and we've got the hat trick. Come on.'

Everything around us was burning. Even the ground under our feet was burning. Even through my fireproof suit, I was burning. Stinging sweat ran down into my eyes. I was drenched.

The building was massive and it seemed to take ages for us to get around the perimeter. We couldn't get too close. We zigzagged around, trying to find the tiny door on the north side.

'Fifty minutes remaining to terminal event.'

'There,' said Markham. 'There's the door.' He had to

shout to make himself heard over the sudden frenzied bleeping of our tag readers. Bloody things. They only ever work properly when if your target is either easily visible or only twenty feet in front of you. Jumping up and down shouting, 'Hey, hey, I'm over here!' is often quite helpful, too.

But, our only stroke of luck that day, on this side of the building, only the upper part of the scaffolding was in flames, so apart from lumps of burning wood falling on us from a great height – no problem.

I heard a crackly voice in my ear. Major Guthrie. 'Max? Is that you?'

'No. Who's Max?'

'Very funny. The door's locked. We can't get out.'

'Are you still in the crypt?'

'No, we're only on the other side of the outside door. We're all ready to go. We just can't get the bloody thing open.'

Markham shone his torch around the doorframe.

No, they couldn't get the door open because a bright shiny chain secured the latch. And that chain was secured with a heavy-duty padlock. Someone had not intended that door to open easily.

Markham used the pick end of his fire axe to attack the padlock and I kicked odd bits of burning wood away from the door, which didn't do my knee any good at all.

'Forty-five minutes remaining to terminal event.'

'How're you doing?' I yelled, kicking the last piece of wood away.

'No use. Here. Shove your end in here.' I inserted my fire axe as instructed and we both strained to prise open the padlock. The very substantial padlock.

No luck.

More debris fell down around us. We cowered in the shelter of the wall. God, it was so hot …

Guthrie's voice in my ear. 'Report.'

'Still working on getting the door open. Are you on fire in there?'

'Not yet, but it's very smoky. Get a move on.'

'On it.'

We strained again, making no impact at all. I tried prising apart the links on the chain but couldn't get a proper purchase. Nothing we were doing was making any difference.

'Forty minutes remaining to terminal event.'

Markham reversed his axe and began to hack at the chain. He fetched it a number of powerful blows then stepped aside for me. I did my best, but it was a very substantial chain. I was gasping for breath all the time. Sweat ran down into my eyes. I couldn't see properly and I was sure most of my blows were going astray. We were wasting our time.

Another enormous explosion rocked the ground under our feet. More lumps of burning wood showered past us. 'Shit,' shouted Markham, dancing around and slapping his smouldering fire suit. I pushed him against the door for the tiny amount of protection the lintel would give us and crowded in after him.

'Thirty-five minutes remaining to terminal event.'

I was melting. And not in a good way. I couldn't breathe. Couldn't see. Couldn't stand. I was dissolving in my own sweat. I wondered idly whether the melting point of the human body was greater or lesser than that of padlocks. It didn't really matter. People, padlocks-... We'd all burn in the end.

We both had the same idea at the same time.

'We're idiots,' I said, unshouldering my blaster.

'Careful,' he warned. 'Direct your beam.'

We played liquid fire over the padlock and chain. Nothing seemed to happen.

I blinked furiously to clear my eyes but the sweat stung viciously. I tried to sniff, but no good. Tears and snot mingled with the sweat running down my face. My mouth, on the other hand, was as dry as the Sahara and tasted like it. I was so dehydrated that it was very possible that I would never pee again.

The padlock was holding. I could have screamed from frustration. The heat was melting the lead on the roof but the bloody padlock was still holding. I had a sudden vision of a huge heap of a burned-out St Paul's with a bright, shiny padlock still nestling smugly atop the smouldering pile.

Markham shut down his blaster and tried again with his fire axe. 'Yes,' he shouted. 'It's softening.' He fetched it a hefty blow with his fire axe. 'Come on, you bitch!'

He rained down blows in a frenzy. I stepped back to give him room and he went at like a madman until I stopped him.

'Take a break. I'll give it a go.'

He'd definitely made an impact. The padlock hung askew. I didn't have any strength to waste, so I took my time, lining up each blow carefully.

'Thirty minutes remaining to terminal event.'

'Can't you shut that off? It's really getting on my nerves.'

'It's so I can get you out in time.'

'I'm not going anywhere without them,' I grunted, redoubling my efforts.

'They might die if you leave, but they'll definitely die if you stay. We all will, so no arguments,' he said tersely. 'Move over. My turn.'

He was a lot stronger than he looked. Half a dozen swift blows and the padlock clattered to the ground. At last. He tore at the chain.

I activated my com. 'Major?'

'Yes.'

'We're getting the door open. Be ready to move.'

'We're ready. Just give the word.'

Markham gave a final yank to the chain, which went the way of the padlock.

He seized the latch and gritted his teeth against the pain in his hands. Even through his gloves, what with the fire and then our blasters, it must have been nearly red-hot. He pulled.

Nothing happened.

'Twenty-five minutes remaining.'

'Can you please shut that thing off?'

'No. A little help here?'

I couldn't do anything. There was only an iron ring so small only one person could grasp it.

I called Major Guthrie again. 'Major, you need to push from your side.'

'Copy that.'

A series of thuds from the other side of the door

139

indicated that they were, indeed, pushing. I took a moment just to check that the door did actually open outwards because we are St Mary's after all, but yes, the door opened outwards. Or it should do. Mystified, I stared at it. There was no lock. I could see the door shudder with every impact. It just wasn't opening.

'Wait,' I shouted over the noise. 'Stop a minute.'

Ignoring my protesting knee and splitting headache, I crouched for a close look. I was right. A small piece of wood had somehow got wedged under the door, preventing it from opening.

'Major – pull. Pull the door towards you.'

'What?'

'Twenty minutes remaining to terminal event.'

'Shut up,' I shouted. 'No, not you, Major.'

A huge piece of burning wood crashed to the ground between us, reminding us that we really didn't have much time. Because, of course, that had completely slipped our minds.

Markham kicked it away. 'Don't argue, sir. Just bloody do it.'

I saw the door move back an inch or so and began to work at the wedge with my axe. I had to do it by guesswork because I couldn't see a thing and I was struggling for every breath. I suspected I wasn't going to last much longer.

'Move over,' said Markham, impatiently. He shoved me aside and began to work on the wedge.

'OK. Got it.'

He seized the ring at exactly the same time as what seemed like everyone behind the door threw their

140

weight at it.

The door flew open. All right, I was wearing a helmet, but nail-studded oak is still nail-studded oak. I flew backwards and hit the ground with a crash that knocked the breath out of me. I lay gasping while St Mary's erupted out of the doorway, Dieter, Roberts, Peterson and Van Owen in the lead, alternately treading on or falling over me. Only at St Mary's do the rescuees try to trample the rescuers. Bloody ingratitude.

I sat up painfully and lifted my visor. 'You stupid bunch of pillocks! This is what happens when I'm not around. The whole thing goes tits up and you have to be rescued like a bunch of little girls.'

'Fifteen minutes remaining to terminal event.'

I turned to Markham in exasperation. I was burned and breathless. I had a splitting headache. My knee was killing me. I had at least three people on top of me. The last thing I needed was to listen to a well-modulated voice counting down to disaster. 'Will you stop it doing that? It's getting on my nerves.'

Markham ignored me, heaving people to their feet. 'Come on, Max. Time to go.'

'Did you manage to salvage anything?' I gasped, displaying the correct grasp of priorities.

Van Owen rolled off me and shouted something about Schiller.

Markham was yelling at me. 'Come on, Max. We have to get out of here.'

We were all shrieking at each other over the noise of the roaring flames. Somewhere to my left another explosion, further off this time, sent a huge fireball into the sky. Sparks and small burning pieces of stuff rained down on us.

'Wait, wait,' shouted Guthrie, gesturing. 'Come back inside a moment.'

It was a good idea. We stepped back into the comparative calm of the cathedral. I took a moment and stared.

It was packed. Jam-packed. Packed solid with piles of paper, books, wooden boxes, furniture, and household goods. This was no hasty last minute, hurl-it-in-any-old-how-we'll-sort-it-all-out-later, stacking. Everything was neatly piled. Narrow walkways threaded their way between the stacks. Massive pillars arose out of towering piles of books piled around their bases. Tarpaulins covered the more valuable items. The whole place reeked of wood, tar, dry paper, dust – and smoke. If someone had said, 'How can we ensure St Paul's is completely destroyed in the coming conflagration?' they could not have made a better job or it. A huge space filled with every inflammable material known to man and encased outside with a wooden framework. Great job, guys!

I dragged my mind back. 'What's this about Schiller? Where is she? Who saw her last? And where?'

No one seemed sure.

Van Owen spoke up. 'We'd formed a chain and were passing stuff up from the crypt. She was at the top of the steps. I didn't see her leave. Did anyone?'

People shook their heads.

I said, 'Could she be in here somewhere? Unconscious? Do we need to search? Or is she out there in the flames?'

No one knew. All attempts to raise her had met with failure.

I could have screamed at them. I would scream at them. But not now. Guthrie was already organising search teams. They dispersed, calling to each other through the smoky gloom.

I sagged against a pile of books. An arm appeared with a bottle of water.

'Drink,' said Dr Foster and disappeared.

'Let's have a look at your hands,' I said to Markham.

He grimaced at his shredded gloves. I could see burned flesh. 'Actually, Max, no offence, but I think it's best to leave them for the moment. No time. We must go.'

'Not until I know Schiller's safe.'

'Not your problem, Max. You've done what you came to do. Time to go.'

'I've got fifteen minutes yet.'

'No. There's a burning churchyard to negotiate. It's hell out there. It's going to take us twice as long to get back as it did to get here.'

'Schiller ...'

'Is not your problem. Time to go.' He spoke into his com. 'Major, I have to get Max back to St Mary's. We're leaving.'

'Copy that. Thanks for your help, Max. We'll revise our jump times and see you back at St Mary's in a couple of days.'

I tried again. 'Schiller ...'

'We'll find her. Leave your gear. We'll pick it up. Get out of here. Run.'

Markham was physically pulling me towards the door.

143

'Come on, Max.'

I shook off his arm. 'What is the matter with you?'

He stood in the doorway, looking out at the hell that was London on 3rd September 1666. We'd both pushed up our visors. I could see he was white-faced with pain and drenched with sweat and there was a strange expression on his face.

'Ten minutes remaining to terminal event.'

'We're leaving. Now.'

'Just a few minutes. Please. Schiller's missing.'

He pulled his gun and slapped in a clip. 'No. One way or another, you're leaving.'

I said slowly, 'What are you doing?'

He swallowed. 'He's not a stupid man, is he? Dr Bairstow, I mean.'

'I don't understand.'

He drew himself up and was suddenly different. 'He foresaw all this. He knew something had gone wrong. He knew you'd refuse to leave. That you wouldn't be able to help yourself, so I'm telling you, Maxwell – no arguing, no nothing – get your arse out of that door and back to Number Six.'

I'd never heard him use that tone before. 'Markham?'

He raised the gun. 'I'm begging you, Max, please. Don't make me do this.'

'Do what? I don't understand.'

But I did.

'Dr Bairstow's instructions. If you refuse to leave before the countdown expires, or you're prevented from leaving for some reason – then I'm to shoot you. Dead. Only one living person etc.'

144

I stared at him. 'You'd do that?'

'You know I would. So I'm saying, Max. Don't make me do it.'

I stared at him in shock. His small, determined face and the pain in his eyes. Yes, he would do it. Only one version of one person could be present at any given time. One living person. If I couldn't or wouldn't leave then he would shoot me. Only one living person ...

I nodded.

'Five minutes remaining to terminal event.'

'Bollocks,' he said, grabbing my arm. 'Move.'

We moved. We really moved. It wasn't far as the crow flies but our path was not an easy one. We should have picked our way between the piles of burning rubble, eased our way carefully around dangerously leaning buildings, dodged the burning debris dropping from the sky, and we did none of that.

We really motored, kicking aside the smaller stuff, running straight over the top of the bigger stuff. I could feel the heat searing through my boots. My face was scorched. My lungs were scorched. My gloves were in shreds. My boots were melting. And all the time, we ran.

'Four minutes remaining to terminal event.'

We weren't going to make it.

Markham seized my arm and tugged. I held the other up to protect my face. We'd left blasters, fire axes, everything behind us so we could move more quickly.

'Three minutes remaining to terminal event.'

We ran for our lives. Ducking, dodging, weaving. My lungs were heaving and my rasping breath was hurting my throat. Worse, Markham was limping. He was doing his best to hide it, but his leg was still weak.

'Two minutes remaining to terminal event.'

Actually, we were running for my life. Because he would do it. I knew he would. How he'd cope afterwards, I had no idea, but, whatever the cost, he would carry out his instructions from Dr Bairstow. He wouldn't even need to take my body back. They could just leave it here to be consumed in the fiery holocaust that was London.

'One minute remaining to terminal event.'

I panted, 'That bloody countdown thing might be faulty, you know.' He didn't bother with an answer.

We raced through Paul's Gate. Even now, there was the possibility that our pod was buried under the burning remains of someone's house and if it was then I was finished. The other pods were far too far away to reach in the little time remaining to us.

'Thirty seconds remaining to terminal event.'

'Jesus,' said Markham. 'Run, Max.'

We ran. My whole attention was fixed on Number Six. It wasn't that far away but it didn't seem to be getting any closer. I felt an old, familiar pain in my chest.

'Twenty seconds remaining to terminal event.'

My legs were failing. No matter how hard I pumped, I wasn't covering the ground. My lungs were failing. I couldn't see. Time, for so long my friend, was now my enemy. Time was spilling away and taking my life with it.

'Ten seconds remaining to terminal event.'

I wasn't going to make it. It was just too far away. Markham let go of my arm. He was going to shoot me.

'Nine seconds.'

'I'm sorry, Max. I don't want to do this.'

'Eight seconds.'

This time I grabbed him. 'We can do it.'

'Seven seconds.'

We skidded together over the rough ground.

'Six seconds.'

'Five seconds.'

I shouted, 'Door.'

'Four seconds.'

The door opened, I could see inside the pod. See the console lights blinking a welcome.

So near and yet so far.

'Three seconds.'

Something hit me hard in the small of my back. I fell forwards, my momentum giving me that little extra spurt of speed. I shouted, 'Computer ...'

'Two seconds.'

We crashed headlong into the pod. Markham was already shouting for the door.

'One second.'

'...emergency extraction...'

'Zero.'

'...Now.'

The world went black.

Our landing was a bit of a disaster.

We landed so hard, we slid off the plinth completely, skidding across the hangar, leaving smoking grooves in the concrete floor.

Markham and I were both on the floor anyway but I swear we bounced. The locker doors flew open but worst of all, the toilet exploded, which wasn't something that had ever happened before. A great tsunami of blue water surged across the floor where it was absorbed into the carpet at a rate that would gladden the heart of any producer of sanitary product commercials.

Sadly, we didn't stop with just a couple of bounces. The pod slithered on, spinning across Hawking, colliding heavily with Number Two, and knocking it half off its plinth where it lay at a crazy angle. Our own pod tilted precariously and finally rocked to a bone-breaking halt.

Something inside the console went bang. The lights flickered wildly and the fire extinguisher fell off the wall, missing Markham's head by a fraction of an inch. He uttered a curse, which probably curdled milk for a half-mile radius, and the console coughed out another bang, which made me jump. Smoke spiralled from the front panels. The pod was suddenly full of the smell of burning fish, mixed with the chemical smell of the toilet. Apart from all that, we were back safely.

Silence fell.

'Shit,' said Markham, faintly, possibly having exhausted his repertoire of more colourful expletives.

'Well, at least we're not on fire,' I said, in an effort to look on the bright side. He refused to be comforted.

'For God's sake, Max, look at this place. Look out there.' I rolled over and looked at the screen. 'It's total devastation. We're going to be paying for this lot for the rest of our lives. I'm going to have to have at least forty kids to inherit the debt.'

Fortunately, at that moment, Mr Lindstrom's voice came over the com. 'Max? Markham? Can you hear me?'

'Tell them I'm dead,' said Markham, making no move to get up off the floor.

'I'm fine, but Markham says he's dead.'

'He will be when Chief Farrell sees this little lot.'

Markham groaned.

'Is Dr Bairstow there?'

Of course he was. 'Doctor Maxwell. Another of your spectacular landings?'

Two. I've had two bad landings. Just two. Well, three now. Compare that with Peterson who bounces his pod every time. Where's the justice?

'What bad landing, sir?'

'Ah. I must have been mistaken and this … devastation … is in no way related to your recent remarkable appearance.'

'Personally sir, I blame Mr Lindstrom. Who leaves all these pods lying around anyway? It's just asking for trouble. Incidentally, sir, mission accomplished.'

'I never doubted it for one moment,' he said calmly and inaccurately, and closed the link.

They kept us overnight in Sick Bay. We were both sprayed with medical plastic and rehydrated. I dictated my report for Dr Bairstow and then settled back for a quiet evening.

I kept expecting them to bring in Mary Schiller. They'd find her. She was almost certainly in another part of the cathedral. Where else could she be? Injured or unconscious, obviously, since she wasn't answering her com, but they'd find her.

Markham limped in to see me. I'd been waiting for him.

Unexpectedly, he dumped a bottle of Syrup of Figs on my bedside table.

I stared at it. 'I've already been once this year. At the summer solstice, if memory serves.'

'Oh God, no,' he said hastily, and unscrewed the cap. Tequila fumes floated across the bed. 'Your very own Margarita. Compliments of Mr Lindstrom. Look he's even rubbed salt around the lip.'

'My compliments to Mr Lindstrom. He is now officially my second favourite techie.'

A silence fell between us.

'Max, my report is for Dr Bairstow's eyes only.'

'That's OK.'

He fiddled around with the things on my bedside table. 'I would have done it, you know.'

'I do know.'

151

'And if it had been the other way around, so would you.'

'Yes, I would. Although I don't know what I would have done afterwards.'

'I don't know either.'

'Did he think of that, I wonder?'

'Who?'

Dr Bairstow.'

'He gave me a choice. When I stayed behind after our meeting. He told me that if I felt I couldn't do it then there would be no rescue mission. He weighed the survival of his unit on one hand against the survival of the timeline on the other and made exactly the right decision. And if you or I would have hated ourselves afterwards, think how he would have felt.'

I shivered.

'But,' he said, suddenly cheerful. 'That's us. We're St Mary's. From total disaster to resounding success with but a single bound.'

'What about Mary Schiller?'

'She'll turn up,' said Markham. 'Stop worrying. And Van Owen will tear the place apart to find her.' He paused. 'You do know they're ... together, don't you?'

I nodded. I did know.

He continued. 'They'll find her and go straight on to the second site to bury the stuff they got from Old St Paul's. Stop worrying.'

But they didn't. Find her, I mean.

Two days later, as promised, they were back. Markham and I bruised, scorched, and still smelling faintly of chemical toilet cleaner, assembled with the rest of the unit to welcome them home and celebrate their triumph.

The Technical Section had levered Number Two back onto its plinth. One side was dented and part of the stone casing had come away. And then there were the long black skid marks across the floor. We could only hope that in the excitement of their return, no one would notice.

The pods materialised almost simultaneously. After a minute, the doors opened and they filed out.

I knew immediately.

They hadn't found her.

Around me, people fell silent.

They looked terrible. When we last saw them, they were singed and smoke damaged. Now they were soaked to the skin, muddy, and exhausted. I counted heads. One missing.

Shit.

I went down to speak to Van Owen who was thanking them individually for a job well done. They nodded quietly and allowed the medical team to usher them away.

I caught Leon's eye and smiled. He nodded towards the damaged pod and raised an eyebrow. I indulged in a complicated piece of mime, which indicated it had all been Markham's fault.

He smiled for me alone and was led away with the others.

Van Owen was sitting on the plinth outside Number Three. She sat with her forearms on her knees, her head bowed, like a puppet whose strings had been cut. I sat beside her. 'Greta, talk to me.'

She took a deep breath and came back from wherever

she'd been. 'We didn't find her, Max and it was too dangerous. Guthrie pulled us out. We had to leave her.'

'We'll go back,' I said, without thinking. 'We're St Mary's. We never leave our people behind. We'll find her.'

'Who?' she said, angrily. 'Who will find her? Who will go back? We've all been there once. There's no one else left. Whom would we send? Mr Strong? A couple of typists?'

I said nothing.

She calmed down. 'Sorry.'

'It's OK.'

'Actually, Max, it doesn't matter. You could send an army and you'd never find her. Things were bad when you were there, but they got much worse very quickly. If she was in St Paul's, she died when the roof came down. If she was outside the building then she was caught in a raging inferno. Or perhaps she was crushed under a pile of burning rubble. There was nothing on the tag reader. She's gone, Max.'

'Greta, I'm so sorry. I know the two of you were very close.'

She shrugged. We sat in silence for a while. I fingered her wet clothes. 'So why are you so wet?'

'Oh,' she gave a short laugh. 'When we jumped to 17th-century St Mary's, it was pissing down. Seriously, Max, you've never seen rain like it. One minute we're all burning to death and the next we're half drowned.' She pushed her wet hair back off her face. 'But we got it done, Max. It's all out there.' She nodded in the direction of the gardens. 'Safely buried one hundred and twenty-five yards from the south west corner of the Great Hall. Just waiting for us to dig it all up again.'

'Good job, Greta. Thank you. And Dr Bairstow will want to congratulate you personally. He'll talk to you about Mary, as well. Listen to him. Let him help you.'

She nodded.

'You should get yourself upstairs.'

She nodded again.

'Would you like me to walk up with you?'

'Yes. Yes, I would, please.'

Mary Schiller's memorial service was two days later. We assembled in the chapel. Full formal uniform. I looked at the serious faces around me. Van Owen sat on my right, her face very solemn under her hat. Everyone looked solemn. Schiller had been a popular and respected member of the unit.

Dr Bairstow spoke, as he always did. He spoke movingly and well. As always, I was astonished at how well he knew his people. He took good care to appear remote and distant, but he knew us all better than we knew ourselves. I saw him speaking to Van Owen afterwards. People moved away to give them some privacy. I couldn't hear what he said, but I knew his words would be just right and she would be comforted and supported.

Then we got on with things.

Next up was the 'discovery' of the buried treasure in our grounds. The plan was that the Chancellor and other members of the senior faculty would be invited to lunch, plied mercilessly with alcohol, and while this was going on, a team of technicians, heavily disguised as people who actually worked for a living, would make an astonishing and exciting discovery while digging a channel for a new pipe. Or cable TV. Or something. They were still arguing about it. As if anyone would be interested.

I did offer to take over from Van Owen if she wanted to step back from this one, but she refused, with thanks, and I think she was right.

'So tell me,' I said, feet up on my desk, drinking tea. 'I haven't had time to ask. What did we actually manage to salvage?'

'A mixed bag,' she said, leaning back in her chair with her mug and putting her feet up on my desk as well. She looked tired and heavy-eyed, but she was functioning. Work always helps.

'There wasn't much in the way of religious stuff knocking around. With so many people in and out all day long, it would have been asking for trouble. I suspect they only got the good stuff out on high days and holidays. However, we did get some very nice candlesticks, a couple of large pewter collection plates – empty, of course – some tapestries and hangings, a leather-bound Bible and the wooden book rest affair it was standing on. The rest of it was just small stuff that was lying around. Some wooden boxes – one had some rather nice fretwork – which turned out to contain someone's treasured memories in the form of letters and locks of children's hair. Some were deed boxes with hearth records and the like, which Thirsk will find useful. We grabbed as many books as we could, of course, because they were everywhere. There's no saying what they are and we didn't have time to look at all of them. Everything's wrapped in waterproof cloth and stored in a lead chest. There's no treasure, I'm afraid. The value comes from it having been rescued from St Paul's, but it's a good haul, Max. Thirsk will be pleased.'

'I certainly hope so. Speaking of pleasing Thirsk – are you still up for the sidesaddle demonstration? I'll understand if you want to back out.'

'No, I'm looking forward to it. Besides, we'll need someone to distract the crowd when you and Turk part company. As you always do.'

'Hey,' I said, stung, but it was good to see her smile again. 'I've been practising.'

She snorted.

The Chancellor and her crew came to lunch. They ate in the dining-room along with us peasants, possibly in a spirit of democracy, but more likely so we could admire their capacity.

'Bloody hell,' said Peterson, anxiously, as yet more bottles were broached. 'They're going to drink us out of house and home.'

'Unlikely,' I said. 'I've been down in the basement and there's an entire reservoir of alcohol down there.'

'Enough for a bunch of senior academics out on a jolly at someone else's expense?'

'Good point. Yes. Probably. Almost certainly. I hope so.'

We were distracted from our anxious musings by a familiar voice.

Max!'

I turned round. 'Eddie!'

Professor Eddington Penrose was an old friend and fellow-disaster magnet. He'd proved himself during a public riot in 17th-century Cambridge and again when we found ourselves inexplicably at what might possibly have been the end of the universe. As a physicist, he'd been over the moon with excitement. Even when we nearly died.

He shook my hand enthusiastically and cocked an eyebrow at Leon. 'Dare I hope you are no longer ...?'

'No, you may not,' he said.

'Ignore Mr Grumpy,' I said, giving him a hug. 'How are you?'

'Absolutely top-hole, Max.' His round blue eyes sparkled appreciatively. 'I talked Madam Chancellor into including me in this little jaunt.'

'You're interested in Old St Paul's?'

'Good heavens, no. Not in the slightest. I'm here to suss out the opposition.'

Enlightenment dawned.

'You're building their boat! Eddie how could you?'

'They asked me,' he said, simply.

Fair enough, I suppose.

He was craning his neck, trying to see out of the window to the lake. 'So how's the St Mary's effort going, Max?'

'Excellently,' I said, before Leon was overcome with the need to tell the truth. 'You will be as flotsam – or jetsam, I never know the difference – in our wake.'

'Indeed,' he said, in beaming disbelief. 'Would you

care to mount a small wager?'

'Bring it on, Eddie!'

It was just possible that Leon might have been making no, no, no gestures. I don't know. I wasn't looking.

'So what's the wager, then?'

He twinkled with pure mischief.

'Me.'

'You?'

'Yes, me. If we lose, you, my dear Max, have the benefit of me for say, seven days. Sadly, I'm not as young as I was,' he confided in an undertone. 'And if you lose, I get you. Only for seven days, of course. Again, not as young, etc.'

'Eddie!' I said, half laughing, half horrified.

He didn't miss a thing, did Eddie. 'Ah, I see. The boat not going quite that excellently, then?

'Of course it is,' I said defiantly, ignoring not only Leon, but Dieter and Lindstrom as well.

Peterson did his best. 'Professor, you can't bet a person ... I'm pretty sure that's illegal ...'

I waved this away. 'We're not going to lose, so I say now, in front of witnesses, the loser gets the services of the other for a period of seven days.'

'Capital,' he said, rubbing his hands together.

Heads swivelled towards Leon who was looking unflatteringly unperturbed.

'Are you ... I mean ... are you ...?' stammered Dieter.

'Am I what?' he said, calmly finishing his coffee and getting up.

'Professor Penrose ... and Max?'

'Well, as I see it, a no-lose situation for me. If we win,

we benefit from the unrivalled expertise of Professor Penrose for seven days and if we lose then Max is shunted off to Thirsk for them to benefit from her unrivalled expertise for the same period of time. It seems a fair trade to me, although my heart does go out to them.'

He returned their stares blandly and said, 'Why, what did you think they were wagering?'

He waited a while, but nobody seemed inclined to say anything. 'And, at last, I'll get to watch *Match of the Day* in peace. Knock yourself out, Professor.'

I waited until everyone was busy discussing boat building and then shot off in something of a panic. Straight to Professor Rapson.

'Ah, Max,' he said, straightening up from his cluttered workbench. 'How delightful. Um – did we have an appointment? Should I be somewhere else?'

'No, Professor, it's OK. I just need a quick update and some reassurance. How's the ship going?'

'Boat, Max. It's a boat.'

'Boat, then. How's it going?'

'It's all going very well.'

'You do know Thirsk have got Professor Penrose on their side?'

'A bit of a double-edged weapon, Max. He's more than capable of sitting down to design and build a record-beating craft of some kind, doodle for ten minutes on the back of an envelope, and solve the problem of cold fusion instead. He's very easily distracted you know and – oh look, there it is. I've been looking everywhere for this and – what was I saying?'

'If we lose, I've sold myself to Thirsk for seven days.'

'Goodness gracious, but there's no cause for alarm. We're not going to lose.'

I looked around at the boat-free chaos of his workshop. There were no visible signs of construction. 'Have you started yet? Where is it? Why haven't you started yet?'

He regarded me pityingly. 'We're building it outside, Max. If we build it in here then we won't be able to get it down the stairs.'

'I knew that,' I said, quickly. 'I'm just concerned about the opposition. They've modelled their boat on a pirate ship, you know. It's called *The Black Carbuncle*.'

'Most amusing. Ours, however, is based on the design of those master mariners, the Vikings, and will prove to be immensely superior. Faster, more manoeuvrable, and with a few hidden surprises built in.'

'We're weaponised?'

'Well, yes, of course, Max. Why wouldn't we be?'

'Please tell me you haven't invented a Death Ray.'

'Not yet,' he said, regretfully. 'There are still a few small flaws to iron out. Guidance. Range. Tendency to explode. However, we do have a giant catapult. And our rather nifty underwater ramming device based on the – well never mind that. Loose lips sink ships, you know. And a water cannon. And flour bombs. And water pistols.'

I would be horrified if I hadn't known that the evil brain of Professor Penrose was working along exactly the same lines.

Seeking a distraction, I rooted around amongst some sketches on his workbench. They appeared to be of dragons.

'What's this?'

'Oh, these are designs for our figurehead. We must have one. I thought a dragon. Or a Valkyrie, maybe.'

'Well, since we're the Institute of History ...' I said, cunningly, 'why not have History herself at the front bit? Sweeping aside all obstacles and clearing our path to victory.'

He stopped dead and peered at something that could only be seen by someone with a Professor Rapson-type brain. 'Yes. Yes. Kleio, the Muse of History.'

'In papier-mâché,' I said, giving the pot a good stir, just to liven things up a bit.

'Or polystyrene foam,' he said, getting into the swing of things. 'Yes ...'

Ho ho ho ...

Twenty minutes later, at three o'clock on the dot, I trotted outside, one hundred and twenty-five yards from the south-west corner of the Great Hall, to where Leon and his team were waiting with a small digger, a pile of fresh earth and a large hole.

'It is in there, isn't it?' I said anxiously. 'Nothing must go wrong.'

'It's there,' he said, reassuringly. 'We found it yesterday, checked it was untouched, and covered it back up again. We're ready to "discover" it as soon as our leaders can peel themselves away from lunch. Relax. Nothing can go wrong.'

I looked across the grass. Dr Bairstow and the Thirsk team were just appearing on the terrace, presumably to enjoy some much-needed coffee.

I said to Leon, 'You're up,' and stepped back.

It all went like clockwork.

Van Owen and I stood a little apart, ostensibly supervising the operation, but in reality, just getting in everyone's way.

The digging-tool-thingy clanked on something metal. Someone shouted artistically and waved their arms, indicating excitement.

Van Owen and I rushed forwards theatrically to look into the hole. It was like one of those old silent movies. We telegraphed astonishment and surprise. On the terrace, heads went up and the next minute, they were all surging across the grass to see what was happening. Other members of St Mary's, who had been vaguely hanging around waiting to be involved, turned up as well, so we had a good crowd for our moment of discovery.

We stood breathlessly as the digger got its digging-tool-thingy under the chest and prised it free of the hole. Lead is heavy. We couldn't possibly have lifted it out ourselves. Van Owen said they'd all nearly had a collective hernia getting it in there in the first place.

The chest was laid gently on the ground and everyone looked at it for a moment.

I caught Dr Bairstow's eye and he nodded. This was going well. In a moment, they'd break the lock, gently peel back the wrappings, and expose the treasures we'd salvaged four hundred years ago. Or last Monday – however you wanted to look at it. This would be a huge triumph. Another prestigious find for Thirsk University. Another world-headline event for them. They would love us again. Well, they would until we blew their arses out of the water in the Raft Race.

I allowed myself a small sag of relief and looked across at Van Owen, who was sagging similarly. She gave me a quiet smile and a thumbs up.

Dieter stepped forwards with a spade. With one blow, he knocked off the lock.

Everyone paused, savouring the moment.

I took a moment to look around. The Chancellor stood beside Dr Bairstow. She was a little flushed, but that would be the excitement and not in any way connected with the vast quantities of alcohol consumed at lunchtime. Everyone was staring at the chest. Dieter crouched at one end and Leon at the other. Professor Rapson was dancing with excitement. Dr Dowson was issuing a series of instructions. With a great deal of straining, the top of the lead chest came free and was gently lifted away.

We all craned forwards. There was complete silence. I could hear people breathing.

Leon and Dieter moved back and somewhat stiffly, Dr Dowson knelt alongside the chest. Very gently and delicately, he began to peel back the coverings.

I know, we should have taken it inside and opened it more carefully and discreetly, but we were the victims of our own excitement. Everyone wanted to see what was in the box and we wanted to see it now.

The Chancellor was no better than the rest of us. She and her team stood right behind Dr Dowson, eager – desperate even – for that first look. That first glimpse of artefacts that hadn't seen the light of day for four hundred years. Whose last sight had been of Old St Paul's burning around them.

Dr Dowson gently pulled aside the last layer and we all leaned forward to look.

A moment frozen in time. No one moved. No one spoke.

I remember it was a grey day. A day without weather. No wind. No sun. Not hot. Not cold. Just a milk-white sky looking down on us as we stood, all of us, rigid with shock.

We stood for several lifetimes. From nowhere, a sharp little wind sprang up, ruffled our hair, and was as suddenly gone. As if her spirit, imprisoned underground for all those years, seized its freedom and fled, never to return.

Movement came back into the world. A huge gasp of shock ran around those assembled. I felt my heart turn over. Van Owen gave a small cry and put her hands over her face. Peterson and Clerk were on either side of her, holding her up. Someone burst into tears.

Quick as a flash, Dr Dowson flicked the covers back again but it was far, far too late for that. We'd all seen it. None of us would ever forget the sight.

They'd had to fold up the body to get it in. It lay in an impossible position. Jagged yellow bone poked through fragments of rotting clothing that had once been an orange firesuit.

The head – the skull, rather – was almost buried amongst a quantity of pale blonde hair, but the bullet hole in the centre of the forehead was clearly visible.

We'd found Mary Schiller.

She'd been here all along.

She'd been here for four hundred years, waiting for us to find her.

The moment passed. The Chancellor, after the first shock, exchanged a look with Dr Bairstow, rounded up her people, and took them quietly back inside St Mary's.

Peterson and Clerk helped Van Owen away. Helen went with them.

Dr Dowson still knelt beside the chest, distressed and shocked. He made several futile attempts to rise, but he was trembling to such an extent that he couldn't get up.

Professor Rapson put his hand on his shoulder and said gently, 'Never mind, Occy. Let's get you inside, shall we?' and helped him to his feet. Dr Dowson paused for a moment, said, with tremendous dignity, 'I shall be in my office should anyone require me,' and the two of them walked quietly away. Leon took his silent team back into Hawking, leaving just Dr Bairstow and the rest of the History Department, who were standing as if we'd never move again.

Dr Bairstow stirred. 'I would like you all to go back inside, please. Miss Prentiss, if you would be so good as to ask Dr Foster to join me when she can be spared from Miss Van Owen. Dr Maxwell, would you remain here, please.'

We watched them walk away.

'Are you all right, Max?'

I nodded. My voice wasn't working.

'See to your people, Max. Try to keep a lid on any high emotions. We don't know anything yet. Try to keep everyone calm. I shall attend to our friends from Thirsk. Please join me in my office in one hour.'

I had to clear my throat. 'We're in trouble now, aren't we?'

'Yes, we are. But let's get through today, first.'

It's one thing to grieve for a colleague and friend you think has been lost in the line of duty. It's quite another to find she's been murdered. Murdered and brutally folded in two and then callously shoved into a lead chest by someone whose idea of revenge is so cold and calculating that he was willing to wait four hundred years for it to come to fruition.

Even before we found the message carefully left for us to find amongst the wrappings, I knew it was Ronan. What I wasn't prepared for was the other signature on the letter.

Bloody Isabella Bitchface Barclay.

I blamed myself. I'd had a chance to shoot her last year at the Battle of St Mary's and I hadn't. She'd escaped, leaving me a note saying she'd be back one day, but I'd never dreamed she'd do anything like this. How had she and Ronan found each other? And how had they found us? So many questions. So many questions and no answers at all. We had nothing except for the pathetic remains of Mary Schiller left here all those years ago for us to find today.

With hindsight, it was all so clear. They'd attacked David Sands, accessed the coordinates from Number Eight, followed behind, waited until St Mary's jumped away, dug up the chest, stolen the contents, and left Schiller instead. Never mind the possibly fatal damage to our reputation and prestige, the thought in my mind – in everyone's mind – was that we'd been here for years, living, working, arguing, playing football and she'd been here all that time. In the cold. In the dark. All alone, while St Mary's walked, unheeding, over her grave.

I met with Peterson while we discussed what we were going to say. He offered me a drink, but I declined. I wanted one quite desperately, but I needed to be stone cold sober for this. There was no dodging reality today.

My chest heaved in a dry sob. I couldn't help it. Peterson, who didn't look much better than I did, took my hand. 'Not your fault, Max. You weren't even on the assignment. In fact, if it wasn't for you and Markham, we'd all have died there.'

'I know. I'm thinking of Van Owen. She was just beginning to lift her head and come to terms with losing Schiller. And now – this. Can you imagine anything more cruel? To leave that gloating note. Where they knew we'd find it. What are we going to do now?'

'Nothing,' he said. 'We don't know where they are or when. There's nothing we can do until we encounter them again. In the meantime, we get on with the job.'

'I'm off to talk to my people now. Van Owen's under sedation. I'll see her tomorrow.'

'Thank God we don't have any trainees,' he said,

draining his glass. 'They'd be stampeding for the hills even as we speak. Come on. I'll go with you, even though you don't need me. They're a good bunch.'

They were. I let them talk. I let them vent their hopeless, helpless anger, pouring a drink or two where I thought it would help. I listened. I put in a word here or there when I thought they'd listen. Gradually, things subsided.

Finally, Clerk said, 'What happens now, Max? Not only do we not have anything for Thirsk, they've just witnessed our greatest disaster.'

'First,' I said, 'we bury Miss Schiller with full honours. Then we take a bit of a rest. The Open Day is almost upon us. I know most of us don't feel like it at the moment, but we're St Mary's and we can do this. I'll start looking for a salvage operation so brilliant that Thirsk will forget all about this. It's going to be a rough couple of weeks, but we'll get through them. Miss Van Owen will probably return within a day or so. She's now our only Senior Historian and I know I don't have to ask you to do what you can to make things a little easier for her.'

I was sitting in my room, hugging my knees and trying to pull my thoughts together when Leon appeared.

'What are you thinking about?'

We had promised we would always talk to each other, so I answered honestly. 'About death and loss.'

'Come here.'

I shunted across the sofa and we sat together. I rested my head on his shoulder. As always, he felt warm and solid. Today, he smelled of fresh earth, fabric conditioner and soap. Slowly, I felt some of the tension drain away.

'Tell me.'

'I was thinking of everyone I've lost here. Kevin Grant. Remember him? And our baby. Our little baby who never even lived at all.'

He raised my hand to his lips and kissed it. I turned his hand around and held it to my cheek for a moment then continued.

'And Tom Baverstock. And you.'

Leon himself, lost and then miraculously restored to me as I had been to him.

'Jenny Fields. Karl Ritter. Robbie Weller. Young Esterhazy. The list just goes on and on. And now Mary Schiller.'

I remembered the work she and Van Owen had done on Mary Stuart – how they'd burst into my office, faces alight with triumph and excitement because they'd found the answer. Schiller had gone with us to 16th-century Edinburgh. I remembered the two of us giggling because she'd tied my bum roll on upside down and back to front. I looked like a pregnant frog. She couldn't move for laughing and then we couldn't get the knots undone, which hadn't helped at all, and finally she had to go off for a knife.

She'd stood beside me, quiet and alert at the court of Mary Stuart, whispering names and brief descriptions in my ear as we negotiated that social minefield. She'd fought at the Battle of St Mary's. I remember her being shoved around by the Time Police – hot, angry, and dirty. And now ...

'They killed her and stuffed her into a box for us to

discover now. Today. Leon, she's been here for hundreds of years and nobody knew.'

'Shh,' he said, tucking stray bits of hair behind my years. 'For what it's worth, she died instantly. I suspect they grabbed her at the top of the steps to the crypt and she never knew anything about it. Then they locked the door on us and jumped away. I know – I know – it's no consolation but she didn't burn to death. Nor was she trapped somewhere waiting to be engulfed by flames. She died doing what she loved. The fault does not lie with you, who planned the mission. Nor Dr Bairstow who authorised it. Or with me because I provided the pods. Nor with Ian Guthrie who provided the security. The fault lies with Clive Ronan and Isabella Barclay. Blame them, not yourself.'

He was right.

'I mean it, Max. You must do that, because you have to get out there and pull your department together. You have to help them pick themselves up without seeming uncaring. You have to move them on without pushing them too far or too fast.'

'It won't be easy.'

'No, it won't. Good job you're exactly the right person for the job, then.'

He dropped a kiss on top of my head. 'Use me, Max. Whenever you want to shout or scream or cry or kick the furniture – use me. I'm always around.'

'Have I told you …?'

'Yes, yes,' he said, quickly. 'You're always boring on about how wonderful I am. Actually, it's becoming a bit of a drag.'

I never thought I would say this, but thank heavens for the Open Day. It gave us something else on which to focus. I allocated responsibilities, imposed deadlines, and chased them all ruthlessly.

Van Owen returned, quiet but functioning, and I watched my department close ranks around her. I know Dr Bairstow had offered her a transfer to Thirsk should she wish it, but she had declined with thanks.

For myself, I needed to give some thought to my ever-shrinking department. We were down to just five historians. We'd had fewer – back in the day, it had been just Kal, Peterson, and me, but we're established for twelve. I also needed to consider whether to replace Schiller as Senior Historian. Peterson and I were Chief Officers. Van Owen was the other Senior Historian. I didn't want to be in a position where we had more chiefs than Indians. Our manpower shortage was becoming serious.

Two weeks later, I had an update for Dr Bairstow, who questioned me closely on the progress of our ship. Boat. I was pleased to report the flat bit was completed. Or the deck was laid. One or the other.

'I am requested by Professor Rapson to invite you to crack a bottle over the front bit the day after tomorrow, sir.'

'Ah – the launching ceremony. Excellent. I like to see these old traditions kept up.'

'Well, if you really want traditions, sir, I believe the established procedure is to launch the boat over the living body of a virgin, thus propitiating the gods and anointing the boat with sacrificial blood. To bring it good luck.'

'Well, we could certainly do with some at the moment.' He looked thoughtful. 'I wonder ...?'

'Sir?' I said, not completely convinced he was joking.

He sighed. 'You're right. So, what of the race itself?'

'Across the lake, sir. There and back again. That way, everyone gets a good view. I understand Thirsk will be bringing a number of supporters whose dastardly schemes will, we hope, be neutralised by the Security Section who will be keeping a very close eye on them.'

'And what will the other members of my unit be doing while this takes place?'

This was not knowledge with which he should be burdened. It's always vital for Senior Managers to be able to maintain plausible deniability. I hastened to distract him.

'Cheering on their team, sir.'

'What? All of them?'

No – was the answer to that one. Apparently, small but carefully selected groups of St Mary's personnel would be posting themselves at strategic points around the lake, all the better, they said, to facilitate the St Mary's Path to Victory, which would have worried me considerably if I hadn't known that Thirsk themselves would post similar numbers of evil-minded saboteurs – sorry, students – for exactly the same purpose.

'A substantial number of people intend to indulge in the art of "cheerleading" as I believe it's known.'

He blinked. 'Cheerleading?'

'Yes, sir. An American custom, I understand.'

'And of what does this custom consist?'

'As far as I can ascertain, sir, it consists mainly of hurling young women through the air to the accompaniment of a rhythmical chant.'

He blinked again. 'Exactly how far through the air are these young women hurled? And of what does the rhythmical chant consist?'

'Oh, I don't know, sir. Something along the lines of "Go, Beavers, Go".'

'Go where?'

'I don't think they're being directed to a physical location as such, sir, it's more a kind of generic encouragement.'

'And exactly who are these ... er ... Beavers?'

'A hastily chosen example of a typically named American team, sir. I believe they're very fond of naming themselves after animals – Rams, Lions, Dolphins ...'

'Marmosets, Prawns ...?'

'Exactly, sir.'

'And are these cries actually uttered by the airborne young women? Are we sure they are not simply ejaculating in fear?'

'Probably not, sir. The cries are generally uttered by those with at least one foot on the ground.'

'Astonishing.'

Mrs Partridge coughed again and in the interests of sparing him mental disquiet, I veered away from the promising subject of pom-poms and their implementation.

He emerged from his reverie. 'This is an American custom, you say?'

'Yes sir. Of quite recent introduction, I believe.'

'So the early settlers did not, in fact, throw their young women around in this manner?'

'Just accused them of being witches and hanged them, as far as I can see, sir.'

He sighed. 'With some trepidation, I enquire as to the possibility of this unit remembering that its behaviour should, at all times, reflect the gravitas and decorum of an internationally renowned academic establishment?'

'Oh, I think we both know the answer to that one, sir.'

We attended Dr Bairstow's pre-Open Day briefing, in which he ran over final details and timetable. It seemed to take forever. I suspected the Normandy landings were less complicated. Bearing in mind the way he'd ambushed me in the first place, Peterson and I were giving him our full attention.

He finished with a typical instruction.

'Please bear in mind there will be a large number of undergraduates attending our event and many of them could be potential members of St Mary's. I would be grateful if the benefits of working at this particular establishment could be made clear to them on every conceivable occasion.'

'I'd be grateful if they could be made clear to me,' murmured David Sands, behind me.

I turned and fixed him with my best 'I'm your head of department and don't you forget it' look.

'Is there a problem, Dr Maxwell?' asked Dr Bairstow. A little unfairly, I thought.

'On the contrary, sir. The entire History department, motivated by the inspirational words of its director, has just indicated its enthusiasm by volunteering, unanimously, to undertake the clearing-up process afterwards. However unpleasant a task that may be.'

'Ah. Excellent,' said Dr Bairstow, nobody's fool. 'Are there any other volunteers for this valuable though undoubtedly lengthy and messy undertaking?'

Total silence at St Mary's is such a rare thing.

10

All right – here we go. Open Day 101. Watch and learn, people.

At exactly 2.00 p.m. – or 1400 hours for the more military minded – the Boss opened the proceedings with the traditional ear-splitting howl as the sound-system registered its protest. We got that sorted out and he made his speech of welcome. Wisely, given the attention span of his audience, he made it brief. Very brief. I timed him at seventeen seconds and five of those were applause.

Duty done, he made himself scarce, (rumour had it he'd prepared an underground bunker for this very event), and the crowd scattered, hopefully to avail themselves of the many opportunities to spend vast amounts of money.

Apart from the sidesaddle demo, I hadn't tied myself to anything in particular and spent some time wandering around the place and trying to stay out of trouble. There was plenty of excitement around – some of it planned and some of it not.

Professor Rapson had set up his trebuchet at the eastern end of the lake; the purpose of which was to hit the floating targets. Members of R&D were loading up with small rocks and simultaneously fighting off a not-inconsiderable number of small boys who were volunteering to be human missiles. I moved hurriedly on.

Screams and shouts emanated from the marquee where the IT crowd were showing our dinosaur holo. I could see the shadows of fighting reptiles jerking on the sides of the tent. Ear-splitting roars rent the air and that was just the audience. The queue for the next performance stretched all the way to the tea tent.

Over on the football pitch, a medieval tournament area had been set up. The Security Section's colours were green and white. They'd tossed a coin, lost, and were relegated to the area near the toilet tent. The History department, wearing blue and green, had, for some inexplicable reason, chosen the end next to the beer tent. The participants were warming up for their sword fighting demonstration. I'd warned them all – 'It's a demonstration, not a war. Understand?' and they'd solemnly nodded and ignored me. There would be four individual bouts and then a rest period during which volunteers from the audience would be invited to brandish a dummy sword or two. On strict instructions from Dr Bairstow, no one was to be maimed. Helen had uttered a snort of disbelief over that one and gone off, presumably to mug up on every type of sword wound, up to and including but not necessarily limited to, decapitation. Good luck to her. After the individual bouts, the four of them, uttering blood-curdling cries, would indulge in the closest thing four people could get to a melee and then the last man standing would limp away to the beer tent, job well done.

Another enormous queue was forming for Dr Dowson's tour of St Mary's. His working title had been

180

'A History of Country House Architecture from the 17th Century to the Present Day.' Sadly, this had crumbled beneath the weight of overwhelming indifference, been renamed, 'Blood, Disease, and Torture through the Ages,' and risen, phoenix-like from the ashes. Several members of the Security Section (with suspicious alacrity) had covered themselves in gore and volunteered to be chained to the walls at strategic points of the tour. Evans had gone the extra mile and glued a stuffed rat to his chest. Naturally, at the end of the day, it refused to be unglued, and after losing painful amounts of chest hair, he'd given up and named it Archie. I was later told that for several days afterwards, members of St Mary's were treated to the sight of Archie peering coyly over the top of his T-shirt, until eventually, he (Archie) dropped off of his own accord.

Streaks of wet 'blood' splashed artistically up the walls and a soundtrack of agonised screams echoed around the building. The whole thing was rather similar to one of Dr Bairstow's lengthier all-staff briefings. (I had an unfamiliar fit of self-preservation and did not, in any way, mention this resemblance to the Boss.)

Back outside, several people had fallen into the lake. Hunter was keeping a careful tally. Bets had been placed on the final total and a lot of money was riding on this.

I spent some time trying to avoid SPOHB, who wanted to talk at me, the Chancellor and her crew who wanted to boast about their boat, and Dr Bairstow who wanted me to assist at the prize-giving in the Great Hall. Like that was ever going to happen.

Since I was somewhat conspicuous in my blue velvet

riding habit, I stood quietly at the back and watched him present the prize for Best Picture of an Historical Event to Class 5 of Whittington Junior School for their picture of the Black Death wiping out nearly every living thing in their village in 1348. They'd put their hearts and souls into depicting, in enormous detail, the scabs, sores, buboes, gangrenous limbs ... it was an amazing piece of work. I was very impressed.

He presented the prize to an angel-faced tot who, apparently, was responsible for the bloodstained rat climbing out of a skull's left eye. I didn't mind betting we'd see her here at St Mary's one day. Either as an historian, or, more likely, a member of the kitchen staff.

I left before he could summon me to do something I didn't want to do and bumped into Helen, busy dealing with injuries relating to overenthusiasm on the bouncy castle. She seemed to be disentangling two fathers, a mum, and a frisky septuagenarian. I know there was an age limit of fourteen, so God knows what had been going on there.

By way of a change, I went to visit the donkeys from the local sanctuary. They'd been tethered in the shade, looked incredibly cute and in contrast to the human-induced mayhem all around, doing no harm at all. I could have happily stayed there all afternoon, handing them the odd carrot and twitching my skin to keep the flies off. Mr Strong, when not enthusiastically directing the traffic with two table-tennis bats, was rushing to and from the compost heaps with buckets full of donkey-related product.

Comforted and calmed, I made the mistake of walking past a small blue and red striped tent and was pounced on by Madame Zara, All-Seeing Daughter of the Gods, who, apparently, just knew I would be walking past at that moment.

I told him I had no silver with which to cross his palm and he indicated, cheerfully, that this was no problem – he took all major credit cards.

I asked where, in a tightly fitting-blue velvet riding habit he expected me to keep a credit card, and would have moved on.

'Oh come on, Max, just for a minute. Then you can stand outside and say loudly that I'm the best fortune teller you've ever been to.'

'You're the only ...'

'Please ...'

I sighed. 'All right.

We entered his gloomy tent.

'What's that awful smell?'

'Isn't it incense?'

'I'm pretty sure it's not.'

'Oh, I thought it was. Never mind. Sit down and give me your hand.'

I held out my hand while he poured over it, making artistic passes, and breathing heavily. The smoke curled around his head. I began to feel giddy so God knows what it was doing to him and it wasn't as if he was normal to begin with.

He seemed to spend a very long time peering at my palm. My hands are quite small. There's not that much to see, surely. His breathing deepened – he appeared to be in some kind of trance, although with Markham, it's hard to tell.

Whispered words drifted around the dim tent, as insubstantial as the evil-smelling smoke from his candles.

'*Watch your back.*'

'What?' I said, confused by his departure from the script.

'What?' he said, blinking.

'What was that all about?'

'I told you. You will meet a tall, dark stranger ...'

'That's not what you said.'

'What did I say?'

'Something about watching my back.'

'No, I didn't. I said you would meet a tall, dark stranger and you will travel across water.'

'We've got to stop clouting you around the side of the head. It's not doing you as much good as we hoped.'

Somewhat unnerved, I left him.

Small boys aged eighteen and upwards were admiring the display of vintage cars. I shook my head at such folly and passed on.

Things were hotting up in the local farmers' market where smelly cheese and oddly shaped sausages were being purchased with enthusiasm, especially after sampling thimblefuls of assorted murky and very sticky drinks, which invariably resulted in a sharp intake of breath, a momentary loss of vision, and utterances of 'Wow! I'll definitely have a bottle of that! No, make it two!' People were staggering away with slightly less control over their limbs than they had previously enjoyed.

Away in the distance, the Rushford and District Brass

Band were belting out 'The Floral Dance' with considerable enthusiasm and much less rhythm. The sun shone down, birds sang, the house and gardens looked wonderful. How long could this last?

I wanted to have a clear look at the two boats, both now proudly moored alongside each other at the south end of the lake and guarded by rival squads from each organisation who gazed at each other with such hostility that I half expected a good number of bodies to be floating face down in the water already. Happily, not yet, but give it time.

Both ships were bigger than I expected. The word raft was misleading. True, they weren't ocean-going liners, but they were substantial vessels.

The Black Carbuncle towered malevolently, her skull and crossbones flag fluttering in the wind. Yes, technically she was a raft, but somehow, they'd managed to build two floors.

'Decks,' said Professor Rapson, materialising alongside (I'm told 'alongside' is another nautical term).

'Doesn't that make it a bit top-heavy?'

'Surprisingly, no. I suspect there's something attached below the waterline. I can't make it out and they won't let us get close enough to look.'

'What are those things at the front bit?'

'Prow. And they're modified bull bars.'

'Bull bars? For God's sake, this isn't the school run.' I was suddenly anxious. 'Professor, we're not going to lose, are we? I really don't want to be paraded around Thirsk behind the Chancellor's chariot, exposed to the jeers of the mob – sorry, students – and knowing I'm heading for ritual strangling.'

His eyes twinkled. 'Have a little faith, Max.'

He stepped aside and for the first time, I saw *The Valkyrie* close up.

Again, yes, technically a raft. But only technically.

'Modelled on a Viking longship,' he said, enthusiastically. 'Lean, mean, fast, and manoeuvrable. It can go backwards and forwards. Although not at the same time, obviously.'

'Professor, it's magnificent.'

And it was. It was bloody wonderful. Our boys had done us proud. They'd even built a stubby mast with a red-and-white-striped sail. Colourful papier-mâché shields were slung along each side, each one with its own lovingly painted personal symbol. Crossed spanners for the Technical Section. A scroll for the History department. The caduceus for the Medical Section. A red, green, blue, and yellow window-shaped symbol for the IT people. You know the one I mean. The international warning sign for explosions for R & D. Even the Security Section, never normally recognised for their sense of humour, was represented by crossed shields. Yes, shields on a shield. All right, they'd managed the humour, but still had to work on imagination.

The best bit, however, was at the front.

'Prow,' said the professor, wearily.

'A figurehead,' I said in delight.

'Yes. Come and see.'

He grasped my arm.

'I took your advice, Max.'

Oh wonderful! After all these years, now they start

taking my advice and they start with this.

'The Muse of History,' he said proudly. 'Kleio herself. What do you think?'

Frankly, I was amazed the boat hadn't tipped over. Completely by accident, they'd achieved a more than passing likeness to the Muse of History. Except for one very important area. Actually, two very important areas.

I said carefully, 'Wow!'

'Yes,' he said. 'We had a lot of papier-mâché left over and didn't quite know what to do with it.'

'So you thought ...'

'Well,' he said, cheerfully, 'she'll never sink.'

'Not with those flotation devices, no. Has Dr Bairstow seen this?'

'Oh yes, yes. He was here earlier.'

'Was he ... did he ... Was he alone?'

'Oh no,' he said vaguely. 'I think Mrs Partridge was with him.'

'How delightful. And did she pass any sort of comment?'

'No, now you come to mention it. She was very quiet. I think perhaps she was struck dumb with admiration.'

'Nearly right, Professor. Just to be clear, she didn't say anything at all?'

'Well, just as she was leaving, she did ask if anyone knew of your whereabouts. I believe she wanted a quick word.'

'Jolly good,' I said, weakly, wondering how long it would take me to find my passport and just how far I'd be allowed to get.

'Anyway,' he continued briskly, 'let me walk you

187

around the weapons systems.' He pointed to a giant piece of rubber, mounted on the deck. 'Giant catapult. Water cannons – one to port, one to starboard. Simple to set up. One end sucks up the water, the other end blows it out again. Water pistols for hand-to-hand combat when we board them. Over here, plastic bags for water bombs. A crate of well-past-their-best fruit and vegetables, kindly donated by the kitchen department. Ditto a supply of eggs. And flour bombs – and let's face it Max, who does flour bombs better than St Mary's?'

Flour, eggs, and water. The whole lake would become one vast lump of pizza dough.

'And the crate of beer?'

He pushed his spectacles up his nose. 'For the crew, of course, Max. What else?'

I sighed. Silly me.

'So what exactly is involved here, Professor?'

'They row, or paddle, or punt, or whatever, straight across the lake. See those two trees over there? There are two rosettes secured to their trunks. They must seize one and bring it back. First one back here is the winner and it will be us, because if you look carefully, you will see that our boat is reversible. As I said, it can go forwards and backwards; the crew just have to about-face and row like hell. *The Black Carbuncle*, however, must be physically turned. I think we've found their Achilles heel, Max.'

I suspected *The Black Carbuncle* didn't need to be turned because our sh – boat – would have been long since despatched to the bottom. She had an air of black menace about her. I was certain the evil brain of Professor Penrose – surely a candidate for the world's next supervillain – would have devised cruel and unusual devices that would send us to the bottom of the lake in the first ten minutes or so.

As the person nominally responsible for the Open Day, and given the capacity for potential disaster, I felt it was my duty to perform a quick risk assessment. I dived straight to the heart of the matter.

Scanning the lake, I said, 'Where are the swans?'

He looked around vaguely, as if he expected to see them roosting in a tree somewhere.

'No idea. I expect they've gone wherever swans go. Africa, maybe?'

No. In times of crisis, our swans head for the library – their traditional refuge in any sort of emergency. Since it was currently occupied by pupils and parents, they might have headed off to complain personally to the King.

Meanwhile, the crews were arriving. Everyone was wearing life jackets and hard hats. Dr Bairstow and the Chancellor, both knowing their people and their capabilities well, had insisted upon it. From the corner of my eye, I could see Helen and the medical team setting up an emergency treatment station. Crowds of people milled everywhere, seeking the best vantage points so the kids would get a good view of the drowning nutters. I suspected many of them had brought their own missiles. Even by St Mary's standards, it was going to be carnage.

The Thirsk crew were daunting just to look at. Eight enormous young men, each of whom could almost certainly lift a horse by himself, should he ever choose to do so. They wore black hard hats. Even their life jackets were black. They loomed. The young men, I mean, not the life jackets.

Our boys, on the other hand, presented a much more ... eclectic ... image. They'd obviously rummaged around Wardrobe. Leon and Guthrie wore WW1 helmets, probably genuine. Peterson wore a Greek helmet with a moth-eaten crest. Possibly not genuine, but with him, you never knew. Evans wore a Norman helmet with a long nose guard. Probably not genuine. Randall wore a motor cycle helmet. Almost certainly genuine. The rest of them wore assorted knights' helmets from which the visors had been removed. Definitely not genuine. In his search for authenticity, Mr Markham, now divested of his Madame Zara, All Seeing etc. persona, appeared to be wearing a small pink Tupperware bowl with two cardboard horns glued thereon. I was determined not to comment.

The crowd cheered both teams impartially as they prepared to board.

Beside me, Professor Rapson and Professor Penrose were eyeballing each other. Things could get ugly.

A hand fell on my shoulder. Oh God, Mrs Partridge had found me.

'It wasn't me,' I said wildly. 'It was just a suggestion. I never thought ...'

Leon was grinning at me. 'What?'

'Nothing,' I said quickly.

'Do me a favour, will you? Nip round to those trees over there and make sure nothing happens to those rosettes. There are people here today who have even fewer scruples we do.'

'Good thought,' I said, seeing Dr Bairstow and the

Chancellor approaching to start the race.

The crowd roared their enthusiasm.

Suddenly, everyone was at their oars and we were ready for the start of the race – a traditional St Mary's demonstration of entropy – from order to disorder. In the words of the song – *Nobody does it better.*

Believe it or not, there were rules. Everyone needs rules. After all, how can you break what doesn't exist? Rules give anarchy something to aim at.

Points would be awarded for design, construction, innovation, teamwork, enthusiasm, and stamina. Since our boys were already making inroads into the beer, I had my doubts about the stamina. On the other hand, no one could fault their enthusiasm in knocking it back.

Anyway, each craft, ostensibly eschewing violence, cheating, dangerous rowing practices, etc., was to row across the lake, retrieve their rosette, avoid hand-to-hand fighting with any enemy forces secreting themselves nearby, and return to the jetty. Given that neither craft might survive the experience, it had been decided that the first team simply to hand their rosette to the Chancellor would be the winner. Personally, I would have just unpinned the stupid thing and strolled gently back around the lake to arrive some thirty minutes before any surviving ships pitched up. It seemed the logical thing to do. You can see now why both teams were exclusively male.

The Chancellor stood on the jetty and raised her arm above her head. The crowd, egged on by Dr Dowson over the PA system, counted down. The gun fired and in a sudden fury of boiling white water, they were off.

As was I.

I strolled slowly around the side of the lake, picking my way through excited family groups baying for blood. If we ever did this again – over Dr Bairstow's dead body, probably – building a mock Coliseum and staging a gladiatorial combat might be extremely popular. I filed that away for future reference.

The first person I saw was Van Owen, very conspicuously not wearing a blue velvet riding habit.

'You're not changed,' I said, accusingly.

She was staring over my shoulder. 'Just on my way,' she said vaguely. 'I was helping Dr Dowson and didn't want to get blood all over it.'

'Good thought.'

She stared over my shoulder for so long that I turned myself. 'Problem?'

She seemed to return from a great distance. 'No. Sorry. Miles away. Where are you off to?'

'Rosette protection duty.'

She smiled with a huge effort. 'Very wise. Well, I'd better get changed.'

'Greta, is everything all right?'

'Yes. Oh, yes.'

'I can do it alone, you know.'

'No you can't. I'm the star of the show. You and that rat-tailed apology for a horse are just there to make me look good.' She paused. 'Wait for me, Max. I'll meet you here in twenty minutes and we'll go to the stables together.'

She set off in a hurry.

'You're going the wrong way.'

'No, it's OK. I'll nip through Security and take the back stairs.'

She disappeared, and I carried on around the lake.

Across the water, *The Valkyrie* was engaging with the enemy. Leon and Dieter, chins on their chests, were pulling doggedly across the lake, protected by Evans and Roberts, who held shields over their heads. Peterson and Clerk were loading the catapult and subjecting *The Black Carbuncle* to an unending rain of root vegetables.

The ancient and venerable seat of learning based in Thirsk was not, however, taking things lying down. At a given signal, they turned left – parboiled, or whatever left is called in nautical terms – and increased their rate to ramming speed. Professor Rapson was beside himself on the jetty, jumping up and down in a frenzy. Dr Dowson was shrieking contradictory instructions over the public address system. The crowd shouted a warning, but too late. There was a massive collision – or whatever the nautical word is for massive collision. Both boats seemed fused together.

Markham, still wearing his very fetching pink Tupperware bowl, and brandishing what he probably thought was a cutlass, bellowed 'St Mary's' and threw himself at the crew of *The Black Carbuncle*, who immediately picked him up and hurled him straight into the water. He sank like an anvil. Two or three pirates followed him in, although whether to rescue him or finish him off completely, I never was able to ascertain.

Because at that moment, someone put a cold, hard gun to the back of my neck and said, 'Stand very, very still, because the one thing I want to do more than anything else in the entire world is to blow your stupid, ugly head off your stupid, ugly shoulders.'

Isabella Bitchface Barclay was back.

I had a sudden picture in my head. A small, concrete room, smothered in white fluffy filling and a dismembered teddy bear pinned to the wall with a knife through his eye together with a note telling me this wasn't over.

Sick Bay had put me back together again after the Battle of St Mary's and Mrs Enderby had done the same for Bear 2.0 – Leon's special gift to me. He'd taken time out from saving the world just to bring him to me. A brief glimmer of light in a dark time. Now I was back to what passed for normal and Bear spent his days on my windowsill, smiling at the world. I'd let my guard down and here she was.

There was nothing I could do. She was behind me. There were people all around us. I felt a sudden anger that no one was looking at what was going on under their noses. She'd chosen her moment well. Everyone was watching the Raft Race. I could hear cheers, boos, laughter. No one was watching what was happening here.

I stood very still because I didn't want my stupid, ugly head blown off my stupid, ugly shoulders, either. I said nothing. She wasn't the most stable person on the planet and this is me saying that.

She jabbed the gun.

'Walk.'

In the absence of more detailed instructions, I turned and set off towards St Mary's and got the jab again.

'Not that way.'

Well, it was worth a try.

I set off again, away from the lake. Away from the noise, the activity, the people, the possibility of any chance of help.

'The barn.'

Half hidden behind a group of trees was our old barn. Now that we had proper stables and a feed store, it had fallen into disuse. Mr Strong kept his grass cutters there and a bunch of miscellaneous tat which, being a man, he was incapable of throwing away, because, of course, it might come in useful one day.

The sound of large numbers of people having a great time slowly died away as I headed towards the barn. I could hear her walking behind me. We could have been the only two people in the world. Shortly to have that number reduced by half.

I stepped out of the sunshine and into the dim darkness of the barn. It smelled of straw, oil, and earth. Dust danced in the sunlight filtering in through holes in the roof. I walked into the centre and stood still. Waiting.

She stood well back in the shadows. In a quiet, deadly little voice, she said, 'I'm going to kill you.'

'Well, yes, Izzie, obviously.'

'You ruined my life.'

I opened my mouth to say, 'Glad to have been of service,' but something stopped me.

'Actually, Izzie, I think you did that yourself. You're the one who betrayed St Mary's. You're the one who picked the losing side. People are dead because of you. People don't like you. You're actually very unlikeable.'

Yes, good move, Maxwell. Winding up the unstable woman with the gun who's always hated you, in an out-of-the-way place where no one will come to your aid. On the other hand, I'd known her a long time and she did like the sound of her own voice. She probably had a lot more to say before finally putting a bullet in me.

I continued. 'The bear's fine, by the way. Just a few stitches and he was as right as rain.'

I turned as I spoke and finally got a good look at her. 'Which is more than can be said for you, Izzie. You really should have got that nose seen to.'

I was exaggerating to wind her up. I'd broken her nose but the slight bend was barely noticeable and then only if you were looking for it.

She said nothing. The gun was rock steady in her hand. This was a new Barclay. One completely in control of her emotions. I wondered if she'd been taking lessons from Clive Ronan. Speaking of whom …

I looked around. 'All on your own today? Don't say he's dumped you already. What is it with you, Izzie? You just can't hang onto your men, can you?'

As I'd hoped, that was a red rag to her bull. Her voice rang around the barn.

'You stole my life. He was mine. He loved me. I was everything to him. And then you came along and it was as if we never existed.'

We? Hang on a minute. Just hang on a minute … That wasn't right.

The gun came up. This was it. She was too far away for me to reach her. There was no one else around. I was completely unarmed. This really was it. I was going to die. I'd killed her. She'd killed me. Now, after all our duels over the long years, she was finally going to come out on top.

'Wait,' I said, desperately. 'Just wait a minute. Can we please stop killing each other and just talk for a moment? You keep saying this and I don't think I've been listening properly. When you say "I stole your life" what do you actually mean?'

She scoffed. 'It's a little late to pretend ignorance now. You know what I'm talking about.'

'No,' I said, quietly. 'No, I don't. Tell me.'

For a second I thought she'd just go ahead and shoot me anyway. Outside in the distance, I could hear the shouts and cheers as the Raft Race continued towards its chaotic end, but in here, the silence was like a blanket. Everything hung in the balance, and then she shrugged.

I let my own shoulders drop. So far so good. I spoke quietly. Anything to reduce the emotional temperature. Up in the hayloft, something scuttled over our heads.

'I've heard you say this before, Izzie. I always assumed you meant I'd stolen Leon Farrell from you and that maybe I'd somehow stolen your career at St Mary's as well. Is that what you mean?'

She stared at me. 'No, of course it isn't. Don't pretend you don't know what I'm talking about.'

'Izzie, I honestly have no idea. Please – for once – can

we just talk to each other?'

Without waiting for a reply, I deliberately turned my back on her and walked over to a convenient hay bale, which meant I was even further from the door and from her, too. I felt her relax a little at the increased distance between us.

She watched me sit and arrange my riding habit in folds around my feet. I waited in silence. She would have to speak first.

After a long while, she joined me, perching opposite on an old metal corn bin. She still had the gun but now it rested quietly in her lap. We looked at each other.

For the first time ever, she spoke to me as an equal. No sneering. No abuse. She spoke almost like a little girl. 'Did he never mention me at all?'

Thank God, I had the sense to top and think. I had a sudden revelation. This wasn't about Leon. Or anyone at St Mary's. And there had only been one other man in my life. My heart began to thump because surely she couldn't be talking about ...?

It was no more than a whisper because my throat closed so hard I could barely get the words out at all.

'Who's "he"? Who do you mean?'

She swallowed hard and her voice wasn't steady either.

'My father.'

My world fractured into a hundred thousand glittering fragments. A hundred thousand glittering fragments rearranged themselves into a new pattern and fell back into place leaving me adrift in a suddenly unfamiliar world.

'Are you talking about ...? Do you mean ...?' I couldn't finish the sentence.

'John Maxwell. Yes, of course I am. My father.' She drew a deep, shuddering breath. 'Our father.'

Never mind trying to find words. They could come later. In a hundred years or so. I stared at her and struggled for calm. Really struggled. And what was I going to say to her when I could speak?

It didn't matter. She had more than enough words for both of us. They just tumbled out. She couldn't get them out fast enough. It was as if something deep inside her had given way and whatever it had been holding back couldn't be contained for another moment.

'He was my father first. We were a family. We were happy. We were. I adored him. He was so big and handsome, he would sweep me up in his arms, and I was his little princess. And then he was gone and my mother wouldn't stop crying and there was never enough money and we had to live in a horrible house and my new school was horrible as well and she kept trying to talk to him but he just cut us out of his life because now he had a new little princess and it should have been me. You stole my life.'

I stared at her. I know mine had not been a functional family, but I had no idea about any of this. That my father been married before. Or if not married, had been in some sort of relationship. A serious relationship that had produced Isabella Barclay. No idea at all. No idea I had a sister ...

She was crying now, overwhelmed by whatever pent-up emotions were raging within her. The gun was weaving all over the place.

'For God's sake be careful, Izzie. You'll blow your own feet off in a minute.'

She snapped. Her head flew up.

'Shut up! Just shut up! Everything is a joke to you, isn't it? You've never had to struggle the way I did. Do you know how many jobs I had to take to get myself through uni? How much student debt I racked up? And I had to send money home to my mother. Because she never got over him. He ruined her life as well. But not you. You just cruise effortlessly through your perfect life, don't you?'

Her mouth made ugly shapes. Bitter words flew across the gaping chasm that would forever lie between us. 'And then I came here. I was going to show him ... make him proud ... make him see me ...Then you turned up and everything I'd worked for slowly slipped away. Is it deliberate? Do you deliberately follow me wherever I go – wrecking my life?'

I stared at her and the tears just ran down my cheeks. Not only from shock and fear, but pity. Pity for her. And anger. Because she was the one who got away and I hadn't.

It came out as a whisper. 'Oh, Izzie, if only you knew ...'

'What? If only I knew what?'

I could see it now. Now that I knew, it was easy. She was short, just like me. She had ginger hair, just like me. People had remarked on the resemblance in a casual sort of way. Even I'd noticed it. We were like two peas in a pod. Except she was the one who got away.

'If only you knew how lucky you've been.'

'Lucky? You call me lucky?'

'Yes, I do. You had the luckiest escape of your life when John Maxwell left your mother.'

She barked a harsh, contemptuous laugh and rage boiled up inside me. I couldn't hold it in. I forgot to be conciliating. Forgot the threat. Forgot the gun. Forgot everything.

'You haven't got a clue, have you? You stand there, dripping with self-pity over your supposedly tough life and you don't have a bloody clue. You had a home and a mother who loved you. You grew up free from fear. Yes, money might have been tight but there are worse nightmares. There was no John Maxwell in your life. Because he was in mine instead. Do you remember your ninth birthday? Well, I remember mine but not for the same reasons, I'm sure. Yes, I had two parents but one was a monster and the other was a waste of space. Don't tell me your mother wouldn't have fought for you like a lion. Any mother would. Well, I wasn't so lucky. Mine just let him get on with it. And I was going to hell in a handbag. I lost count of the times I was suspended from school. If one of my teachers hadn't taken me in hand, I'd be in a prison cell or dead by now. And don't talk to me about getting through uni. Three jobs, Izzie! Three! And that was with a scholarship. Whereas you ...' I was desperately trying to keep it all together but my voice had deteriorated into some dreadful rasp that hurt my throat. 'You never had to hide in a wardrobe. You didn't have to cope with the pain, the shame, the overwhelming, always present fear. Yes, you could have had my life. Any time you cared to ask for it. Why didn't you? Why didn't you come and take it? You could have banged on my door anytime and I would have given it to you as a gift.'

My voice cracked and I couldn't go on. In the silence, I could hear us both breathing.

Her face was a mask. 'What are you saying?'

I struggled for some control over my voice. 'You know damned well what I'm saying. And it happened to me, Izzie. It all happened to me. Because you're the one who got away.'

More silence. She'd put the gun down. I could probably have made a grab for it but I was shaking as much as she was and there were more important things going on here.

I wiped my nose on my sleeve, dragged in some deep breaths, and tried to calm down. 'How old are you, Izzie?'

'What?'

'How old are you?'

'I'm forty next year.'

'Listen to me. This is important. Neither you nor I are the villain here. That's John Maxwell. He ruined both our lives, but I walked away from him and built a new life and you can do the same. You still have half your life ahead of you. Stop obsessing over the past. Walk away from all your bitterness and resentment and hatred and build yourself a new life. Live abroad. Start again. Don't let him poison your life any longer. Please. I implore you, Isabella, not just for my sake but for yours as well. Walk away now. Let it all go and be happy.'

My words rang around the barn. Something skittered again.

I sat quietly and let her think. I could imagine exactly the thoughts going through her head. Whether strong or weak, when the foundations on which you've built your life are kicked away, the result is exactly the same. Everything comes crashing down around your ears. She was struggling to re-evaluate her life as I was struggling to re-evaluate mine. Looking at past events through new eyes. Hearing new voices. Adrift in a sea of uncertainty. And in my case, vowing future vengeance on the man who so casually ruined so many lives. One day I would ... And then I shook myself. Yes, great move, Maxwell. Allowing John Maxwell power over your life again. As if I didn't have Leon, and Dr Bairstow, and Peterson, and Guthrie to show me that there will always be decent men in this world. I could let it go.

But could she?

She drew a deep, shuddering breath and looked down at the gun as if seeing it for the first time.

We stared at each other. What now? Where could we possibly go from here?

I spoke again, more quietly this time. 'I meant what I said, Isabella. Take a few days. Think about it. Change your life. Do something wonderful with it.'

Silence. She wasn't even looking at me. She was still staring at the gun in her lap. She'd hated me nearly all her life. Was it too late for her to change now?

In the distance, out there in a world a million miles away from this one, I could hear shouts, cheers, and a series of explosions. The Raft Race was ending. The next event was the musical sidesaddle demonstration. I should be going. If I didn't turn up, they'd come looking for me and suddenly, I didn't want them to find her. Suddenly – God knows why after everything she'd done over the years – I wanted her to be free. To start again somewhere. To defeat her own demons. Not to let John Maxwell win. I didn't know why it was so important to me. I just knew it was.

I stood up slowly. She still didn't move.

I said very quietly, 'I'm going now. I'm going to walk away and take a chance on whether you'll let me. Whether you'll take the first step of your new life. Today. Now. Whether you can leave all the shit behind you and move on. Goodbye, Isabella. I wish you the very best of luck. Be amazing.'

I stepped past her and she still didn't move. I took two more paces and then looked back at her, sitting on the corn bin, her hair, so like mine, lit up in a shaft of sunlight shining through a chink in the roof. As if she felt my gaze, she lifted her head. We looked at each other for a long time and then she smiled, uncertainly. I smiled back at her. A bit of a first for both of us. I felt a sudden conviction. She would make it. She was tough. She could start again.

I walked across the barn, heading for the open doorway. Back towards the sunshine. People. The rest of my life.

I turned my back on her.

And then the bitch shot me.

I've been wounded several times. I've had my fair share of being stretched out on the ground, wondering what the hell just happened, and always with that voice in my head screaming at me to get up. But not this time. This time it was as if the connection between mind and body had been severed. No messages were being received. I wasn't even sure they were being sent out.

I lay on my stomach where I'd fallen. I could feel cold hard earth under one cheek. I could see a hand on the end of an out-flung blue velvet arm. In the absence of anyone else, I supposed it must be mine.

Even as I stared at it, trying to piece together what was going on, I felt and heard slow footsteps approach. I saw a pair of mud-splattered Timberlands come to a halt about two feet away.

'Look at me.'

There was no chance. I could hardly move my eyes, let alone my head. Realising this, she took several steps backwards and knelt. Now I could see all of her. Especially her face, frighteningly blank, her eyes empty, completely in control of herself.

She calmly took out the clip, inspected it, and shoved it back in again. Prolonging the moment. Her hands were quite steady.

So was her voice. 'I've always hated you, Maxwell. You're scum, but I never thought even you would try to buy your life by spewing such filth. You're a poisonous bitch. You wreck people's lives. You contaminate everything you touch and I really can't allow you to live any longer.'

She raised the gun.

I refused to close my eyes. Actually, I wasn't even sure I could. There didn't seem to be a single part of me that was working properly. I wasn't even sure I was breathing. Perhaps I was already dead and these were my last thoughts slowly spilling away …

I stared up at the gun, her arm, her face, those eyes … There was no one else in the world … I saw her finger tighten …

The gunshot sounded loud. Incredibly loud, even to me. For long seconds I stared up at her.

She knelt, motionless, and then, with shocking suddenness, a thin, red line of blood ran from the corner of her mouth. Her arm dropped to her side as if, all at once, she was too weary to hold it up any longer. Then, as I watched, she fell forwards onto her face. She thudded into the earth and because that's the way the gods like to do things, her face was about eighteen inches away from mine. Dying, we each looked into the other's eyes.

I felt no emotion. No fear. No shock.

There were more footsteps, slowly approaching. Someone else was here.

Not that it mattered. Still we stared at each other. The last thing either of us was going to see was each other.

The gods must be laughing their heads off.

Someone kicked away her gun. Someone stood behind me. I saw her body jerk with the impact of the first shot. And again. And again. Someone was ending her life and still she wouldn't look away from me, hanging on to her hatred, even in her last seconds.

Someone emptied an entire clip of ammunition into her.

She died between the fourth and fifth shots. I saw the change. Dead eyes now. And still her body jerked and spasmed as bullet after bullet penetrated her now-dead body. Blood and worse splattered my face as the thing that had been Barclay slowly disintegrated in front of me.

I didn't stay for the end. Somewhere around the ninth or tenth shot, I closed my eyes and let go.

I was out of the game for a very long time.

I know that in fiction, the brave protagonist throws aside the bedclothes, leaps from the bed announcing that he/she/it/everything is absolutely fine, and gets out there and solves the crime/ catches the villain/ saves the world/whatever.

I did none of that.

I lay, staring up at the ceiling or, when they sat me up, out of the window instead. I barely moved. I didn't speak. There was so much banging around in my head and I hadn't a clue how to deal with any of it, so I didn't deal with it at all. I just sat and stared at nothing, unable to comprehend what had happened and unwilling to try, until one day I felt the bed sag. I withdrew my thoughts from wherever they had been and focused to find Leon sitting on the bed, pale and shadowed with worry. He took my hand.

'Enough. Come back to me.'

I stared for a long time while questions surfaced and sank again in the seething cauldron of my mind, but I had to say something. I made huge effort and returned to the land of the living.

My voice was hoarse with disuse. 'Who won the Raft Race?'

'Debatable. Our boat sank first, but after everyone had fought their way to land, it was discovered that Mr Markham had, in fact, swum underwater, reached the rosettes, grabbed both of them, and presented them to the Chancellor. By that time you'd been discovered and no one cared anyway.'

'Does everyone know?'

'No. The Open Day carried on around you.'

'Did we make any money?'

'Yes.'

I ran out of questions I could use to avoid the issue.

He waited.

'Who found me?'

'Van Owen. You didn't turn up for the musical ride. She came looking.'

I nodded carefully.

He waited some more.

Finally, since I obviously wasn't going to say anything, he said, 'What happened, Max? Tell me. How did you and Barclay get into that barn? I assume she shot you. Who shot her?'

I shook my head. 'The shooter was behind me. I never saw him.'

'Do you remember what happened?'

Reluctantly, I nodded. I wasn't going to lie to him, but if he didn't ask the right questions, then I wasn't going to put him right.

He waited. He was doing a lot of that. Where to begin? What to say? How could I possibly deal with the guilt, the self-blame? How could anyone manage to get her whole life so wrong?

'She ambushed me while I was watching the race. She had a gun. We went to the barn. She shot me. Someone shot her.'

'She shot you in the back. At close range. You turned your back on her, Max. What aren't you telling me?'

I drew a deep ragged breath that hurt my chest and still couldn't get enough oxygen into my lungs.

'We promised we would always talk to each other, Max. You and I have been through a great deal together and I know this is difficult for you, so I'm saying this. Tell me now and I'll tell those that need to know. You won't ever have to say another word if you don't want to. Helen won't like it, but I'll make everything right with her. And Dr Bairstow. So tell me what happened and then we'll never speak of it again.'

I still couldn't breathe properly. Somewhere, something bleeped. I heard the door open.

'Not now,' he said, quietly enough, but with that note in his voice, and the door closed again.

He smiled reassuringly. 'Well, that's both of us in trouble, now.'

I gripped his hand. Hard.

'I thought I'd got through to her. I really did think I had got through to her. I thought it was over. I thought she would go away and start a new life. That because I had done that, she could too. It was her chance to start all over again. To leave everything behind her. To go away. I really thought she would do it, because her hatred was consuming her. It was burning her up. She said I ruined her life and she was right. Only I had it wrong because I never listen properly and it wasn't you she was talking about. But I never knew. Until she told me, I had no idea. And then she told me and everything changed.'

He said carefully, 'I think I got most of that but I need clues. What did she tell you?

'That ... that she was my sister.'

There. It was out. What would happen now?

He wrapped both his warm hands around mine.

'No, she wasn't.'

'Yes, she was. And as soon as she said it, I could see ...'

'No, sweetheart, she wasn't. She was not your sister. She never was your sister. Isabella Barclay is – was – the only daughter of prosperous parents, Patricia and Robert Barclay. She went to school in Stoke-on-Trent and from there she studied computer sciences at the London College of Computer Technology. She spent a few years in the private sector and then came to St Mary's. Don't you think Dr Bairstow does an extensive background check on everyone here? There is no way she could be your sister and he not know about it. It was just something she said to mess with your head and it worked. You

212

turned your back on her, just as she planned, and she shot you, and if that other, unknown person hadn't been there, she would have got away with it. The final victory would have been hers.'

I stared at him. 'Not ...?'

'Not your sister, no.'

'She said ...'

'All lies.'

All ... lies. The words drummed in my head. All ... lies. Picking up speed. All lies. I'd been manipulated. How she must have laughed inside as I sat before her, earnestly imploring her to leave it all behind and start again. I'd bared my soul to her. Told her my secrets. And that tentative little smile she'd given me as I got up to go ... the one that convinced me she had heard my words ... So that I would turn to go .... She'd staged the whole thing and I'd made it easy for her and it was ... all ... lies. Something was building inside me. Something that had been lying dormant for years and was big and ugly and looking for something to hurt ...

'Leon, you should leave now.'

All lies.

'No.'

All lies.

'I mean it. You must go.'

'No.'

Lies. Lies. Lies.'

He got up off the bed and walked to the door. He was leaving after all. No, he wasn't. He locked the door and returned to the bed.

All the time, something was coming. Something was

213

coming fast. Something red and hot and huge and all-consuming and uncontrollable ... Doors that had remained safely closed for years were flying open ...

'Here.' He handed me the water jug.

And then – suddenly – it was here.

Rage. Pure and primal. A desire for violence ...

I screamed. It hurt my throat and I didn't care. I hurled the water jug across the room. It shattered against the wall and made a satisfying dent in the plaster, too. But not satisfying enough for me.

I've had one or two occasions in my life when the proverbial red mist has descended. I'm not proud of them, but they happen occasionally. This was one of those occasions. I have no memory of getting out of bed, or even of the next few minutes at all, but when, finally, I came to rest, I was standing, panting and in pain, by the window, tangled in tubes, with IV drips on the floor, the fruit bowl in tiny fragments, the window broken, the bedclothes on the floor, and one of the pillows ripped to shreds and bits of it floating everywhere.

Silence settled along with the filling.

I slowly became aware of people pounding on the door.

Leon approached, holding a blanket, although a chair and whip might have been more appropriate.

'Better now?' he said, calmly.

I was still shaking in the aftermath, although whether with shock, cold, or relief, I couldn't have said. He wrapped the blanket around my shoulders and I sat on the window seat, exhausted.

He opened the door. I braced myself because this was

unacceptable behaviour and God knows what was going to happen now, but he simply picked me up and carried me into the empty isolation ward down the corridor. The bed was warm and soft. I vaguely remember people disentangling tubes and things, and drawing the curtains. Voices came and went. I lay for a while with my eyes closed, gently closing the doors on now empty rooms as silence finally fell.

I felt Leon curl himself around me and knew I was safe.

'No hanky-panky,' said Helen's voice from a million miles away. 'We're not licenced.'

I slept.

He was as good as his word. I don't know what he did or what he said, but with one exception, no one ever mentioned Isabella Barclay in my hearing ever again.

Kal and Dieter came to visit and we all pretended everything was normal.

I had important questions. 'Did we make any money?'

'Masses,' said Kal, writing 'NIL BY MOUTH' and pasting it over the bed. 'Apparently we could have made even more, but Dr Bairstow vetoed the plan to charge people to view your body. We did suggest a chalk outline and letting people visit the crime scene but he said it would be in poor taste, and I suppose what with the Chief Constable being there we had to behave ourselves ...'

She tailed off.

'Shame,' I said.

Dieter nodded. 'We thought so, yes.'

*

My next visitor was Markham. I was so pleased to see him.

'Hey!'

He deposited the entire supply of chocolate for the northern hemisphere on my bed. 'There! That should see you through to lunchtime.'

I laughed for the first time in what seemed like ages. 'Good to see you'

'Good to see you, too.'

He sat on the bed and smacked me a huge kiss, just as Leon entered.

He shot to his feet. 'Whoops. Here's Chief Farrell. Do you think he saw anything?'

'No, you're quite safe. He never notices when other men kiss me.'

Leon sighed. 'I'm almost afraid of the answer, but might I enquire why you are kissing the Chief Operations Officer?

Markham beamed, unabashed. 'Sorry, Chief. I didn't mean to make you feel left out. Deepest apologies.'

He threw his arms around Leon, kissed him soundly on the cheek, and released him.

I stared at the pattern on the curtains. Blue stripe, green stripe, cream stripe, don't laugh ...

Leon stood stunned. In fact, he made Mrs Lot look like bowl of quivering jelly.

Cream stripe, green stripe ...

He dropped his flowers on the bedside table and turned to Markham. 'Seriously, is that the best you can do? No wonder Hunter won't give you the time of day. *This* is how you really kiss a girl.'

I smiled and lifted up my face, but he seized Markham in his arms, bent him over backwards, planted him one firmly on the lips, and in walked Nurse Hunter.

I waited with interest to see what would happen next.

She said, 'For God's sake, you two, get a room,' and walked out. Markham tore himself free and raced after her.

Leon called after him. 'Don't tell me the magic's worn off already.' He turned to me. 'What are you laughing at?'

'Well, if you don't know the answer to that one ...'

That evening, Hunter turned up with double-strength Horlicks and a selection of films.

'*Eat, Pray, Love*?'

'Dear God, no.'

'*The Haunting of Hill House*? Original version.'

'Maybe ...'

'*Tremors*?'

That's the one.'

Barely had the first giant slug eaten his first victim, however, when I had a visitor. Van Owen. My heart sank. This couldn't possibly be good.

Hunter switched off the TV, glanced at both of us, and quietly disappeared.

We looked at each other. She looked dreadful. I was supposed to be the invalid and she looked far worse than I did. She'd cut off her long hair and looked, at the same time, both younger and older. Her pansy-purple eyes had matching shadows underneath. She was seeing things she would rather forget. Gentle, pretty Van Owen. Who

217

would have thought?

Why had she done it? I wouldn't have thought her capable of such savagery. If she'd just shot Barclay once or twice then she'd have got away with saving my life as her defence, but sending all those bullets into a body – to keep firing long after life had departed – it hadn't been a pretty sight.

I checked no one could possibly overhear and then said, urgently, 'Where's the gun?'

'Middle of the lake.'

'You're sure it's safe?'

'Yes. It's in pieces. No one will ever find it.'

I let my head fall back on the pillows. 'I have to thank you, Greta.'

'No need. I'm just sorry I didn't get there sooner.'

'How did you know she was here?'

'I didn't. I thought I saw her in the crowd. I didn't believe it at first, because ... well because I was convinced I was imagining it. That I was seeing what I wanted to see. Then I saw her again and it was definitely her. Then I had to acquire a weapon.'

I didn't ask from where she'd got it. Ignorance is bliss. For the first time, I noticed her clothes. Jeans and boots. A long parka. Backpack by the door.

'Are you going away?'

'I'm leaving St Mary's.'

'Greta, no, there's no need.' I said with careful emphasis, 'I don't remember a thing that happened.'

She shook her head. 'Sadly, I can remember everything. I can't stay. Too many memories.' She smiled. 'Sorry to leave you with no senior historians.'

'If you don't go then I won't be without any senior historians.'

She carried on as if I hadn't spoken. 'My time here was … golden. Whatever happens to me next, nothing in my life will ever be this good again. To have been here – to have found love – to have fitted in … I'll always look back on these years … I'll miss it dreadfully. And all the people. But I can't stay. New start. New life. You understand?'

I nodded. I did understand.

'I'm sorry, Greta. It's my fault. I believed every word she said. And then, just for a moment at the end, when she smiled at me I really thought that perhaps …'

'Don't waste your thoughts on her, Max. She was pure evil. What she did to Schiller was inhuman. She deserved to die and when I saw her standing over you … Thank God she never was a very good shot.'

I saw the scene again. Barclay's body, jerking and jumping as bullet after bullet thudded into her. Even after she was dead, they still kept coming, showering me with warm blood …

I sighed. She was dead and still causing grief. I changed the subject. 'What does Dr Bairstow say about you leaving?'

Her chin wobbled. 'Oh, Max. He was so very kind. He said just the right things. I'm afraid I cried all over him. He's sending me to Thirsk for three months as a research assistant while I look around and decide what to do next. He told me I could come back anytime. That there will always be a place for me.'

'And will you?'

'I don't know. I might. I just don't know.'

'Do you need anything?'

'No. He's given me six months' pay. I nearly fell over. And then he thanked me for my service.'

'As do I.' I held out my hand. 'I owe you, Greta. I won't forget.'

'Goodbye, Max. I know you'll struggle with the concept, but take care of yourself. And thanks for everything.'

I swallowed hard. 'An honour and a privilege.'

She heaved her pack onto her shoulder and walked out of the door.

I appreciated that Hunter left me alone for an hour.

Two weeks later, I thought I was ready to go back to work and found that actually, I wasn't.

I stood in the gallery for a long time, looking down on the historians working below in the Hall. Prentiss and Roberts stood at a whiteboard, prioritising bullet points. Clerk and Sands were building a data stack. They all had their heads down. I'd never known the place to be so quiet.

No Schiller. No Van Owen.

I should move. I really should go down there and face them.

'Are you going to stand here all day?' said a voice behind me, shaving several decades off my life expectancy.

When I was certain I could present a reasonably normal exterior, I turned to confront Miss Lee, on her way around the gallery with an armful of files and just for one brief moment, looking like a real admin assistant.

'I'm sorry, Miss Lee. I didn't recognise you. You're working and it confused me.'

'Everything confuses you. And yes, one of us is working while the other is just standing around staring into space. Let's see if we can work out which one is which, shall we?' She looked down at her armful of files. 'Oh yes, now I've got it.'

I really didn't need this.

She scowled. 'So – are you going to stand there all day?'

'I might,' I said, quietly and for a moment, I actually contemplated doing just that. Spending the rest of my life here, between two worlds – no stress, no decisions to make, no friends to grieve for.

She shifted her position and I braced myself for whatever was coming next.

'No you won't,' she said. 'I'm fed up with doing all the work around here. I don't think you realise how difficult it is to do two people's work.'

'How would you know? You struggle to do any work at all.'

'Here are last month's time-sheets for you to sign. Professor Rapson has requisitioned twenty-five dead rabbits and three cowhides and I'm not getting involved in any of that. Chief Farrell is requesting your comments on next month's pod schedule. Major Guthrie wants a word about your entire department's failure to submit their form 23Bs. Mrs Enderby says …'

'Go away,' I said.

She heaved the sigh of the oppressed and shifted her

weight to her other hip.

'Listen. If I can face them on a daily basis then you can do the same.'

'What?' What did that mean?

'If you want my advice ...'

Oh God, I was taking crisis management tips from Rosie Lee. For a moment, I wondered if I was still back in Sick Bay, sitting on my pink, fluffy cloud of confusion.

'What's that, then?'

She grinned and suddenly was a different person altogether.

'Whatever it is, you need to face it down. You give it a good kicking, because that's what you have to do. Then you walk away. And then you turn around, walk back and give it an even bigger one, just because you can.'

She heaved her files into my arms and I sagged under the weight.

'I'm an invalid, you know.'

She snorted rudely. 'I'm going now. Unlike you, I'm quite busy this morning.'

'Are you sure you can remember where my office is. Should I get someone to show you the way?'

I was wasting my breath.

'Dr Bairstow wants to see you. I'm going for my lunch now.'

Then she was gone.

I hadn't been the only one keeping secrets. Dr Bairstow had bad news for me.

He asked me how I was and I said fine, and then, having exhausted his tiny Caring Manager repertoire, he brought me up to speed.

Things were not going well for St Mary's. Schiller's death, our recent spectacular failure at rescuing the treasures of Old St Paul's, me being shot, Van Owen's sudden departure – no one was very happy with us at the moment. I was instructed to get us back on track and to be quick about it.

'I'm sorry, sir. I'm responsible for all this. The idea was mine – as was all the planning, the allocation of personnel ...'

' ... And the responsibility is mine.' He smiled sadly. 'Yes, the mission was your idea. You are the Chief Operations Officer – it was supposed to be, but the final approval for every mission is mine. Always mine. Only mine. And the responsibility for the tragic aftermath of the Old St Paul's assignment, up to and including your being shot – is also mine.'

He looked out of the window for a moment and then the moment passed.

'However, the responsibility for raising morale in your department, ensuring that it continues to operate as usual, coming up with something to get us all back on track, and placating our overlords rests solely with you. Why are you still sitting there, Dr Maxwell?'

Not having the strength to face the maelstrom of paperwork on my desk, I took a cup of tea into the library, sat by the empty fireplace in one of the big armchairs, and had a bit of a think.

We should never have gone for Old St Paul's. I could see that now. If only my normal vision was as good as my hindsight. The risk/reward ratio had been all wrong. Braving the flames for a few unimportant artefacts had been a mistake. My mistake. Now I had to put it right.

We needed something more spectacular. In terms of reward, that was. Something with a big reward and comparatively small risk. Maybe this time, not so much a citywide conflagration – more a small bonfire.

The jolt of inspiration nearly blew me out of my chair.

I went off for another cup of tea and to find some paper.

I made a list, stared at it for a while, and then started to delete. Occasionally, I added another line. Then deleted it again. After thirty minutes, I had just one remaining item.

I drew a square, carefully coloured it in, and started to write. I scribbled thoughts all over the page and then joined them together. A route through our next assignment.

Pulling a selection of books from the shelves, I made notes, thought for a while, and then began to build my data stack. I listed the aims and objectives, the client, the personnel, the pods, the equipment, the methodology.

I was still at it when Leon came looking for me. Apparently, I'd missed a meal and he was concerned I might be dead. He looked at the stack for a while, rotated it slowly, and said, 'You've got to be kidding.'

'Of course I'm not. It's perfectly doable.'

'Yes, but not by you.'

'Why not?'

'Where have you been for the last four weeks? Do you not remember being in hospital at all? Because I remember it very vividly and I really don't think I could do that again.'

'You won't have to. She's dead.'

'And so is Schiller. And Ronan's still out there, somewhere.'

'Leon, I'm not hiding at St Mary's for the rest of my life.'

'That's not what I'm saying. I'm saying you should take it easy for the next month or so. By all means plan assignments, but let others take the strain for a bit.'

'I can't do that. I don't have any senior historians left. Clerk is the most experienced historian I have at the moment, but there's only one of him. Prentiss and Roberts are brilliant but still inexperienced. There's no way around this. If the Boss presented me with half a dozen fully qualified trainees tomorrow, someone would still have to supervise them. And we have to get moving, Leon. As far as Thirsk is concerned, we're back to being a bunch of certifiable nutters. All our good work over the years, Alexandria, Troy, Nineveh, the Cretaceous period – it's not counting for very much at the moment. We have to get back out there and we need something spectacular for them. If we can pull this off ...'

'I understand all that. I'm just saying it shouldn't be you pulling it off.'

'It won't be. I intend that my role will be purely supervisory. I'll point. Others will do the heavy lifting. That's what junior staff are for. Come on. I'm hungry.'

He sighed. He wasn't happy.

*

225

That wasn't the only thing he wasn't happy about. Back in my room, he caught me balancing on the back of the sofa trying to change the overhead light bulb. I stopped listening after a while.

He wouldn't let me lift anything heavier than a teaspoon and when he heard I'd started running again, I thought I'd never hear the end of it. This wasn't like him at all. I tried to be patient. I know it's not easy, waiting beside a hospital bed for someone to wake up, but it wasn't as if he hadn't done it before.

The final straw was when I reached for him one night and he drew back. I sat up and switched on the light. 'Are you ill?'

'No, of course not. I've just had a long day and so have you. You need to take things easy. Go to sleep.'

I lay down again and listened to him breathe in the darkness. He wasn't asleep either.

We had a problem.

I should have realised this might happen. I'd been injured before and he usually coped with it by offering his own brand of bracing hard work and verbal abuse, but this time I'd been badly hurt. He'd spent a few days sitting by my bed, not knowing one way or the other. Despite my assurances to the contrary, I knew I wasn't yet fully up to spec, but he was being overprotective. A natural enough reaction – but annoying.

Normal people talk through their problems. Alternatively – first choice as far as I as concerned – I could arrange a practical demonstration.

I thought I'd better check first with Helen. Just to be on the safe side.

Did I just say that?

She was sitting on the windowsill of her office, puffing cigarette smoke out of the window. She scowled heavily as I entered, but I ignored her. Since it was Helen and she has the people skills of a root vegetable, I went straight to it.

'Am I dying?'

'We are all dying,' she intoned, blue smoke wreathing around her head. The effect was more than disconcerting. No wonder people will only visit Sick Bay in a pack. 'The path of men is thorny and filled with pain.'

'Well, it is if you have anything to do with it. No, listen — is there anything you're not telling me?'

'The world is full of things I'm not telling you, Max. Be more specific.'

'Well ... um ... I am fine now, aren't I?'

'As far as I know,' she said, lighting another cigarette and puffing her smoke out of the window.

I looked up at the smoke detector. She read my mind.

'Of course it's got a battery in it. To have a detector without a battery would be irresponsible.'

'And does the battery work?'

'God, I hope not. Looking after you lot has got me up to thirty a day again.'

'Speaking of looking after us ...'

'Yes. Right. No, as far as I can see by running my eyes over you, you're fine. About ten pounds overweight, of course, and I want to test your eyes sometime, and your left knee isn't up to spec, and your bowels move slightly more slowly than continental drift ...'

'Yes, all right,' I said, interrupting this depressing litany. It would be a miracle if I made it through the night at this rate. 'The thing is ...'

'Yes?'

'The thing is ...'

'Yes?'

I struggled for words. 'Leon is being ... cautious.' I sat back, quite pleased with my choice of words.

Complete waste of time.

'You're not getting any, are you?'

'No. I thought you could help.'

'Forget it. I'm not having sex with you.'

'I don't want sex with you. I want sex with Leon!'

I hadn't realised I'd raised my voice until Hunter stuck her hear round the door. 'Everything all right?'

'Yes, it's just Maxwell going through a dry period.'

I said coldly, 'Don't let me keep you from your duties.'

Hunter grinned and pushed off.

'Well?' I said to Helen. 'Any suggestions?'

'Have sex.'

'Yes, very helpful.'

'What else do you want from me?'

'I wondered if you could do me a certificate or something.'

'What sort of certificate?'

'I don't know. Something to say I'm roadworthy.'

'This is not an MOT centre.'

'Helen ...'

'Look, I'm not saying you're as you were – you're not. However, you are perfectly capable of having sex without anything dropping off. Well, not dropping off you, at any rate. Just sit down and talk to Leon. He's just a little nervous about you at the moment.' She hesitated a moment. 'Perhaps you don't know what it was like for him, sitting by your bed, waiting for you to wake up.'

'But what has that to do with not wanting to have sex. Does he think it'll kill me?'

'He might not be thinking very clearly at the moment. Talk to him. Tell him you can't die of sex.'

I said darkly, 'You can the way I do it.'

'Just get out of here and take your ego with you.'

'I'm going to tell Leon your battery's flat.'

'Do that and I'll have you flat on your back and your legs akimbo while I do something interesting with ten feet of rubber tubing.'

'I thought you said you didn't want to have sex with me.'

She blew more smoke. 'Just … go, will you?'

All right, that could have gone better, but it had given me an idea. Racing off to the kitchen, I found Mrs Mack. 'Do we have any doughnuts left?'

'I think so, yes, three or four.'

'I'll take two please.'

I spent rest of the afternoon doing everything I could to wind him up.

'Look,' I said, 'I have a major assignment coming up and I don't want to be let down by the Technical Section.'

229

'What?' he said, outraged.

I went on to demand immediate updates on the readiness state of every pod in the place. I argued over the servicing schedule. I showered him with unreasonable demands. He was everything that was patient and reasonable and I really had to work at it, but by close of play, he was hanging on to his self-control by a thread. There would be Words later on.

Back in in my room, I showered and put on my old Thirsk sweats. I was just pulling out two wine glasses and a plate when he banged on my door – rather more vigorously than I thought necessary.

'Come on in.' I said, apparently oblivious of today's thundercloud look. 'Can you open this for me?'

We sat at the table, sipping. The wine was rather good, but I didn't want to give him time to relax. The more wound up he was, the better for my purposes. I looked at him. He'd showered too and was wearing the most dilapidated sweats I'd ever seen and that included even mine. They were obviously cherished. The logo was so faded as to be indecipherable. I stared at it. 'What the hell is that?'

'This?' He squinted down at his sweatshirt. 'These were awarded to – well, there's only six in existence.' He smoothed the material gently with his hand.

I snorted derisively. 'Yes, but they're not Thirsk, are they?'

'Well, no, they were awarded by a French establishment.'

'Oh,' I said politely, 'French. Well, never mind, so long as you like them.'

He twitched a little but let it go.

'Cheer up,' I said insensitively.

'I'm fine.'

'Your face says otherwise.'

'No, it doesn't.'

I leaned back in my chair and sipped my wine, wearing the expression I use on the Boss occasionally.

He frowned. 'What is the matter with you today?'

'There's a coincidence. I was just about to say the same to you.'

We sipped in silence.

I got out the doughnuts and put them on a plate.

'What are you doing?'

'Well, it's rude to scarf them straight out of the bag. Just because you're in a bloody awful mood today doesn't mean I should let standards slip.'

'Are you going to eat both of them?'

'Yes, I am, because I don't think you're yet ready for – Ta-Dah! The Doughnut Challenge!'

'The what?'

'Ta-Dah! The Doughnut Challenge! Do you not have doughnuts in the Technical Section?'

'Yes,' he said tersely and knocked back his wine. 'I'm just not familiar with The Doughnut Challenge.'

'You mean – Ta-Dah! The Doughnut Challenge! Well, you wouldn't be, really, would you? This one really separates the historians from lesser mortals.'

'Oh. Really?

I nodded and gazed absently out of the window. The two doughnuts continued to occupy their place in the space-time continuum.

231

He sighed. 'All right, I'll ask. What is – Ta-Dah! The Doughnut Challenge?

'It's not easy …'

'To explain or to do?'

'OK, it's this.' I pushed the plate to the middle of the table. 'You pick up your doughnut. You're the beginner, so you get first choice.'

He nodded, apparently taking this Himalayan-high pile of crap seriously.

'You pick it up with your right hand – unless you're a leftie of course. You take one bite, just one, and put the doughnut back on the plate. Your opponent – that will be me – does exactly the same thing at exactly the same time.'

There was a pause. 'And … that's it?'

'What were you expecting?'

'Well … more.'

'Just one tiny thing. You cannot, must not, under any circumstances, lick the sugar off your lips. Lip-licking is forbidden.'

'And that's it?'

'Well, when you've finished your mouthful you take another bite obviously, but yes, that's it. The challenge is to eat an entire doughnut without once licking your lips.'

'You've done this before?'

'Every Friday, in the History department. The Weekend Starts Here sort of thing.

'Who usually wins?'

I looked as smug as I could, which is a lot, leaned forward and said softly, 'I'm very, very good. You're going down, buster.'

His eyes darkened. 'We'll see about that.'

'So, you're up for it then?'

'Bring it on,' he said, grimly.

'OK, get your top off.'

'What?'

'It's the stake. Thirsk versus – whatever that thing is. Did I not mention that?'

'No.'

'Changed your mind?'

Silence.

'Welching on a bet?'

He sighed. 'No.'

I indicated that he should hand it over.

Slowly, reluctantly, he pulled it over his head and tossed it to me. It was still warm and I could faintly catch his smell on it. It had been a long time ... Concentrate, Maxwell.

'What are you going to do with it?'

'Nothing much. I'm just going to nail it to the wall and torture it.'

I dangled his cherished sweat carelessly from one finger and let it drop to the floor. He watched it fall and set his teeth. I tilted my head to one side, gave him the full, shit-filled grin, and wondered how much longer he'd let me get away with this.

'And what about you?'

I unzipped mine and shimmied it off. Breasts – Nature's built-in advantage. I had also made sure I wasn't wearing the regulation grey sports bra that looked as if it could double as the Humber Bridge in its spare time, but my favourite wisp of satin and lace. The catalogue described the colour as 'crushed raspberry'. Just about the same shade as his suddenly flushed face, and, if truth be told, just slightly too small for me. My cups runneth over. Do I like to win or what? He went very quiet and very still. I saw him glance at the door and shoved the plate in his direction before he could make a run for it.

'On three. Remember, first one to lick their lips is the loser.'

'I really don't think you should …'

I mocked. 'Giving up without a struggle. How typically techie,' and pulled the plate towards me.

He pulled it back again and took his doughnut.

Here we go …

'One, two … three,' and bit into my doughnut.

The secret is to avoid the jam. I chewed slowly and carefully and concentrated on ignoring the increasing desire to lick my lips, which, actually, is not easy. Try it sometime, but pick a different partner. You're not having mine.

He never took his eyes off me. To distract myself I found myself staring at his chest hair and the way that intriguing dark line disappeared down his belly to all points south. Very useful; even someone with my poor sense of direction rarely lost her way. I lifted my eyes and watched his mouth, then let them wander across his face to those eyes; those blue, blue eyes, then back down to his lips again. His sugar-encrusted lips.

Oh God … He wasn't supposed to have this much control. I'd deliberately left a giant loophole in the rules. How much longer before he picked up on it?

He stood up suddenly and for one nasty moment, I

thought he was going to make a run for it and I was going to have to chase him through St Mary's in my bra, but no, St Mary's was safe. He knocked his chair over backwards with a clatter, shoved the table roughly out of the way, and grabbed me. Not gently. He ran his tongue across my bottom lip and sucked off the sugar. My world slid sideways and flew into a million shining pieces.

'You never said I can't lick the sugar off someone else's lips,' he whispered and we concentrated on removing every last grain. I ran my hands over him. He was broad and solid. I ran a fingernail across his chest and he shuddered, I hoped for all the right reasons. My own breathing was suddenly all over the place. He was hard and hot and I couldn't wait any longer. I slid my hand inside his pants. His breathing was fast and shallow, like a cat, and he was very, very pleased to see me.

I started to ease down his pants. He caught my wrists and said into my hair, 'It's too soon. I don't want to hurt you.'

'Oh Leon, don't you know by now? I don't break that easily.'

Which was true enough, but that didn't stop him touching me as if I was the most precious object on this earth. His hands, always sensitive, glided feather-light over my body, leaving me gasping and shuddering for more. I closed my eyes and breathed him in, feeling all control slip away. He was everything that was gentle and considerate and after five minutes, I slapped his arm and told him to get a move on.

He lifted his head and informed me he was doing some

of his best work here and a little appreciation would be nice.

I told him I'd known him do better.

I was challenged to cite my source.

After four or five minutes, he said, yes all right, but he believed in quality over quantity.

I told him I preferred deeds over words.

He demanded to know why historians were always in such a hurry.

I told him historians have a short attention span and who was he again?

He grinned down at me, his blue eyes dark and very bright. 'Let me remind you,' and a couple of frantic minutes later, I had forgotten who I was, too.

Afterwards, when we could speak coherently again, I said to him, 'Now. What's all this, "I'll lift that – it's much too heavy for little old you", rubbish?'

He buried his head in my hair so I couldn't see his face. 'I love you, but I can't always tell you how much. I can't always tell you how much I worry about you. I'm not much good at telling you about things that mean a great deal to me and you do mean a great deal to me, Max. More than anything in the world. And you were so badly hurt. I know you're bouncing around the place these days like Tigger on a trampoline, but every time I look at you, I see you lying there, white, helpless, hurt … I just worry you'll do too much.'

I opened my mouth to tell him I'd be fine and then had a second thought.

'In that case, I'll slow down a little. Just for you. If you like, we can go back to having lunch together outside Hawking. Sitting in the sun as we used to. That way, you can check me over every day and I'll pretend not to notice.'

He laughed and reached for me again. 'Deal.'

First time I've never finished a doughnut.

I didn't waste any time, making an appointment to see Dr Bairstow the very next day. We desperately needed something to restore our confidence and prestige. In our own eyes, as well as those of other people.

He didn't immediately look up from his writing. Not a problem. I could wait him out.

Eventually, when it became clear I wasn't going to go away, he looked up.

I grinned at him. He closed his eyes.

'I believe I have, on several occasions, requested you not to do that, Dr Maxwell.'

'Sorry, sir.' I rearranged my features into an expression of funereal gloom. I wouldn't have thought it possible, but he managed to look even more disapproving.

He frowned. 'I'm sure this is a question we will both regret me asking, but why are you here? Did I send for you?'

'I don't think so, sir. Not unless you despatched Mrs Partridge to swoop down on me, rather in the manner of a Valkyrie scooping a fallen warrior from the battlefield, and she's missed me.'

'Both scenarios are equally unlikely, Dr Maxwell. State your purpose.'

'To blow your socks off, sir.'

'I should perhaps warn you that these days, my socks are not that easily blown off.'

'Glad to hear that, sir. I like a challenge.'

He laid down his pen. 'Proceed.'

So I did. I brought up my data stack, gave him a second to assimilate the contents, and took him through everything from beginning to end. He listened in complete silence, but then, he always did. His method was to allow me to dig my own hole, unimpeded, and then bury me with the flaws, inconsistencies, and weak spots.

I wound down to a halt and waited. Still not speaking, he held out a hand for my notes. I passed them over. He read through everything from beginning to end, went back, re-read a section, checked it against the data stack, laid the file on his desk, and regarded me.

I regarded him right back again.

He spoke. 'You don't feel that after recent events, something a little less high profile might be more appropriate?'

'No, sir, I don't. We screwed up big time. We can spend years taking small, safe steps to restore our reputation or we can hit them with the biggest coup of the century.'

'And if it doesn't come off?'

'We're no worse off, sir.'

'You don't feel a cautious approach might be indicated?'

'This is the cautious approach, sir. As you will see, I've recommended we only inform Thirsk *after* we've successfully concluded the assignment. If we fail then

240

they'll never know. But we won't. Fail, I mean.'

'We did last time.'

'Actually, sir, we didn't. Your people performed perfectly. It was Ronan and Barclay who killed Miss Schiller and went on to steal our artefacts and substitute her body.' I took a deep breath. 'To prevent that happening again, I propose we deploy the entire Security Section at the second site. For protection. I don't think historians at the first site will be in any jeopardy, sir. There are no advancing armies or burning buildings. We'll be fine.'

'I think you underestimate the History department. I have yet to learn that any historian requires an advancing army or a burning building to get herself into trouble, Dr Maxwell.'

I said nothing. He was coming around. The best thing I could do now was to keep my mouth shut.

He stared hard at his desk for a while. 'I will give provisional permission. Present me with a mission plan within five days and I will give it full consideration.'

'Yes, sir.'

I seized the file and data stick and was out of there before he could change his mind.

He said yes. Eventually. He just really made me work for it. And I did. I put together an assignment in near-record time. I raced around the building, involving as many people as possible because we needed this. We needed not just any old salvage mission but something spectacular. Something to get us back in the game. With the History department waiting anxiously downstairs, I marched into his office with my completed mission plan and talked for nearly an hour.

The Man from St Mary's – he say yes!

I held a full briefing in the Hall. Everyone was there. The whole History department, the Security Section, most of IT and the Technical Section, even Mrs Mack and the kitchen crew, because they were going to have to feed us. I even included the Admin Section who would be assisting Dr Dowson and Professor Rapson in their research. They sat at the back, eager and attentive, in direct contrast to the historians lounging at the front, pretending to be cool about the whole thing.

I stood on the stairs and looked down at their heads, bent over scratchpads and scribblepads. Mr Strong had set up the big screen for the visuals and Mrs Partridge and Miss Lee were distributing the background info. I waited patiently and eventually, silence fell.

'Good morning, everyone. Thank you for coming. Our purpose today is to discuss our upcoming assignment. I know a lot of you have already contributed a great deal of time and effort. Thank you for that. I shall brief you on the background to this assignment, give details of the teams and their pods, work out a timetable, and answer any questions at the end. Everyone set?'

They nodded. Here we go.

I brought up the first images.

'Site One. Florence – 1497. Specifically, the 7th February 1497. The Bonfire of the Vanities.'

A ripple ran through the room. Someone, somewhere at the back said, 'Yes!'

I continued. 'It's the height of the Renaissance. The city of Florence is at the forefront. The old ways are being discarded. The invention of printing means new ideas and new ways of thinking are accessible to the masses. It's a period of incredible advancement and change and it's happening all across Europe, but it's especially happening in Florence. It's no coincidence that Da Vinci, Botticelli, and Raphael were all born in this area.

'Or rather, it *was* all happening in Florence. Unfortunately, the city has fallen under the influence of the monk, Girolamo Savonarola. His stated mission is to destroy all "frivolous and sinful pursuits", which, according to him, is just about everything excluding breathing and eating and even those two only in moderation. He's a powerful preacher and under his influence, draconian laws are introduced forbidding fine clothes, art, music, homosexuality, and the old favourite, "moral transgressions".

'It's a dreadful time. And it's not just the adults who are involved. Children, over a thousand of them, will march through the streets collecting items for the Bonfire. They've been brought up to shop their parents, their relatives, their friends, everyone. To report all instances of frivolity or luxury. They even snitch on each other. They get people beaten up and arrested. Even being overweight is considered a sin. These are not nice kids. There is a record somewhere of them parading through the streets, singing hymns and carrying candles. Forget it. These are kids in the grip of religious fervour and in a position of power over adults. Do not underestimate them. We will need to tread very carefully.

'Under Savanarola's influence, almost everything – cosmetics, books, statues, fine clothes, playing cards, chess sets, jewellery, wigs, musical instruments, even false teeth are to be burned. And, of course, works of art. Which brings me to our assignment. The influence of Savanarola is such that even the artist, Sandro Botticelli, caught up in the moment, volunteers some of his paintings to be cast into the flames.'

I paused and took a deep breath. 'That's what we're after, folks. And everything else we can lay our hands on, of course, but basically, we're there to bag a Botticelli.'

Silence.

'So what's the plan?' asked Evans. 'Just knock on his door and shout the Florentine equivalent of "Penny for the Guy?" Paintings for the Bonfire?'

'Yes.'

Silence.

'How many paintings were destroyed?' asked Dieter.

'No idea. It could be one or it could be twenty.'

'Wow,' said someone. Again.

'Problem?' I said.

'Oh, no …'

'I think we may be overestimating the difficulties. It won't be a case of wrenching them from an overprotective artist. He's so completely under the spell of Savonarola that he'll probably give them to anyone who asks for them. We just have to make sure it's us doing the asking. All we need do then is to convey them safely to the second site, where Dr Dowson and his team will dispose of them in such a way as to enable discovery by a University of Thirsk funded excavation in the near future.

'So – the teams. Two teams for Site One. Clerk, Maxwell, and Sands in Number Eight, and Peterson, Prentiss, and Roberts are in Number Five. This part of the assignment will be under my control, or failing me, Dr Peterson.

'The third team will be headed by Professor Rapson and is responsible for procuring contemporary storage materials because, as always, all items are to be sourced locally.

'The fourth team, headed by Dr Dowson and his archivists, will be waiting for us at Site Two. Also on site will be the Security Section, for obvious reasons, and a small team of technicians, just in case we break something. These teams will all be in TB2. Doctor Dowson, if you would like to give us the details of Site Two, please.'

He bounded to his feet and joined me on the staircase, shedding a blizzard of papers in all directions.

'Thank you, Max. Firstly, I must tell everyone that the usual rules apply – the artefacts will not leave their country of origin. They are Florentine treasures and will therefore be discovered – we hope – near the city.'

He brought up a map on the big screen.

'We were rather spoiled for choice when it came to selecting a suitable hiding place for our recovered paintings, but after a certain amount of reconnaissance we have selected, as Site Two, the Belverde caves near Monte Cetona. These are a range of naturally occurring caves and there is widespread evidence of prehistoric settlements. We feel it is perfectly possible that 15th-century treasures could have been sent there for safe keeping and then forgotten about until a joint Thirsk/Italian dig will shortly stumble upon them, to worldwide astonishment and acclaim.' He smiled at me. 'We hope.'

I smiled back. 'Listen up, people. We're St Mary's and we're not bright, but we learn from our mistakes and we will be taking certain precautions. There will be absolutely no possibility of anyone following us this time. As I said, almost all the Security Section will be deployed at the caves. Let me remind all of you, they are there for our protection. Please do not ask them to fetch and carry, give you a hand to lift something heavy, or just hold this for a moment. They are there to keep us safe. Allow them to do so. Yes, this is a big assignment, and if we pull it off there's no doubt we'll be back to flavour of the month, but it's not as important as the safety of everyone there. Therefore, everyone, including me, will be answerable to the Security Section. I'll ask now – does anyone anticipate any difficulties with that?'

Sometimes, you just have to get right in people's faces and tell them, but apparently, no one had any difficulties at all.

'The usual sterile conditions will apply at Site Two. These finds will be subject to intense archaeological scrutiny, especially if we do manage to bag a Botticelli. Paper suits, hairnets, and cotton gloves will be supplied and are to be worn at all times in the working areas. By everyone. I don't want an over-zealous archaeologist discovering that not only did women in the 15th-century dye their hair Sunkissed Blonde, but smothered it in extra-strong-control mousse as well.'

I paused again. 'Any questions?'

'Language?' asked Peterson.

'Well, most of us will need a crash course from Dr Dowson, but we're fortunate in that Dante Alighieri wrote his famous *Comedies* in the Florentine dialect, and this became the basis of the Italian language, so anyone who can speak Italian stands a good chance of being understood. Mr Sands does, I believe?'

He nodded. Roberts raised his hand as well. 'Me too – a little.'

'Excellent. The rest of us will mug up on the basics. OK, then. Those who need to, report to Wardrobe and get kitted out. Mr Dieter, if you could be kind enough to ensure sufficient paper suits and booties are loaded into TB2, please. Everyone is to report to Sick Bay for a check-up. By Thursday, please. Dr Dowson and Professor Rapson, if you could let me have details of your teams asap, please. That's it for the time being. Thank you, everyone.'

We assembled in Hawking. Historians waited outside Number Five. A quivering Dr Dowson and his crew stood by TB2. There wasn't a great deal of chatter. People were very carefully not thinking about the last time we did this.

'Change of plan,' said Leon, materialising beside me. 'Dieter's going with the R & D crew – I'm going with you. Just in case.'

'In case of what?'

'In case anything needs dismantling, reassembling, fixing, whatever. And no, I'm not talking about historians wrecking everything they touch – although they do – I'm also available for heavy lifting and crowd control.'

'Glad to have you,' I said, because I was. Disregarding the completely inaccurate remark about historians breaking everything – as if! – he was right. We might have to take things apart to get them into the pods and if you hand a screwdriver to an historian, two seconds later he'll have blinded himself with it.

I ran my eyes over everyone for one last check. I wore a shapeless sack in a coarsely-woven brown material that itched. I was pretty pissed about it and so was Prentiss, already looking acutely uncomfortable in a similar outfit, scratching herself, and complaining bitterly.

We adjusted each other's headdress – just a simple linen hood for this trip – I wasn't sure how severe the dress code would be, but it seemed simpler to have no hair showing at all. We didn't want to end up on the Bonfire ourselves.

Peterson gave me the thumbs up. Dieter indicated that now would be a good time for Dr Dowson to enter TB2 and helped him up the ramp. I ushered my own team into Number Eight.

'Whenever you're ready, Mr Sands.'

The world went white.

We landed in a tiny unnamed square faced with blank, brick walls. Over in the corner, an outer wooden staircase leaned against the wall for support. At the top, a bricked-up doorway gave no clue as to the building or its function.

The day was grey and chilly. It had been raining and all the paving glistened wetly. Brown weeds struggled to survive in the gaps between the uneven cobbles.

I could see Number Five, sitting quietly against the left hand wall. Sands angled all the cameras and Clerk checked the proximities.

'We're fine,' he reported. 'Ready to go when you give the word, Max.'

'OK,' I said. 'Let's do it.'

'Good luck,' said Leon, sitting back comfortably.

I was surprised. 'Are you not coming?'

'I'm on pod protection detail. Besides, it's cold and wet out there.'

'I'm sorry; I forget that at your age, inclement weather can be a problem for you.'

'Play nicely, children. No biting.'

I gave the word and we all assembled outside. Peterson consulted his map while Roberts struggled with the wooden handcart we'd optimistically brought with us to handle the vast numbers of artefacts we hoped to acquire.

We emerged cautiously from the square and sorted ourselves out. We put Peterson in front with Clerk and Sands behind him. As the junior member of the team, Roberts pushed the cart and Prentiss and I, knowing our places, fell in behind. As always, I would be leading from the rear, standing safely behind everyone at all times. Like a wartime politician. We all assumed expressions of terminal piety and set off.

We'd landed near the dark mass of San Spirito. With our backs to the church, we headed for the river, turned right, and made our way along the riverbank. The Arno flowed darkly and silently, swollen with winter rains. Five minutes later, we arrived at the fabled Ponte Vecchio.

The best thing about being at the back is that you can

blindly follow the people in front and spend your time usefully looking at the wonders all around. I was in Florence! Best of all, I was in Renaissance Florence. The city of the Medici. The city at the centre of the flowering of artistic culture and yes, currently in the grip of a disastrous religious fervour, but that was why we were here, after all. To rescue what we could. To redress the balance in some small way. There's something very satisfying about outwitting religious fanaticism.

Ahead of us, the Ponte Vecchio, newly rebuilt in stone, gleamed wetly in the chilly February day. Each side was lined with modern goldsmiths' and jewellers' shops. Previously, this area had been occupied by butchers and fishmongers, all of whom were famous for dumping their rotting produce daily into the River Arno. Without thinking, I mentioned this.

'That's offal,' said Sands, and was immediately forbidden to speak again during this assignment.

We picked our way cautiously across the bridge. Roberts was not always in complete control of his handcart, likening it to a supermarket trolley with a wobbly wheel and the central walkway was quite narrow. Normally, progress would be deliberately slow as pedestrians were tempted back and forth across the street by merchants displaying their wares. Today, wisely, the counters were bare and most of the shops were locked and shuttered. Only an idiot would display anything beautiful on today of all days.

Ahead of me, I could hear Peterson in his role as training officer, informing Roberts that this was the origin of the term bankruptcy. When a man could no longer pay his debts, the soldiers would seize the tabletop he would be using to display his wares (banco) and break it (rotta). Hence, bankruptcy. Mr Roberts, intent on not letting his cart sideswipe a group of soberly clad men discussing something or other in serious tones, nodded absently.

We emerged from the bridge into the main part of the city. Peterson guided us to a convenient doorway and we stopped to take it all in.

This was Florence and it was beautiful.

The skyline, dotted with towers and spires like broken teeth was dominated by Brunelleschi's magnificent dome. I was quite surprised that piece of groundbreaking architecture hadn't been one of the first things to go up in flames. Around us, steps led away in mysterious directions; beautifully carved wooden balconies overhung the lower stories; porticos and graceful archways abounded. Shallow roofs were mostly clad in clay roof tiles. Many buildings were of brick or stone, but some were rendered and painted in shades of terracotta, ochre, cream, a gentle yellow or, on this miserable winter's day, a rather dingy white. Wooden shutters covered many windows.

It was a still day. A thick pall of Renaissance smog hung sullenly over the city with no wind to disperse it. Over there, quite nearby, a thick pillar of black smoke rose vertically, carrying the soul of beauty up to heaven. We'd found the Bonfire.

We set off towards it, passing wonderful buildings with perfect proportions. Churches, public buildings, palaces, all decorated with friezes full of life and movement. Some were badly hacked about as the Church

251

unavailingly tried to quash the outpourings of new ideas and new thinking. To reduce beauty and splendour to its lowest common denominator. To ignorance. Dull, dingy, unimaginative, safe ignorance.

The pillar of smoke reminded me why we were here. I pulled myself together. It all happened a long time ago. Yes, Savonarola put the brakes on for a while, but in the end, there was no holding progress. The Renaissance was followed by the Age of Reason as slowly but surely, people emerged from the dark clutches of religious fanaticism.

I've never visited Florence, although I certainly will one day, so the size of the Piazza Della Signoria came as a bit of a shock. It was far bigger than I expected. This was the site of public feasts and tournaments. And bonfires, of course.

I could see it from where I stood behind my menfolk. My heart sank. This wasn't just a pile of junk, haphazardly heaped up in the middle of the square and torched. They'd done this properly. A great tongue of wood, about three feet high and six feet wide, jutted some way out into the centre of the square, culminating in the giant Bonfire several times the size of a man. A heat haze shimmered around it, even on this cool February day. Red and orange flames were the only colour in this drab town and just in case anyone was in any doubt over who was responsible, an enormous crucifix presided over the scene.

All along the long, wooden platform, a team of ten or twelve pious-faced monks passed treasures from hand to hand until, at the end, a huge, sweating man, stripped to the waist, unceremoniously hurled them into the heart of the blaze. Such was the intense heat that they flared only briefly and then were gone forever.

Another group of monks, also clutching a crucifix, stood as close to the flames as they could safely get and alternately prayed and chanted, presumably to prevent pious citizens being contaminated by any fumes or smoke emanating from these soul-imperilling vanities.

Standing on tiptoe behind Sands, I could see framed canvases, small items of furniture, bolts of cloth, and many other unidentifiable objects making their sad way along the platform to the bonfire.

I looked around. It was heartbreaking. Who knew what was being destroyed. Pictures, literature, statues, all going up in smoke because some monk was going too far. And books. Beautiful books, full of knowledge and beauty and ideas. All lost, thanks to a mad monk who, in the end, became a little too mad even for the church he served.

Groups of people, all men, stood watching and talking in subdued tones. Soldiers stood sullenly outside the Palazzo Vecchio. Whether they disapproved of the goings on or whether it was just traditional soldier sullenness, I had no idea.

All the time, more and more treasures, some quite large, were being heaved into the square by sweating men, and passed on to the monks for destruction. I was conscious of a sudden need to hurry. Any one of those pictures might be a Botticelli. They could be burning now as I stood uselessly, condemning actions I could not prevent.

As discreetly as I could, I looked around for the man himself, Girolamo Savonarola. I could not believe he wouldn't be here somewhere. Unless, of course, he was out directing operations elsewhere, urging his followers on to greater and greater efforts of destruction.

No, he was over there. I saw Peterson nudge Sands and nod over to the right. A black-clad figure stood close to the bonfire, but a little apart from everyone, his hands thrust into the sleeves of his robe. A large wooden cross hung around his neck. His nose was prominent and his fleshy lips contrasted with sharp cheekbones in a face made sallow by abstinence. The face of a fanatic. I suspected he stood alone not through choice but from fear. Those who passed by showed deference to him and hurried on as quickly as they could. With the cruel irony so beloved by Fate, I rather thought he was standing on the exact spot on which his own bonfire would burn. In just twelve months' time, his own pillar of smoke would rise towards the heavens. I wondered what sort of reception he would get when he arrived.

However, I had a day's pay to earn.

It was very obvious that anything that got as far as the chain of monks on the wooden tongue was doomed. There was no escaping the bonfire's flames.

'Right,' I said, quietly. 'The team from Number Five is to take the cart and try to intercept any artefacts before they make it as far as the square. Offer to relieve men of their burdens. Follow them for a few paces and then peel away. Do it quietly, discreetly, and above all, safely. Pay particular attention to any canvases or panels you come across. My team will head out and try to track down Botticelli himself, to see if we can't acquire the paintings at source. We will stay in our teams and keep our coms open. There doesn't seem to be any violence anywhere, but I'm sure we'll encounter street gangs, looters, and fanatics as well as ordinary citizens. Good luck, everyone.'

We split up. Peterson's team wheeled away and the rest of us left the square and headed towards the Duomo.

The rest of us had had to undergo one of Dr Dowson's crash courses in linguistics, but Mr Sands already had beautiful Italian and very passable Latin and was able to make himself understood with little difficulty. He stopped two men, both hugging their warm russet cloaks tightly around themselves against the chill. I noticed a slightly darker area around the hems from where the fur trim had been removed. They wore plain, close-fitting hats, pulled down low over their foreheads. Mr Sands enquired, very civilly for the house of Sandro Botticelli or, giving him his real name, Alessandro di Mariano Filipepi. With the type of luck rarely encountered at St Mary's, both men instantly turned and gestured behind them. A torrent of Italian followed, but, as with most people, they unconsciously mimed their directions as they spoke, angling their arms right, left, and straight on in a way that even we could follow.

With even more luck, it wasn't far. Botticelli lived in the maze of tiny streets between the Duomo and the massive building site that would one day be the Palazzo Strozzi, in the Street of the Five Fountains. I don't know why it was called that. When we arrived, there wasn't a fountain to be seen. It was probably named by an ancestor of those idiot town planners who strew the landscape with the ugliest urban housing estates conceivable, then name them Green Pastures or The Orchard or Cherry Blossom, and name all the roads after trees that will never grow there. If I ever retire, I'm going to buy a house in the centre of town somewhere and name it Sea View, just to give people something to worry about.

We picked our way around dirty puddles, following the directions we'd been given. Far from being the bustling centre of commerce I had expected, the streets were very quiet, with doors and shutters firmly closed. This could be the easiest salvage operation we'd ever undertaken.

I could smell wet plaster, wet stone, wet straw, woodsmoke, horse droppings, and wet clothes. A fine rain hung in the air, leaving glistening drops on our clothing. Somewhere to my right, I could hear the odd mournful drip as water trickled down into an old barrel.

The ground floor apartments were all given over to shops, but an anonymous green door opening off the street led into a small courtyard. We paused and looked around. This had once been a garden. Beautiful glazed pots stood against the walls but now were cracked, crumbling, and contained only dead bushes and weeds. A broken wooden bench had been overturned and lay forlornly on its side. Perhaps even gardens were considered sinful.

Sands indicated upwards, so we turned left and climbed a flight of outside steps, walked around a narrow gallery, and there it was. We stopped at the end of the gallery. A pair of double doors confronted us. Sands thumped on the door with his gloved fist, but there was no reply. He banged again. The sound was very loud in this quiet place. No one flung open a door or window and demanded to know what was going on. We checked around. Nothing and no one.

Sands took a deep breath and banged at the door again. 'Master Botticelli? Sir, could you open the door, please?'

There was a long silence. I was about to suggest pushing on this door too, on the off chance it might be open, when we heard the sound of slow footsteps, dragging their way across a wooden floor.

A thick voice, barely audible informed us that yes, yes, he was coming and to hold our water, for the Lord's sake.

Clerk and Sands exchanged a glance. 'Bet you anything you like he's as pissed as a newt,' whispered Sands.

'Surely not,' said Clerk. 'That's the sort of thing that would really lead to trouble with the Church. Especially today of all days.'

I said nothing. He was an artist and today he was surrendering his work for destruction and no matter how much he was under the spell of Girolamo Savonarola, parting with his paintings, his own creations, couldn't possibly be easy for him. I could imagine him needing something from a bottle to help him on the way.

On the other side of the door, a metal bolt was drawn back, and eventually, the door opened.

And there he was.

14

We all have our illusions. Whether consciously or not, we all have pictures in our heads. People, places, events, we see these things in our mind's eye and carry these images with us throughout our lives.

I don't know why, but given the ethereal nature of his paintings, somehow I'd expected an aesthetic, modestly dressed man with penetrating eyes that looked at the world and saw what others could not, and whose long, slender fingers would translate that vision into the wonderful, luminous paintings for which he was so famous.

The dishevelled figure leaning against the doorframe and breathing great gusts of wine fumes all over us was about as far from my imagined picture as it was possible to get.

For a start, he wasn't tall and slender. He wasn't even stocky. Leon was stocky. Botticelli was, in fact, built like a barrel, with a deep, wide chest and broad shoulders. Perhaps that must be how he earned his nickname, 'Botticelli'. Little Barrels. He wasn't much taller than me and I'm definitely not tall.

His heavily lidded hazel eyes were made even heavier by the enormous amount of alcohol he'd obviously consumed. Empty flagons rolled around the wooden floor and the smell of stale wine was almost pungent enough to overcome the ever-present odours of linseed oil, turpentine, walnut oil, fresh wood, paint, old food, and the world's worst body odour.

Nobody recoiled. I was proud of them.

We stared at him. I don't think anyone could think of anything to say. The silence rolled on.

'Well,' he said eventually, slurring his words so badly that I could hardly make them out. 'What are you waiting for? They're over there.'

For a moment, none of us moved. I couldn't believe it. He was going to give them to us. He was going to give us his paintings. We didn't have to lie, or club him over the head, or trick him – or even ask him. He was actually going to give us his paintings!

He gestured backwards with his head, which was a bit of a mistake because he overbalanced and started to topple. It was like watching a tree fall. He didn't bend at all. Sands and Peterson leaped forwards, steadied him, and walked him backwards into his studio. I followed them in and closed the door behind us.

'Over here,' grunted Clerk, and they deposited him in the nearest chair, an ornate wooden affair with arms, currently serving as a model's throne. A bolt of dark red satin frothed at his feet, making him look like the Demon King.

I left them to minister to him, stepped behind him where he couldn't see me, and activated my recorder. I wanted to get all of this. I paint – a little – when I can, and I would never, ever again have an opportunity to study the

260

studio and working methods of one of the greatest painters of all time.

We were standing in a big, square room. The only windows looked north out over the courtyard. A number of ornate wooden easels stood nearby. Disappointingly, all were empty.

On the opposite wall, a long, paint-stained table was covered in paint-making equipment, dry pigments, mortars and pestles, palettes, brushes, odd pieces of panel, paint-covered rags, plates of stale food, and even more empty flagons. Yes, an artist definitely lived here.

Two doors led off this room. One appeared to be a storeroom of some kind and through the other door, half open, I could see a couch with blankets. Clothes littered the floor. One boot was propping the door open.

Over in the corner, four comfortable chairs stood on an exquisite carpet. Small tables were within easy reach. This would be where he entertained his clients, to discuss commissions, or possibly for them to watch the progress of his latest work.

This place would normally be full of people with apprentices and assistants scurrying around preparing panels and paint. Tempera doesn't keep overnight, and Botticelli's technique was to apply layer after layer of luminescent paint. He would need a small army of apprentices to keep up with him. Friends would drop in and out on an hourly basis. Fellow artists would do the same, come to snoop, to criticise, to pinch ideas, to drink ... The room would be noisy and lively, and in the middle of it all, like a king in his court, the artist himself, holding forth, demonstrating his skills.

Never again. Those days were done for this man. For him, nothing would ever be the same after today. He would produce a little more work, but the glory days were gone. When they burned his paintings, even though they did it with his blessing, a large part of him would go with them.

Speaking of paintings ...

I panned discreetly around the room. He'd said they were ready for collection and they were, propped against the fourth wall, three of them, covered in old cloths.

Heart beating, I handed the recorder to Mr Sands, stepped over, and twitched the first cover aside.

I stared and stared. I don't know what I'd been expecting. Given his fascination with the Madonna and the number of paintings on that subject, I suppose I'd thought it would be something along those lines. Or maybe another 'Portrait of a Young Lady' which was Botticelli-speak for another portrait of Simonetta Vespucci, his lost love, dead these many years. But no, of course it wouldn't be. There would be no reason for those to be destroyed. He'd painted his other passion – Greek and Roman mythology.

I gazed at the first painting, drinking it in. The subject was easily recognisable. The Judgement of Paris. The moment when Paris awards the golden apple to Aphrodite and supposedly kick-starts the Trojan Wars.

Three goddesses, naked apart from the usual useless wisp of material draped over one arm, parade themselves before him. Athena, remote and reluctant, stares vaguely out of the picture, her mind obviously elsewhere. Hera stands in the middle, a little older than the others and possibly trying too hard because of it. And there, off to one side, carefully framed by arching trees, stands Aphrodite, effortless, glorious, with translucent skin and long, light hair. She is smiling at Paris and that smile will secure the fall of Troy.

Paris is dark and muscular. He too is naked, but for some reason, even though he's depicted as a shepherd, he's wearing a metal helmet with a red horsehair crest. He is holding the golden apple high. The moment of judgement is seconds away. In the background stand a couple of very bored-looking sheep, who, not surprisingly, have no idea of the significance of the occasion.

I uncovered the next picture.

Paris and Helen.

Whew! I could see why this one might be banned, even without Savonarola. Two figures are in a garden, late in the evening. The light is fading and the picture is full of shadows and mystery. Paris is leaning over a reclining Helen and it's very apparent what both of them have in mind. Between them, they're wearing about six square inches of material. The impression given is that no sooner has the viewer moved away than they will fall on each other. A tiny part of my mind wondered whether he would take off his helmet. Sensuality just oozed from the image. He'd painted the promise of sex. The background was full of trees with their limbs twisted erotically around each other and everywhere you looked, there was rounded, gleaming flesh.

'Wow,' said Clerk, unable to drag his eyes away.

The third portrayed the death of Paris.

He lies, sprawled and broken with his head in Helen's lap. It's unclear how he died – there's not a mark on him. I suspect Botticelli didn't want to mar the perfection of his body. Helen is wearing (barely) something white and diaphanous with intricate draping, beautifully painted. Her head is bowed in grief. We cannot see her face. A heavily built Menelaus (I assume it's him because he'd been painted with red hair and in the Middle Ages, it was a popular belief that the devil had red hair) leans threateningly over Paris's fallen body towards Helen. The three figures form a perfect triangle. It's a masterpiece of composition.

I stepped back and contemplated these three pictures. I could have looked at them all afternoon. For the rest of my life even, but time was short. I felt a rage that these could have been lost. Burned in the Bonfire of the Vanities. That would not happen. Not while there was still breath in my body. I was determined we would save them.

But how? They were huge. Why the bloody hell couldn't he have painted small, intimate pictures that we could just shove down the front of our tunics and run like hell. We were fortunate, however, that they weren't the biggest things he'd ever done *The Primavera* was seven feet by ten feet for God's sake. These weren't that big, but there was no way we could conceal any of them. The best thing would be to get them on the cart, and back to the pods as quickly as possible.

I issued a series of quiet instructions and for the next few minutes, we were very busy.

All this time, the artist hadn't moved. He slumped in his chair, unmoving. I couldn't tell if it was despair or resignation. I sought in my head for something to say to him. Some word of hope, but there was nothing. He would never paint anything miraculous again. There would be a few nativity scenes, but the spark was gone, and the strict rules laid down by the church as to how religious subjects were to be portrayed wouldn't help, either. He would sit on a committee to discuss, I think, the positioning of Michelangelo's David, but he would die, early in the next century, in conditions of great distress and poverty, having been unable to recapture his former brilliance. Still, he never painted lewd or lascivious subjects again, so that was all right, then.

Sands and Clerk were manhandling the last piece of panel out of the door. I could hear them cursing as they struggled down the stairs, and believe me, when historians curse, they don't mess about. There was the sound of voices as Peterson and his gang turned up, and they began to load the cart.

I should go.

I walked back to the still unmoving figure. His eyes had the familiar blind look of one in great emotional distress. I hadn't noticed the wooden crucifix hanging on a chain around his neck. He clutched it with one hand, as one clutching a lifeline. Given that the other hand still had a grip on his flagon, he seemed to have all bases covered.

I did what I could.

'Sir, these paintings are going to a better place.'

Silence. Apart from water, dripping somewhere.

'Sir …'

It was useless. I don't think he was hearing me and I couldn't say any more. If he bounded from his chair now, miraculously restored and seized a brush then I'd be changing History and then we'd all be in trouble and my Italian was nowhere near good enough for this anyway. I should leave well alone and just go.

I walked over to the table and began to pick up flagons, looking for one that wasn't empty. The least I could do for him was cushion this day with alcohol. I found two that were about half-full. I did remember to unstopper them and sniff the contents. I didn't want him chugging back turpentine. I moved a small table within his reach and placed the flagons upon it.

He still hadn't moved. I looked around. After we'd moved all that stuff out, the room was nearly empty. Like his life.

I crouched again and placed one hand over his cold one. Someone else with hands as cold as mine.

He jumped a little at the touch and, for the first time, looked at me properly.

'Simonetta?'

'No,' I said, very gently. 'Simonetta is dead. Remember?'

He nodded. A solitary tear ran down his cheek. He had nothing left.

I hated to leave him, but Peterson was yammering away in my ear. It was time to go.

'Go,' I said to Peterson. 'I'll catch up with you.'

At the door, I took one last look back. He hadn't even reached for the flagons. I wondered if he was actually ill. The oil paints of the time were full of mercury, arsenic, and lead. Were his own paints poisoning him? No, not likely. As far as I could remember, he didn't use oil paints that much; tempera on board was his favourite medium.

I could have cried for him. What could he have gone on to achieve? What had the world lost today?

I retreated out of the door, leaving him to his sad, empty world, and clattered off down the wooden staircase.

We were just manhandling the cart back into the street when we heard voices approaching. Of course we did. Everything had been far too easy up until now. These would be the real men despatched to pick up these paintings. These were the men he'd been waiting for.

I looked at my teams; Peterson, Roberts, and Prentiss with their cart stacked high with three big, very carefully wrapped panels. I signalled to Sands and Clerk, also similarly burdened, to step back into the courtyard. It would be a disaster if all of us were arrested. They melted away.

'Go,' I said to Peterson. 'Head back towards the square. You know what to do.'

He nodded. 'For God's sake, Max. Try and stay out of trouble.'

'Not a problem. We'll take a different route back to the pod and see you there. Now go. Quickly.'

They heaved the cart into motion and set off down the street, rattling over the cobbles. Someone in the crowd shouted after them. Following instructions, they increased their speed and the crowd set off after the cart.

'Will they be all right?' enquired Clerk, anxiously, as he and Sands emerged back into the street.

'Of course,' I said with confidence. 'To all intents and purposes, they're just a bunch of concerned citizens conveying frivolous items to the Bonfire. How commendable.'

'And what happens when they don't stop at the Bonfire?'

'Peterson will think of something,' I said with slightly less confidence. Although he probably would. Think of something, I mean. 'Right, you two. You know what to do if we get separated?'

'Get back to the pod. Avoid the square. Stay out of trouble.'

'Three simple instructions even we should have no trouble carrying out,' I said, because I never learn. 'Avanti!'

Mr Sands winced.

'What?' I said.

He shifted his load for a better grip. 'Nothing. Hey, toc-toc.'

'What?'

'It's Italian for knock-knock.'

'What?'

'No,' he said, in exasperation. 'Concentrate, Max. You never get this bit right, do you? You don't say, "What", you say, "Who's there?" Honestly, how many times have we been over this?'

I closed my eyes and when I opened them again, the two of them were just turning the corner at the end of the street. I picked up my skirts and trotted after them.

We were fine for nearly three streets. Then we weren't.

On the face of it, they were just a bunch of kids and they too were collecting stuff for the Bonfire. Small items. One or two of them clutched pots. One had a small bundle of material. Most were aged between about eight and fourteen. Only three or four of them were older boys.

Heads turned as we approached.

'Keep going,' I said. 'Don't catch anyone's eye.'

'Max ...'

'We discussed this. Back to the pod, gentlemen.'

'What are you going to do?'

'Watch your backs. Go.'

They went.

I paused, just to keep an eye on the kids and make sure no one followed.

As I said before, these were not nice children. They were encouraged to spy on their parents and all those around them. All of Florence lived in an atmosphere of fear and betrayal. Like the witch trials. And communism in America. Accuse before you yourself are accused. The church had enlisted their help and they'd been very useful, but at the end of the day, I told myself, these were just kids. With the attention span of an historian.

I recognised a familiar scene. A little girl stood with her back against the wall surrounded by a mob of shouting children. At least they were still shouting. It's when they go quiet that the trouble really starts. Every now and then one of them would dart forwards and slap her or pull at her clothing. She was aged about eleven. She stood defiantly, but every now and then, a tear tracked through the dirt on her cheeks.

We all looked at each other.

I should have followed on after Clerk and Sands. That few minutes start would be all they needed and this was nothing to do with me. Just a bit of childhood bullying. It happens to everyone. A child's world is divided between the bullies and the bullied. This was the moment when I should have left and I would have, but just as I turned away, someone twitched off her dirty linen hood and a great quantity of matted red hair tumbled to her shoulders.

I stopped. Without warning, I was back in the school playground.

I was alone, as usual, standing in the angle between the music room and the main building. I was leaning against the wall, and, just for once, not doing any harm to anyone, when Georgia Woods and her cohorts found me. They were big girls, two or three years ahead of me and I thought, initially, they were on their way to ruin someone else's day, but no, today was my turn. It is the unerring instinct of the pack to pick on the weakest, but they got it wrong that day.

They started on about my hair. All right, yes, sometimes it looks as if I've been in the European Wind Tunnel, but those were the days of Big Hair and I'd seen worse. Apparently, it was the colour that was ruining their day.

I stared at them with silent contempt and turned away. I already had detentions stretching into the next century, and some instinct was warning me my behaviour would not be tolerated forever.

Meanwhile, according to this gaggle of teenage Barbies, only stupid people have red hair. Only evil people have red hair. Judas Iscariot had red hair.

I said good for him. I'd always been a fan.

They replied that red-haired people were descended from Satan.

I replied that in that case so were Elizabeth Tudor, Titian, Mary Stuart, Henry VIII, Barbara Villiers, Nell Gwynne, Matisse, Emma Hamilton, General Custer, and Christopher Columbus.

Their blank faces indicated they hadn't heard of any of these. I wasn't surprised. Non-redheads lack brain cells. I might have mentioned that to them.

Out came the scissors and I realised this was planned. They hadn't just been causally wandering past. I was going to have an impromptu haircut, and whereas other people might have proper parents who would descend upon the school in an avalanche of righteous wrath and demand retribution for this sort of thing – I hadn't. I was on my own and they knew it.

I stopped leaning against the wall and slowly straightened up, moving into fighting mode and summing up the opposition. There were four of them, but one was definitely unwilling. She hung back and didn't want to be involved at all. One was fairly unwilling – she would only join in when there was no danger to herself. One was the leader – she might not want to get involved personally – but the last one was her enforcer – a big girl who would make two of me and who played hockey with all the brutal fervour of one who intends to play for the county one day and won't let anyone or anything get in her way.

I reviewed my own resources. On the plus side, I had a lot of hair. On the debit side, I had the muscle tone of lettuce.

They closed in and things might have gone badly – although for whom, we'll never know – because a prefect turned up.

Five minutes and quite a lot of shouting later, we were all in front of Mrs De Winter, the Head Teacher. She didn't usually deal with disciplinary issues, so I knew I was in trouble this time. I assumed my traditional expression of sullen disinterest and stared out of the window. She was surprisingly brief and they all filed out, encumbered with detentions. I went to leave as well, but she stopped me.

'Sit down, please.'

This was a new departure. Warily, I sat.

She looked at me for a long time. 'I can help you.'

I gestured at the door, which had just closed behind Barbie and her bullies. 'I can look after myself.'

'That wasn't what I was talking about.'

I sat very quietly, not moving a muscle. As do small animals when confronted by some unknown peril.

The silence went on. The bell for the next lesson rang and we both ignored it. A little voice inside my head said, 'This is important. Don't screw it up.'

We looked at each other. Something was about to happen. I was about to have the most important moment of my entire life. The one that changed everything. The one that set me on the path to St Mary's. When someone told me I had worth.

However – the point I'm taking so long to make – is that from the beginning of time there's always been a worldwide prejudice against red heads.

'Better dead than red,' they would shout at school. To which I would reply:

'Blondes will cry.
Brunettes will pooh.

But here is what a redhead will do.'

Usually just prior to smacking them one. Now, in another time and another place, here was some other kid on the receiving end.

We need to be clear on this. I don't like children. There isn't an orifice that doesn't exude something unpleasant. Sometimes, all of them exude simultaneously. And this was not a waif-like elf with huge, appealing eyes. She was small because she was malnourished, and a waterfall of yellow snot bubbled from one nostril to solidify in the crease above her top lip. Occasionally, she licked it. I am continually astonished that people actually choose to have children! To be honest, if she hadn't been small and ginger, I would probably have walked straight on. But she was ...

I weighed up the opposition. They were only kids, after all and children always do what adults tell them to do.

You can tell I'm not a parent.

I was only a couple of hundred yards from the pods. Just a quick sprint over the Ponte Vecchio and straight to San Spirito. No problemo.

I shouldered my way through the crowd, picked up her hood and handed it back, making sure I stood between them and her. A narrow alleyway opened up a few feet to her left. I took her hand, barged through the kids that didn't get out of the way quickly enough, led her to it, said, 'Go home,' and watched her run away.

Her footsteps echoed for a while and then she was gone. I should have followed her then. I should have got out of there while I could.

I turned back, all ready to make myself scarce, and it was too late. Children had closed in around me. The silence had a sinister quality. I felt a sudden moment of fear and pushed it aside. These were kids, for God's sake. What could they do to me?

Quite a lot – as I was about to find out.

I had a choice. If I called for help, both teams would drop everything and come to pull me out and we'd lose everything. We couldn't do that. Apart from the fact that the future of St Mary's was riding on this, I couldn't, just couldn't, abandon those paintings to the mob of religious bigots and bullies that comprised Florentine citizenry on this day.

A voice spoke in my ear. Peterson.

'Max, they've got the cart. We couldn't outrun them.'

I could hear raised voices and the sounds of a scuffle.

There was nothing anyone could do.

'We planned for this. Let them have what they want. Walk away. No one gets hurt. Just walk away. Sands and Clerk are just ahead of me. Find them and get back to the pods.'

'Copy that.'

I stuck my chin in the air and prepared to shoulder my way out and chase after the others. Back to safety. But suddenly, all the little kids were in a ring around me and everyone was ominously quiet.

I still wasn't that scared. What could they do to me? They were children. Some of them barely reached my waist.

Whenever I look back at this, I wonder if it wasn't History trying to teach me a lesson. Not to interfere. Don't get involved. We're always being told: don't get involved. There's always a price to pay and usually it's a life. Do what you have to do and get out. That little girl had been in no desperate peril, but suddenly, I was. Because – and what were the odds of this happening – as I eased my way along the slimy, wet wall, trying to get past them, my coif caught on something – a nail, maybe – and as I moved away, the stupid thing fell off. I made a grab for it, but too late. A gasp went up. More red hair. They probably thought they were being overrun by Satan's minions.

Something caught me on the arm and I couldn't think what it was until another stone whizzed past my face. I barely had time to jerk my head out of the way.

I said, indignantly, 'Ow!' because I still had no idea how much trouble I was in. I backed myself hard against the wall for support and protection. Not the best move because now I was really trapped, but there were now so many of them that there was no other direction in which to go.

I don't know why I didn't call for help there and then. I think part of me couldn't believe this was serious. They were children, for God's sake, throwing a few stones. Someone would open a window and yell at them, they'd all run away laughing. I'd rub my arm, curse a bit, and get back to the pods.

More stones clattered around me. Some of the ones thrown by the smaller children never made it as far as me, but the older ones had found their range. A lucky shot hit my knee in exactly the wrong spot and a sharp stabbing pain ripped through my leg. I felt it buckle beneath me and how it really was serious. I wouldn't be running anywhere anytime soon. Time to get help.

I fumbled with my com and whispered. 'This is Maxwell. Code Red. Code ...'

I felt stones rain down on my head, my shoulders. They weren't large rocks. People don't sling boulders because it only takes two or three of those and then you're unconscious, which is no fun at all. You have to suffer first. It's probably good for the soul; so they threw smaller stones – pebbles found in the street. Which was a bit of a bugger because that meant there was an unlimited supply and they wouldn't be running out of ammo anytime soon.

I tried again. 'Man down. Behind the Villa Strozzi.'

Some of these pebbles had sharp edges but fortunately for me, the thick brown dress I was wearing offered a certain amount of protection. I made make myself as small as possible and hoped for rescue because there was no way out. Nowhere to run to and, in my case, no left leg to run with. There were far too many of them to engage. Yes, I had a stun gun, but even I recoiled at the thought of tasering a bunch of kids – nasty little buggers though they were. I needed to keep as much distance as possible. Deep down, I think I was still hoping they weren't that serious. Just a bit of a stoning, just to teach me a lesson and then everyone goes merrily on their way. To church, probably, for their reward. Even deeper down, I knew I was kidding myself. I wasn't going to get out of this without help.

Not everyone was throwing stones, but everyone was urging them on, baying for my blood, cheering the hits. The sound of high-pitched, childish voices was terrifying. There was no mercy to be shown here.

Only the wall was holding me up. I told myself I had

to stay on my feet because once I was on the ground, they would close in, and then things would really become unpleasant.

Vaguely I could hear someone talking in my ear, but my knee was throbbing so much that I was sick with the pain of it. My head swam. My knee would no longer hold my weight. Like a voice from the past, I could hear Helen saying, 'I told you that knee of yours would let you down one day.' On the other hand, it seemed unlikely I would live long enough to regret not getting it fixed. There's always a bright side if you take the time and trouble to look.

I had what seemed a good idea at the time, and bent to pick up a stone myself. After all, there were plenty of them around – and threw it back. Yes, I know, but I think I've already said I'm not fond of kids, especially this bunch of 15th-century ASBO contenders encircling me. I blame the parents. And I didn't throw it hard – more a kind of gentle toss, really, but someone out there took exception. You're not supposed to fight back.

Something hard slammed into the side of my face. My head jerked round and I lost my earpiece. My vision blurred. The world tilted. I was falling. My face scraped down the rough wall. I scrabbled for some sort of handhold to keep me on my feet. I tried to cover my head. My knee was on fire. Probably more seriously, there was that deep internal pain that tells you that things inside are not as they should be. There was blood every-where and it was mine. It ran down into my eyes, blinding me.

I heard a man's voice. With my luck, this would be the

parents turning up to yell at me for chucking stones at their innocent children, because they were good kids really, and the whole thing was just an unfortunate situation that got out of hand. I became aware that someone was shouting in my face. Nothing new there, then.

A familiar voice cut through the hubbub.

'Get behind me.'

He pushed me roughly behind him but despite all my best efforts, my legs just wouldn't hold me up any longer. I began to slither down the wall and as I did so, my elbow caught on a kind of latch. There was a click and something behind me gave way. I fell backwards and grabbed instinctively at the figure in front of me, which did no good at all, because I fell heavily onto a cold, stone floor and jarring my knee quite badly, and whoever it was landed on top of me, because, of course, I just wasn't damaged enough, was I?

I think everyone on the street was just as surprised as me. One moment we were there and the next minute – we weren't.

Their astonishment gave him just enough time to stagger painfully to his feet, slam the door closed, and fumble the bar into place. We were safe. Relatively speaking.

Blearily, I tried to lift my head and focus. Someone knelt beside me. It *was* Leon and he too, looked bloody and bruised. St Mary's was taking a real battering today. We seemed to be in some sort of small storeroom. The warm smell of spices enveloped me. It would have been rather pleasant just to drift away, but I could hear the mob outside, pounding at the door. This was just a temporary respite.

I tried to say hello but it didn't come out that way at all.

I tried to focus on something – anything – but I really couldn't see that clearly. Well enough, however, to see that other than the door, there was no way out.

The blinding light above my head resolved itself into a skylight. He pulled over a barrel and climbed up, but it was way above his head. He might be able to pull himself up, but there was no chance for me and it was only a matter of time before those outside discovered they could get in that way. We'd bought ourselves a few minutes, nothing more.

He jumped down and came to kneel beside me.

Catching his sleeve, I said thickly, 'You. Go.'

'No.'

'Leon …'

'Not leaving you, Max. Save your breath.'

Sometimes, there's no arguing with him. He gets that note in his voice, that look on his face …

Outside, they were battering away at the door.

He activated his com and said calmly, 'Gentlemen, your urgent assistance is required, please. Can you stand up? No, not you, Peterson. Quick as you can, please. No, not you, Max. You stay there. No, not you, Miss Prentiss. Look – will everyone who isn't the Chief Technical Officer please shut up. Thank you. Peterson, you, Clerk, and Roberts get back here, asap. Yes, same location. Prentiss, you and Mr Sands remain at the pods, please. Prep for the usual hasty getaway. Everyone move now.

No, not you, Max. You just stay where you are.'

I was busy wiping the blood off my face, and when I could see a little better, pulled up my skirts to expose the black and purple melon that had once been my knee.

Bollocks! I wasn't going to be skipping anywhere this afternoon. I hastily pulled down my skirt before he saw it.

He was inspecting the door. Without turning, he said, 'It's your knee, isn't it? How badly does it hurt?'

'Hardly at all,' I said, with a complete absence of accuracy. 'An icepack or two and it will be absolutely fine.'

To this day, I'm still not sure what set him off, but he went up like a rocket. We stood – well, sprawled, in my case – in that dirty, musty storeroom with half of Florence trying to batter its way through the door, and with every chance that rescue would arrive too late, and had a conversation that would change our lives.

Attack is always the best form of defence, so I made sure I opened the batting. 'What are you doing here? You were supposed to remain with the pods.'

'I'm not even going to answer that.'

'But the paintings …'

'Forget about the bloody paintings, will you. Let's talk about why you can't even get from A to B without starting a riot on the way.'

I was righteously incensed. 'This is a search and rescue mission. We were here for those paintings. You should be at the pods now, assisting. Why aren't you at the pods now, assisting?'

'Those paintings are not the most important things in Florence.'

I tried to keep it light. 'Yes they are. Historians are two a penny, but there's only one Botticelli.'

'You are not two a penny. There is only one of you, too. You are not worth less than a splash of paint on a bit of wood.'

Typical techie. They have all the artistic appreciation of people who spend every day hitting metal with a lump hammer.

'You can't say that. Those painting will touch millions of people's lives in a way I never could.'

'You touch people's lives, Max. Not in the millions, but that doesn't make you less valid than a wooden panel. People are always more important than things.'

Unable to stand still, he was prowling around the tiny storeroom, looking for non-existent ways out. 'You mean a lot to me. Why doesn't that mean a lot to you?'

I opened my mouth, but he swept on.

'You still don't get it, do you? Even after all this time. After all that's happened to us. From the moment I met you, when you stood in front of me with that hair and those eyes and that attitude ... You've been wreaking havoc in my life ever since. You dance around the timeline, escaping disaster by a hair's breadth and sometimes not even by that much. You leave a trail of catastrophe and devastation strung out behind you like a comet tail.'

I was so flabbergasted by this injustice that I could hardly speak. Definitely a first there.

I regrouped. 'I don't believe you. You're standing in front of me now, spouting some gibberish about me risking life and limb and you're far worse than I could ever be. Who got himself lost in the Cretaceous? I had to steal a pod to get you out. Who got himself snatched by Clive Ronan and carted off into the future? If it wasn't for me you'd still be naked and tied to a bed.' I stopped to consider that for a moment and then got back on track. 'Who fell in a ditch and was nearly eaten by Nile crocodiles last year? It took three of us to get you out. Who would have had a burning cathedral fall on his stupid head if Markham and I hadn't got the door open?' I raised my voice to be heard over the repeated hammering on the door. 'And now – instead of one of us being stuck in a Florentine cellar, there's two of us stuck in a Florentine cellar. Is there a way out? No, there is not. Are we trapped? Yes, it would appear so. The whole point of this assignment was to recover ...'

I got no further. He seized my shoulders, twisted me round to face him, and kissed me hard. Really hard. It was one of his better efforts – as I might have mentioned when I got my breath back.

He ignored me. 'You just won't be happy until you've driven me completely insane, will you? I'm a reasonable man. I don't ask for much. Just someone who can get through the working day without imperilling herself, or those around her, or the timeline ... Why couldn't you just follow Clerk and Sands back to the pod? And don't give me any of your usual crap about being overtaken by events. You just couldn't walk past, could you? You just couldn't leave well alone?'

I opened my mouth to protest at the injustice of this, but the shouting in the street kicked up a notch and from the way lumps of plaster were falling away from the doorjamb, the whole lot was going to come away any minute now.

Somehow, he had wrapped himself around me and was taking my weight. I leaned back against his solid warmth. I could feel his heart and it was racing away. As was mine. I turned my head to see him better. I would have liked a little longer to savour the moment, but that door was coming down any moment now.

He took my hand and rubbed his thumb over my knuckles. I rested my head back on his shoulder and looked up at the grey light seeping through the grille. Escape – so near and yet so far. I made no further attempt to persuade him to leave. He wouldn't go. I wouldn't have gone either, so I was in no position to criticise.

One of the hinges was working loose. I could hear shouting and the sounds of bodies thudding against the door. We had only a few minutes left before...

'Do you think ...? The thing is ... Would you like to marry me?'

The door trembled, but not anywhere near as much as me. There was a long, long silence.

Because, with those few words, wherever they came from, my life changed forever. Everything stopped dead. Even the hammering on the door seemed to recede. The world just stopped. I stood on the edge. The future was unfamiliar and far more frightening than anything on the other side of that door was. Unexplored territory. Terror Firma.

With a crash, the door latch broke clear of the wall. The doorframe shuddered. Daylight appeared. The whole thing was coming down. We had only seconds left.

'Yes. Yes, I would. Very much.'

'I ... don't know why I said that.'

'I don't care. You asked. I said yes and I'm holding you to it.'

The entire door, frame, hinges, bar, everything, crashed into the storeroom in a shower of dust and debris.

I balanced unsteadily on one leg and pulled out my stun gun.

'This isn't going to be much fun,' he said.

'Don't worry; I won't hurt them too much.'

He moved away a little, to give us both room.

'It's been an honour and a privilege, Max.'

'For me, too.'

Three bulky figures fought their way through the dust, crunching over the broken bricks and plaster. They had scarves tied tightly around their faces and carried heavy wooden staffs. They looked big and mean and they meant business.

The one in front pulled down his scarf and prepared to enjoy the one of the greatest moments of his life.

'Toc-toc!'

I opened my eyes. It didn't make the slightest difference. I couldn't see a thing. I would have panicked but whatever it is that Dr Foster pumps into people on these occasions was doing its job beautifully. There was one thing, however, that was vitally important.

'The paintings? Did we get them?'

Someone said something I couldn't make out. Great. Now I couldn't hear, either.

I tried again, getting cross because no one was answering me.

Something cold slid into my hand.

I must remember to tell Helen to stop doing that.

Finally, I opened my eyes. Some people see angels. I got Peterson. Scarfing down my grapes. I stared at him reproachfully through my one working eye and rearranged my priorities.

'Leon?'

'At Site Two.

'Is anyone else hurt?'

'Not compared with you, no. Just minor bits and pieces.'

I nodded.

'For you, however, a bit more serious. Bruised kidney. You have excitingly coloured wee. Extensive bruising and lacerations. A magnificent black eye. Minor concussion. Helen's had a go at your knee. Shall I go on?'

'No. Bored.'

Silence. I peered Cyclopically at him.

He grinned. 'Do you want me to put you out of your misery?'

'Go on, then.'

He couldn't keep it in. 'We got them, Max. All three of them.'

I was grinning so much it hurt.

'You were right. They followed the cart and we led them a merry dance, I can tell you. They caught us up in the end and had a good poke around, only to find a bunch of not very exciting pots and pans and three blank panels. They confiscated the lot, of course, so we lost the cart. Not quite sure what that will do to the timeline. Let's hope it ended up on the Bonfire at the end of the day.'

He helped himself to the last of my grapes and began poking around the apples.

'Good plan of yours. Clerk and Sands got back to the pod with the real panels, no trouble at all. We got your call. Leon set off at the speed of light. Showing the correct grasp of priorities – and knowing we'd have to answer to you afterwards – we secured the paintings first and followed on behind, only to find you about to be beaten up by a group of small children. I have to say, if you had any street cred before, you certainly don't now.' He looked sideways at me. 'Congratulations, by the way.'

I played dumb. 'What for?'

He looked at me, still going at the apple like a starving rabbit. 'Leon left his com open. We heard every word. You would not believe the huge amounts of money changing hands around this place. I'm taking Helen out to dinner with mine.'

Oh my God. Oh my God. What had I done? I was engaged to be married. 'Does everyone know?'

'Of course. Except for Dr Bairstow.'

'Bet you he does,' I said, displaying possibly slightly more gloom than was appropriate for a recently engaged person.

'Of course he does, but nobody wants to be the person to tell him officially. We'll leave that to the engaged couple. Good luck there. Any idea what he'll say?'

'You have thirty minutes to pack your belongings and be gone' was the most likely option. 'No. Can we talk about something else?'

'Well – back to the paintings. You should have been there. We had a hell of a job getting them through the pod door. It was just like one those spatial awareness tests we give recruits – and as it turned out, we all we all failed that one, but we got them in eventually. Prentiss and Sands stayed put and we all cantered off to your rescue, thoroughly enjoying the in-flight entertainment on the way. Was Leon really once tied naked to a bed? No, don't answer that. Let me live with the image. Tell him that one has passed into St Mary's legend. That'll cheer him up. Anyway, the paintings and everyone else have gone on to Site Two and I brought you back here as quickly as I could.'

He read my mind.

'The entire Security Section is guarding the caves, Max. A mouse couldn't get past them let alone Clive Ronan. Barring natural accidents and disasters, the panels will be fine. Dr Bairstow's talking to Thirsk at this moment. He sends you his regards and has asked me to remind you that you've exceeded your sick-leave limit for this year already and it's only September.'

'I didn't know there was a limit.'

'I think he's imposed one especially for you.'

He bit into his apple again and said indistinctly, 'The thing is, Max ... the thing is ... you're in trouble.'

'What?'

Outraged, I tried to sit up, dislodged something important inside, and fell back on my pillows, coughing and feeling every inch of me protest.

He glanced nervously over his shoulder. 'Shh, for God's sake, or we'll have Hunter in here. Or worse – Helen.'

I said in a painful whisper, 'How can I be in trouble? We've just saved what are about to be the three most famous paintings in History. What more does he want from me? Why is it ...?

He was so agitated that he actually put down the apple.

'No, listen, will you. I don't mean that sort of trouble. Max, he's talking about sending you to Thirsk for three months, minimum. Probably six. Maybe even a year.'

I was bewildered. 'But why?'

'Well, for God's sake, look at you. You've had a rough year. He's offering you a period of light duties. To recover.'

'I can't leave St Mary's for a year. Who would run my

department? I have no senior historians. It would be a disaster.' I tried to sit up. 'I must talk to him.'

He picked up his apple again. 'No, you don't. I have a better idea.'

'You?'

'Yes,' he said defensively. 'And why not? Listen to me. I think we can help each other out here. I don't want you to go to Thirsk, either, but there's no getting around the fact you're not up to factory spec at the moment. Nor are you likely to be for some time. Face it, Max, you've had a shit year. All that stuff with the Time Police. The Battle of St Mary's. Then you were shot. Now this. But I agree that for you to leave even for three months could be a disaster for the History department, so I've had a brilliant idea.'

He finished his apple and bowled the core accurately into the waste bin.

'Howzat!'

It really is quite difficult to keep historians on track, sometimes.

I prompted him. 'Brilliant idea?'

'Ah. Yes. How do you fancy a spot of swinging?'

Now I was baffled. 'What?'

'You know, you chuck your office keys into a hat and I chuck mine, and we swap.'

I tried to pull the bedclothes up to my chin. 'Swap what?'

'Jobs. You take my job. I take yours.'

'No, listen,' he said as I opened my mouth to protest. 'You take my job. Chief Training Officer. There are no trainees at the moment, so it's not particularly onerous, but it will give you the chance to do the thing you're really good at, which is to plan. If you go to Thirsk then I'll have to run both departments, or at least oversee your replacement. I won't have time to do either properly, so the future of my department is at stake as well, so what I'm saying is that you take over the training post. You'll be off the active list for a while so you'll have the time to sit down and devise a completely new training plan. The previous one was far too long and cumbersome. We need to get them out there as soon as possible, Max, and without frightening the shit out of them at the same time. Our dropout rate is unsustainable and I need you to address that. So sit down and come up with something. I'll help. You can pick my brains at any time. In the meantime, I'll take over your department. With your input, I'll plan their upcoming assignments and allocate personnel. We'll work closely together – well, we always do anyway – and everyone's a winner. You have to think about this, Max, otherwise it's Thirsk for you, and you won't know St Mary's when you come back.'

If I came back. Neither of us said it.

Now he was eyeing up the pile of chocolate on my bedside table.

I reached out painfully and stuffed it all under my pillow, out of his reach.

'Tim, this is serious.'

'Yes, I know. It's serious for both of us, but I think we could take this to Dr Bairstow and he'd jump at it. It's the ideal solution.'

'Will you speak to him or will I?'

'I will,' he said. 'I have a modicum of tact and

discretion. If you try to do it, he'll open a branch of St Mary's in Ulan Bator and the two of us will be staffing it until the end of time. He'll be along to see you tomorrow. If we put our heads together now, we can have something to offer him then and with luck, he'll change his mind.'

We talked for the next hour. He took notes on his scratchpad and left it with me when he departed.

I was so unsettled that I actually forgot the chocolate under my pillow, which was discovered the next day by Hunter when she made the bed. Spending the night under my pillow had not done it any good at all. I didn't bother listening, telling her I'd always wondered what Markham saw in her, and relations between us were temporarily severed.

Left to myself, I got to grips with the whole matrimony issue by ignoring it. I pulled out Peterson's scratchpad and spent an hour or so reading through what we'd come up with so far, adding comments and suggestions of my own.

Hunter brought in tea and was so incensed at finding me working that she forgot we weren't speaking and more than made up for lost time. I let her run down and then asked for a data table. She slammed the door behind her.

I don't know what Peterson said to Dr Bairstow, but it appeared to have been successful. He turned up the next day.

'Good afternoon, sir.'

'Dr Maxwell. I believe there is something you wish to say to me.'

My heart slid sideways in panic. How did he know?

Had someone blabbed? Where was Leon when I needed him? Oh yes, a thousand miles and six hundred years away.

I brazened it out. 'Yes, sir. Something very important.'

'Indeed? Then please proceed.'

He was laughing at me – I knew it. However, he'd invited me to proceed, so I did.

I laid out the work I'd done so far on the new training schedule. He took the scratchpad and carefully read it through.

'It's only preliminary thoughts, sir.'

'Yes,' he said thoughtfully. 'You appear to be introducing our trainees to the joys of actual assignments much earlier in the training process than before. Do you feel that is wise?'

'I think, sir, that they should be made aware of the realities of the job quite early on. We don't want to spend a fortune training someone only to have them bottle out on their first assignment. I'll build in safety measures, of course, but if you agree, then that is the direction in which I would wish to proceed.'

He handed me back the scratchpad.

'There are some interesting ideas there, Dr Maxwell. I look forward to seeing what else you and Dr Peterson manage to come up with. Yes, you may proceed. Was there anything else?'

'Not at this moment, sir.'

'Do I assume there will be something else in the near future?'

'Bound to be, sir.'

He gave me one of his enigmatic looks and left the

room. Well, that had been easier than I thought it would be. It was only afterwards that I wondered whether Peterson and I swapping jobs had been what he intended all along. Sometimes I think he quite enjoys being the puppet master.

I recovered surprisingly quickly, but, as Helen said, I wasn't ill. There was just a problem with my knee, which had been repaired. Once I'd recovered from the operation, everything was fine. I was heaved to my feet less than twenty-four hours later. The next day I was on crutches. They chucked me out after three days. I still limped a lot, especially when I wanted sympathy and I couldn't run – yet – but that would come. My urine returned to its previously unexciting hue and I was unleashed back into the world.

They returned from Site Two five days later. Provided I did it sitting down, I was allowed up to watch their return from the gantry. They filed out of their pods, looking grubby and tired, but they'd been successful. You can always tell.

Leon was last out. He closed the ramp behind him, looked up, smiled for me alone, and something inside me eased a little.

We discussed the details later over a bottle of wine. The paintings were safely concealed. Thirsk had been advised. An expedition would set out next year. We were back on track.

Most importantly, Dr Bairstow was, if not in a sunny mood, at least a little less frosty than usual and Leon said that now was the ideal time to break the news of the matrimonial trauma heading his way.

I was less sure but we couldn't put it off forever.

We limped to his office. Well, obviously, I limped, Leon walked normally. Albeit very slowly. I'd had crutches and become so fed up with the jokes (you've never heard unsophisticated humour until you've heard St Mary's apparently unending supply of crutch jokes) that I'd gone to see Professor Rapson and demanded to be upgraded to a stick and please would he make me one.

The result was one lean, mean, made-to-measure walking stick; matte black and with red and orange flames curling around it. I'd wanted a swordstick – who wouldn't? – but he'd said no, he'd had instructions from Dr Bairstow, so I had something similar to David Sands. Stun gun, built-in compass, weighted handle for those blunt-instrument traumas, and a little compartment containing something fiery for the little emergencies life continually tosses my way. I was delighted with it. David Sands had given me a few handy tips on stick wielding and, up until this very moment, I'd been ready for anything.

Now, as we headed for Dr Bairstow's office, I wasn't so sure.

Mrs Partridge waved us straight in.

He looked up as we entered. 'Goodness me. Both of you. To what do I owe this pleasure, I wonder? As it happens, I was just about to send for you. The Chancellor has just telephoned to say the joint Thirsk/Italian expedition has been set for the coming March. She would like to know if anyone from St Mary's would care to join them. She felt it would be appropriate for St Mary's to have a presence. I don't need to tell you what an honour that is. Max, perhaps you could give that some thought, please.'

I nodded.

'So, what can I do for both of you today?'

Leon opened the batting. He had to. I'd forgotten how to speak.

'Sir, Dr Maxwell and I are to be married.'

I wouldn't have put it that bluntly myself. Actually, I'd have sent him an email. From Venezuela. I braced myself. He put down his pen and regarded us with some amusement. 'Who asked whom, I wonder?'

Since Peterson, Prentiss, Sands, Clerk, and Roberts had promised to take that particular piece of information to the grave, we declined to comment.

Leon said carefully, 'If you feel this course of action is inappropriate, then we will, with huge regret, tender our resignations.'

'I'm not sure such a sacrifice will be necessary for any of us, especially given our current perilous staffing levels. I do insist, however, that as senior officers, you continue to live on campus. Is this likely to be a problem?'

'Not for us, sir.'

'Then I shall give some thought to your accommodation arrangements.'

The door opened behind us and Mrs Partridge entered bearing not the traditional tea tray, but champagne and glasses.

How does she know these things?

He stood up. 'I hope you will allow me to offer my

congratulations and best wishes to you both.'

We drank a toast.

'Well,' said Dr Bairstow, accepting a refill, 'that accounts for the bewilderingly large sums of money being distributed around the building. I understand Messrs Markham and Roberts are boasting they have enough to retire on.'

We all smiled politely at the joke and I thought thoughts that would not only considerably shorten the lifespan of Messrs Markham and Roberts, but bypass the need for a retirement fund altogether.

16

I packed up my meagre possessions and moved into Peterson's office. Since it was just down the corridor, this took about ten minutes.

I'd said goodbye to Rosie Lee.

'You'll only be next door,' she said. 'It's not Antarctica.'

'Bet you'll miss me.'

'All bosses are interchangeable. The only difference is how they like their tea.'

'Since you've never made me a cup of tea in your life, how would you know that?'

She informed me that since she'd been overwhelmed by her massive workload from the moment she walked through the door, it was hard to see when she would have found the time to pander to my insatiable desire for the stuff.

I advised her that my abnormal needs were as nothing compared with those of Dr Peterson.

She asked if I was still talking about tea and I left before I dotted her one with her own keyboard.

There was good and bad in this new job.

Peterson's office – no, my office now – had a great view of the lake – good.

It was nearer to Dr Bairstow – bad.

Which meant it was also nearer to Mrs Partridge – even worse.

However, it was further from R & D and the greater the distance from the blast zone, the greater the chances of survival – good.

I'd left Rosie Lee behind – good.

And I'd gained Mrs Shaw – best of all.

She welcomed me with tea and a plate of cakes. Peterson was probably welcomed with a blizzard of paperwork to sign, the pious hope that he would be of a higher standard than her last boss, and a request for three weeks' leave. Starting now.

'Thank you, Mrs Shaw. You do know I may never leave this office again?'

She smiled at me. She was considerably older than Miss Lee, with wavy grey hair and blue eyes. She bustled around the place, round-faced, plump; a quietly spoken grandmother whose only time off was to visit her grandchildren occasionally.

'What do they think you do?'

'Oh, they think I potter about in my little job, or do my knitting, or work in my garden. I always make sure I lose my spectacles whenever I stay with them, just to reinforce the stereotype.' Her eyes twinkled.

'How long have you been here?'

'Almost since the beginning.'

'Did Dr Bairstow recruit you?'

'No, he recruited Mavis – Mrs Enderby – and she recommended me.'

I was surprised. 'Had you known her long?'

'We were in the same underground unit.'

'You fought? Like Mrs Mack? Did you know her, as well?'

'I was only on the front line at the end. When things went bad. Mostly I worked in code breaking and Mavis was in logistics. We didn't know Theresa Mack personally. We knew of her, of course. Especially when the Fascists were forced out of Cardiff. They all poured across the Severn and Mavis and I were in Gloucester at the time. We stood behind the barricades in Westgate, but they were too strong for us. We fell back to the cathedral and made our final stand in College Green. We turned them back, they ran, and it all ended three weeks later at the Battersea Barricades.'

I looked at the quiet, motherly little figure in front of me and reflected, not for the first time, that appearances can be very deceptive.

'And then, you all fought together again at St Mary's, last year.'

She hesitated. 'Except for Miss Lee, of course.'

There was something there, but the phone rang at that moment and I forgot it.

I unpacked my few things, wandered around my new office, got my bearings, sat down at my new desk, fired up the data table, and made a start. It was years since I'd been a trainee and the training procedures hadn't changed much since my day. Now I'd had the go-ahead from the Boss, I intended to ditch the existing programme. I would scrap the whole lot and start again with new ideas and new ways of doing things. Best of all, if I spent my time on this then I wouldn't have to think about the other new and frightening part of my life.

I called up the schedule of upcoming assignments and started sifting through them – looking for the easy stuff – something that wouldn't get trainees killed as soon as they stuck their heads out of the pod.

Mrs Shaw printed out individual assignments for me and I was laying them out on my meetings table when Peterson stuck his head round the door.

'Can I buy you a drink?'

'Do bears shit in the woods?'

We settled ourselves in a quiet corner of the bar and clinked glasses.

'Your very good health, Max.'

'Thank you. Yours too.'

He sat back, sighed, and stretched out his long legs, resting his feet on the coffee table in front of us. He had something to say. I recognised the signs. I sipped my Margarita, sucked the salt off my bottom lip, and waited. Either for him to speak or the room to blur, whichever came first.

'So, Dr Bairstow let you live about this marriage thing?'

'Yes. He seemed amused but calm.'

'I never thought you'd be the first to marry.'

'I never thought I'd marry at all.'

'Will you live away from St Mary's?'

'No. We're to have two adjoining rooms on the west landing. There's a connecting door. Either we have a room each or one's a bedroom and the other a sitting room. I haven't really thought about it.'

'When's the ceremony?'

'Not sure. Soon, I expect.'

'Where's it to be?'

'Um ...'

'Do you have a dress yet?'

'I think I have several.'

'I mean a wedding dress.'

'Not just at the moment.'

He stared at me in exasperation.

I stared back. 'What?'

'Weddings don't just organise themselves, you know.'

'I don't see why not. We don't want anything elaborate.'

'Let me guess. A short ceremony – somewhere – followed by a drink in the bar and then everyone back to work?'

Some instinct warned me not to utter, 'What's wrong with that?'

'Why is this so important?'

'Max, it's your wedding.'

I stared at him. 'This is Kal, isn't it? Kal and Helen have put you up to this. And don't sit there looking pathetic and sorry for yourself because that won't save you. If you choose to hang out with the two most terrifying women in the universe then that's your problem.'

'Three.'

'What?'

'Nothing.' He gestured for two more drinks. 'Have you actually given this any sort of thought at all?

'Well ...'

'I mean, where will the actual ceremony take place?

301

Church? Register Office? Swanky hotel?'

'I do know Leon wants a religious ceremony,' I said, glad to be able to report something positive. 'It means a lot to him and I don't mind, so …'

I tailed off.

'Have you even thought about what you'll wear?'

'Um …'

'Max!'

'Well, not one of those enormous, white puffy dresses, obviously.'

'God, no,' he said. 'You'd look ridiculous, but what about flowers? And the reception?'

'I don't know,' I said, miserably. 'How can anything be so complicated and at the same time so unimportant?'

'Max, you've planned multi-part assignments which have spread over centuries. Millennia, even. Why is planning one small wedding throwing you into such turmoil?'

'I don't know. I always think a wedding is a bit like dying, don't you?'

'No,' he said, carefully. 'No, I don't think that thought has ever occurred to me.'

'Well, it is. It's unpleasant, messy, and complicated, but it's something you have to go through to find out what happens next. It would be nice if I could just wake up and find marriage had happened overnight. While I was asleep.'

'Have you discussed this with Leon?'

'Oh, no. He'd think I don't want to go through with it and that's not true at all. I just wish it was all over with.'

'Look,' he said. 'You need to get to grips with this.

Have the ceremony here – if the Boss doesn't object and why should he? – It would be rather nice to be filing into the chapel for something a bit more cheerful than the usual memorial services. Although possibly not for you, of course. Honestly, Max, the way you're carrying on, you'd think it was one of those medieval trials by ordeal.'

'Well, it is a bit, isn't it? It's a bit like Earl Godwin being accused of murdering the King's brother and saying, "If I am guilty then let this bread choke me", and he took a bite and it choked him and he died.'

He stared at me. 'No it's not. It's nothing like that at all. Will you pull yourself together? I've never seen you so all over the place and remember I once saw you chased by a T-Rex.'

I nodded and chugged back the rest of my drink.

He signalled for another refill.

'Right. List of things to do. Sort out the venue. Speak to Mrs Mack about the catering. I think she'd be delighted to prepare something other than Toad in the Hole or Spotted Dick. Talk to Mrs Enderby who knows clothes better than anyone does. I bet you any money she has half a dozen designs tucked away all ready for you. Don't worry about flowers because Mr Strong will help you out there. Don't worry about invites – I'm assuming you don't have any family to invite?'

'God, no.'

'Tell people they can wear what they please. The men will wear their uniforms because it's the easy option and the girls will probably wear long dresses because they don't get the chance to dress up very often. Don't worry about seating plans and things. When have you ever

303

known St Mary's experience difficulty sitting down for a meal? And that's pretty well it. Sorted.'

'I'm impressed. And I don't have to do a wedding list because we don't want any presents.'

'Ah yes, that reminds me of the second part of my mission.'

'What mission?'

'Nothing,' he said, soothingly. 'No mission at all. Allow me to ply you with more alcohol.'

'Are you plying? I hadn't noticed.'

'You're on your third Margarita and wouldn't notice if Markham and Roberts performed the handkerchief dance, naked, on the coffee table in front of you.'

'No. There aren't enough Margaritas in the world for me to miss that. What do you want?'

'Look, this may be the alcohol talking …'

'That's all right. It's certainly the alcohol listening … What do you want?'

'You.'

I frowned. 'Flattering, but I'm spoken for. Haven't we just been discussing the preliminaries to making it official?'

'No, idiot, I'm here to discuss my gift to you.'

'Tim, there's no need. I don't want …'

'Thermopylae.'

'… to miss that. Are you serious? How did you swing that?'

'You gave up your jump so that we could sort out Markham's ghost so it's only fair. Consider it St Mary's gift to you.'

'And Dr Bairstow said yes? What about my knee?'

'Dr Foster says no running, no jumping, no kneeling – you know the sort of thing. However, so long as you just sit on a rock and record, there shouldn't be a problem.'

'Wow!' A thought struck me. I should be thinking for two now. 'What about Leon?'

'He's not coming.'

'No, I mean what about Leon's gift?'

'Oh, I believe he's getting a new screwdriver.'

'What?'

'Well, some sort of special piece of kit he's been after for some time. The techies are over the moon about it. You do know that if you change your mind the entire Technical Section will kidnap you and forcibly marry you to Leon – like it or not.'

Which reminded me again of this wedding hanging over me like the Sword of Damocles.

'I'm being got rid of, aren't I?'

He looked shifty.

'What's going on?'

He said nothing.

'Oh my God, Kal's coming to organise things, isn't she? Isn't she?'

'Cheer up,' he said, thrusting another Margarita my way. 'It's all academic anyway. You probably won't make it through Thermopylae. Just think about it – being killed by your own wedding present. How bizarre would that be? Even for you.'

'Cheers, Tim.

Leon had clearly announced he would be wearing his uniform and anyone who so wished could do the same.

Lucky devil. All he had to do was have a haircut, not cut himself shaving that morning, and he was done. My preparations, alas, were somewhat more complex. And, as I kept pointing out to an uncaring world, I had my Botticelli report to write, my Thermopylae assignment to prepare for, a whole new training schedule to create, to say nothing of daily and exhausting physiotherapy which, yes, I was going to get around to any day now.

It all fell on stony ground but despite Tim's motivational speech, I just couldn't get any enthusiasm going at all and then Kal arrived from Thirsk and set about organising the universe back into line.

I fled to Thermopylae.

17

We thought we'd hold a briefing for Markham, who was coming with us, which just went to show what we knew, because he ended up briefing us.

I don't think Peterson quite believed his claim that he was familiar with the facts. 'All of them?'

'Of course. The Battle of Thermopylae was required reading.'

'For what?'

He paused and then said evasively, 'For me.'

'In what capacity?'

'During training.'

'It's like pulling teeth,' said Peterson. He fixed Markham with what he probably imagined was a penetrating stare. 'For what were you training?'

Silence. Markham shifted uneasily.

'Hang on a minute, weren't you in the army?'

'How did you know that?'

'You told us, cloth head.'

If, like me, you were sitting well back and watching very carefully, you could just see the flicker of amusement in Markham's eyes.

'Did I?'

'Hold on,' I said. 'Were you studying tactics and

things at – what do they call it – officer school?'

'Not for very long.'

'You surely didn't set fire to that as well?'

'No, of course not,' he said, wounded to the core. 'Not the whole thing. It's a big place, you know.'

'So just a small corner of it?'

'Barely even that. Just a few rooms. Maybe a bit of corridor. There was plenty of building left so I don't know why they made such a fuss.'

'So they chucked you out?'

'Of course not. We all put it down to youthful high spirits.'

'So why did you leave?'

'I was recruited?'

'What? By St Mary's?'

'Of course.'

'Dr Bairstow recruited you?'

'No,' he said, patiently. 'I told you. He recruited Major Guthrie and I came with him. A complete package. But, to drag you back on topic, before all that, we studied assorted battles and Thermopylae was one of them.'

Peterson turned to me. 'It's like discovering a diamond in a compost heap.'

He was indignant. 'You can't call me a compost heap. I'm almost certain that's against rules and regs.'

'He's not calling you a compost heap, idiot. He's calling you a diamond.'

'Oh.' He settled down. 'Well, that's all right, then.'

Peterson settled back and put his feet up. 'Go on then. Give us Thermopylae.'

Markham cleared his throat.

'OK. 480BC. The Persian King, Xerxes, is marching on what is now Greece, intent on making them part of his vast empire. No one's anticipating any real difficulties. Greece is a collection of tiny city-states, whose leaders can't even comfortably be in the same room as each other, let alone form an effective alliance. However, needs must when the devil drives, and the Greeks manage to put aside their differences and assemble their forces. Unfortunately, the Spartans were the only country with any sort of professional troops and as the massive Persian army approaches, they're celebrating some sort of religious festival –'

'The Carneia,' I murmured.

'That's the one. Anyway, because it was a bit of an emergency, Leonidas of Sparta is allowed to take three hundred of his bodyguard to block the pass at Thermopylae. Legend says they knew they were all going to their deaths, so the order was "Sires only". In other words, only Spartans with living sons could fight. So off they set, picking up reinforcements as they went.'

He paused for a glug of tea and to snaffle the last chocolate biscuit from under Peterson's nose.

'I can't remember the names of all the allies and their armies, but they reckon there were about seven thousand of them when they arrived at the Hot Gates. Xerxes, apparently, tried to bribe his way past them and when they laughed at him, he ordered them to hand over their arms. To which the Spartans replied, "Come and get them!"

'Anyway, the Spartans chose their ground well. Cliffs on one side and rough seas on the other. There are three

309

sets of gates, one at each end of the pass, and one in the middle and Leonidas set up camp at the middle one.

'The Persians attack – the battle lasts three days with the Spartans giving a good account of themselves and Xerxes apparently having hissy fits because his magnificent army can't get past. He has huge logistical problems keeping them all fed and watered, *and* he's fretting about his fleet, which is out there somewhere.'

'However ...' said Peterson, unwrapping my emergency packet of Hob Nobs.

'However,' said Markham, helping himself to the top three without even seeming to move, 'they're betrayed by some bloke ...'

'Ephialtes of Trachis,' murmured Peterson,

'Yes, him, and he leads a force around the back and the Persians fall on them from the rear and they all die. An important lesson, they told us, in how a secure position can suddenly become a trap. We had to write essays, draw diagrams, the lot. It was good.

'Anyway, it seems those few days they held the Persians back were just long enough for the Greeks to get their fleet operational and not long enough for any of them actually to fall out and start killing each other, instead of the enemy. The Persians were eventually finished off at the Battle of Platea. Everyone agrees the Spartans were very brave and they made a cracking, but not very accurate, film out of it.'

He busied himself with the biscuits again.

Peterson and I looked at each other.

'Masterful,' said Peterson.

'Yeah,' he said, spraying crumbs all over my office. 'I

310

got good marks.'

'You also got expelled.'

'I told you – I left,' he said with dignity. 'Having received a job offer commensurate with my qualifications and talents ...'

'You mean St Mary's – a place where setting fire to things is actually considered a qualification.'

'That's the one,' he agreed.

It's always the dust that I remember. In my eyes. In my hair. The smell of it. The feel of it making everything gritty to the touch. And it was hot. So hot. A brazen sun hung in a sky from which the heat had leached all colour. An eagle hovered on a thermal, high above our heads.

Huge, forbidding cliffs hugged the coastline, leaving just a narrow passageway barely wide enough for a single chariot to pass through, let alone an army. Rough seas chopped incessantly at this narrow place, throwing spray into the air. In a few days, these waters would run red with blood as bodies and bits of bodies bobbed about in the choppy waters.

We stood above the Pass of Thermopylae in what today is modern Greece. Even from all the way up here, I could see the steaming pools that gave the Hot Gates their name. I could smell the sulphur on the breeze. Just as in Troy, this was a place where the unseen presence of the gods cast long shadows. For the Spartans, these Hot Gates were the gateway to the next world.

Their only weakness was the infamous goat track that ran behind them, impassable to heavy troops or cavalry but easily accessible by foot soldiers. The legend says that the Spartans were caught unawares, but Leonidas was perfectly well aware of its existence and had despatched a thousand Phocians to block their path. With hindsight, this was a mistake. If he had strengthened this force with even a few Spartans, the whole course of the battle might have been different. Unable to spare even a single man, however, he mistakenly placed his faith in the Phocians and kept his own men where he thought they were needed most. His force consisted of his bodyguard; about five thousand other troops, mostly from the Peloponnese; seven hundred men from Thespiae; and about four hundred from Thebes.

The Persians waited on the plain to the west. Leonidas and his men waited at the Gates. The Greek fleet waited on the beach at Euboea, watching to see which way the Persian fleet would turn. Everyone was waiting. And it was August. The heat was blistering, beating down on us like a hammer on an anvil.

I turned west to face the sun.

A huge dust haze on the horizon signalled the position of the Great King and his massive army. Herodotus puts the figure at two point six million; the Greek poet Simonides at nearly four million. Another contemporary estimated about eight hundred thousand. Modern estimates, with their tendency to downplay ancient glories, generally reckon between about a hundred thousand to three hundred thousand. All of them facing seven thousand Greeks. At night, we could see the tiny flecks of light that were the Persian campfires, stretching to the distant horizon. As if all the stars in the heavens had fallen to earth. Reports spoke of rivers being drunk dry. Looking down on that vast force now, it was easy to believe.

We knew there would be a five-day pause, while both armies took stock, surveyed each other, and waited. Xerxes would use the time to send out spies who would report back that the Spartans, famously, were indulging in a little light exercise, oiling their bodies, and combing their hair. Traditional pastimes for an army that boasted it looked forward to battle – warfare was far less strenuous than their regular training regime. Leonidas, of course, had no incentive to attack, but Xerxes, with, at a conservative estimate, a hundred thousand mouths to feed, could not afford to linger. His supply lines must have been perilously long.

We hung camouflage nets around the pod, checked over all our gear, and then ventured forth to search out the best vantage points, settling finally on a small, north facing plateau on the lower slopes of Kallidromus, about a hundred yards from the pod. As things went, it was comparatively rock-free, offered an excellent view of the Middle Gate, and was protected from behind by a small cliff wall.

We could do nothing more, because, as we had known it would, the weather began to change. The wind veered and became stronger. We swallowed even more dust and took refuge inside the pod. Our position was sheltered, but we knew a storm was coming. A big one. Every year, at this time, the notorious Hellespont wind would arrive and this year it was late.

The next day, the wind was gone but there was no relief. An oppressive stillness settled everywhere. The sky was like a bruise. All birds had disappeared. Clouds of choking dust hung in the air. The heat was massive, every movement a huge effort. With the benefit of hindsight, we knew this was, literally, the calm before the storm. We checked again that everything was secure, including ourselves, and waited it out. We could do nothing else. None of us could.

Towards nightfall, a screaming wind – the Hellesponter – came out of nowhere. The storm was spectacular. The sea boiled and crashed down on the narrow path. Foam flew skywards. I could taste salt on my lips, even all the way up here. Lightning split the sky in jagged flashes. Thunder crashed and boomed.

For the Spartans, this was good news. Their flank was safe. No Persian fleet could move in these waters.

The storm lasted the best part of two days. We took refuge in the pod, recorded what we could, and waited.

'It's like *Wuthering Heights*,' said Markham.

We stared at him. 'Which limb had you broken that time?'

'Appendix.'

'Ah.'

On the third day, I awoke from a restless sleep to find that the storm had blown itself out. It was still hot – steam curled from wet rocks as the sun appeared through the clouds, but the air was fresher. And that wasn't the only benefit. Looking across to the bay, we could see pieces of driftwood bobbing about in the always-restless waves.

Over there was a broken mast, still tangled in its own ropes. And another. Sodden sails twisted in the water. Broken oars littered the shoreline. The Persian ships, caught in the storm, would not be assisting Xerxes' land forces at Thermopylae. They hadn't fared well and now Xerxes, who had a huge army to provision, had a problem. He couldn't afford to wait. He must move now.

We watched the Spartans spend what little was left of the day and most of the night making themselves and their weapons ready for battle. We catnapped, waking at the slightest sound.

Just before dawn, the Greek contingent marched forwards to the narrowest point of the path. Men spread themselves between the cliff wall and the sea. They stood easily, leaning on their spears, exchanging the odd word. Waiting.

'Nervous?' asked Peterson.

'I wouldn't think so. This is what they were born to do.'

'Not them, imbecile.'

I paused. Was I?

'Yes. Yes, I am.'

'Me too.'

'Me three,' said Markham. 'Let's not forget there's a lot resting on this.'

'You mean the fate of the western world?'

'No, I mean my own much more important personal fate if I don't get you back safely to Chief Farrell.'

'I wouldn't worry too much,' said Peterson. 'He's known her a long time. His expectations won't be high.'

'Yeah, but I gave my word.'

'I'll be fine,' I said, slightly annoyed. 'We'll all be fine. We're all the way up here. What could go wrong?'

What indeed?

At dawn on the fifth day, a vast, dirty cloud signified the approach of the Persian army. Even on the side of the mountain, we could feel the vibration of thousands and thousands and thousands of approaching feet. It was Xerxes' proud boast that he would cause the land to shake at his approach and he certainly had achieved that. All around us, we could hear small stones tumbling as the tramp of his army dislodged them.

I had all my recorders trained on the Greeks. Peterson was doing the same to the Persians. Markham crouched off to one side, watching out for us. We were all wearing wide-brimmed hats, mottled grey and green fatigues to blend in, boots to prevent snake bites and scorpion stings, sunglasses, and four or five buckets each of sun cream. We could only hope no shepherd stumbled across us.

Below us, a single voice barked a command and there it was, miraculously assembled within seconds – the famous phalanx. Four densely packed ranks of men, stretching from one side of the path to the other. From the cliff to the sea. A mouse couldn't have got past them. There were the crested helmets. There were the scarlet cloaks. There were the infamous bronze Spartan shields with their inverted V. They weighed about thirty pounds each and should a Spartan ever be careless enough to have lost his weapons, he could easily use it to bludgeon a man to death. No Spartan would lose his shield. You came home with it – or on it.

Each man was armed with a spear some eight feet long. Each man carried two swords; the short xiphos – excellent for groin and throat damage; and the kopis, a curved sword used for hacking – heads, limbs, whatever. Each man extended his spear over the shoulder of the man in front. Each man planted his feet in the ground. Each man had implicit faith in his comrades. No man would budge. To me, they looked impregnable.

Until I turned my head to watch the approaching Persians. The ground shook with the majesty of their approach. The tiny Greek army stood firm. What were they thinking at that moment?

Whatever it was, they weren't thinking it for long. The Persians halted and only seconds later, the sky darkened as hail after hail of arrows hissed viciously through the air, bringing sudden death from the skies.

Except that they didn't. Almost contemptuously, the Spartans crouched and raised their big bronze shields and these, together with their helmets were easily able to deflect most of the arrows. A few men fell and were carried away. Their comrades shuffled up to cover the gaps as reinforcements arrived from the rear.

The barrage continued for some minutes until someone must have reported back to Xerxes that he was wasting time, effort, and arrows and it ceased.

Silence fell.

'Are you getting this?' said Peterson, softly, all his attention fixed on the Persians.

'Yes,' I said, all my attention fixed on the Greeks.

'I'm fine too,' said Markham from somewhere vaguely behind us.

317

Trumpets sounded and it was time for the main event. Having failed to soften up the Greeks, Xerxes now sent the Medes to march upon the Greek lines, obviously reckoning ten thousand of them should be more than enough to do the trick.

My equipment was working fine, so I was able to spare them a quick glance. The Medes were good soldiers, well armoured, with dome-shaped helmets and chain mail over brightly coloured tunic and trousers. Good soldiers they might be, but they were outmatched from the start. Their short swords were no match for long Spartan spears and those who did actually manage to reach the Spartan lines found their light wicker shields couldn't turn back the Spartan weapons. They went down in their scores. The Spartans had an effortless rhythm. Stamp, stab, and twist. Stamp, stab, and twist. The Persian front rows fell, dying. Those behind slipped and fell in the gore. There were Persian bodies everywhere, twisted and tangled together in their own blood.

All the time, the sun beat down mercilessly. Xerxes' superior numbers meant he was never short of fresh soldiers and he hurled wave after wave of them into the attack. Leonidas rotated his troops, regularly sending them back for rest and water. Unlike the Great King who had thousands to choose from, he had no spares.

Hours passed in what seemed like minutes and the Persians had made no progress at all. The sun passed its blistering zenith and began to drop in the sky. Now was the time when Xerxes might expect the Greeks to be tiring as they toiled in the endless heat, so he sent in the most dreaded of all his soldiers.

The Immortals.

So named because they all wore blank metal facemasks and one could not possibly be distinguished from another. When one fell, another identical soldier would immediately take his place, apparently unkillable. Hence their nickname – The Immortals.

Leonidas responded by sending his Spartan bodyguard to the front. The fighting was fierce for a while, and then, suddenly overwhelmed, the Spartans turned and ran. The Immortals broke ranks and streamed after them. At a single shouted command, the Spartans turned as one, raised their shields, and the entire Persian front rank, unable to stop, impaled themselves upon their spears. It was over in seconds. The Spartans regrouped.

Wave after wave of Immortals advanced and every time, the Spartans turned them back. The huge numbers of dead and dying began to make it almost impossible for them to reach the Greek lines. The light was fading. Xerxes called it a day.

So did we. We checked over our equipment, pulled out the used tapes, shut everything down for the night, took it all back to the pod, and had something to eat. Markham made the tea while Peterson and I reviewed the tapes, making sure our angles were good. That took half the night. We ate and worked at the same time. Markham was ordered to get his head down because at least one of us should be fresh in the morning.

That night there was another thunderstorm. I listened to the rain drumming on the roof and spared a thought for all the soldiers out there, unable to light a fire, wrapped in their cloaks, trying to keep their weapons dry, watching all that dust around them turn to mud.

'Here's a thought,' said Peterson, raising his voice above the wind and rain. 'How about Markham and me nipping west tomorrow, to catch Ephialtes and the Immortals crossing the River Asopus? We might actually get a glimpse of his face. What do you think?'

'Brilliant idea,' I said, when actually a better phrase would have been, 'Bloody stupid idea, that's just asking for trouble.'

We stumbled from the pod in the pre-dawn gloom, burdened with food, water, more tapes, spares for just about every piece of equipment we possessed, and a first aid kit.

Both camps were already busy. I wondered how much sleep the Greeks had had. Probably not very much, except for the Spartans who were so used to this way of life they could probably have slept during the battle itself.

The second day was a repeat of the first. Xerxes probably hoped the tiny Greek force would have worn itself out after their efforts of the previous day, but that turned out to be wishful thinking on his part. Once again, the Greeks resisted everything he threw at them and in the end, the Great King called a halt and returned to his camp, presumably for a bit of a rethink. And, of course, to meet his surprise visitor, the traitor Ephialtes who would offer to guide the Persian army along the goat track to the rear of the Spartans.

Halfway through the afternoon, Peterson and Markham had packed up their gear and set off across the rocky hillside. They left their com open and I could hear them, slipping, sliding, and cursing their way across the landscape, until eventually, as the light began to leave the sky, they arrived.

'We're here,' said Markham. I heard faint sounds as they bedded themselves down behind a rock.

'Can you see anything?'

'Are you kidding?' said Peterson, and I could hear the excitement in his voice. 'There's a bloody great column of soldiers crossing the river at this very moment.'

'Is he there? Can you see Ephialtes?'

'Hold on. There's a small band advancing up the hill towards us.'

That made sense. Hydarnes, the general commanding this expedition, would send out a token force in case of ambush. No one trusts a traitor.

Markham intervened. 'They'll pass very close to us, Max. Radio silence.' Everything went quiet. I sat at the console and waited for them to re-establish contact.

And waited.

I wasn't too worried. Ten thousand men would take a long time to pass by. Peterson would be recording. Markham would keep him safe. No, I wasn't too worried.

'Max?' Just a whisper.

'Yes?' I said, stifling the instinct to whisper myself.

'Markham's missing.'

'You've lost Markham? How the hell did you manage that?'

'He had to go.'

'Where?'

'No, he had to go.'

'For God's sake – didn't you go before you came out?'

'Of course,' he said, defensively. 'We are professionals, you know.'

'Where could he possibly have gone?'

'How should I know? Knowing Markham, he's been stung by a giant scorpion or even snatched by aliens. I'm going to check.'

'OK.'

He kept the link open, so I could hear every word.

I could hear his heavy breathing as he eased his way cautiously through the rocks.

'Shit!'

'What?' I said, more alarmed than I would admit.

'Shit!'

'What?' I nearly shrieked, frantic by now.

'Bloody hell, Markham!'

'What? What's going on?'

'Max. We're in trouble.'

'What's happened? For God's sake, tell me.'

'I've found Markham.'

'Is he all right?'

'*He's* fine, yes.'

'Then what's the bloody problem.'

Silence, and then he said. 'Tell you what – I'll let him explain things himself.'

There was a short pause and then Markham said tentatively, 'Max?'

'What the f – I mean, what's happening? Tell me or die.'

He told me.

I decided I'd kill him anyway.

18

People think that Leonidas was the most important person at Thermopylae; or possibly the Great King, Xerxes; but actually, the most important person at Thermopylae was that bastard Ephialtes. The traitor. The man whose name, even now, is Greek for 'nightmare'. The man who led the Persian troops over the mountains so they could fall on Leonidas from the rear as dawn broke. Without Ephialtes, the whole course of History might have been different. You could certainly say Ephialtes was *the* key player.

So, when Markham inadvertently slugged someone with a rock, thus rendering him deeply unconscious for the best part of twenty-four hours – guess what his name was.

'What were you thinking?' demanded Peterson, which for him was the equivalent of a thundering bollocking.

'I couldn't help it,' he said defensively. 'You know what it's like. You squat there with your tunic up round your waist, making sure to avoid the prickly plants, and worrying about scorpions and snakes ... It's always a bit of a nightmare for me, so when this bloke suddenly came round that big rock there with his todger in his hand and fell over me just as I was having a bit of a vulnerable moment, I thumped him one with a rock before he could raise the alarm. It really wasn't my fault at all. It was instinct.'

'Shit,' said Peterson, again.

I sat at the console -and tried to think. Even if he opened his eyes now – this very moment – there was no way Ephialtes was ever going to be in any condition to lead the Persians over a rough mountain track. In the dark.

I sat, appalled, trying to force my brain to think of a way out of this situation. I even considered pulling us all out now – damage limitation – and leaving the Persians to find him, assume he'd fallen amongst the rocks, and try to find their own way around the mountain. There was a full moon tonight. Once they crossed the river and found the path, they could probably do it.

I was kidding myself. If they could have found their own way across the mountain then they would have done so by now. No, they needed Ephialtes to show them the way.

'First things first,' I said. 'Is he still alive?'

'Yes,' said Peterson.

'Right. Keep him that way. Check his airways and roll him into the recovery position.'

'Done that.'

'OK. How bad is the wound?'

'Not deep – he's not bleeding like a stuck pig. Breathing deep and regular. Pulse not too bad. He's not going to die. On the other hand, he's not going to be leading the Persians, either.'

Silence.

I heard the sounds of movement and Peterson say to Markham, 'Help me.'

'What are you doing?' I asked, suddenly scared to death, because I knew exactly what he was doing.

'I'm going to take his place. I'll guide them over the mountain. We've recced the area. I know where the path is. We know the Phocians don't hold the pass. I'll get the Persians there and then –'

'And then they'll kill you.'

'No they won't. They didn't kill Ephialtes.'

'You're not Ephialtes.'

'They won't know that. Only a few high-ranking officers will have seen him face to face and then only for a few minutes. I bet that to them, one Greek looks very much like another. Especially in the dark.'

'You don't speak good Greek.'

'They won't understand good Greek.'

'They'll be hugely suspicious. For all they know Ephialtes is leading them into a trap. And you barely know the area. If you get lost they will kill you.'

'He won't get lost,' said Markham.

'You don't know that.'

'Yes I do. I'll be there, guiding him.'

'How?'

'Night vision,' he said, simply. 'I'll follow on a parallel course and keep you on the path. And if things do go horribly wrong then I'll pull him out as quickly as possible and we'll think of something else.'

'They'll have scouts out,' I said, in despair. 'You're only one person.'

'This is my fault,' he said quietly. 'You have to let me help put it right. You would do the same.'

He was right but I was in no mood to concede any

325

points. I appealed to the marginally most sensible member of the team.

'Tim, you can't do this. It's madness. And this is me saying that.'

'I have to. This has to happen. This isn't us changing History. This is us putting it right.

You don't need to do this. Let them find their own way.'

'I can't. Suppose they get lost on the way. This is one of the pivotal events of the Ancient World. This must Happen.'

I was frantic. 'Tim, listen to me. The Spartans can't hold the Hot Gates. Without the ambush from the rear, they might hold on for a week or so, but they will fall eventually. Nothing will change.'

'You know that's not true. Yes, they'll be defeated eventually, but the three days they hold the Persians here are critical. Three days are just long enough for the Greek fleet to get its act together, but not long enough for them to start falling out with each other. That must not happen. The weaker ones, the ones with less resolve, will drift away. The alliance will break up. Everyone will concentrate on defending just their own city and Xerxes will pick them off one by one. And that means that Greece will fall. And if Greece falls then there might be no Rome. No Rome – no civilisation of Europe. No Europe – no American colonies. Everything changes, Max. Everything.'

'I didn't save you from the Black Death last year so you can throw your life away now.'

'Just because you once saved my life it doesn't

mean you own me.'

'Yes it does, sunshine. I own you, body and soul.'

Markham interrupted. 'If we're doing this it must be now. They'll be getting suspicious if someone doesn't emerge from these rocks soon.'

Peterson sighed. 'I have to do this. It obviously can't be you, Max. You're the wrong sex and you don't have enough working knees. And Markham doesn't speak Greek so it has to be me. I have to guide the Persians through the mountains so that Leonidas can lead his army to glorious defeat.'

I was crying with frustration. He wouldn't make it. He knew it. I knew it. This was just some desperate last-minute attempt to get things back on course. It wouldn't work. How could it?

'I won't let you do this. History can repair itself. If we weren't here then it would have to. I'm mission controller, Tim, and I'm telling you now. Get back to the pod.'

'If we weren't here then we wouldn't have to do it. Ephialtes would have had a quick slash behind a rock and they'd all be on their way by now. I'll be fine. And I've got Markham.'

He sounded breathless.

'What are you doing?'

'Swapping clothes. Markham's dressing Ephialtes in my gear.'

'What for?'

'I'm not lugging a naked man about,' said Markham, primly. 'That sort of thing can be open to misinterpretation. We can't leave him here to raise the alarm when he comes round and we can't kill him. I'll get

327

him back to the pod and you can keep an eye on him there and record the battle at the same time. Either he recovers or he doesn't. The main thing is that the Persians get over the mountain tonight. Everything else is irrelevant, really.'

He was right. There was an awkward silence and then I heard Markham grunt as he heaved Ephialtes over his shoulder. He said to Peterson, 'It'll take them a while to get ten thousand men across the river and Hydarnes will want all his men safely on this side before they set off. I should easily be able to catch you up when I've dropped off buggerlugs here.'

What could I say? They were both of them almost certainly going to their deaths and I couldn't be there with them.

'We'll try to leave our links open, but don't call us, Max. We'll call you.'

'Understood. Good luck, both of you.'

'It'll be a piece of piss,' said Markham. 'You just wait and see.'

The link went silent as they parted. Markham on his way back to me, and Peterson to whatever awaited him down by the river.

Markham arrived far more quickly than I thought he would. He dumped Ephialtes at the Kallidromus site because we didn't want him anywhere near the pod, and I arranged him in the recovery position. He was still out cold, breathing heavily. Markham donned armour and packed himself some extra water and a few high-energy biscuits. I passed him my stun gun.

'Here, take this.'

'I can't leave you unprotected.'

'I'm not. I've still got my trusty pepper spray.'

'Max …'

'No, I'm not important. If Peterson doesn't get them over the mountain then I don't know what we'll do. What happens to me is pretty irrelevant.'

He took it.

'Please, take care of him.'

'I will. And you, Max, don't you get into any trouble. I really don't want to have to explain to Chief Farrell that I fell down on the job.'

He was good. I looked up from Ephialtes to find he'd faded away completely. I listened, but even with him moving around in all this loose rock, I couldn't hear a thing.

Left to myself, I checked the patient – no change – and curled up against a rock. To my left were the Persian campfires. Down below, I could see the Greek lights. Somewhere out there, Peterson was leading ten thousand men through the night with only Markham to get him out of any trouble. By this time tomorrow, it would all be over. How many of us would still be alive?

It was a long and lonely night.

Peterson was necessarily silent, but he'd left his link open and I could hear everything that was happening around him. Murmuring voices. Feet sliding on rock. The odd curse from someone nearby. The faint chink of armour. His own heavy breathing as he struggled up the mountain. Given their numbers, they moved surprisingly silently, but these were the Immortals, Xerxes' mountain troops, completely at home in this sort of terrain. There

329

was no shouting and no sounds of violence, which I interpreted as a good sign.

Markham, on the other hand, was very chatty, guiding Peterson through the night, instructing him to bear a little more to his right, or turn left around that rocky outcrop. The moon was full and bright; Peterson should have no visibility problems. I think Markham was doing it for reassurance. Occasionally, he remembered to spare a word for me, reporting everything was going well.

I stared up at the same full moon that was lighting their way. Then I looked down at the stertorously breathing Ephialtes and wondered if we would ever be able to put things back on track.

The hours passed. I listened to Markham guiding Peterson guiding the Persians through the night. Surely if the Persians had any suspicions, they would have acted by now. Was it possible this would actually work? I watched the moon travel across the sky. How long till dawn?

And then it all went wrong.

All I could hear through my earpiece was a sound like waves, breaking on the shore. Surely, Peterson hadn't got lost and found himself down on the coastal plain? No, of course not. As Herodotus recounts, they were making their way through an oak wood and this was the sound of ten thousand men kicking up the fallen leaves. Any minute now, they would encounter the Phocians, despatched by Leonidas to guard the path. They shouldn't be a problem. They would assume the Persians had come for them and strategically retreat to higher ground where they would be safe. This, however, would leave the way open for the Persians who would sweep contemptuously past them and vanish into the night.

'Bollocks!' said Markham in my ear, his voice high with agitation and alarm. 'No, no, no. That's not right. Bloody hell! Max, can you hear me?'

'What,' I whispered, frantic with worry. 'What's not right? What's going on?'

You're just supposed to say, 'Report.' I always forget that.

'The Phocians – they're going to fight. They're gearing up and advancing.'

'What? No! They can't do that. They're supposed to run away. They're not supposed to fight.'

Bloody hell. If they fight … if they hold the pass … if the Persians don't get through … My mind skidded all over the place with the implications. We were here – at a major point in History and everything was changing around us. How can everything go so wrong so quickly?

'It's all right,' said Markham, in my ear. 'I've had an idea.'

'What? What are you going to do?'

'I'm going to get them to pull back.'

I opened my mouth to tell him no – and closed it again. He'd been with St Mary's for years now. He knew the score. You don't mess with History. Lives are always lost when you do. And we'd messed with History. We'd slugged Ephialtes, the most important man here tonight. We'd changed History and we had to put it back. Whatever the cost. I knew what he was thinking. This was his fault. He should make it right. In his place, I would do exactly the same thing. The best thing I could do for him was let him get on with it. Whatever he was going to do.

331

'How?'

'I'm going to attack. I've been sweating cobs underneath this armour all night, so I might as well get some use out of it. I can't use my blaster on them, but I can spray some fire around. I'm going to frighten the living shit out of them. I suspect that now they've actually seen the Immortals in front of them, they're halfway there, already. I attack the Phocians and by the time they realise it's a trick, the Immortals will be well on their way and they won't be able to do a thing about it.'

My heart sank. One man. He was only one man. What could he possibly do?

'What about the Immortals themselves?'

'My guess is that Xerxes' orders are to let nothing stop them getting over this mountain. Unless they're directly attacked, they won't stop for anyone. That's what I'm counting on, anyway.'

'Good plan,' I said, as calmly as I could. I took a second or two to get my voice steady. 'Report back to me when you've finished.'

'Copy that. Max ...'

I swallowed. 'Yes?'

He paused. I had the impression he was groping for words. I could hear him breathing. 'Hunter ...'

I closed my eyes. 'Yes. I'll ...' I took a deep breath. 'I'll ...' What would I do? 'I'll tell her.'

'Thanks. Tell her I ... well, you know. And tell her as well that if she ... Well, that ugly bugger Randall's been sniffing around and ...'

I nodded, even though he couldn't see me. 'Are you asking me to tell her it's OK to ... to ...?'

332

'She won't want to,' he said with confidence. 'I'm a hard act to follow, you know. I'm the standard against which all other men are measured.'

My eyes blurred. 'Just get up that bloody hill,' I said.

He laughed. 'I'm going to close the link, Max. I think that's best. You need to concentrate on your bit. Peterson, I'm going to have to leave you now. Good luck, everyone.'

I heard Peterson grunt an acknowledgement. It was all he could do. All the links went dead.

I sniffed hard and went to check on Ephialtes, who was still very deeply asleep. He lay on his side, his breathing was regular and his pulse strong. He was going to survive.

Which was more than could be said of Peterson and Markham. We'd joked about me being killed by my own wedding present. It never occurred to me it could be fatal for them, too. They could be dying at this very moment and there was nothing I could do about it.

I decided to concentrate on the things I could do something about. I moved a little way from our site, picking my way through the rocks, and drawing nearer to the edge of the plateau. I wanted to see if there was any movement yet from the Greeks. Dawn could surely not be far off. I found a comparatively flat piece of ground and wriggled forwards on my stomach.

I lay motionless for a long time, listening to the sounds of the night. An occasional insect whirred past my head, but mostly, all I could hear was the distinctive song of the every male cicada in the area. There must have been hundreds of them around to be making that amount of noise.

333

And then – quite suddenly – it stopped. Stopped dead. Absolute silence. Something was here. Something had disturbed them. I felt the hairs rise on the back of my neck.

My first thought was that Ephialtes had come round but no – conscious he might be, but walking was going to be beyond him for a good few hours yet. Which left ...

I was an idiot. I'd made a terrible mistake. How stupid to assume the Spartans wouldn't take advantage of the moon to send out scouting parties. Of course, they wouldn't sit passively behind their lines. Leonidas would want as much information regarding the disposition and numbers of the enemy as he could get. The whole hillside was probably crawling with invisible Spartans. And they were good at it. Spartans moved as easily through the night as they did through the day. During training, boys would be sent out alone for long periods to fend for themselves. Anything was permitted. Murder was encouraged. Some poor helot would have his throat cut for any food he was carrying and never know what hit him.

This little plateau had an excellent view of events below. That was why we were here. And that was why the Spartans were here, too.

Ephialtes still lay like a dead man, concealed among the rocks. I sent up a prayer to the god of historians. Don't let him wake up now. Or snort. Or grunt.

I was prone on my stomach, facing out over the Gulf of Malia. I had no idea what was going on behind me and if I twisted my head to find out, it would be the last thing I ever did. My face was filthy so that wasn't a problem. My clothes were a sensible mottled green-grey mix. Just lie still, Maxwell, and fade into the earth. I tried to slow my breathing and not listen to my heart going like a hammer.

I cut my eyes to the right and there they were.

Nothing chinked and there was no sound of breathing but suddenly, they were here. What I thought was a dark mass of rock resolved itself into a group of three or four men. They even stood like rocks – not upright because then they'd be silhouetted against the skyline, but unevenly, at strange angles. Not man shaped at all. Blending in. Each one becoming part of the landscape. They weren't wearing helmets and they'd left their spears behind. Each man wore just a brief tunic and carried his xiphos. They were almost right on top of me and I hadn't even known they were there. If I hadn't been lying motionless myself ...

On the plus side, they obviously didn't know I was here, either, or I'd be dead. There was no question of making a run for it. If I was very lucky, I might get perhaps five or six inches before they cut my throat. I tried not to hold my breath because they'd hear the gasp when I had to breathe in again. Just breathe slowly and quietly. I was on the ground, vulnerable, exposed, and helpless. Long seconds dragged by. I waited either to be pulled to my feet or for the sword thrust that would kill me. My face was in the dust. I breathed through my mouth so I wouldn't sneeze. At ground level, I was squinting up at them, and from that angle, they looked absolutely bloody massive.

They stood stock-still. Watching. Listening.

I swear time stopped.

I felt the sweat break out all over me. The urge to get up and run was overwhelming. Could they see me? How could they miss me? I was lying almost at their feet. I could smell them. Sweat. Leather. A faint whiff of oil.

The seemingly never-ending silence was killing me. Were they watching me to see what I would do? Was one of them even now raising his sword? My eyes stung with sweat. I daren't blink, even. I lay, still as the corpse that I might soon become, awaiting the red-hot, ice-cold agonising explosion of pain as a sword thrust skewered me into the dirt.

Silently one detached himself and took two steps towards me. I closed my eyes and that was all I could do as he planted his right foot firmly on my left hand.

Don't move. Don't pull away. Don't gasp with pain. Don't do anything.

I bit my bottom lip and tried to think of something else other than my bones grinding together under his boot and I might – just might – have been successful, only the bastard fumbled for a moment and then peed on me.

Seriously – what is it with men and peeing on things? Can they not help themselves? Trees. Rocks. Walls. Me. You name it and the next minute there's a bloke peeing all over it. Peterson has peed on me at least twice and he's supposed to be a friend.

Another little known fact I can contribute to our knowledge of the Spartans is that they don't do the traditional bloke splash and dash. A seemingly never-ending stream of warm, asparagus-smelling wee splashed off the rock onto my head and shoulders. For God's sake! The only good thing about this was that he wasn't looking what he was doing. Sword in one hand, todger in the other, he was constantly scanning around him. This was a war zone and his attention was on everything but what was happening at ground level.

He did that funny thing that men do when they've finished, eased his weight backwards, which did my hand no good at all, and finally, finally, stepped back. For some reason, my hand hurt even more once he removed his foot.

I never heard them go. I certainly never saw them go. I wasn't even sure they had gone. I ran through various courses of action and discarded them all in favour of just lying still. Other than the breeze, I could hear nothing. Of course I wouldn't. The entire Spartan army might be sitting in a circle watching me and I would never know.

I lay, not moving, for a long, long time, straining my eyes, straining my ears.

Nothing.

I rolled my eyes around, but at ground level, you can't see much.

Eventually, what passes for common sense reasserted itself. If they knew I was here, I would have been long since dead. Lifting my head a fraction, I looked around. Rocks. The obligatory prickly bushes. Dust. The damp patch I was lying in. Nothing else. No dark mass of Spartan warriors blending effortlessly into the landscape. I was alone.

Apart from bloody Ephialtes, of course. It would be entirely typical if he were the only one of us to survive the events of today. We knew they didn't kill him. Ephialtes lived long enough to collect his reward from the Great

King and enjoy it. His name would become synonymous with traitor. All sorts of rewards were offered for him and he fled. He died some years later in, I believe, a non-Thermopylae related incident, but the Spartans paid the reward anyway.

Slowly, the sky lightened in the east and I shivered in the pre-dawn chill. I could make out individual rocks and the lump that was Ephialtes. He was too big to move by myself, so I dropped a blanket over him to protect him from the coming sun and considered my compassionate duty done.

I considered calling either Markham or Peterson but if they were in trouble, they wouldn't want me gabbling away at them. They would call when they were OK. If they were dead then they wouldn't. It wasn't rocket science.

I sat down, glugged some water, and examined my hand, which throbbed, but not hugely. I'd had worse. I wondered when I'd last slept. Or when I'd last eaten, and it wasn't going to be now, because the trumpets sounded below. The alarm was being given. Word was out that the Immortals had made it across the mountain. I was torn between anguish for the Greeks, all of whom were now doomed; relief for Peterson, and near-demented concern for Markham. However, both of them were perfectly capable of looking after themselves and I should get busy. If they were dead then this was the best way to ensure they hadn't died in vain.

I activated all the recorders and not a moment too soon, because the Greek force was splitting up.

I knew what was happening here. Everyone but the Spartans was being ordered to retreat. The Thespians would refuse. The Great King's army had already overrun their city. They preferred to die with the Spartans. The Thebans would remain too, somehow become separated from the main body of the army, and surrender almost immediately.

Disciplined as always, the remaining Greeks assembled themselves for battle. Tiredly heaving their dented shields into place one last time, they clustered together, spears bristling. The plumes were gone from their helmets. They were white with dust, through which trails of red blood made a shocking contrast.

Men shouted. Trumpets sounded. Without waiting for the ten thousand Immortals bearing down on them from the rear, the roaring Greek army left the Middle Gate and charged full tilt at Xerxes' light infantry and cavalry. Both sides met with a crash that reverberated off the cliffs. There was no battle plan. Everyone's aim was simple. To kill as many of the opposing side as possible.

The fighting was vicious. The Spartans were fighting for their country and the lives of their countrymen as well as their own. The Persians were driven forwards by their own officers wielding whips. There was no quarter – no mercy was shown by either side.

The Spartans fought with their spears and when those were gone, they drew their swords. When they were broken or shattered, they laid about them with their shields. When they were gone, they threw rocks or fought hand-to-hand, using fists and feet. When they were gone, they used their teeth. When they couldn't stand any longer, they fought on their knees. One by one they fell, bleeding from a dozen wounds, finally overwhelmed by the sheer numbers surrounding them.

I watched one Spartan, helmet gone, hair flying behind him, run, roaring, full tilt at a group of fully armed infantrymen. He'd lost both hands, but he hurled himself on them, beating them about their heads with his bloody stumps, snarling and biting. Unstoppable. It took four of them to wrestle him to the ground and more than four of them to kill him.

I didn't see Leonidas die, but I did watch the desperate scramble to retrieve his body.

As the Immortals approached from the rear, the few remaining Greeks retreated and took up position on Kolonos Hill behind the wall. There, they clustered into a rough circle, broken spears bristling. Waiting for the end.

All right, they weren't a pleasant race. Their lifestyle was ruthless. Mercy and compassion were a weakness that had long since been bred out of them. Their treatment of slaves and indeed, any non-Spartan was brutal. But they were the right people in the right place at the right time. As if History had prepared them for this one moment, and then, having no further use for them, discarded them. A few centuries later, they would be gone. But this was their moment. This was their bright, shining, blood-soaked moment.

Xerxes, in his fury, sent his troops to tear down the Phocian wall and as it disappeared in a heap of rubble and even more dust, they moved in. Thousands upon thousands of Persian soldiers surrounded the tiny hill and even then, despite the whips of their officers, none would approach.

Finally, the order was given and Persian arrows rained down upon them, wave upon wave, turning day into night, until every last Greek was dead and Xerxes entered the Hot Gates at last.

19

I sat back against a rock, drew a deep, shaky breath, and wiped the sweat off my face. My hands weren't steady. I made myself take a moment and sip some water. Looking up at the sky, I could see the sun was beginning to go down. Hours had passed and I'd been oblivious.

I suddenly realised I'd still heard nothing from Peterson or Markham. Should I try to contact them? No. There were Persians swarming everywhere and they shouldn't be distracted. I should trust them to look after themselves. My job was here, recording events and keeping an eye on Ephialtes. There wasn't a single thing I could do for either of them, so I concentrated on the task in hand.

Down below, the Persians were building huge funeral pyres to bury their dead. I watched with interest, because Xerxes, usually quite punctilious in observing respectful funeral rites for his enemies, would order that no such courtesy be extended to the tiny force who had withstood his magnificent army for three long days. Leonidas' hideously disfigured head was impaled on a stake and left for the whole world to see. The rest of his army was simply left as carrion.

The Persian funeral rites took all day. They lighted the

funeral pyres at dusk and I lay and watched the fires burn all night. At around midnight, Markham called in. His voice was just a hoarse and dusty whisper.

'Max. You OK? Is it over?'

I closed my eyes briefly, took a breath, and made sure my voice was steady.

'Yes. The funeral rites have been completed. I imagine they'll move out at dawn.' I tried to swallow in a mouth suddenly too dry to do so. I was almost afraid to ask. 'Where's Peterson? Is he alive?'

'He's here, with me. We've taken cover. He's been a bit knocked about, I'm afraid. You said that no one liked a traitor and you were right. They gave him a bit of a kicking and then left him at the side of the trail. I've been too busy lugging him to safety to call and there are Phocians everywhere.'

I wiped my eyes and gave quiet thanks to the god of historians. 'Do you need a hand with him?'

'No, if you're safe, stay where you are. I'll get him down, don't worry.'

He closed the link. I shut my eyes.

And opened them again.

Shit! I'd forgotten about Ephialtes.

He was awake. No, that's not quite right. His eyes were open, but at that moment there was no one home. I squatted beside him, waiting, and gradually, some spark of intelligence came back into his eyes.

I'd wondered how much he would remember and the answer was everything, because he uttered a cry, struggled to his feet, staggered heavily, sat down on a rock for support, held his head, and threw up. Great.

More bodily fluids.

Finally, his eyes cleared and he looked around, trying to establish where he was. I handed him a goatskin of water and made him sip it slowly.

When I thought he could, I indicated he should get to his feet. I don't think he had the faintest idea who or what I was, but he stood up, followed me to the edge of the plateau, and looked down at the fires below. He might have missed the last twenty-four hours, but he could see the Spartans had fallen. I wanted to see his reaction.

He stood for a long time, looking down. Even in the moonlight, which traditionally drains all colour from the landscape and everything in it, he looked pale and haunted. Several times his lips moved as if he was struggling for words. Maybe he was praying to the gods, although I suspected there wasn't a god on Olympus who would touch him with a barge pole after today's events. He would be an outcast for the rest of his life. Albeit a rich one.

I know it was unjust. He'd be reviled all his life for something he hadn't done. On the other hand, he'd also be handsomely rewarded for something he hadn't done. And he had planned to do it. Without our intervention, he would actually be the traitor History declared him to be. I wasted no pity on him.

At last, he turned and looked at me. Perhaps he was looking for a word of kindness. Or of comfort. Or understanding. He stretched out a hand to me in silent pleading.

I saw the Spartans in their brave, red cloaks, never giving ground. Heard the clash of metal as they raised their shields in the phalanx. Felt the ground shake as they stamped their defiance in the dust. Saw that one, last, armless Spartan, spitting, biting, and kicking as they took him down …

I'd long since assembled the words I wanted to say. I drew myself up and turned from the scene below. Slowly and clearly, I said, 'Ephialtes, your name will live forever,' and I could see he understood exactly what I was saying.

I couldn't be bothered with him any longer. I walked away and began to gather up my belongings. When I looked back, he had gone. I never saw him again. I assumed he was off to the Persian camp to collect his reward.

Bastard!

At dawn, the Persian Army began to move. It was quite a sight.

First to pull out was Xerxes' enormous personal baggage train, escorted by several squads of infantrymen.

This was followed by the Immortals, row upon row of them. Each anonymous and identical. Even after days of suicidally hurling themselves at the Spartans, their ranks were not noticeably depleted.

Behind them came what I assumed was the sacred chariot of Ahuramazda, the Persian god, empty, but drawn by four snow-white horses. Gold and jewels glittered in the early-morning sun.

Now came Xerxes himself, heavily escorted. I strained for a glimpse of his face. I had set up three recorders in different locations and could only hope that one of them was able to get the details. He was riding a horse, not being carted around on a luxurious divan, and his only concession to luxury was the four mounted slaves carrying a sunshade over his head. He wore purple and that was about all I was able to get. I kept my fingers crossed that the recorders would get better images.

After Xerxes marched the infantry, row upon row, throwing up so much dust that I could barely make them out. Their ranks went on and on forever. I sat up and chugged back some water. I disappeared round the back of a rock for a while and when I came back, the infantry were still marching past. I even think I might have dozed off for a few minutes. For God's sake, don't tell anyone that.

The cavalry followed the infantry. Endlessly. I had long since lost count of rows and columns and the dust was making my eyes sting. I could hardly wait to get back, review the recordings, and try for an accurate estimation of their numbers. I could easily see how anyone watching this lot pass by would have put their numbers in the millions.

Then more Immortals. Cloned ranks stamping through the dust, making the ground shake.

Even then, it wasn't over. Bringing up what I suppose could be called the rear, were the support teams. Members of his court. Administrators and courtesans. Blacksmiths, armourers, cooks, spare horses, wagon upon wagon loaded with provisions – food, drink, firewood, spares for absolutely everything and everyone.

Hours and hours went by. I ran out of water and still didn't dare leave.

Finally, the ranks began to thin. Here came herds of cows, sheep, and goats, all being driven along the same path as the army. And the camp followers, most of them on foot, bundles balanced on their heads, choking in the dust. Dogs ran around, barking.

The sun was dropping in the sky, and still they came. I wondered how many miles there were between the head of the army and these last few souls bringing up the rear. Finally, the last figures were lost in the dust.

I heaved a sigh in the sudden silence.

The sun was a fiery red ball when I stopped off at the pod for more water and then scrambled carefully down the rocky hillside. My knee didn't like it much, competing with my hand in the throbbing competition, and I had to zigzag around to find the easiest route. I was soaked with sweat when I finally arrived at sea level and looked around me.

I've been at this job for years and sometimes, even now, I'm still overwhelmed. I stared about me, unable to believe I was actually here. Unable to believe I was standing at the Hot Gates. Not in modern times, as a tourist, but actually here – the site of the famous Spartan stand at Thermopylae.

Not that there was evidence to that effect. Looking around, there was virtually no trace that any Spartan had ever been here. There wasn't a body in sight anywhere. The Persian army had marched straight over the top of them. Their remains had been totally obliterated under the victorious tramp of Persian feet. There wasn't even a grease stain across the path.

Acrid smoke from the funeral pyres mixed with the

settling white dust that covered everything, including – yes, there it was – off to one side. Leonidas's head, still impaled on a leaning stake, stood under the long shadows of the cliffs. I drew closer and stood looking at the most famous Spartan of them all. It was impossible to see how he had once looked. His hair and beard were dark and that was about all I could say. Flies crawled across his one remaining eyeball.

I heard a shout behind me, and whirled around, cursing myself for not having my pepper spray ready, but it was Markham, slithering down the slope from the opposite direction and supporting Peterson as best he could.

I blinked a couple of times, swallowed, and then tapped my wrist, significantly. 'You're late. It was all over with hours ago. Did you get lost?'

He lowered Peterson to the ground in the shade and leaned forwards to put his hands on his knees to ease his back. He looked appallingly battered and dishevelled, even for him. I passed him some water and knelt to take a look at Peterson.

His face was a mess. Xerxes might well have offered untold riches, but the Immortals had obviously held him in complete contempt. Any soldier would.

'Tim?'

His voice was thick but he knew me. 'Hey, Max. Did you get it?'

'Yes, I got it all. You took them over the mountain, then?'

'Yeah. Ungrateful bastards.'

I helped him drink some water. His nose was broken, but his teeth and cheekbones were intact.

'How do I look?'

'You're still pretty. Helen will still love you.'

'Don't see how she can help it,' he slurred. 'I'm a hero.'

I hugged him. Very gently. 'Yes, you are.' I turned to Markham. 'And you are too. Although a very dirty one. Did you seriously chase off a thousand Phocians?'

'No, of course not,' he said, wetting his face with water and just spreading the dirt over a larger area. 'I chased off the ten at the front. They turned and ran and then everyone else turned and ran too. It was easy. But I'm still a hero as well, right?'

'Why can I smell asparagus?' said Peterson, squinting at me.

'No idea.'

The three of us sat against the cliff and watched the setting sun turn the sky blood red. It was incredibly hot and still. I could hear the endless rhythm of the sea. There were a few broken weapons scattered around and the settling dust was turning everything white, including us, but otherwise, you could hardly believe so bloody a battle had been fought on this very spot.

Markham was fishing around in his pack.

'Have you still got it?' asked Peterson, anxiously, trying to sit up.

'Of course.' He pulled out a flask of wine.

'Come on,' said Peterson. We helped him to his feet and stood for a moment. In this narrow place, the heat was stifling. Unbelievably, men had fought here for three days.

We stood in front of King Leonidas of the Spartans

and poured the first cupful for the gods. The ground was beaten so hard that it couldn't absorb the liquid, which just lay in a red puddle on the dusty earth.

We poured the second to appease any shades that might still be hanging around this place – Persian or Spartan.

The third cup was for us. We shared. A few sips each. It wasn't until I drank that I realised how thirsty I was.

I sat on a rock and looked around me. No birds sang here. The only sounds were of the sea and the lonely wind. Markham was fishing in his pack again, coming up with a can of spray paint.

I swallowed the last of my wine in a hurry.

'What are you doing?'

'Vandalising an important historical site.'

He shook the can and passed it to Peterson. I could hardly believe my eyes.

'You can't …'

'Yes,' said Peterson, with all the dogged intent of one at the end of his physical strength, 'I can.'

We helped him up and propped him up in front of the cliff. He unfolded a piece of paper, squinted at it carefully, and in flawless Greek sprayed:

Go tell the Spartans, stranger passing by,
That here, obedient to their laws, we lie.

The famous tribute to the Spartans that in various forms would be taken up by poets and storytellers and echo down the ages. Monuments would be erected here, including a fine statue of Leonidas himself, and another to the Thespians who died with them and are often forgotten. Everyone would remember the words that Tim had

351

written here today; all the more poignant, because, of course, tragically, most of the Spartans didn't lie here. A few would, but most of them were just something unpleasant on the bottom of their enemy's sandals. They had deserved better and Peterson had given it to them.

We stood, bareheaded for a minute, the hot wind ruffling our hair and then we turned to go. Markham pulled Peterson's arm around his shoulder and I picked up their gear. They set off.

I let them get a little ahead and then turned back to Leonidas for one last look. It must have been a trick of this lonely place, but for a moment, just for a moment, I thought I heard a faint echo of his voice, borne on the wind off the sea, urging his men onwards to glorious defeat.

I said quietly, 'Thank you,' and my words were lost on the same wind. I like to think he heard them.

I followed the others back to the pod.

The FOD plod lasted half a day. That's the Foreign Object Drop plod, when we have to make sure we haven't left anything behind. It took half a day because our stuff was scattered everywhere. On the slopes of Kallidromus above the battleground. Down at the river where Markham had slugged Ephialtes. All around the pod. Just everywhere.

We made Peterson stay inside out of the sun, so mostly it was Markham and me, and I was still limping so mostly it was Markham, but we got it done eventually.

Back inside the pod, we had a hugely deserved cup of tea. The first didn't even touch the sides, so we had another one, just to keep it company. We tried to tidy ourselves up a bit. Historians never go back looking scruffy. Apart from Markham who looked scruffy when he set out and had deteriorated somewhat since them. He sunnily informed us this was because he was beyond improvement.

We fervently agreed.

'So,' he said, putting his feet up on the console. 'Are you going to go through with it, then? I only ask because I have a vested interest.'

'Go through with what?'

'This wedding, of course.'

'Yes,' I said, shortly. 'You've been placing bets, haven't you?'

'No! Well, yes, but mostly I need to know because I've been elected Gatekeeper.'

We stared at him.

'Do you mean usher?'

'I don't think so. My job is to slam the doors shut once you're inside so you can't get out. Dr Black and Dr Foster will follow you up the aisle, ready to intercept any suspicious movements on your part, and we all hand you over to Chief Farrell. After that, of course, it's up to him.'

I had mixed feelings about being home again.

We were checked over. Peterson was admitted and Markham and I were remanded for the statutory twelve hours' observation.

'Why can I smell asparagus, too?' demanded Markham.

'Really?' said Hunter, picking up a scanner. 'A distorted sense of smell is sometimes indicative of a concussion. Have you been hitting yourself on the head again?'

'Don't think so.'

'How many fingers am I holding up?'

'I don't know,' he said, putting an artistic hand to his supposedly fevered brow. 'Why don't you take your clothes off and see if that helps me to concentrate.'

I don't know why he bothers. Far from achieving his heart's desire, he'd just opened himself up to a world of pain.

'Bath,' I said, heading in that direction.

They looked at the state of me.

'I recommend a shower,' said Hunter. 'Or maybe two.'

'Have you ever tried to drink a Margarita in a shower?'

'No alcohol allowed.'

355

'Oh, what a shame,' I said, secure in the knowledge that my previously prepared bottle of 'Essence of Lavender Relaxing Foam Bath – Guaranteed to Calm and Soothe,' would be far more relaxing, calming, and soothing than the manufacturers could ever take credit for. Although there might be singing later on.

On the downside, there was now nothing between marriage and me. I couldn't procrastinate any longer. In my absence, Kal and Helen had been busy.

We visited Mrs Mack who bundled us into her office. I shunted the kitchen cat, Vortigern, off a chair and we sat down.

'Menus,' she announced, putting on her spectacles and laying various bits of paper in front of me.

I stared blindly, trying not to panic, but there's an established routine for this sort of ignorance and I fell back on it now.

'Do you have any recommendations, Mrs Mack?'

'Yes. This one.'

I scanned the page.

'Yes, I like this one too.'

'Excellent. And wine?'

'Yes.'

They stared at me.

'Certainly,' I said, to reinforce the point. Just in case of confusion.

'What sort?' said Mrs Mack, patiently.

I pulled myself together. 'Red and white. Two glasses each. After that, they pay for their own.'

'And the toast?'

'Champagne,' said Kal, firmly.

Mrs Mack nodded. 'Venue?'

That was easy. I could do that. 'In the dining room. Overspill on the terrace. Inside if wet.'

She scribbled a note and closed the file. 'Thank you, ladies.'

I was escorted out and we set off to Mrs Enderby.

'I shall look like a lampshade,' I said, gloomily as we clattered up the stairs. 'Or a mushroom. Or a small pudding bowl. And I'm *not* wearing heels.'

'For God's sake,' said Kal, pulling open the door to Wardrobe. 'You clump about all day in a blue sack and with your hair in a sock bun. A pudding bowl would be a huge improvement. Stop whingeing and smile at Mrs Enderby.'

Mrs Enderby was gently reassuring and, in her own way, easily as remorseless as Kalinda and Mrs Mack. 'I think you'll find, when you see yourself in the mirror, Max, that you don't look like a pudding bowl at all.'

I kicked off my boots and undressed, muttered a bit, and allowed myself to be eased into a dress. I put my arms in the sleeves and was neatly zipped up.

I saw Kal and Mrs Enderby exchange glances.

'Slip these shoes on, dear,' said Mrs Enderby. 'Just so I can get the hem right.'

I eyed them suspiciously. 'Heels.'

'Just very small ones – just to give us an idea of the length.'

'It's like shoeing a horse,' said Kal, as I lifted first one foot and then another. I was all set to protest, but they were actually quite pretty. And fairly comfortable. Not as comfy as my boots, of course, but even I could see the boots were a bit of a no-no at a wedding. Even sprayed with silver, like Cinderella's slippers. I mentioned this to Kal.

'Yes,' she said. 'A princess with glass boots. How could any prince resist? Now then – flowers?' She was holding a checklist.

'Yellow roses,' I said. One of the things I was sure about. 'Mr Strong will provide.'

'Commendably decisive. Hair?'

'Barring accidents, almost certainly.'

'I mean – up? Down? Sideways?'

'Piled up to give you height and then falling to your shoulders to contrast against the gold of the dress,' said Mrs Enderby. 'Make-up?'

'No,' I said.

'Yes,' said Kal. 'Ignore her.'

'I *am* the bride, you know.'

She handed me the checklist. 'Get on with it then.'

I handed it back again. 'Fine. I'll wear makeup.'

'Would you like to see yourself?' asked Mrs Enderby who had finished twitching my skirts into place.

I braced myself. Perhaps the fat meringue look was fashionable this year. Turning to the mirror, I beheld a vision. I knew it was me, because of the lop-sided bun and terrified expression, but otherwise a complete stranger stared back at me. Mrs Enderby had based the style on the late Renaissance. A straight dress of soft gold, gathered under the bust, fell in gentle folds behind me. The sleeves were long and elegant. A low V-neck gave me a small cleavage but not excessively so. After all, I didn't want to be struck down by an enraged deity right in the middle of a religious ceremony.

Kal dismantled my bun and rearranged my hair into something a little gentler.

'Well,' said Mrs Enderby, softly. 'What do you think?'

I tore my eyes away. 'I think it's lovely, Mrs Enderby. Absolutely beautiful. You're a genius.'

'Yes,' said Kal. 'Now, we just need to get the shoes shorted. I'll run you into Rushford and we'll visit two or three shoe shops.'

'No need,' I said, glancing down at the really quite comfortable shoes I was already wearing. 'These are just fine.'

'Oh good,' said Kal, in no way glancing at Mrs Enderby. 'That's very convenient, isn't it?'

'Yes, said Mrs Enderby, staring at the ceiling. 'Very.'

I stared at them, but they were both perfectly straight-faced, so I let it go.

There was, however, a task that only I could perform. I walked very slowly to the Boss's office, rehearsing words in my mind. Mrs Partridge waved me through.

The Boss was sitting at his desk, surrounded by multi-coloured files. Blue from the History department, green from Security, orange from the Technical Section, the back of an envelope from R & D ...

'Sorry, sir.'

He pushed aside his paperwork. 'Please come in, Dr Maxwell.'

'I can come back later.'

'I order you to enter my office and interrupt me. Please

sit down.'

'I wanted to ask … I wanted to say …'

This was ridiculous. I'd sat here hundreds of times, bombarding him with words, talking him into assignments, talking myself out of trouble (and sometimes straight back into it again) and now, when I particularly needed them, the words just wouldn't come.

I took several deep breaths and said, 'Sir, I would be greatly honoured if you would give me away at my wedding.'

Silence.

Shit. Had I contravened some rule or reg? Yes, almost certainly. It's what I do.

He sat back and smiled. 'The honour would be mine, Max. I shall be delighted to do so.'

Relief flowed off me like … like something relief flows off from a lot. My brain wasn't working that clearly.

'Thank you, sir. That's a huge weight off my mind.'

And it was. Suddenly, I felt a whole lot better.

He smiled again. Twice in one day. Matrimony must be having a mellowing effect on him as well. 'I must confess, I was rather hoping you would ask. I've asked Wardrobe to send my uniform to the cleaners, just in case, and Mrs Partridge has been running me through the formalities. There seems to be a great deal to do.'

I said gloomily, 'You should try being the bride, sir.'

'Yes, I can see that you are dancing through the days in a rapture of dizzy anticipation.'

I sighed and sought to change the subject. 'That reminds me, sir, while I'm here, shall I sign the paperwork?'

'I'm sorry?'

'The invoices, sir. Or will you deduct things directly?'

'Deduct what directly?'

'My share of the wedding expenses, sir.'

'I'm afraid I am unable to comply, having been instructed by Chief Farrell that all expenses will be met by him, and I have to say, Max, that since I'm far more frightened of him than I am of you, I shall obey.'

'But they must be massive.'

'No, I don't believe so. Your requests actually seem to me to be very modest.'

'I don't want a spectacle, sir. Just two people exchanging their vows in front of their friends who join them in a small celebration afterwards.'

'Yes,' he said thoughtfully. 'I'm not sure St Mary's is completely up to speed with the phrase "*small celebration*," but we shall see.'

I stared at my hands and he watched me for a while.

'Max, what is it? What is causing you this unease?'

I floundered helplessly in a sea of unspoken words. Nothing came out.

'He is a good man, Max. You know that.'

'I do know that, sir. It's just – I worry I'm not a good woman.'

He got up and limped around the table. I stood up and he took my hand.

'Neither Leon nor I harbour any doubts on that score. You make him happy.'

I swallowed.

'Of course, you also make him angry, frustrated,

impatient, exasperated, despairing, and furious. Emotions in which I sometimes share, but I, like Leon, wouldn't change a hair on your head.'

I hung my unchanged head and whispered, 'Thank you, sir.'

He stepped back behind his desk. 'There was something else – what was it? Ah, yes. A set of desert fatigues appear to have gone missing. Are you able to shed any light on this sorry matter?'

'Peterson, sir,' I said, abandoning him to the wrath of Dr Bairstow without any hesitation whatsoever. 'He took off his clothes when we met Ephialtes and we forgot to get them back.'

'Really? How extraordinary. I personally find a formal handshake usually suffices, but obviously, Dr Peterson has his own very unique way of forming new acquaintanceships. Carry on, Dr Maxwell.'

The day came. We were to be married in the early evening. At dusk. That magical time between day and night.

I was dressed, made-up, hair done, and waiting for something to go wrong.

I didn't know what – my anxiety wasn't related to anything specific – just an all-encompassing, gut-churning expectation that something dreadful would happen. In an effort to allay my fears, I thought I would compile a list of everything that could possibly happen, read it aloud to myself, see how stupid I was being, and then cathartically consign it to the WPB file with a practised throw.

I worked my way through Leon falling through some

sort of temporal crack – I don't know, any sort of temporal crack; Markham accidentally setting fire to the chapel; some idiot raising their hand at the 'just cause or impediment' bit; Clive Ronan swinging by, just to cause trouble; Dr Bairstow forbidding the marriage; my being shot again …

Normal people just have to worry about the flowers not turning up or Uncle Henry goosing the bridesmaids …

'What have you got there?' said Kal, twitching my list out of my hand. 'Oh for God's sake, Max. Helen, listen to this …'

I twitched it back again. 'Why are you here?'

'We're your bridesmaids.'

'I've changed my mind. I'm not having any.'

'Yes you are.'

'And if I was, it wouldn't be you two.'

'But we're in our posh frocks and Helen's put on lipstick.'

I drew breath, but someone knocked at the door, possibly to tell me that the chapel had been the on the receiving end of a direct nuclear strike.

It was Mr Strong, clutching a bunch of perfect yellow roses. At some point, they'd passed through Mrs Enderby's hands because they were wrapped in a long, trailing bow made of the same golden material as my dress.

The sight of the flowers hit me hard. This was a bridal bouquet. I was getting married. I was actually getting married. The enveloping panic made my head spin.

'Alcohol, quick.' said Kal, looking around the room. 'There's bound to be some somewhere.'

363

She was out of luck. All my gear had been carted off to my new room. The one I would share with Leon. After we were married. Oh God, I was getting married …

Another knock at the door. This was it.

Helen opened the door to Dr Bairstow.

'Good evening, sir.'

'Dr Foster, Dr Black, good evening. And how is the patient?'

'Panicking, sir.'

'Only to be expected.' He flourished a bottle of something. 'Ladies, you are relieved.'

They picked up their skirts. I could hear their footsteps clattering off down the stairs and we were alone.

'Well, Max, how are you feeling?'

'Very nervous, sir.'

'Well, of course you are. It's a big step.'

'Into the unknown.'

'That shouldn't frighten you, of all people. It's what you do. You took a step into the unknown when you placed your trust in Mrs De Winter. You took another jump into the unknown when you were recruited by St Mary's. You took a giant leap into the unknown after Agincourt and I have no doubt that when the time comes, at the end of a long and happy life, you will positively hurl yourself into the next world. I have no fears for you. None at all. The unknown is your playground.'

He picked up the piece of paper.

'What's this?'

'Oh, that's my disaster list, sir. You know me, always prepared for any eventuality.'

'Really? I must have missed that over the years. What

a shame. Let me see ...' He scanned down my list of potential catastrophes. 'No. No. Good heavens! Possibly. No. Probably not. No. No. Yes, almost certainly. No.' He screwed up the list. 'I think, on balance of probability, Max, almost nothing to worry about.'

I changed the subject. 'Did I see a bottle, sir?'

'You did indeed. Anticipating a certain level of apprehension, I came prepared.'

'And glasses, too. I'm impressed, sir.'

He sighed. 'I have been in charge of this unit for a great many years now. I know what is required of me.'

As he spoke, he opened the bottle and poured the fire juice.

'Just a very little for you, Max. I can't have you drunk on my watch. Never mind what Leon would say, Dr Black would almost certainly come looking for me afterwards.'

He handed me a glass and we looked at each other.

'Well,' he said, eventually. 'Did you ever think this day would come?'

I shook my head.

'I still remember your first day here. The day we met. You stumped into my office with, as I believe I remarked to Mrs Partridge afterwards, an armful of qualifications and a bucketful of attitude and nothing has ever been quite the same since.'

'Nor for me.' I took a deep, wobbly breath. 'Sir, if I had ever been able to choose my own father ...'

He said softly, 'It's been an honour and a privilege, Max.'

'And for me too, sir.'

We clinked glasses. I sipped very cautiously. Sometimes, you never knew what he was handing you. We stood together as the shadows crept across the darkening room. My last few minutes as a single person.

His watch beeped.

'We're under starter's orders, Max. Time to go. Are you ready?'

'I am, sir.'

He offered me his arm.

'May I say, my dear, that you look quite beautiful.'

'Thank you, sir. May I say that at this moment, there is no one I would rather have with me.'

He cleared his throat and patted my hand.

'Off we go, then.'

We negotiated the stairs and set off across the deserted hall. Voices came back to me from down the years, whispering in the shadows.

'David Sands, don't go into Rushford today.'

'Ladies and gentlemen, we're going to Troy!'

'Miss Black, there are two "p"s in oppressed and only one "n" in minority. You are neither.'

'You left them to die, you traitorous bitch!'

'Enemy at the gates! Good luck everyone!'

I shook myself a little. Old ghosts.

Together, we moved slowly across the Hall towards the chapel.

The click of Dr Bairstow's stick sounded very loud on the stone floor.

The tiny chapel glowed in the gentle candlelight. Built originally for the family in residence and their servants, today it was packed. I was vaguely aware of the murmur of many people. I saw Leon, standing by the altar with Dieter. Even as I looked, he turned around and smiled for me alone, and all my doubts and fears suddenly became as insubstantial as early morning mist.

Silence fell.

Someone coughed.

The music started.

Everyone was looking at me.

'Remember,' whispered Dr Bairstow. 'Slow and stately.'

I nodded.

'We should, perhaps, synchronise our limps.'

I choked out a laugh.

'Are you ready, Max?'

I lifted my chin. 'I am.'

'Then let us begin.'

I kept my eyes on Leon the whole time.

He said his vows. I said mine. He held my hands throughout and never looked away. His hands were warm and steady. Like his voice. And his eyes.

I, alas, vibrated like a tuning fork all the way through the ceremony.

When it was done, we turned, walked back down the aisle, and stepped out into the magical dusk. Into an enchanted world of white lanterns, candles, and tea lights. Fairy lights lit a golden path ahead of us. White ribbons had been tied around every tree trunk. In the distance, soft music drifted across the darkening gardens.

I stood, entranced. No wonder I'd been confined to my room all day. That they had done all this for us …

I was gobsmacked. St Mary's, global capital of noise and disaster and explosions had not only done romance, but done it perfectly, converting our slightly battered environment into a golden world of magic and wonder and fairy-tale beauty.

Leon's grip tightened. I turned to face him. He smiled down at me and whispered, 'Always remember this moment, Max because it won't always be like this. There will be days when you're cross and I'm grumpy and doors will be slammed, but that won't really be us. This is us. This is how we really are, so always remember this moment.'

I nodded.

I blinked in the hailstorm of flashes as people took photographs and then we followed the runway of lights around to the front terrace where Mrs Mack had set up the reception area.

All around us, people were laughing and joking. Markham and Hunter danced past us. Helen and Tim walked quietly together. Helen was smiling. Kal and Dieter held hands. Her eyes were brighter than the thousands of stars in the heavens above us.

Snowy white cloths covered tables laden with plates. White balloons hung, ghostly in the dusk, ready to terrify the living daylights out of everyone after their fourth drink.

Dr Bairstow spoke. There were toasts. I remember cutting a cake.

The fireworks started and we slipped away.

We had tossed a coin to see who would be the designated driver and I had won. Leon had groaned and rolled his eyes. I told him to suck it up – we were only going forty miles or so. (Actually, we were booked into the Stuyvesant – an international hotel on the coast, famed for its quiet luxury, because, said Leon, when you spend your working days sleeping in the dirt, and peeing behind a rock, indoor plumbing is a pearl beyond any price. I would have been happy with any establishment that just provided soft toilet paper, but this was Leon's choice and I was happy to agree.)

In a further effort to ally his fears, I'd added that the roads would be quiet, and my driving was much improved and I hardly hit anything these days. He had said nothing in a way that said everything.

I was a little taken aback when I discovered the Boss had loaned us his Bentley. We had history with that car.

I pulled very slowly down the drive and looked back as we waited for the gates to open.

I could see a small fire. Probably, one of the Professor's fireworks had exceeded expectations. It was only a small fire, but there was a disproportionate amount of shouting.

'Nothing to do with us,' said Leon, as I nosed the car cautiously through the gates and pulled more or less smoothly away. We drove slowly down the twisty lane, the headlights picking out glittering eyes in the hedgerows. A rabbit, caught in the headlights, stared panic-stricken as disaster bore down upon it before dashing for cover. I knew exactly how it felt.

'Challenging times ahead,' he said.

I agreed. 'Yes, but I think it'll be fine if we just take it slowly. Baby steps, you know.'

'Yes, as you say, baby steps.'

'The most important thing is to get them out there on proper assignments as soon as possible, but without frightening the living daylights out of them.'

He sighed. 'It may be possible we're talking about two entirely different things.'

'Why? What were you talking about?'

'Have the events of the last few hours faded from your tiny historian memory already?'

'Sorry. I was talking about something important.'

'You're winding me up, aren't you?'

I grinned at him. 'So easy.'

'Just concentrate on your driving, please.'

'I told you not to have that third glass of wine.'

'Half an hour into the marriage and you've turned into a nag.'

'Yes, I'm amazed it took so long, too. Be prepared for years and years of mental and physical abuse.'

His voice came out of the darkness. 'Could we start now?'

He turned towards me and touched my breast. Very, very gently at first, and then increasing the pressure, moving his fingers in the way he knew I liked so much. The car's interior was suddenly very dark and very hot. I gripped the steering wheel as if my life depended upon it.

We hit a tree.

Not very hard, thank God. We sat in silence for a moment, listening to the metal tick. Miraculously, both headlights were undamaged and by their light, I could see a shower of autumn leaves, dislodged by the impact, slowly fluttering around us. It was quite pretty.

'Well, for God's sake,' he said, climbing out of the car and going to inspect the damage.

'Are you all right?' I said, anxiously, not wanting to figure in the tabloids as the bride who killed the groom even before the honeymoon had begun.

He pulled open my door and helped me out. 'I'm fine. Are you?'

'Of course. It takes far more than a minor bump to …'

I got no further. He backed me against the car and kissed me hard. He tasted of wine and Leon, and my little heart, already pumping like a piston, went into overdrive. I could feel him against me.

'Leon …'

He held my face between his hands.

'Right here,' he whispered. 'Right now. Across the bonnet of this car. We've done it before. For old time's sake.'

'Yes,' I said, breathlessly, remembering. 'Oh God, yes.'

He growled under his breath, twisted his hand in my hair, and pulled my head back. Every sense I had kicked up a gear or two. I reached down for him. This was going to be good.

A brilliantly blinding light enveloped everything and a female voice said, 'Is everything all right here?'

What?

'Behave yourself,' whispered Leon. 'The Force is with us.'

I made a huge effort to look normal.

'Good evening,' he said, calmly. 'As you can see, we've had a small bump. I was just checking this lady for whiplash.'

The light turned on me.

'Are you all right? Do you require an ambulance?'

'No,' I said, blinking. 'I'm absolutely fine, thank you.'

Sadly, this cheerful reassurance did not speed her on her way. In fact, now the other policeman emerged from the car and began to inspect our stricken vehicle. 'A very nice car, sir. Is it yours?'

'No,' said Leon, always inconveniently truthful. 'We borrowed it.'

'With or without the owner's consent, sir?'

'Oh, with,' I said. 'Definitely with.'

'Well, there's not too much damage,' he announced. 'But you won't be going anywhere in this tonight. Do you have someone you can call?'

Leon sighed and pulled out his phone.

'Dieter! Dieter, can you hear me? ... Well, move away from the music, then ... Can you hear me now? ... Crank up the low-loader, can you? ... Yes, we've had a bit of an accident ... On the Whittington road ... No, we're fine ... Yes, the police are here. (This was Leon-speak for "For God's sake, find someone not entirely insensible with drink.") ... Yes, OK. Thirty minutes then.'

'Perhaps,' said the female sergeant, 'you could tell us what happened? Who was driving?'

'I was,' I volunteered. 'I'm awfully sorry. There was an animal in the road and I swerved to avoid it.'

'What sort of animal?'

'A rabbit,' said Leon.

'A deer,' I said, simultaneously.

They regarded us suspiciously. God knows why.

'Have either of you been drinking?'

'I have,' said Leon.

'I haven't,' I said, virtuously. 'You can't drink and drive.'

'You can't drive at all,' said Leon, a little unkindly I thought.

'I can,' I said indignantly. 'It was the rabbit's fault.'

They pounced.

'I thought you said it was a deer.'

Bollocks.

'It was a rabbit that looked like a deer,' I said, making things worse with every word and any minute now I was going to be commanded to blow into this, please.

'Stop talking,' said Leon. He turned to the police people. 'The best thing we can do is go back to St Mary's with the low loader and start again with another car.'

'You're from St Mary's?'

There was no point in denying it. On this road, where else could we have come from? I sighed. Sometimes, our credibility with the police is not very high.

'I think you had better accompany us back to the station, sir and madam.'

What?

Leon pulled out his phone again.

'Dr Bairstow? ... Yes, good evening, sir ... Ah, you've heard. Only minor damage ... Yes, I know, but that was a long time ago ... No, we're both fine, but we've been arrested.'

'Not yet,' interrupted the sergeant.

'Sorry – apparently, we're still assisting the police with their enquiries. As it's your car, perhaps you could

373

have a word? Thank you, sir.'

We sat in the back of the police car while Dr Bairstow talked at the policeman and the sergeant prepared whatever it was I was going to have to blow into.

'We're never going to live this down, are we?'

He shrugged. 'Just building the legend.'

'What legend?'

'My legend, of course. You're probably not aware of this, but I'm generally reckoned to be awesome.'

'What about me?'

'You're just a catastrophe. Different type of legend. You're more a kind of horrible warning.'

I peered through the window to see what the police were doing. 'So what happens now?'

'Well, unless they have conjugal cells – not a lot.'

'I can't believe I'm spending my wedding night in gaol.'

'Good job they didn't turn up thirty seconds later.'

'Seriously, you would have lasted that long?'

'A special effort for my wedding night.' He sighed. 'It's always going to be like this, isn't it?'

'Well I hope so. I like exciting, unexpected, and slightly dangerous.'

'And that's just your driving. Don't get me started on your cooking.'

'Well, if you'd been able to control yourself ...'

'Hey, I'm not the one who hit the tree.'

The policeman stuck his head into the car. 'They're on their way.'

'They? Who's they?'

He shrugged. 'All of them, as far as I can tell.'

Oh, no.

Leon leaned forwards. 'Arrest us now. Take us away, I'm begging you.'

The policeman straightened up and looked back up the road. A dazzling array of headlights was bearing down on us. Red and orange lights strobed from the low loader. A variety of horns sounded a fanfare. Somewhere a sound system was thumping out 'Livin' La Vida Loca'. Which wouldn't have been too bad if what sounded like a small army hadn't been singing 'Dancing Queen' at the same time. It was not an harmonious duet.

'Dear God,' said the policeman. 'Get out of the car.'

I stared up the road at the advancing cavalcade. 'What? No. You can't leave us here.'

'It would seem your guvnor's had a word with my guvnor. I said – out.'

We climbed out. They started their engine.

'Take us with you,' I wailed. 'I have vital information, I know who killed Sennacherib.'

They put the car in gear and drove away. They were laughing their bloody heads off. What happened to 'Protect and Serve'?

Our doom bore noisily down upon us. There was no escape.

A figure stepped suddenly out of the darkness, giving us both a minor heart attack.

'Here. I think you might need these.'

He handed me a set of car keys and Leon a torch. 'Just down that track. Go now.'

I stared at him, amazed. He must have moved like lightning to get here ahead of the others.

'Ian …'

He held my gaze. 'One good turn deserves another, Max.'

'There is a place in historian heaven reserved especially for you.'

'God, I hope not. The only thing that keeps me going is the thought of an historian-free afterlife. Both of you – get out of here. I'll deal with this.'

I took his hand. 'Thank you.'

I caught a brief flash of his rare smile.

'An honour and a privilege, Max.'

THE END

ACKNOWLEDGMENTS

As usual, I'd like to thank all the wonderful people at Accent Press, especially my editor, Cat Camacho. Grateful thanks also to Suze and Suzie for their comments and support; and to my neighbour Aly, who has to put up with me suddenly staring into space and then starting to scribble on the nearest horizontal surface – a bit of paper, the back of my hand, her dog …

Want to know what happens next?
Catch up with Max and the disaster magnets in

'To do what I do – go where I go – see what I see – it's a wonderful, unique, never-to-be-taken-for-granted privilege.'

With great privilege comes great responsibility, something Max knows only too well, and as newly appointed Chief Training Officer at the St Mary's Institute of Historical Research, it's up to her to drum this guiding principle into her five new recruits.

With a training programme that includes Joan of Arc, an illegal mammoth, a duplicitous Father of History, a bombed rat, Stone Age hunters and Dick the Turd, the question everyone is asking themselves is – what could possibly go wrong?

HEADLINE

Lies, Damned Lies, and History

*'I've done some stupid things in my time. I've been reckless.
I've broken a few rules. But never before have I ruined so
many lives or left such a trail of destruction behind me.'*

Max has never been one for rules.
They tend to happen to other people.

But this time she's gone too far. And everyone
at St Mary's is paying the price.

With the History Department disintegrating around
her and grounded until the end of time, how can
she ever put things right?

HEADLINE

AND THE REST IS HISTORY

*'Because, my dear Max, you dance on the edge
of darkness . . . and I don't think it would take very
much for you to dance my way.'*

When an old enemy appears out of nowhere with an
astonishing proposition for Max – a proposition that
could change everything – Max is tempted. Very tempted.

With an end to an old conflict finally in sight,
it looks as if St Mary's problems are over.
Can they all now live happily ever after?

As everything hangs in the balance, Max and
St Mary's find themselves engulfed in tragedies
worse than they could ever imagine.

Is this the end?

HEADLINE

An Argumentation of Historians

They say you shouldn't push your luck. Max gives her own luck a massive shove every day – and it's only a matter of time until luck pushes back . . .

January 1536. The day of Henry VIII's infamous jousting accident. Historians from St Mary's are there in force, recording and documenting. And, arguing – obviously.

A chance meeting between Max and the Time Police leads to a plan of action. And, it's one that will have very serious consequences – especially for Max. Her private life is already more than a little rocky. But with Leon recovering and Matthew safe in the future there will never be a better opportunity to bring down Clive Ronan, once and for all.

From Tudor England to the burning city of Persepolis – and from a medieval siege to a very nasty case of 19th century incarceration – Max is determined that this time, Ronan will not escape.

HEADLINE

Hope for the Best

*You can't change History. History doesn't like it.
There are always consequences.*

Max is no stranger to taking matters into her own
hands. Especially when she's had A Brilliant Idea.
Yes, it will mean breaking a few rules, but – as
Max always says – they're not her rules.

Seconded to the Time Police to join in the hunt
for the renegade Clive Ronan, Max is a long way from
St Mary's. But life in the future does have its plus points
– although not for long.

You know what they say. Hope for the best.
But plan for the worst.

HEADLINE

HISTORY WILL NEVER BE THE SAME AGAIN...

BOOK ONE

BOOK TWO

BOOK THREE

BOOK FOUR

BOOK FIVE

BOOK SIX

BOOK SEVEN

BOOK EIGHT

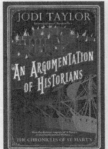

BOOK NINE

BOOK TEN

SHORT STORIES

THE CHRONICLES OF ST MARY'S